T0004312

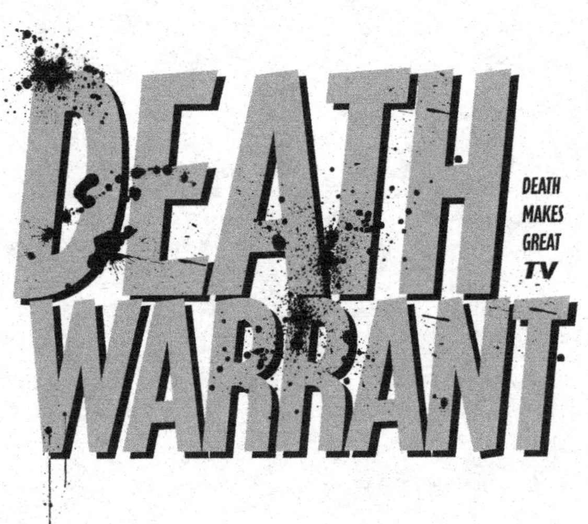
DEATH
WARRANT
DEATH
MAKES
GREAT
TV

BRYAN JOHNSTON

CamCat Publishing, LLC
Brentwood, Tennessee 37027
camcatpublishing.com

This is a work of fiction. Names, characters, places, and incidents are either products of the author's imagination or are used fictitiously.

Hardcover ISBN 9780744305081
Paperback ISBN 9780744305241
Large-Print Paperback ISBN 9780744305326
eBook ISBN 9780744305333
Audiobook ISBN 9780744305371

Library of Congress Control Number: 2021951333

Cover and book design by Maryann Appel

5 3 1 2 4

Dedicated to

Boots, Trixie, Rocco, Pisken, Bella, Lakota, Leo,
Sadie, Petey, and Rookie.

Furry friends forever.

PROLOGUE

Jesus, thought Joey, stopping to catch his breath while simultaneously chastising himself for using the Lord's name in vain. They'd said the hike was challenging, even by hardy Norwegian mountaineering standards. But he didn't realize "challenging" was code for "your lungs will be bleeding." Probably not too demanding for a younger person, but he grudgingly admitted he no longer fit that demographic. Those advancing "middle-years" made his little adventures even more important to him. He took a swig from his water bottle and checked his watch. He'd been making good time. "That's why you trained for six months, dummy," he reminded himself for the umpteenth time, not that anyone could hear him. He'd seen a few hikers coming back down the mountain, but to his surprise he hadn't seen anyone else making the ascent. He'd purposefully picked the least touristy season that didn't include several feet of snow to make his bucket list trip, but still, he'd expected to see a few more people. Not that he was complaining; he was enjoying the solitude. With one last cleansing breath and the taste of copper dissipating from his mouth, he got to his feet for the final push.

On the climb he'd taken to talking to himself, carrying on conversations out loud, playing the part of all parties involved. He'd found it highly entertaining, and it helped keep his mind off the lactic acid burning in his thighs over the five-hour climb.

"Why in heaven's name does it have to be Norway? It's so far away," Joey said out loud in the closest resemblance of his wife Joanie's patented exasperated tone. He'd had thirty years of marriage to fine tune it.

"Because that's where the Trolltunga is, hon!" Joey replied.

He vividly remembered when the holo-brochure had arrived. "Have you ever seen anything like it?" he'd asked her. She hadn't. The 3D image projected by the brochure had been impressive, and even his wife couldn't deny that. The Trolltunga was a rock formation that sprang 2,000 feet straight up above the north end of a Norwegian lake whose name Joanie never could pronounce and was topped with a cliff that jutted out preposterously far, like an enormous plank of a pirate ship. Watching the image slowly rotating over the brochure on their dining table had sealed the deal. Joey could taste the copper again but powered through. He knew he was almost there.

"Should have brought the stick, genius," he grumbled to himself. "That's what hiking staffs are for." But he'd been afraid some careless baggage handler would damage it. The staff had been too important to him. The entire Boy Scout Troop had carved their names into it along with the final inscription, "Thanks for all your years of service." He wasn't sure who was prouder of the gift, him, or Joanie. Regardless, the staff would have been a help.

His research showed that the round-trip climb would be about 22 kilometers—45,000 steps—and the equivalent of climbing and descending 341 floors. He guessed he was right around floor 170. Almost there.

As he rounded a large boulder, he thought back on all his training, preparation, and admittedly, the inconveniences he'd put Joanie through, and recited one of his wife's favorite admonitions, "Joey Dahl, I swear you will be the death of me." But then what he saw stopped him in his tracks. At that moment Joey felt complete validation. He also instantly understood what made the Trolltunga such a draw for thrill seekers. The cliff's edge reached out so far that the photo op was one for the books, the type of picture you frame and hang in your den. A conversation starter.

Bragging rights. The other church deacons were going to be sick of hearing about it.

"Oh, babe," Joey said, more to himself this time, "I wish you were here to see this." But even six months ago he knew that was never going to happen, what with her condition, but she was never going to begrudge him this trip. He'd been dreaming about it for years.

It took a certain person, one immune to heights and vertigo, to walk to that cliff's edge and look out. Joey was one of those people. He set up the small, portable tripod he'd brought and mounted his mobile device, his optic, to take pictures and video remotely. He couldn't wait to show it to Joanie and the kids. Through a little trial and error, he eventually got the framing right and strode out to the edge. He turned to face the camera and spread his arms wide in a "look at what I achieved" pose. The optic's camera lens clicked once, twice, three times.

And then the bullet hit him right above the left eye.

Joey Dahl dropped like Icarus, toppling backwards off the cliff, falling into space. Like a base jumper without a wingsuit or parachute. His body tumbled down the sheer cliff face, yet he never quite hit the side. His body stayed clear of the rocky wall, due to the sharp drafts from the lake below. The constant pushing away from the wall, managed to keep him undamaged, bullet wound aside, until he finally met the ground below, by a lake whose name his wife never could pronounce. By then, however, he'd been long dead.

SIX THOUSAND MILES away, a room full of people in finely tailored suits and skirts were watching intently, applauding with their approval. One of them, a woman with severe bangs, all business, smoothly pivoted from the wall of monitors, her eyes drawn to another, smaller screen where a series of numbers were appearing in real time. She allowed herself a trace of a smile. The ratings were in. Perhaps not matching those of the pop star's demise from last summer, but still better than management had expected. Enough to trigger her bonus. Maybe she'd take the kids to Six Flags.

CHAPTER 1
JANUARY

If you're going to be summarily executed, you'd at least want the place that's arranging your death to have a couple of nice rugs. Just for appearances. Nobody wants to be offed by some fly-by-night outfit that considers Ikea the height of corporate décor. As it turns out, I needn't have worried. I really didn't know what to expect, they don't show the offices on the commercials. I knew it probably wouldn't be like walking into a tax-prep firm in a strip mall—some tiny space filled with cheap furniture, all pleather and particleboard. It is anything but, and instantly fills me with a good vibe and reinforces my belief that I am making the right choice. The entry doors are an artistic combination of rich amber-hued wood, glass, and burnished metal, most likely brass, but buffed dull to appear understated. Classy. You feel like you are walking into a place of importance, where critical decisions are made on a by-minute basis, which I guess they are. Upon entering I'm greeted by a kindly gentleman with open arms.

"Welcome, Ms. Percival, we're so pleased to see you," he says with utter sincerity. "Our receptionist will take care of your every need."

It takes me a second to realize the man is a hologram. I take a step closer and poke at it, which the holographic gentleman tolerates with a smile. Only the subtlest flicker gives away its true identity. From more than a few feet away you'd swear the man was flesh and blood. Holos are common these days, but this one takes the cake. The technology they have here obviously is top shelf stuff. Based on the greeting, they had me scanned and identified the moment I stepped through the front door.

I immediately pick up on the smell: lavender. It's subtle but noticeable. Upon deeper consideration, the perfect scent. It's probably the world's most relaxing smell. Smells have a stronger link to memories than any of the senses, and I can feel myself imprinting the scent with the experience. What did my high school teacher always say? Smells ring bells. True that. I'll probably go to my grave associating that smell with this place. Ha, go to my grave, bad choice of words for this visit.

The lobby floor is a combination of real hardwoods and Persian rugs so soft you instantly want to take your shoes off for the sheer sensory experience. The space feels more like the lobby of a four-star hotel: tasteful, elegant, contemporary without pressing the issue. The woman behind the reception desk is perfectly in line with the ambience. She is probably in her late thirties, attractive but non-threatening. I like the cut of her jib, as my mom used to say. Her clothes are professional but still fashionable. If I were to guess, they were most likely chosen for her by a consultant, like news anchors choose their clothes to project an image of trustworthiness. When I approach the desk, her face lights up with one of the most endearing smiles I have ever witnessed. I lean in a bit and squint to make sure she's real. Yep, carbon-based life form.

"How may I help you?" she asks, and I absolutely believe she means it.

"I'm here to get whacked." I mimic guns with my fingers, firing off a couple rounds at her before blowing the non-existent smoke from the barrels. When I'm nervous I say stupid stuff. Stupid or snarky. Stupid, snarky, or sarcastic. I've been attempting to pare it down to just one for the last ten years with mixed results. I try to sound like being here is no biggie, but my voice sounds shrill in my ears, and I seriously doubt my anti-perspirant is up to the challenge.

The woman, unfazed by my cavalier attitude, nods with a soft, endearing smile. "Of course. You can speak with one of our sales associates. Please take a seat. Someone will be with you in a moment."

She gestures to a cozy waiting area with a half-dozen comfortable looking chairs, one of them occupied by a distinguished looking woman idly paging through an issue of Vanity Fair, one of the last media hold outs that still clings to the quaint notion of publishing on paper. I can see an A-list actress of some substance gracing the cover, dressed in a bold red riding jacket, khaki jodhpurs and knee-high boots. I can practically hear the baying of the hounds. The actress is currently all the rage and the expected shoo-in come award time for her role in a recent high-profile drama that has captured the country's imagination. A period piece that boasts betrayal, star-crossed love, and overcoming staggering odds in the face of adversity. Or at least that's what the trailers led me to believe.

I turn back to the receptionist. "So, how's it work?"

"Pardon?" she asks innocently.

"I mean, do you get to choose? Sniper shot? Blown up? Pitched into a vat of acid? There was one episode, brutal, they dropped a piano on the guy, like in a cartoon." I also yap when I'm nervous.

The receptionist's smile doesn't waver. "I remember it well." She gives me a polite nod and says, "Your sales associate will answer all of your questions," and then tips her head in the direction of where the woman with the magazine is sitting.

With a wink I fire off another round at the receptionist, holster my hands in my pockets, and turn toward the waiting area. Jesus, she must think I'm a moron. I take a seat several chairs away from my silver-haired counterpart. She glances up at me and gives the tiniest of polite smiles—held a beat longer than is socially necessary—before turning her attention back to her magazine. In that singular moment we become confederates, there for the same reason, and she is acknowledging to me with that brief exchange that regardless of my race, sex, social standing, or political leanings, that I—we—are about to become members of a rather unique club. All for one, one for all.

My distinguished clubmate looks, well, prominent. The cut of her suit speaks of dinner parties of the well-heeled, where talk of debutantes and cotillions is not simply language of earlier generations. And that's what's puzzling. I'd simply assumed this place was not frequented by the 1 percent. I mean, why would they need to resort to this measure? They're all loaded. They've got the means to provide for their family members without going to the extremes this joint provides. It then dawns on me that maybe not everyone here is doing this for the money. But why else? Fame? Boredom?

A moment later, a slim middle-aged woman with flawless hair approaches and addresses my clubmate. She rises to her feet, shakes the proffered associate's hand, and off they go. It is now just me and the glossy A-lister.

I don't even have a chance to pick up the magazine before my appointed sales associate arrives to greet me. If there ever was a physical embodiment of warmth and compassion, he stands before me. He introduces himself as Benjamin and I can no sooner call him Ben than flap my arms and fly to the moon. To call him Ben would be an affront. This is Benjamin, the type of man who walks one step behind his wife, who enters a room of strangers with his hand on the small of her back to let her know he's right there with her. Benjamin is clearly a man who listens more than he speaks and gives careful consideration before he does. This is my three-second impression.

Benjamin appears to be maybe a decade older than me, in the early throes of middle age with salt-and-pepper hair, receding, in baseball terms, at the power-alleys of his forehead.

He wears a nice-fitting suit of deep blue with the thinnest of pinstripes. His shoes, brown, match his eyes. It's the eyes that support everything. His whole demeanor, his warmth, radiates from those dark twins. But I can see upon further review that the smile that rides along with them is what seals the deal. The smile and eyes work in tandem. One without the other, strong, but together, unimpeachable. I would buy a Rolex out of the trunk of this guy's car.

Benjamin shakes my hand and asks me to join him in his office where we can chat. That's what he says—chat, not talk. The perfect word to set my mind at ease.

Just two pals.

His office is small but nicely appointed and has a window overlooking a wooded urban park. The lavender scent follows us into the room, which I appreciate. Benjamin offers me a seat in front of his desk and takes the chair behind it. The desk is tidy, with nothing but a couple of framed family photos, a World's Most Okayest Employee mug, and a glass computer tablet mounted on a small, low-profile frame to keep it upright when he chooses to use it in that position.

Benjamin steeples his hands on his desk and fixes me with those molten lava cake eyes.

"So, Frances," he begins. Not Ms. Percival, but Frances. "You'd like to learn more about . . ." He glances at his glass tablet and looks up with a small smile. ". . . how to get whacked."

"Pretty much. And by the way, you can call me Frankie."

"Then Frankie it is. And by the way, it's okay, you can call it by its official name, a death warrant."

"Fair enough."

"How much do you know about the process?" Benjamin asks evenly. He says process with a long o. Benjamin has what used to be called a Trans-Atlantic accent. You'd hear it all the time in ancient movies with actors like Katherine Hepburn and Cary Grant. It's halfway between a British and American accent. Like something taught at a New England boarding school. It sounds divine.

I shrug. "Not much. How come there's hardly anything about it on the Internet? I mean, that's pretty crazy that you're able to keep it so hush-hush."

Benjamin nods and smiles compassionately. "It is rather amazing, isn't it? You'd think someone would talk. Somebody always talks. I'm embarrassed to say I really don't know."

And I believe him.

"And yet virtually nothing shows up in the media," I observe, probably a little more pointedly than intended.

But Benjamin doesn't seem to mind. He holds his hands out, shoulders arched in the classic *Beats me* pose. "Those are the interior machinations of the machine that are a mystery even to me. Ask me what time it is, and I can tell you. Ask me how the watch works, and I can't. Much of the information is purely on a need-to-know basis."

"And you don't need to know?" I ask.

"Way above my paygrade. We're highly compartmentalized." He can see my skepticism. "Rest assured; I can answer most of your questions."

He settles back into his chair and that's when it occurs to me. The eyes. Brown. The receptionist's eyes were brown. The other sales associate's eyes were brown. Don't ask me how I notice this, it's what I do. I notice things. Little stuff that often is of no consequence. That's why I was always a fan of Sherlock Holmes mysteries. He noticed things. While others saw, he observed. I thought that was cool. We were kindred spirits. Of course, his gift of observation made nonsense of mine, but the one thing I have going for me is that I am nonfiction. I live in the real world. What I don't have is the benefit of Sir Arthur Conan-Doyle ensuring that I can spot a scuff on a shoe and divine that the culprit had brushed it against a curb in a rush to catch the number five bus. It's bullshit, but it's entertaining bullshit.

Instead, my ability to notice things on a high but more realistic level has made me reasonably successful in my career—I'm a mentalist. My job is to observe. Take note. Listen and connect dots that others don't see. I suppose I could be a cop or a private investigator, but that seems like work. Being a mentalist, on the other hand, is fun. We're like magicians, but without the corny patter. Do I really have the gift of divination and clairvoyance? Sometimes it sure as hell feels like it. Let's just say I've got a knack. However, a byproduct of my keen perception is an overactive imagination. I'll sometimes see things for more than they are. But it does make life more interesting.

Back to the brown eyes. Of course. Brown eyes are soft, they're compassionate. Blue eyes are striking, but in a place like this you don't want striking, you want everything to be the Xanax of appearance. Calming. I'll bet every public-facing employee here has brown eyes. In fact, I would imagine they're all screened by a team of consultants to within an inch of their lives to fit specific criteria. A place like this probably only hires people who radiate kindness. I wonder how they measure that? There's got to be some way to quantify a person's level of kindness and compassion beyond spending five minutes in a room with them. With today's technology, I'm sure someone's found a way to figure out the analytics. To make it measurable.

Benjamin breaks into a smile no less cozy than an electric blanket. "So, what would you like to know?"

"Uh, how about you tell me what you can, and I'll ask questions as they come to me."

Benjamin gives a short nod. "Certainly. Let's begin with the 30,000-foot view, and for clarity's sake, I will use vernacular that I'm technically not supposed to: You will be killed, and your death will be televised."

"Pretty damn clear vernacular," I say.

Benjamin is all smiles. "I know, right? Gets to the meat of it pretty quick."

"What did you mean by vernacular you're not supposed to use?" I ask.

"Part of our internal policies. Company culture." Benjamin says amiably. "Our programs are to be referred to as 'episodes,' not 'shows.' There are no 'victims,' but 'participants' or 'souls.' And all 'participants' will be shown the highest respect and dignity."

"Mighty neighborly of you."

"Thank you," says Benjamin, looking sincerely appreciative of my comment, despite its snark. "Let me see if I can guess your next question," he asks. "How does it work?"

"You've done this before, Benjamin."

"Once or twice. We've got plenty of packages to choose from, depending on your budget, time frame, and other factors."

"What kind of factors?"

Benjamin turns his eyes to his glass tablet, makes a few taps and swipes to call up the necessary information.

"Do you care if it's clean or messy? Quick and painless or would you rather feel the experience? Do you want a run-of-the-mill termination or something more exotic?"

"Who the hell wants to feel the experience of dying?"

"You'd be surprised. There are some people who want to embrace their last moments on earth. I'm told they think that's when they feel most alive."

"That's whacko."

"Preaching to the choir here, Frankie." Just a couple of pals.

"What do you mean by exotic?"

Benjamin leans back in his chair and stares up at the ceiling for a moment, collecting his thoughts. "Well, there was one we did a few years back that struck me as outside the lines, as well as being spectacularly challenging."

"What was that?"

"Piranha attack. And he lived in the city."

"No shit?"

"That one took some serious production to pull off. We had to bring in twice our normal crew. But it was worth it; the ratings were outstanding."

"How outstanding?" I ask.

"Are you familiar with ratings?"

"A little."

Benjamin taps on his glass tablet. "Piranha attack . . . 48.8 rating, 71 share."

He informs me that a rating point is a percentage of the total viewing population being polled and the share is the percentage of that population that's watching at that moment. So that meant almost half of the country was watching and 70 percent of those who had their TVs, computers, or optics on were tuned in. I wonder what the other 30 percent were watching.

"Holy crap! Those are Super World Bowl numbers."

"Actually, a little higher."

"And I read that a thirty-second ad in that game runs for ten million dollars."

Benjamin ruminates for a beat. "10.2, last I checked."

This is where the rubber meets the road, where the money comes into play.

"So, how does it work? Money-wise, I mean."

Benjamin clasps his hands in front of him and his face takes on an astonishing look of grace. I don't know what they are paying him, but it isn't enough.

My brain is having a difficult time reconciling the fact that this man who looks and sounds like a warm bath works for a company that kills people for profit.

"Certainly," he says. "This is why you've come in. So your family will be sufficiently provided for after your passing."

His demeanor strikes me as that of a funeral director talking costs for the casket, flowers, and organist. A tricky balancing act.

Put the client at ease while doing your job to assure you're keeping the company in the black, so the owner can continue to pay his gas bill, the mortgage, and take his kids to Disneyland.

"If you choose to move forward with our services you will pay a fee, earnest money, as it were, again based on some of the criteria I listed earlier—time frame, complexity." Benjamin pauses for an instant, like it's important to him that the following line land properly. "The up-front fee is to ensure we aren't seen as preying on the desperate."

"I can see how some might get that impression," I reply with a straight face.

Benjamin smiles at my understanding. "Once our service is rendered and your passing is confirmed, your designee—the dependent, as it were—will receive a percentage of the advertising revenue brought in by the televised production."

"And I'm guessing the more elaborate the production, the higher the ratings, and therefore more money for the . . . what did you call it? The designee?"

Benjamin cocks an eyebrow. "Usually, but not necessarily. I've seen some pretty pedestrian terminations receive quite robust ratings because of the backstory involved."

"Backstory?"

"Well, a background that may give the episode a little more drama. Let me give you an example." Benjamin does the glance-at-the-ceiling thing again, drawing on memories. "There was one episode where the method of death was a simple blow up. Explosives set to go off at a designated time and location. Nothing overly dramatic. But what gave it an extra twist was that on the day of the scheduled event our client decided to take his dog for a walk. An unexpected deviation from his normal schedule. We were embarrassingly unprepared for this. All our research gave us a 99 percent chance that he would be alone at the time of detonation. But as fate would have it, that miscue on our part became a ratings bonanza."

"What did taking his dog for a walk have to do with any of that?" I ask.

CHRIS MILLER HAD no idea Max, the gray-muzzled little lab mix padding alongside him, was causing conniptions in a television studio four states away. Well, padding was generous, it was more like limping, or waddling; Max was pushing ninety-eight in people years and built like a kielbasa sausage—mostly due to Chris's soft heart and table scraps. Chris figured Max could eat anything he damn well pleased for as long as he lived. Seven years previously, Chris and Max had been hiking in Zion National Park when Chris fell down a crevasse and was pinned. He only had enough water to last about a day. But Max had run for help, just like in the classic Timmy-fell-down-the-well scenario. Ever since, Chris spoiled his aging mutt mercilessly.

And that's what the people in the television studio hadn't foreseen.

"How long before he's at the optimal detonation coordinates?" asked the director. He dabbed an already moist handkerchief across his brow for the dozenth time in the last fifteen minutes.

"Ten minutes," replied the field producer, an edge to her voice. She was crumpling and uncrumpling a paper cup in her fist that moments earlier had been half filled with water which she had slugged down, desperately wishing it was something stronger. "My team has the space cleared. No civilians present. At least for now. For the time being, everything is go."

Nothing was go, thought the director. Things were far from go. But he had to keep a lid on it. He glanced up at the bank of monitors covering the control room wall. A half dozen or so showed audiences from around the globe watching the action. Most at impromptu *Death Warrant* parties. The public did seem to bond in these instances. The director liked to see how the audience was reacting to the circumstances; it helped him craft the story arc and emotional payout by seeing first-hand what they were responding to. At that moment the audience members were generally freaking out. Nobody wanted to see a cute, albeit fat, little dog blown to bits. In the pre-show the audience is given the opportunity to know the method of termination. It was impossible to guess which way they'd lean from episode to episode. Sometimes they wanted to know, other times they wanted to be surprised.

On this night, however, the votes were for knowing. When the hosts shared that the death would be delivered by explosion, the initial reaction was overwhelmingly positive. Detonation was always a crowd pleaser. But the closer they got to boom-time, the antsier the audience became. They didn't know the exact moment, but they did know that a little dog was more than likely going to be caught in the line of fire.

Thus, the freaking out.

"How could nobody have seen this coming?" shouted a large, imposing executive from the back of the room, a hint of a German accent in his voice. Not a soul dared make eye contact or a feeble excuse; that would have been career suicide. In circumstances like this they resorted to their training, experience, and professionalism, which ran in abundance in this control room. They were the cream of the crop and liked to think they were prepared for any emergency.

The director turned to a small, earnest looking man huddled over a computer screen in the corner of the studio. "Stats. What the hell? Why the dog? He was supposed to be solo."

The lead statistician gave a shrug. "Over the past 245 days since the job was approved, the featured participant made a nightly walk to this park 232 times." The man glanced back down to his monitor. "He always left between 6:00 and 6:10 p.m." The statistician turned back to the director. "It was, to use a more colloquial term, his evening constitutional. You could set your watch by him. Over those 232 times he brought his dog along a grand total of two times." The man pointed at his screen. "Based on our numbers, the odds of the featured participant taking the dog were less than 1 percent. Well below our threshold."

The field producer cleared her throat. "Uh, evidently one of those new doggy cafes just opened on the far side of the park. You know, one of those trendy coffee shops that sell dog biscuits along with cappuccinos? Our, um, best guess is that Mr. Miller may be taking his dog there for a treat."

Back over in the corner, the statistician shrugged again. "Human nature is always the wild card."

Human nature? The director stared the man down until the little statistician crumpled under his gaze and retreated to the safety of his computer screen. *Human nature my ass,* thought the director. They had algorithms up the ying-yang and banks of computers for the sole purpose of mathing the shit out of human nature. He wasn't about to accept shrugs and excuses. He turned his attention to the demolitions expert who was calmly watching three seats over. "What's the circumference of the charge?"

"Conformed to a 20-foot radius," came the reply. "Basically, like a small landmine, except more focused." The demolitions expert never took her eyes off the monitors, her voice never reaching above a calm, measured tone. "I've never lost a civilian to friendly fire. I'm not about to start now."

"Yeah, well, we may lose a dog if we're not careful."

The dog had been a huge factor when Chris had been accepted to participate in the show. The creative team determined that the backstory with the life-saving event at Zion National Park would be just the right emotional hook.

A few of the newer crew members in the booth were no doubt wondering why the team had opted for a termination that might cause collateral damage. The longer tenured crew already knew: people love a good explosion. Especially *Death Warrant* explosions. They took tremendous pride in their craft. This demolitions expert in particular. She'd won an Emmy for her work in the fine art of blowing shit up. It was for an episode the previous year featuring a dental hygienist and a hang glider. Scored outstanding ratings. The demolitions team spent an inordinate amount of time crafting just the right amount of bang for the buck. And it had to be appropriate to the circumstances and look good on TV. That night they'd needed a small charge—just big enough for one person—and still appeal to the senses. Most real detonations caused little fire, unless lot of fuel was involved. Detonations usually just created a big boom and that was it. Because of the special effects in movies, people had become accustomed to seeing fiery explosions. But the munitions team on this job were artists. They had worked for months to create just the right amount of flame in relation to the size of the charge and the sound.

The director leaned over and asked the assistant director, sotto voce, "Did you hear about the size of the charge for this one?" The AD held her thumb and finger an inch apart, most likely an exaggeration, but made the point. The director whistled low. He was as curious as anyone to see the result.

And still, the executive's words kept ringing in his ears: "How could nobody have seen this coming?"

An hour earlier, millions of people across the globe who had the *Death Warrant* app on their optic heard the unmistakable notification ping signifying someone's ticket was soon to be punched. Upon that ping, civilization ground to a halt, and all eyes were glued to screens. The slickly produced opening title sequence reminded viewers that they were now watching the most popular television show in history. The hosts, as always, were personable, professional, and compassionate. The featured participant, Chris Miller, was given a stirring and emotional backstory and had absolutely no idea that he would be dead by show's end.

Chris Miller's sister, the woman who was going to become a multi-millionaire by the time she went to bed, was sitting in a coffee shop with friends when the ping sounded. When she saw that the "soul" scheduled for "termination" was her own flesh and blood, she immediately and hysterically called her brother. She was utterly confounded when the call wouldn't go through. For that matter, thousands of others trying to place calls—other than 911 calls—to anyone within a hundred-mile radius of where Chris and Max were strolling along hit the same invisible barrier and never reached their intended target. Nobody within that zone received the ping either, so the thousands of people within that hundred-mile radius were as ignorant of the coming events as Chris. The team of *Death Warrant* lawyers who managed to negotiate that dead zone with the FCC received hefty bonuses that Christmas. As a result, Chris received no call or warning and had no idea that he would never experience another sunrise.

After weeks of deliberation and dozens of simulations, the consensus was for an hour-long pre-show. You needed enough time to give the audience the necessary backstory and a proper lead up, but the thinking was that if you went to air too far ahead there was more time for random occurrences. Life is unpredictable, as the dog's presence that night illustrated all too clearly. In a live broadcast there's nothing as frustrating to a producer or director than an Act of God.

The countdown clock on the studio wall clicked closer to the scheduled time of detonation while the director slowly ground the enamel from his molars and the AD tapped her pen at sub-sonic speed. Studio executives watching the feed from remote locations, oblivious to the control room drama, thought it was marvelous.

The director glanced at the treasonous clock. He was running out of options, and his mind wandered crazily to the thought of how much he would miss his 401(k) when he got fired.

When suddenly up popped a good old-fashioned Act of God. The good kind.

"Uh, boss?" said one of the associate producers who was tracking the camera fixed on the dog. "Something's up with the dog."

All eyes turned to the portly little mutt who was no longer walking alongside Chris, but had staggered left, then right, and then keeled over, like one of those fainting goats you'd see on nature shows, his tongue lolling out shiny and pink.

"Biometrics!" shouted the director into his headset mic. "What are you showing?"

A medical team in another part of the building were busy tracking Chris's vitals down to his body temperature's third decimal. They quickly turned their scanners to the inert dog. The cost of the collection of scanners aimed at the dog was the equivalent of some third world country's GNP. At that moment, all that insanely expensive technology came to one unequivocal conclusion.

"Shit. He's dead."

The director, a dog lover himself who shamelessly doted on his own wire hair terrier, found himself having to use every ounce of his professionalism to keep from laughing out loud. It wouldn't have mattered; the entire control room burst into a cacophony of cheers and applause, professionalism be damned.

"How close is the target to the designated location?" shouted the director to the producer over the noise.

"Close enough. The area is clear. No one within fifty feet."

The director turned to the executive, who in turn looked to the demolitions expert. The woman gave a quick look to each and nodded. The director broke into a wide smile and cracked his knuckles. He stole a glance at the monitors showing the audience members, many of whom were openly crying at the death of the dog. But would they be crying when the dog's owner got blown to kingdom come? Doubtful. "Fire when ready."

The explosion was breathtaking in its symmetry, sound, and color. A pyrotechnic Mona Lisa. And no civilian casualties.

"I DON'T BELIEVE it," I say.

"Neither did we," replies Benjamin, absolutely glowing. "I mean, we knew it was an old dog, easily fifteen years, and not exactly svelte, if you know what I mean. But seriously, what are the odds that this dog keels over literally T-minus two minutes?

"Astronomical."

Benjamin punches at his tablet. "Our team ran the numbers. 1,353,482 to 1. We should have bought lottery tickets."

"But there's something I don't understand," I say. "The guy stopped. He hadn't reached the place where the bomb was located. They said, 'close enough.'"

Benjamin gives me his all-knowing grin. "Who said it was at a place?"

I think on this for a moment. "The bomb was on him?"

Benjamin gives a single nod. "His pedometer. We're fans of irony."

I sit back, fanning my flushed face. "Wow."

"Wow, indeed. And that's why it drew a 42/67. Made it to our year-end special. Took the people's choice award if I remember correctly."

We sit in comfortable silence for a moment, savoring the story's finish. Finally, I get back to brass tacks. "How much money are we talking about here? The payout, I mean?"

"Again, it all depends on the ratings, but let's say . . ." and he taps and swipes on his tablet again. ". . . you have an average tune in. Say, 35 rating."

"That's average?" I say, truly surprised.

"A tad below average, but a good round number to work with. With a 35 rating the client payout would be somewhere in the neighborhood of . . . (tap, tap, swipe) . . . 7.2 million dollars."

"So, I die, and my designee collects seven million dollars?"

"Point two. Before taxes, yes."

"Better payout than a life insurance policy," I say a bit thoughtfully.

"I would agree. But we take many of the same precautions. For example, we will not take on a client who has been diagnosed with a terminal disease, so they can cash in on their already impending death. They must be, as they say in the last will and testament biz, of sound mind and body."

"Good thinking."

"We believe so."

We're silent for a moment, but the silence is soon broken by a subtle but repetitive squeak.

I'm a nervous rocker. I stop and settle deeper into the chair, legs out, trying to look at ease.

"What are the upfront costs?" I ask with a flip of my hand. "Ballpark. All things being equal."

Benjamin is polite enough to not acknowledge my lame attempts at casualness. "For a typical job, average lead time, I'd say, fifty thousand dollars."

"Fifty thousand to reap a seven-million-dollar benefit? Seems like a steal."

"Seven point two. We believe our service should be available to everyone, regardless of their social status."

"Still, fifty grand isn't exactly chump change. Not everybody has that kind of money lying around."

"You are correct, but we can't exactly have a payment plan."

"Would you take someone with no down payment and accept payment out of the designee's windfall?"

"No, we do not allow that."

"Why not?" I ask.

Benjamin gives his head a brisk shake.

"There's something unseemly about it. We want our clients to have thought this through carefully and planned accordingly. We don't want just anyone coming in off the street looking for an easy way to make a buck. It can't be a spur of the moment consideration. Each of our prospective clients are evaluated by a team of therapists, psychologists, and counselors to make sure they are emotionally prepared to go through with the agreed upon plan."

"Do you take everyone who meets your criteria?" I ask.

"We do not."

My chair resumes its squeaks, but I catch myself and stop rocking, only to replace it with rotating my chair, back and forth.

"Um, how come?"

"You'd be surprised at how many applicants we have. If we took all of them, the show would lose its appeal. Ratings would suffer. We have to be judicious in our selection."

I get the rotating under control and nod sagely. "Makes sense," I say. "Do I get to dictate how I'll die?"

"Unfortunately, no. We can create a plan for many factors, but the method is kept secret until showtime. For obvious reasons."

"What's the most commonly used method?"

"Rifle shot to the head. Not terribly dramatic, but we can do it from a good distance away, it's painless, and it can be accomplished in a crowd."

"Remind me not to be in that crowd," I say with a ridiculous wink and do the finger-gun thing, firing off a couple rounds. Jesus, I'm a spaz. Benjamin merely smiles. I regroup, refocus.

"Where do you draw your talent?"

"We only hire the most accomplished marksmen. Almost all government trained. 'Wet Boys' as they are commonly referred to in CIA parlance. Did you see the episode in Norway? At the Trolltunga? Sheer poetry."

"Ever kill people hand-to-hand? Snap their neck? That kind of thing?" I ask.

"Occasionally, but it's rare and risky. It takes enormous strength to break a person's neck with bare hands," says Benjamin, nodding sagely.

"You said some people want to feel the experience of dying. What's all that about?"

"We've had ex-special forces clients who wanted their death to be up close and personal. An interesting proposition, in my opinion. Not exactly my cup of tea, but who am I to judge." Benjamin pauses for a beat. "They wanted to know it was happening at the last minute."

"Why?"

"Because they wanted to try to survive."

"Wait. What?"

"They're special forces. Huge egos. Think of themselves as the baddest men or women on the planet. They're willing to spend that fifty thousand with the hopes that they can survive the attack."

"But then the person, the, uh . . ."

"The designee."

"Right. The designee doesn't receive the payout."

Benjamin lets slip a small chuckle. "We do not believe that to be a concern."

"Why?"

This seems to give Benjamin pause, like the thought is beyond ridiculous.

"The production and planning that goes into our events . . ." He breaks, searching. "The chances are astronomically low that someone would survive." He indicates to his glass tablet. "I can run the numbers if you like."

"That's okay. I'm good."

"Besides," he goes on, "virtually all our participants want to die. They want to provide financial means for a loved one." His eyes rest on mine. "Yes?"

I purse my lips and glance away. After an uncomfortable beat I turn back.

"So, you're saying no one's cheated death . . . warrant?" I say with a smirk, trying to lighten the mood.

Benjamin accommodates me with a smile. "Ah, no. That would be bad for business. If someone ever survived, I'd be out of a job." He pauses an instant, biting his lip. "Although, one was close. He was a former Navy Seal, about my age, but still in tremendous shape. We had it set up so that our talent took a seat across from him at an outdoor café, gun already drawn and hidden below the table. The Seal looked up, a little puzzled, and then his key word was said."

"Key word?"

Benjamin spreads his hands before Frankie. "Like I said, some people want to know when it's going to happen, but for that to work we have to use a key word that literally wakes them up to the fact that the attack is about to happen."

"I'm confused," I say.

Benjamin warms even more to the conversation. Clearly this is a favorite subject for him.

"Hypnosis," says Benjamin simply.

"Hypnosis?" I reply.

"Are you familiar with the concept?"

"I'm a professional mentalist, so, yeah," I say, with a slight edge of pride to my voice.

"Are you really?" says Benjamin. And he looks sincerely surprised and impressed, even though I have no doubt he already knew that about me. "That must be fascinating!"

"It has its moments," I say.

"Excellent. Well, then, of course you know the general principles. The person is made to be responsive to suggestion. In our case, the responsiveness must go deep. Think of it as hypnosis on steroids. We have developed methods that are exceedingly effective," says Benjamin. "In this case, when our client came in for his initial consultation, he was embedded with a key word that would awake him to the situation at the designated moment."

"So, the client was cued to know that he was about to be attacked," I say.

"Precisely."

"*The Manchurian Candidate* in reverse," I say.

"Pardon?" says Benjamin.

"Sorry. *The Manchurian Candidate*. Old movie. An assassin goes about his life not knowing he's been programmed to kill someone until a certain word—a key word—is mentioned, at which point he carries through with his task. In your case, the victim becomes *aware* of his impending assassination at the given moment. Like I said, *The Manchurian Candidate* in reverse."

Benjamin looks considerably impressed. "Fascinating. I've never heard it referenced in that way before."

"So, what happened?" I ask.

"Oh," said Benjamin, snapping back into his original story. "The client immediately recognized the situation for what it was, ignored all forms of defense, and went straight into attack mode. He threw his water glass into our talent's face and lunged across the table. Our talent fired, and the shot wounded the client but didn't stop him. The client was able to disarm our talent by driving a steak knife into our talent's gun hand. They went at it, hand to hand for a good few seconds, and I'll be frank, it was touch and go. But our talent's youth and training finally got the upper hand. He was able to put him in a choke hold, and eventually drove that same steak knife into the client's eye."

"Yikes."

"Indeed. But it was superb television. I'm surprised you didn't see it. A popular episode."

"My loss," I say, trying to sound honest. The vast majority of the population is addicted to *Death Warrant*. It is the most popular television show on earth. Yet, I'm not quite as enthralled with it as everyone else. It's the most binge-watched program in history. I don't remember when we as a society became inured to death. It was a slow process, creeping up on us over decades, but when *Death Warrant* aired for the first time, the reaction was sweeping and instantaneous. You would think there would be some part of civilization, some faction who still held life in high regard, but if they existed, they didn't make their presence felt. Who knows, maybe this show would have been a hit fifty years ago and we didn't realize how emotionally dead we were until some hot shit pitched the idea to a network executive.

Benjamin continues, "So, a gentleman came in requesting a quick-turn job. The equivalent of a mob hit. Not terribly dramatic. That's why the quick turns don't have the same payout. Sponsors want time for a little more backstory. Although there is something to be said for the element of surprise. The viewers know it's a smash-and-grab job so they're curious to see how we carry out the termination on such short notice."

"Maybe he wanted a quick-turn," I say, "so he wouldn't have to stress about knowing his number was coming up and the grim reaper could be waiting around every corner."

"Ah," says Benjamin and he raises a knowing finger, "here's the beauty of it. They never know, until it's too late."

"What do you mean they never know? If I sign my paperwork and walk out this door, it's going to be on my mind 24/7. I'll always be wondering if any person I see has a bullet with my name on it." I pause a moment, rubbing my temples. "And this is the part that always makes my brain hurt. Everyone who dies on the show never seems to be afraid or paranoid. They don't appear to be looking over their shoulder. How is that even possible? They signed up. They know they're going to die!" I'm working myself into a good lather; this was a mystery that always bugged me.

But my minor freak out doesn't even phase Benjamin as he dials up a level of compassion that could bake cookies. "Frankie, you said yourself that there's virtually no information online about how we do what we do. And have you noticed that no one you've ever spoken with knows anything either? We take our trade secrets very seriously. The broadcast business can be cutthroat; it's dog eat dog. Do you think I'd be telling you all these things if I thought you might walk out of here and share this information with your husband, barber or bartender?"

"Uh, I was wondering about that."

"Remember the Navy Seal, hypnosis?" Benjamin eases back and spreads his hands out, palms up. "There you go."

"Wait," I say. "You mean you're going to hypnotize me?"

Benjamin positively glows. "It's really quite simple. When you leave you won't recall anything we discussed."

"You mean when I walk out the door, I won't remember any of this?" I shouldn't be surprised. It makes perfect sense.

"No details," says Benjamin, quite reasonably. "Can you imagine if we didn't take these measures? It would be terrible. First of all, once word got out on how things work, our ratings would take a tremendous hit. Much of the mystery would be gone. Secondly, it would be cruel. Would you want to always be looking over your shoulder? Some jobs are a year out. We would never participate in causing a client undue stress and suffering for that long a time. It's unconscionable."

"I see your point."

"Compassion is our calling," says Benjamin.

I hit Benjamin with a skeptical eyebrow raise. "So, at the risk of sounding repetitive, before I leave, you'll hypnotize me to forget that I was even here?"

"Precisely."

"What if I came with someone?"

"Same for them."

"I'm familiar with hypnosis. Not everyone is susceptible. Some people can be hypnotized, some can't."

"Technically ours is a combination of hypnosis and biologicals; we believe in redundancy. And as I mentioned before," says Benjamin, "ours is a much deeper, more powerful form of hypnosis. Everyone is susceptible, particularly with the aid of the biological element."

"That sounds dangerous," I say. "What's to stop you guys from pulling a Manchurian Candidate scenario?"

"Programming someone to kill?" Benjamin looks sincerely stung by this consideration. "We would never do anything like that."

"Uh, Benjamin, that's what you guys do. You kill people for a living."

"There's a significant difference. We do not hypnotize anyone to do anything to which they would be morally opposed. Our terminations are all requested—between consenting adults, as it were—and legally sanctioned. However, I can understand your concern. But I can assure you that your suggestion is beyond the pale. The legal ramifications would be catastrophic. We'd lose our license."

"So, you're saying, even capitalism has its limits."

"Just so. But beyond that, it's a question of morality. We provide a service."

I wasn't done yet.

"What if . . ." I tap my chin, staring at the ceiling. Dammit, I was gonna find some hole if it was the last thing I did. "What if I told someone I was coming?" (Ah hah!) "That person would know I was here and when I came back with no memory of it that could get really messy. Lots of questions."

Again, my question appears to bounce off Benjamin harmlessly. "As I mentioned earlier, the moment you arrive you are scanned, and a full background report is generated. A team member has already checked your phone records to see who you have called within the last few weeks, and another team member has already gone to your home."

"So, your goon squad shows up at my door to see if I spilled the beans to someone else that I was coming here, and if someone's there you hypnotize them too? What if my confidant is a mixed martial arts champion and Green Beret who can kill you in twenty-three different ways in less than five minutes?"

Benjamin smiles without the least bit of condescension. "We never resort to physical confrontations. If there is a person or persons, they will be hypnotized as well, but we use an application process that needs no hands-on involvement. You are a bit of a movie fan, yes?"

"Yep."

"Did you ever see that old movie *Men in Black*?"

"Sure. On my classic movie vid feed."

"The scenes with the flashy-memory-wiping thing? Similar principle."

"Dang."

"As I mentioned, we take our security very seriously."

"Evidently." I'm fresh out of ammo.

Benjamin pauses a moment and fixes me with an earnest and utterly pretention-free gaze. "Why have you chosen to see us?"

My eyes flick to one side as I consider the question in Benjamin's lavender scented office. *Why have I chosen to see them?* The question I knew I would have to answer eventually. But not yet. "I have my reasons."

Benjamin nods slowly, guilelessly. His eyes turn down, passing over his tablet for the briefest of instances. "For your brother, I assume."

I am not prepared for this comment. "How do you know about my brother?"

Benjamin doesn't blink. He holds my gaze with astonishing compassion.

"I told you. The moment you arrive you are scanned, and a full background report is generated." He glances at the glass tablet on his desk, which I assume holds said report. He sees my eyes dart to the tablet and gives a small smile. "I have only a short bio. Not much really. A bird's-eye view, as it were."

"You scanned me. Of course you did. When are any of us not being scanned these days," I say, torn between being miffed and impressed by his candor. "And it's all perfectly legal."

"Absolutely. We take great pains to stay well within the laws of the land."

"Courtesy of a vast and well-seasoned legal department, I would imagine."

"Just so," says Benjamin. "As a matter of fact, scanning and phone record access became legal, I believe, eleven years ago? About year before we went on the air, about the same time monopolistic laws were loosened . . ."

"In your favor," I point out.

"Indeed." Benjamin smiles.

"I've often wondered why you guys are the only game in town. You'd think with all your success, there would be copycat shows galore by now."

Benjamin offers a paternal smile. "As you said, we engage a healthy number of lawyers. Very expensive, very clever, very good lawyers."

"Even lawyers have to eat," I say before pausing for a moment. I wasn't ready to give up yet. "You said that when I leave, I'll have no memory of being here. Okay, fine. But the thought that I wanted to come here in the first place, that desire, will have been in my head, so it's fair to assume that I will consider it again at some point."

"Suppressed," says Benjamin in an almost offhand manner. "You have to understand, we have mastered this technology, methodology, whatever you wish to call it, to such a degree that we can manipulate thoughts with almost surgical precision. We suppress the desire to the point that the applicant will never consider it again. Once you leave here, whether you choose to go through with the process or not, for the rest of your life the thought of coming here will never again cross your mind. Ever."

"This sounds pretty sci-fi," I say. "I have a hard time believing you can manipulate a person's thoughts to that degree. And as mentalist that's my stock in trade."

"You'd be surprised."

Benjamin patiently waits for me to ask more questions, but I am fresh out. Well, almost. "So, what do we do now?"

"Shall I take that as your confirmation that you still wish to move forward with the process?"

This was it. The moment I'd been considering for months now. Fish or cut bait. Am I really prepared to do this? The thought vanishes almost as fast as it had appeared. I know the answer. I'd weighed the pros and cons in my head a thousand times over and I always came to the same conclusion.

"Rock and roll."

Benjamin gives me the warmest, most soothing smile imaginable. He walks around the desk, and, get this, takes a knee. Right there next to my chair. He looks up into my eyes in the way that every woman hopes is followed by a little box and a diamond ring, takes my hand in his, and says, "I want to tell you how proud I am of you. I know this is not a decision you've made lightly, and if you are chosen for the show, the world will be a lesser place without you. But rest assured, something remarkable will come from it. Lives will be changed in ways you've probably never even fathomed. You are going to make a difference. A tremendous difference."

I am not a crier. Not one little bit. It takes serious Hallmark channel sap for me to even offer up a sniffle. The opening sequence in that old animated movie *Up*? Where we see the entire relationship play out between the old man and old lady, from the time they met as little kids until the day she dies? Probably the last time I needed a hanky. Well, no, there were two other times, but still. The valves on my waterworks are well rusted shut from lack of use.

Until now.

With those remarkable eyes and that absurdly real sincerity, I lose it. And I am not the least bit ashamed. It feels good to do a little bawling. I think I am—this is going to sound weird, but—feeling something. Something real and powerful. Wouldn't you know it, the moment I decide to pull the plug is the moment I feel most alive. Exactly like the Navy Seal I mocked. Irony's a bitch.

CHAPTER 2

I punch in the key code to my apartment and hear the familiar snick of the deadbolt releasing. I walk in and behold the beauty that is my home. All 800 square feet of it. I've been living here for . . . it's got to be going on thirteen years now. I grew up in Portland, but after my mom died, I knew it was time to start fresh. Not that I would ever leave my lovely Stumptown. Evidently, around the turn of the century, the town's unofficial slogan was "Keep Portland Weird." I'm glad to say, my city has not lost its quirky identity. It's perfect for me. When I began my search for new digs, I just drove around town with my brother riding shotgun. We'd drive through a neighborhood, and he'd ask, "This one?" And I'd say, "Nope." On to the next neighborhood. Him: "Well?" Me: "Nope." The next. Him: "I'm not going to even bother asking." Me: "Good." Eventually we cruised by this old brick apartment building and my Spidey senses lit up like a Christmas tree. My brother took one look at my face, sighed, and said, "When do you need me to help you move in?"

The small brass sign bolted to the street-facing wall boasted the name the Royal Arms. How can you not want to live in an old brick building called the Royal Arms? I rushed straight into the rental office and offered some variation of "Shut up and take my money," apartment sight-unseen. I'm kind of stupid that way. The apartment manager, an old, short, bent over guy with a name I will remember for the rest of my life simply because it's an awesome name—Rinaldo Pirini—led me up the stairs to the second floor, third door on the right. I peeked in, gave the room an unnecessary once-over, and before I uttered a word, my brother looked at the manager and said, "She'll take it."

My apartment is honestly nothing to write home about, but it fits me. It is the equivalent of that pair of jeans you find in a thrift shop for $20 that are your precise waist and inseam. And already broken in. I toss my coat on my once upon a time emerald green knock-off of a knock-off of a Chippendale sofa that's covered with pillows—way too many for the space—and flick on my off-brand Tiffany-esque lamp that promptly cozies up the space with a soft warm glow. I glance down at my optic to see if there is something pressing that I need to attend to. Nothing. I flop on the couch and take in the row of movie posters hung on the opposite wall; a mechanical engineer couldn't have spaced them more precisely, which satisfies me immensely. Some would call me OCD. I prefer CDO, because the letters are in the proper alphabetical order. As they should be. Another reason I'm a tad obsessive is because it leaves less things to chance. I like predictability, order. If someone moves my shit around, am I going to freak out? No. But I will most likely put it back in its proper place once my guest leaves. Manners trump tidy.

My head swivels to my worktable. Also known as my dining table. It's covered with papers, pencils, scissors, paperclips, and the like, but I always leave an open space just large enough for a plate. However, at this moment the eating space is bare. I will soon rectify that as my tumbly is feeling a bit grumbly. My eyes pass over my scattered paperwork and I absentmindedly suck on my index finger's previous night's paper cut. I'm no artist, but my sketches are clear enough to capture the intent of my project. The prominent shape is a big rectangle surrounded by two Saturn-like rings that crisscross. Surrounding the shapes are assorted measurements and brief notes describing what is what. I could have done all the drawing and schematic work on my optic or tablet but I'm too tactile for that. I can still be awfully analog in a digital world. The drawings are the early stages of what I affectionately refer to as my one serious boyfriend. I call him Bosco. Not named after an old movie star. That I know of. Bosco is my pet project. Bosco is not a person; he is a thing.

He will soon be a part of my act.

Another stomach growl redirects my focus to more pressing matters: din din. In my laughably small kitchen space, I grab a packet of ramen from a cabinet, drop it into a pan of water, and set it on the stove. "High heat, three minutes, please, Charlie." Yes, I named my stove Charlie. And programmed him to have a charming British accent. Everything that I can program to talk back has a name. The stove is Charlie, the shower is Orson, the video and audio system is Spencer. All men, all named after old movie stars. The technology isn't such that the boys can carry on deep conversations with me, but there's enough code in them that we can have a reasonable back and forth. The fact that they can talk is probably why I say please when I ask for something. Yeah, I know, they're inanimate, but still. It's the way I was raised. Growing up, my mom said on more than one occasion, "I don't care if my kids are heroin addicts or criminals, but they will be well mannered." I'm pretty sure she was kidding about the heroin and crime, but the point was well taken.

A few seconds later Charlie gives me a whistle and tells me my ramen is ready. I fish the ramen out of the pot and into a bowl, grab a fork, and almost make it as far as the couch before I realize I've forgotten the most important element of the meal. I scurry back to the fridge and take out a chilled bottle of white wine. A pinot grigio, I think. Frankly, I'm not sure. I check the label. Yep, pinot it is. I grab a glass out of the cupboard and pour a heaping helping. My cupboard is probably the loneliest cupboard on the planet. Inside you will find two plates, two bowls, two drinking glasses, and two wine glasses. It's the Noah's Ark of tableware. The drawer with my flatware is equally sad. And the only reason I even keep a second set of anything is the rare occasion I have a guest over, usually my brother. I'm not big on entertaining. Well, at least when I'm not on stage.

Back at my work table I jab my fork into the ramen and give it a spin to collect a mouthful. Some people like to use chopsticks for eating ramen. Personally, I think that's nuts. I'm not Japanese, don't plan on eating in Japan anytime soon, and, frankly, prefer to get the food into my mouth. I tried chopsticks once and concluded that eating should not be a chore. Halfway through my meal I decide that I don't feel like working tonight, so I put in a call to my BFFH—Best Friend For Hire. It's something I did on a whim, signing up for the service. And I have to say, I love it. From where I'm sitting BFFHs are the greatest thing since screw top wine bottles. You pay a set fee, select what kind of friend you want—girl, boy, straight, gay, tall, short, blonde, brunette, sports fan, opera lover, whatever—and they show up anytime you like. Don't get the wrong idea, BFFHs can't be used for, shall we say, more intimate relations; that's against the law—and creepy. You can kill people on live TV, but screw a BFFH? There are some things you just don't do. My BFFH's name is Audrey. I have no idea if that's her real name. My hunch is it's not. The agency probably fed my profile into a computer, and it spit out an old Hollywood name.

I'm predictable that way.

I speak to my in-house optic, Spencer. "Hey, Spence, call Audrey."

"Will do," says Spence in his typically gruff but friendly manner. I programmed his voice to have a twinge of Wisconsin in it so it's hard for him to ever sound anything but friendly.

A few seconds later, Audrey's face pops up on my wall video screen.

"Frankie! What's up, luv?"

Audrey has short dark hair and the most gorgeous hazel-green eyes imaginable. They are big, almond shaped and impossible to ignore. I peg her at late twenties. A smidge younger than me. Still young enough to have her looks, old enough to have a clue. Her voice has a slight British accent, but I can't tell if it's authentic or affected. Again, with BFFHs, you're never sure what's real and what's not.

"I feel like a movie," I say.

"Well, that's a surprise, innit?" says Audrey. "Let me guess, the Mission?"

The Mission is Portland's oldest movie house, and just a few blocks away. It only plays old movies and is my favorite place in the world.

"Nothing gets past you," I say.

"When?"

"Half-hour?" I ask.

"Brilliant," says Audrey, and her face vanishes from the screen without so much as a by your leave. I like that about Audrey. She doesn't screw around.

The theater is about a five-minute walk, and I still have half a glass of pinot to consider, so I decide to Zen out for a spell.

"Spence, Pink Floyd, *Dark Side of the Moon*, first cut." I like old music too.

"Roger that," says Spence.

For the next fifteen minutes I drift on a white wine cloud and listen to the dulcet tones of "Speak to me," "Breathe," "On the Run," and "Time." I pause it there. If I'm going to listen to the next cut, "The Great Gig in the Sky," I want to have the necessary time to fully appreciate it.

And a fresh bottle.

I FIND AUDREY waiting outside the Mission's front doors, sitting on one of the fire hydrants that have been painted red, white, and blue for the summer's upcoming tricentennial celebration. Audrey is chewing gum, giving her the look of someone ten years younger. Maybe I should try that. Of course, it also gives her the look of someone 50 IQ points lower. Forget what I said about trying that. Audrey likes to dress a bit punky. Despite the northwest winter chill, she's wearing cut off denim shorts over fish net stockings, black boots, and a jean jacket over a colorful tee shirt with the logo of a band I'm not familiar with. With clothing like that you would expect her to go the whole megillah with extra heavy makeup, tats, and piercings. She has none of that. It gives her the ability to clean up well.

She greets me with a girlfriend hug and asks what we're seeing.

"Terminator," I say.

"I'm guessing you've seen it before, yeah?" she asks, already knowing the answer.

"Yep. Have you seen it?"

"Nuh-uh. What's it about?"

"Time travel. Cyborgs. Saving civilization. A cute blonde guy," I say.

"Sold."

We go inside, arm in arm.

The Mission is not your typical movie theater. Half the seats on the main floor are love seats and couches. Old, threadbare, comfy. Like me. The rest of the space is filled with tables and chairs, because at the Mission you don't just watch movies, you also eat and drink. Usually burgers and booze. Yeah, I know, most of the still-existing theaters serve food and cocktails nowadays. In fact, they seemed to have overcompensated. Most theaters now are like flying first class, with crab cocktail, martinis, and recliners with thousand-fingers massage. The Mission doesn't go in for such snooty niceties. The vibe is different. It's got old bones. It's a little nicked up. Just like me. It's—wait for it—cozy. It's the movie theater equivalent of a bar that's got peanut shells all over the floor. No pretense.

Audrey and I pull up to the bar in back and place our orders—the Burley Beef and a Hefeweizen for me, and popcorn, of course. Can't watch a movie without popcorn. I say please and thank you. Audrey orders a slice of pepperoni and a cherry seltzer. How she can stand that stuff is beyond me. It's so bland, it's the taste equivalent of someone yelling "cherry" from the next room. It tastes like video static. I insist on paying but Audrey is having none of that. We end up doing rock, paper, scissors to settle things. I take two out of three, winning the last round with an unexpected paper to beat her rock. In short order, our food and drinks slide across the bar to us, and we find a deep red love seat with a low thrift store coffee table in front of it. My favorite spot, two-thirds of the way back from the screen, about ten feet right of center. I'm surprised they haven't mounted a commemorative plaque on it in my honor, with all the times I've sat there. We've still got a few minutes before the sneak previews, so we dive into our food. It occurs to me for the millionth time that I've never seen Audrey drink before. Alcohol, I mean.

You'd think that would be mandatory for a BFFH, a friend to commiserate with over a drink. But no, Audrey has all the earmarks of a teetotaler, which is fine by me.

I can easily make up the difference if push comes to shove.

We eat in comfortable silence and before long the lights dim. I settle back into the love seat, kick my feet up on the table, and spend the next couple of hours absentmindedly tossing several hundred pieces of popcorn into my mouth.

After Sarah Connor drives off into the desert in her dusty jeep with her trusty German Shepherd and cool 80's headband en route to *Terminator 2*, the lights come up and the sparse crowd begins milling toward the exits. These old movies don't pack them in like the contemporary films. Most here are cinephiles, die hards, or people with nothing better to do on a Wednesday night. Just like me. Outside, Audrey asks me what else I feel like doing. I tell her I'm going to get a toasty caffeinated beverage with gallons of sugar.

"At your regular joint?" she asks.

"Yep," I say.

Like a good BFFH she already knows I prefer going solo and doesn't ask to join.

"Well then, any parting wisdom for me?"

It's a thing we have. I leave her with an inspirational quote. Like what a parent might write on a kid's lunch bag.

"Do not mistake temptation for opportunity," I say sagely.

"Sorry. Me and temptation have got a good thing going and I'm not about to mess with it."

"Suit yourself," I say. "See you 'round." Audrey gives an overly exaggerated curtsy, spins on her heel, and heads off into the night.

CHAPTER 3

THE CHAT WITH MYRNA

Benjamin leaves me in a room that is slightly larger than his office but with no desk. Just a couch, two exceedingly comfortable-looking overstuffed chairs, a coffee table, a lovely mica-shaded standing lamp, and my grandmother. Okay, she isn't really my grandmother, but she might as well be, other than the fact that my grandmother has been dead for twenty years. And was white. The woman in the room couldn't be a day under 70 but holds herself with such poise and assurance I can't take my eyes off her. Her hair is pure white, knotted up in a perfect bun. She isn't wearing what I'd call a business outfit, but her clothes are professional with a cut and fabric that portray no severity whatsoever. Her dark and surprisingly smooth-looking hands are clasped in front of her, and she wears the world's most disarming grin. And of course, her eyes are like polished mahogany surrounded by crinkly laugh lines. I half expect her to whip out a pan of brownies.

Meet Myrna, the kindliest looking woman on God's green earth.

"So, now we talk," she says.

"Okay," I say, trying to sound casually confident. "What shall we talk about? Literature? Film? Fine wine?" There goes my snark again. Dammit.

Myrna glances at her glass tablet, identical to Benjamin's, and taps on it a few times, looking down through her reading glasses. She's looking over my file. I prefer to think of it as a dossier. Sounds more mysterious. That's me, Frankie, international woman of mystery. I look more closely at the tablet, hoping I can see something. I mean, it is transparent, but it's been crafted so that text or images can't be seen from the opposite side. The thing's probably company issue and has a tracking chip in it so that if anyone tries to take it out of the building, alarms go off and security personnel rappel down from the ceiling. I think, perhaps, I see too many movies.

Myrna finally glances back up at me, over her glasses. They're orange. The frames, I mean. Leaning more toward tangerine. The color compliments her dark complexion beautifully. Again, probably selected by a consultant. Not many people need glasses anymore—the eye surgery is supposedly painless, but I'm a big chicken—and those that do still use readers usually go frameless, most likely to make them as invisible as possible. Not Myrna; those tangerine frames are drawing attention. "Hey, look at me," they're saying, "don't I look wise and matronly?" The answer? A resounding yep.

Myrna gives her head a subtle, yet elegant tip to the right. It looks natural, but I can't help but think it's practiced. A look of sincere curiosity.

"Tell me about your job," she says.

I've been asked about my job a zillion times over the years. Understandably, I have an unusual profession. Exotic. As such I've got the elevator pitch down cold.

"I am a mentalist," I say. "A performing artist where I use observation and conversation to guess what people are thinking and perhaps manipulate their actions."

"Like a psychic?" asks Myrna.

"Sometimes, yeah. There are similarities," I say. "Most people think of us as magicians doing tricks."

"Do you think the things you do are tricks?"

"That depends on your definition of a trick," I say. "If you take the power of suggestion and observation for tricks, then yeah, I do. But I don't. I consider them talents."

"Good answer," says Myrna with a sweet smile and a nod. The fact that I said something that makes Myrna smile fills me with immense satisfaction. I can see why she has this job. You want to tell her things. She'd be a great interrogator.

I already know what her next question is going to be. Everyone asks that same question. Myrna doesn't disappoint.

"Can you tell me what I'm thinking right now?" she asks.

I close my eyes tight, hammily place my fingers to my temples, and say, "You're thinking this woman sitting across from you is full of crap."

"Touché."

"It's okay," I say, "nothing I haven't heard before."

"How did you fall into this line of work?" asks Myrna.

The million-dollar question. I could probably come up with a clever lie—something much more interesting than the truth, but Myrna is not someone you lie to. I think I'd feel cheap and ashamed if I tried coloring an answer. I've tossed out some whoppers on how I got into the biz over the years. One time, when this douchey jerkwad was patronizing me, I told him, with an absolutely straight face, mind you, that it all happened when I was in prison (never happened). Just after getting out of three weeks in the hole for busting open some gangbanger's head who tried to cheat me in a game of pinochle, the gangbanger's bitch shivved me with a sharpened toothbrush handle.

I told jerkwad that I lost two pints of blood, was in a coma for five days, and when I came to, I magically had the gift of second sight. Douchbag left me alone after that.

But for Myrna, I cop to the boring-ass truth.

"I've always been observant, even as a kid," I say. My eyes involuntarily shift up and left—the body's default memory reaction—as I begin picturing my six-year-old self. "Before I would talk to another kid, I would watch them for a good ten minutes. How's that for creepy? But I was gathering information. I'd read their body language, the way they'd stand, the way they'd talk, their tone of voice, what they were wearing. I didn't know the term at the time, but I was already focusing on people's micro-expressions, the little twitches and looks in certain directions. And I'd use that information to form a step-by-step route to what they might be thinking."

"Do you find some people are more susceptible than others?" asked Myrna.

"Absolutely. If I get a douchey guy, somebody trying to look cool in front of their friends, and I ask them to pick a random letter I can almost guarantee you it's going to be X, Q or Z."

"Why?" asks Myrna, seriously curious.

I shrug. "They're heavily sexualized letters and he's a douche."

"That's it?" asks Myrna, a little disappointed.

"Sometimes you can't overthink things," I say.

"But you wouldn't make him choose one of those letters through suggestion, that was simply an educated guess."

"Correct," I say. "I just took past experiences and put two and two together. My real bread and butter though is cold reading. That's where the fun is."

"Cold reading?" asks Myrna. I can tell she is completely fascinated, which makes me feel like a million bucks.

"It's also called the Barnum effect, named after the old circus showman P.T. Barnum, way back when they had circuses. It's where people believe what they are told is specific to them, but it could apply to most anyone. You make statements that are vague, and people put their own meaning into the statement, making them personal. I could say to you, for example, that you have a great need for other people to like and admire you. And that you tend to be critical of yourself. And that you often have great ideas that you never have the motivation to follow through on." I look directly at Myrna now. "Would that be accurate for you?"

Myrna shakes her head with amazement.

"Spot on."

"Of course it is," I laugh. "95 percent of the human population can relate to those comments. Just like that, I'm a mind reader."

Myrna smirks a bit and looks back down at the glass tablet, moving down her checklist, I presume. I use the opportunity to redirect.

"Clearly you already know a lot about me, so why are we even having this discussion?"

Myrna is not bothered by my question, or if she is, she's not showing it.

"True, we have a file on you but it's only surface material. Government issue. It's my responsibility to get to know you better, to create a personality profile, and to determine your ratings viability."

"And to make sure I'm not a nut job?" I ask.

Myrna smiles again. "As I'm sure Benjamin told you, we need to assure you are of sound mind and body. This is a major commitment."

"Life changing," I add with a smirk of my own.

"Life ending," says Myrna a little more solemnly than I would have preferred. "It's my responsibility to fully understand your mental state, or at least understand it as much as I can during our time here."

"But can you really get a true sense of who I am in a few hours? If you were my therapist and we were seeing each other twice a week for a few years, yeah, I think you'd know me pretty well. But just chatting like this? I'm not seeing it."

Myrna removes her glasses, grabs the hem of her blouse, absentmindedly cleans the lenses with it, and says with a mischievous grin, "You'd be surprised how much I can learn."

Something in her eyes gives me pause. I glance around the office for a moment and then back to Myrna. "I'm being monitored right now, aren't I." A statement, not a question.

Myrna simply smiles and nods.

"My breathing, heartrate, body temperature, eye movement? My vitals showing up on your tablet there?"

A nod.

I nod back and do a slow clap. "Well done. Well done. A lie detector test."

"Among other things," says Myrna, setting her glasses back upon the bridge of her nose.

I lean in, conspiratorially, and whisper, "How am I doing so far?"

Myrna plays along and whispers back. "So far so good."

We both enjoy the moment.

I sink back into my chair and stare up at the ceiling. I wonder how many people are watching and listening right now. I picture a sterile white room with a team of serious looking men and women in lab coats, their fingers poised over their tablets ready to take note of anything that catches their attention.

Sadly, I have nothing sexy to give them.

It's almost like Myrna is reading my mind. She smoothly crosses one leg over the other, settling in. "We have so much to talk about, and I'm sure you've got some fascinating stories to tell me."

We'll see about that.

CHAPTER 4

Sheila Graveman is sipping a nice cup of Earl Gray when her professional antenna begins to twitch. Her guy down in surveillance who tracked the initial interview with Benjamin had shot her a note to keep an eye on this one. Sheila has been in the viewing room for less than thirty minutes, and with each passing minute she is becoming more and more convinced that her guy is right: this one's a winner. And not just a winner but a flat-out career changer. Unlike Frankie Percival assumed, the viewing studio is not a sterile white room with a team of serious looking men and women in lab coats; it is instead a comfortably appointed space populated with people dressed sharply in suits and skirts. The company has a strict dress code. There is no such thing as casual Friday at the *Death Warrant* offices. Nobody wants to die at the hands of someone in cargo shorts.

The viewing studio is a windowless space about the size of a standard living room. One wall is covered with a host of video displays and physiological monitors. Frankie appears on all the monitors, each showing her from a different angle and distance. There are wide shots, medium shots, close ups, and one extreme close up, where only her eyes fill the screen. There are six people in the room, four men, two women. Frankie was right assuming that several of them are holding glass tablets, comparing data between the tablets and what is showing on the wall-mounted displays. There is a lot of data. A non-stop river of it. Some around the offices quietly wonder if paying this much attention to detail on someone you are going to kill might be a bit much, but Sheila knows that's ignorant.

Data is their life's blood, and you can never have too much information.

Sheila rises from her seat holding her china teacup and saucer, her eyes fixed on the bank of monitors. She slowly walks around the room, stirring her cup with a small silver teaspoon. No plastic cups and flatware at *Death Warrant*. Sheila is thirty-seven years old and recognized as an up-and-comer within the company. Thirty-seven is relatively young in the organization. There are no employees below the age of thirty. Extensive research determined that thirty is the youngest age at which one can fully accept the level of responsibility that comes with this work and have the moral fiber to handle it. The vetting process for landing a job at *Death Warrant* is rigorous. Sheila has been one of the creative directors for three years. Before that she had a lucrative career as a top wedding planner on the west coast. Her weddings were high class events that frequently made headlines. The level of creativity of her weddings had inevitably made her popular in the Hollywood set, which took her income to another level. But she grew weary of bridezillas and after all, you can only do so much with crinoline before it all becomes redundant. And after hearing, "Til death do you part," a few hundred times, the career shift seemed a natural. Sheila has shown a deft touch with her *Death Warrant* assignments. Two of her jobs the previous year had made it into the top-five year-end special. She has a great eye and manages the slippery feat of making her executions theatrical yet authentic. Quite simply, she has the knack. The event that put her on upper management's radar featured a rifle shot on a remote Norwegian mountaintop. She instinctively knew the location would garner attention. It was unexpected, exotic. She also knew the money shot wouldn't be when the bullet hit, but the ensuing fall. She did the math; the body would fall for twelve seconds. Twelve glorious seconds. The ratings were terrific.

Sheila slowly paces the deep carpeted room, her tea still in her hand all but forgotten. She has sharp features that are only highlighted by a severe hairdo. Her bangs are a hard line of pitch-black hair set above eyes that are nearly as dark.

The woman has presence.

Sheila knows that she is respected within the *Death Warrant* halls but still can't shake the feeling that she always has to prove herself. She is convinced that if she were a man, she would have moved up the corporate food chain quicker and higher. There has never been anything overt; she doesn't believe she is being overlooked purposefully because of her sex; gender inequality is simply engrained in the corporate culture. It's been 227 years since the Emancipation Proclamation, and although the world's moving in the right direction, she senses it is still a long way from being a level playing field. It is a cultural shift, she knows, that is akin to turning around a super tanker. Perhaps, she grudgingly admits, it is why she presents herself with a little more of a masculine edge.

"Have you noticed her heart and respiratory rates?" Sheila asks the room.

"Ice in her veins," says Brett Haesham, one of her Associate Creative Directors, a trim blonde man a few years younger than Sheila. His eyes are flitting back and forth between his glass tablet and the vital signs displayed on the monitors.

"That's an understatement," says Sheila. "Her respiratory rate is thirteen breaths per minute and her heartrate is sixty."

"Pretty low," observes Leticia Boronevska, one of the technicians, and the only other woman in the room.

"Does she look like a marathon runner?" asks Sheila rhetorically. "No, she does not," she answers. "She's just committed to being executed on worldwide television and yet she's chatting with Myrna like they're trading gardening tips. Cool as a cucumber." Sheila turns to one of her team. "We did check her for psychotic tendencies, right?"

"Of course. She came back clean as a whistle. She seems to be processing this as normal."

Sheila walks up to the bank of monitors and studies the array of vital signs. "Eye dilation minimal, breathing steady, body temperature normal. She's the unsinkable Molly Brown." No one picks up on the Titanic reference.

Sheila walks back to her chair and eases back down, still stirring her tea. "This is the kind of stuff that makes me glad I get up in the morning."

One of the technicians, a man about forty, but new to the organization, pipes up. "So, you think this one could be pretty good?"

Sheila's eyes never leave the monitors. "You watched her interview with Benjamin."

The technician nods, suddenly self-conscious of his newness. "Yes," he answers tentatively.

Sheila turns to him, knowing this is a teachable moment. "She asked good questions."

"Like?"

"The one about people wanting to feel the experience of dying. That shows she's curious about the human condition. That kind of trait scores well."

"And the fact that she's a mentalist?" asks the technician hopefully.

"Absolutely," replies Sheila. "A point in her favor. Unusual profession."

Over the next few hours Sheila Graveman takes copious notes, noting key words and phrases. By hour two she is already turning over ideas in her head. By hour three she is bouncing around the studio like her tea was laced with amphetamines. She knows she has something special. Frankie Percival has the potential to be her work of art. Her Mona Lisa. Her Starry Night. However, Sheila thinks another comparison may be more appropriate: Edvard Munch's The Scream.

CHAPTER 5

FEBRUARY

My regular joint is a coffee shop in southeast called the Zombean Apocalypse. Whoever came up with that name better know they will never create anything better than that for the rest of their life. That's one of those names where you think, "Damn, I wish I'd thought of that." Don't let the name fool you though, it's a surprisingly cheerful place. The coffee shop features token framed zombie movie posters throughout, a given, but the owners took pains to not go overboard with the zombie motif. It's basically a smiley face version of zombie décor. I walk past the butter yellow wall that's positively glowing from the sun streaming in through the picture windows fronting the place. You'd never know it was forty-five degrees outside. A fireplace at one end is surrounded by mismatched overstuffed chairs, and the tables look like they were purchased at the same second-hand store where the owner of the Mission theater shops. I love the fireplace. Another nice touch is that at every table you will always find an old magazine. I'm not talking a few months or even years old; I mean old old. Like multiple decades old. Mostly mags that don't exist anymore, with titles like Look, Life, People, Time, and Cosmopolitan. The issues of Cosmo are always in hot demand. Who doesn't want to start their day with *The three tricks that will drive your man wild in the sack*. By the way, I read that article and spent the next week questioning my skills and draining half a case of chardonnay. Every morning the coffee shop staff makes it a point to rotate in a different assortment of magazines. In all my years of coming here I've never seen the same magazine from one day to the next. The owner must have a stockpile somewhere or somebody who hooks him up. Regardless, it's a cool touch that adds to the color of the place.

The barista working the counter is an early twenty-something sleepy-eyed cutie by the name of Mitzi. She's there on a regular basis, late-afternoons and evenings. Based on the hours I assumed she was there to help pay for college, but it turns out she's just a late sleeper and the idea of beginning the day before noon is against everything she stands for. That might explain her half-lidded look and borderline "yea, whatever" attitude. Based on our conversations over the months as I placed my orders, I learned that she's not big on elocution—kinda blends her words—and what she stands for is making really good coffee with those nifty little pieces of artwork in the foam, hanging out with her unemployed boyfriend Lloyd, partying into the wee hours of the morning, and then wrapping things up with a solid ten hours of sleep. Rinse and repeat.

I order my standard chai tea, medium, compliment Mitzi on her new haircut, an inverted bob, and grab a seat by the fireplace. The fire's burning low so it's giving off just the right amount of heat. It'll probably be a good fifteen more minutes before they throw another log on, at which point, I'll need to move to another seat, which is fine. I'm a notorious chair-hopper. Usually for the purpose of finding a clear view of a customer. There's one seat in particular that has the best view. It's by the window and from there you can see every table in the shop. I grab it when I can because I like to do more than watch people, I like to study them. That probably sounds creepy, but I assure you it's not the least bit nefarious. My time at the Zombean is precisely that, my time. It's my quiet time, my time to hang, sip and space. And study. The Zombean is my study hall, where I hone my observation skills. Sometimes I'll kick back with a magazine and while away the hours getting caught up on what had tongues wagging a few decades prior—the COVID pandemic, the last mass-produced gas-powered car, the first truly comfortable women's dress shoe. However, more often than not I'm picking out a face in the crowd and trying to divine their story. Of course, most of the time I have no idea if I'm right as I never speak to them, but it still helps me to focus on people's subtleties. Case in point: the couple by the window closest to the door. Two women, both mid-thirties. I probably shouldn't say couple, as they clearly are not a romantic couple. The one on the left in a baggy maroon sweater is chatty and animated. Her friend, no doubt a good friend, a more elegant looking woman wearing a stylish blouse and a haircut to die for, sits quietly stirring her drink and listening intently. Only good friends and salespeople try to look like they're listening that intently. But with this woman it's not an act, you can see it in her body language. She's leaning in slightly, the way you do when you're interested in something but aren't even aware that you're leaning in. Her chatty friend's left hand flits around like a butterfly while her right-hand is wrapped around her forgotten coffee. The cups are paper with those sleeves to keep your hand from getting too hot. That tells me they weren't planning on staying, but taking the drinks to go, but while they were waiting for their orders, the chatty friend must have started a story that both deemed best suited for a sit down. The good listener is sporting an impressive rock on her left-hand ring finger. Even from across the room you can tell it's a stunner. She's absent-mindedly rubbing the ring with the thumb of the same hand while she stirs with the other. She's obviously the married of the two and I'd wager that the chatty one is talking about a man, either a recent date or a boyfriend who's done something that's got her frustrated. I'm going with the boyfriend angle as she's looking a tad too frumpy, which tells me she's no longer on the hunt and has slipped into a comfort zone with this guy. The conversation is probably running along the lines of the guy being marriage-phobic, not being there when she needs him, spending too much time with his buddies, leaving the toilet set up, watching too much football, snoring, or not noticing the five pounds she's lost. With the way the good listener is working that wedding ring, she's most likely thinking how glad she is to be out of the dating game.

I tire of the ladies and glance around to see whom else I can try to read. Frankly, I shouldn't even be here, I should be back at my apartment working on Bosco. How else am I going to become the next big thing in the entertainment world? I promise myself I'll only stick around a couple more minutes and then bail. I continue my scan, trying to make my last minutes count. It's an average crowd, maybe a dozen people scattered throughout, and the majority are riveted to their optics. I've got an optic myself but it's more of a convenience than a source of entertainment, which places me squarely in the extreme minority. I mean, sure, I use it to watch movies and stuff now and then, I'm not Amish for crying out loud, but for some reason that I've never quite been able to pinpoint, I'm not that into the stupid thing. If I had any close friends, friends I'm not paying for, they'd more than likely label me nuts. Whatever. I've concluded that most people live and die by their optic. If their house was on fire and they had to choose between saving their optic or their significant other, my money's on the optic.

I'm about ready to give up and call it a day when my eyes drift over to a man sitting by the center pillar. I notice that his head is not buried in his optic, so he's got that going for him. He's reading an ancient, dog-eared copy of a magazine that appears to be called Tiger Beat, whatever that is. The cover features a young blonde man with feathered hair and a puka shell necklace. I think it's a music magazine but can't be sure. I see a headline partially covered by his fingers holding the magazine that breathlessly shouts in bold text "Leif tells all!" The man must feel the weight of my stare and glances up from the pages. His eyes are blue. Like, nutso blue. He's a bit older than me, but not too much so, and has a ceramic mug steaming to his left. Okay, he's left-handed, which is interesting. Only 10 percent of the population are lefties. I like anomalies. My eyes finish their once over, getting a general sense of the man before being drawn back up to those ridiculous eyes, and get this, he's still looking at me. Weird. Most people when they catch you looking at them immediately avert their eyes, but not this character. He just continues to stare right back at me like it's a game of visual chicken. Eventually he blinks, gives the slightest of smiles, and goes back to reading about Leif telling all. I'm not used to men staring at me for more than a couple of seconds. It doesn't happen often. I'm what I like to call almost pretty. If I was ten pounds lighter, two inches taller, had thinner ankles or thicker hair, I might get a stare every now and then, but that hasn't been the case. I'm the before picture in a shampoo commercial. Kind of like the chatty woman in the baggy maroon sweater I was reading earlier—not quite put together, but I don't have a boyfriend and hence no excuse. I take in the rest of the room to find a suitable target, but my eyes seem to home back in on Tiger Beat guy. Dammit.

I find myself a tiny bit flustered by this. Why am I looking at this guy? It's not like he's drop-dead gorgeous. Okay, his eyes qualify, but the rest is nothing to write home about. He's wearing a blue plaid flannel shirt and I can't help but wonder if he consciously chose it to compliment his eyes. Is he the kind of guy who does that sort of thing? Does he know what his season is? Where he falls on the color wheel? The rest of the ensemble doesn't give that impression: faded blue jeans, non-designer, and worn sneakers. It's late afternoon and yet there's no stubble on his chin so that tells me he shaved that morning, therefore he's most likely gainfully employed. But it must be a job that doesn't have banker's hours. A bartender? No, bartenders don't care if they're clean-shaven. A salesman? Excuse me, account executive. Perhaps an executive? Someone who can choose his own hours? Hmm. Not clean cut enough, his hair's a smidge too shaggy for the average white collar of his age. Portland's a pretty laid-back town, but there are still rules to business dress, and what he's wearing wouldn't even rate business casual. The fact that he had no issue locking eyes with me tells me he has no shortage of confidence, so he could be one of those overachievers where everything comes easy, and his confidence allows him to get away with looking just this side of professional. His hair is blonde with zero product with enough gray in it to suggest he's not overly vain. He's a comfortable level of disheveled. Maybe DEFCON 3.5 on the messy scale—five being wedding day spit and polish, one being hobo living under a bridge. After careful consideration I'm going with entrepreneur. I feel satisfied with my assertation, silently pat myself on the back, and take a rewarding sip of chai.

My attention is drawn away by the two women I was analyzing earlier. They've finished their conversation, if not their coffees, push away from their table, and walk past me, heading to the bathroom. The chatty one seems much more at ease than earlier. Evidently, she needed some good old-fashioned venting. By the time they pass me, I glance back up at Tiger Beat, but he's gone. I look around the coffee shop with a twinge of disappointment just in time to see the front door swinging shut behind him. He's heading directly across the street to parts unknown. I track his progress longer than I should. His head turns left. Was that a glance back? No, just checking traffic to make sure all's clear. He reaches the other side and heads north until I can no longer see him through the window.

CHAPTER 6

Crap. I'm hungover. What the hell? Am I suddenly eighteen again? Annoyed that Mr. Blue Eyes stared at me and then walked out without so much as a glance back, I spent my evening sulking with a bottle of pinot noir and *Dark Side of the Moon*. I roll over and peek outside through slitted eyes. I'm sure it's not physically possible, but the sun feels really loud right now. I curse the daylight and stagger into the bathroom. I look in the mirror and cringe at the creature looking back.

She looks vaguely familiar. Red, watery eyes deeply set in a face that could pass for a piece of fruit that's been left out in the sun for too long, framed by hair that appears to have been styled with a hand mixer.

"Spence," I groan. "What time is it?"

"12:32 p.m.," replies Spencer from a speaker embedded in the mirror.

"12:32? Gawd!"

I take a closer look at my face, open my mouth, and inspect my tongue, half expecting it to be a shade of color not yet discovered by mankind.

"Orson," I say, "Shower on. 102 degrees."

"Certainly," replies the voice from the shower in its rich transcontinental accent.

I peel off my clothes, climb in under the water, spend the next fifteen minutes regaining consciousness. The water feels like tiny Fred Astaires doing a soft shoe on my head, neck, and shoulders. By the time I climb out I feel halfway human again.

"Nice work, Orson," I say.

"My pleasure," it replies.

I trudge to the fridge, open it, stare for a couple of seconds, and close it. Not quite ready for food yet. I stare at the coffee maker and arrive at the same conclusion.

Evidently, I will be going sustenance-free for the time being. I plop down on the couch and stare into space, trying to reestablish my equilibrium, when Spencer pipes up.

"You had a call," he says.

"You're kidding." I never get calls. Well, seldom get calls. "Who was it?"

"Should I play the call?" asks Spencer with a touch of annoyance. I didn't even know he could do annoyance.

"Yeah, sure."

A face appears on the video screen. My agent. And I use the term loosely. I honestly don't remember the last time we talked. I think he's landed me exactly one job in the last five years. His name's Mel Bevaqua, a short, squatty little Italian, mostly bald. He's got to be at least sixty by now. When I started doing mentalism as a profession, I figured I needed an agent to rustle up some bookings, and Mel was the first name I stumbled across. His office was in a nondescript one-story building not far from my apartment. We met, chatted, I showed him a few mentalist bits, he acted sufficiently impressed, we shook hands, and just like that he was my agent.

For the first few years he landed me a fair number of gigs, but then the calls became less and less frequent until they simply stopped. I guess he had other, more promising clients by then. It was no big deal, I had steady work coming in and had figured out the marketing side of the business, so I seldom went too long without a gig. On the video screen he looks and sounds like it has only been days since we last spoke instead of years.

"Frankie, it's Mel. I received a last-minute call for a job that's right up your alley. It pays well, and you'd be in and out in an hour. Give me a call if you're interested. Ciao!"

Frankly, he had me at it pays well. I call him right back.

He answers on the first ring.

"Bevaqua talent, this is Mel, how can I help you?"

That's one of the things I always like about Mel, he's damn courteous.

"Hi, Mel, it's Frankie."

"Frankie! Thank you so much for calling me back so promptly."

I cut to the chase. "What's the gig?"

"A birthday party for a corporate big wig. Evidently, he's got a thing for magicians. The one he had booked cancelled due to an undisclosed medical emergency and his assistant called me looking for a replacement."

"Lucky me," I say. "What else can you tell me?"

"The party is at the gentleman's home in the west hills."

"Swank," I say.

"Indeed. Since they're in a bit of a bind, I charged them a, shall we say, rush fee, a portion of which I will include with your standard fee."

"Uh, Mel, my standard fee is a little higher than it was when last we spoke. Half a decade ago. About 25% higher."

"I would expect nothing less."

That tells me he probably charged 40% more without asking and I don't get to keep the difference.

"So, you'll do it?" he asks.

"Standard show, one hour? Sure. What's the time and address?"

Mel provides me the information, wishes me luck, and hangs up without a single question about what I've been up to for the last five years. All business. I like that about Mel. I feed the address into my optic and Spencer tells me it's only a fifteen minute drive away. After I hang up a thought occurs to me.

"Spence, call Audrey."

A moment later Audrey's face appears on screen looking much fresher and more clear-eyed than I do. She leans into the camera with a squint. "Bloody hell, it looks like someone's feeling a bit dicky today."

"You should have seen me an hour ago," I say.

"Glad I din't," she replies.

"Say, Aud, you got anything going on tonight?"

Without missing a beat, "Dinner with her majesty the Queen," she says. "It's hot dog night."

"Cancel," I say. "Tell her you've got a better offer."

Audrey scrunches up her face and shakes her a head. "I dunno. You did hear me, yeah? It's hot dog night."

"Tell her you've got an opportunity to escort an up-and-coming American entertainment star on what will most likely be a historic performance," I say as I casually curl a lock of my hair with a finger.

"Wait. What?" says Audrey, seriously surprised. "You're inviting me to one of your gigs? You never invite me to your gigs."

"Old dog, new tricks. Feeling lonely. Wanna show off. Hell, pick one. I dunno, I thought you might like it. I got a last-minute call for some big wig's birthday party. You'd probably, you know, have to wear something nice. Makeup and stuff, too."

"Are you kidding me?" says Audrey. "This is a big-ass deal! I'll actually get to wear a dress. And cool shoes! What time and where?"

"I'll pick you up at six."

And with that, I click off and flop back into my couch. It was nice to see Audrey so excited about coming to see me perform. She was right, I've never invited her before. Not exactly sure why. Maybe it's because I pay her to hang out with me. Whatever. That's deeper self-examination than I am interested in at the moment. That and my head still hurts like a mother. I have a few hours to recuperate, so I begin the healing process with Pink Floyd's *Wish you were here*. It's a forty-four-minute album made up of only five songs which gives you plenty of time to fully immerse yourself in a song before it changes. I think I only make it through ten minutes of *Shine on You Crazy Diamond's* thirteen-minute running time before I drift off, buoyed by the shimmering medicinal powers of Floyd.

I awake fully refreshed and ready to kick birthday party ass and astonish the masses. The promise of a big fat check can do that for you. Yesterday's events at the Zombean already a distant memory.

CHAPTER 7

With artificial intelligence as my trusty navigator, I put my car into autonomous mode, and it finds the sweeping elegant home tucked behind an imposing ornate gate a good fifteen minutes before showtime. This is a tax bracket neighborhood I am not accustomed to. Every house looks like it should be featured on an episode of *Oh my God, I wish I owned this home*! The cars parked in the turnaround make my modest little rig look garishly out of place. We walk up the crushed rock pathway that's flanked by a perfectly manicured lawn and immaculate landscaping. I spot a raked gravel garden punctuated by several small boulders. The symmetry is perfect. A few well-trimmed Bonsai, and skeletal, leafless Japanese maples ring the garden.

I silently approve.

Audrey is looking around only slightly more starstruck than me.

"What's the name of our birthday boy?" asks Audrey, bending to sniff a perfect looking flower to see if it is real. It must be fake. It's winter, right? Her reaction gives no hint.

"Uh, I didn't ask," I say.

Audrey looks stunning in a fitted emerald-green gown and gorgeous cream open-toed stilettos. I'm in my standard Frankie attire: khaki slacks, dress-shirt, vest, loose tie, and a men's bolero hat jauntily dipped to one side. I saw a woman dressed like this in a Woody Allen movie from about a century back, and thought it was just my style. I've emulated it ever since. Eclectic-chic is what I call it. I've heard less flattering descriptions over the years, but I couldn't give a rip.

I can hear the low hum of crowd conversation before I knock on the door.

Then, I hear the unmistakable ping of my and Audrey's optics. It's the *Death Warrant* ping. The international heads-up that an episode is about to begin. My gaze snaps to Audrey just as her hand is reaching for her clutch.

"Don't you dare," I say. "Don't you freaking dare. You can go without an episode just this once."

Audrey's face scrunches up like the thought is painful, but she draws her hand away from her clutch. "Okay, okay. Fine. But your bit better be fookin' brilliant if I'm missin' me show."

As if on cue, the door opens and a stately gentleman with astonishing posture, a cutaway waistcoat, and a warm smile greets me.

"Ms. Percival, I presume?" The gentleman glances at Audrey smoothly, "And guest?"

"You presume correctly," I say, trying to match his smile.

He ushers us into a polished bamboo floored foyer that's nearly the size of my apartment. "Please wait here," he says. "Someone will be with you shortly to go over the arrangements." The gentleman gives us a polite nod, and then before he turns to leave, he says, "I understand Mr. Hasagawa is looking forward to your performance."

Audrey turns to me with her Oh-My-God face and says in a stage whisper, "Hasagawa? *The* Hasagawa? Grayson Hasagawa?"

Grayson Hasagawa is one of the most powerful men in America. The proverbial Captain of Industry. He's into tech, pharma, broadcasting, agriculture, you name it. But what put him in the top one percent of the top one percent was developing a cheap, efficient way to take the salt out of seawater. Global water crises over and done with. As a result, the man is richer than God.

I give Audrey my own variation on the Oh-My-God face. She starts scurrying around the foyer space looking closely at all the furnishings, turning around curtains like she's looking for price tags, and running her fingers along the lip of a pair of vases that come up to her waist. "Your agent didn't tell you who you were performing for?" she asked.

"Nope."

"That's messed up, yeah?" she says.

Audrey then does a pirouette in the middle of the room with her eyes closed. "I can't believe I'm doing a pirouette in Grayson Hasagawa's house."

"Yeah," I say, "and you're gonna get us grand jeté'd right into the slammer if you're not careful."

Audrey stops and grabs both my hands, reverting to her way too loud stage whisper, "This is too cool!"

A voice from neither one of us says, "I know the feeling."

We turn, lightning quick, to face the voice. Both of us, our cheeks candy apple red. At that moment a precise looking woman in a crisp white blouse, black pencil skirt and high-sheen pumps enters from an adjoining room. She extends her hand which I take with a single shake. Her hand is so small and delicate my own feels like an oven mitt. Audrey, in full embarrassment mode, shakes her hand like she's working an antique water pump.

The woman, clearly enjoying our embarrassment, smiles and says, "I'm Devon Nichols, Mr. Hasagawa's personal assistant. Please come with me."

We follow a step behind her through a magnificently appointed study, complete with an enormous globe, renaissance art, furniture to die for, and a large wall monitor. The audio is low, but a quick glance reveals the unmistakable opening credits to *Death Warrant. Crap,* I think to myself, *I'm performing for Grayson Hasagawa, and competing against the most popular show in the world. What the hell, you play the hand you're dealt.* I notice Hasagawa's assistant gives the screen a disapproving stare, and sense that she is debating whether to turn the monitor off, but the moment passes. Out the door and into a smaller room we go, which is evidently a library. Bookshelves line two of the walls and an iron and wood ladder mounted on rolling track sits idly waiting for someone to climb aboard to access the lonely books closest to the ceiling.

Ms. Nichols asks us to wait there for a moment and exits through the far door. After the escapade in the foyer, Audrey stands stock still while I take the opportunity to give the place a closer examination, being a bit of a book fiend myself. In the early part of the century, ebooks became a thing, and there were concerns that physical books would go the way of the dinosaurs, but luckily, the fad faded. Evidently, people like the experience of turning pages. Hasagawa included. The shelves are packed to the gills but there's something funky about the books. Normally, in this type of library, every book would be a leather-bound beauty embossed with gold leaf. There is no shortage of those, but I can also see that many of the books look utterly ordinary. Like you might find at your local bookstore or county library. There's even a scattering of paperbacks. And based on their condition, they've all been read. I pull one out and look it over. It's a thriller that was all the rage last summer. Seemed all the stay-at-home-moms had a copy while they sunned by the community pool.

"One of the biggest bazillionaires in the world reads cheap dime-store novels. That is so bad ass."

I set the book back moments before Ms. Nichols re-enters and beckons us with a wave. It's time for the rules of engagement. I've done my share of corporate events and parties; the higher the profile the stricter the rules.

Ms. Nichols says, "Speaking on behalf of Mr. Hasagawa, I would like to thank you again for being available on such short notice."

"No problem," I say. "Glad I can fill the void."

"Mr. Hasagawa is a big fan of your particular line of work and is very much looking forward to your performance."

"That's the best kind of audience," I say.

"Is there anything you will need? A table? Chair? Water?" A beat. "Something stronger," she says with a grin.

"Tempting," I say, "but I'm good. How big is the room and how will it be laid out?"

"I'll take a gin and tonic if you're asking," says Audrey while I die a thousand deaths for her impertinence.

Ms. Nichols doesn't seem to mind the request and nods. "Certainly. There's an open bar in the ballroom." She turns to me. "That is where you will be performing. There are about one hundred people, all sitting at tables."

"And am I to presume Mr. Hasagawa will be sitting at the front?"

"Correct," says a new voice from our left.

I turn to see what by all accounts is a handsome man striding toward us with a pleasant grin. He reaches out his hand which I take, and he steps in and slowly shakes it, his left hand wrapped over the top. It's remarkable how such a simple gesture disarms me and completely puts me at ease.

The assistant nods in the man's direction.

"Mr. Hasagawa, Ms. Percival." She then turns to Audrey. "And . . ."

Audrey steps up and presents her hand like he's supposed to kiss it or something. "Atwood. Audrey Atwood."

Mr. Hasagawa takes her hand and gives her a courteous nod. "Ms. Atwood." I think if Audrey's cheeks were any redder, she might spontaneously combust.

Grayson Hasagawa looks exactly like he does on television. Mid-sixties, salt and pepper hair, still thick and perfectly coiffed. He's wearing a dove gray sports coat over a pale blue oxford, the top button undone. Business casual. He's clearly of Asian descent, Japanese, but not 100 percent. His eyes are almost black, which at any other moment would give him a sober, no-nonsense appearance if it wasn't for his mischievous grin.

Yep, mischievous, that's the best way I can describe it.

"Ms. Percival," he says amiably. "I am so looking forward to your performance." He stops and places a thoughtful index finger to his lip. "Tell me, how long have you been a mentalist?"

"Performing? About ten years."

"And this is your full-time profession?" he asks.

"It's not exactly a nine to five job, but it's what pays the bills. You don't strike me as a nine to fiver yourself." I'm feeling bold.

Hasagawa seems to enjoy the exchange. "Not anymore," he says.

I glance around the room. "You've got a beautiful home here. And I love your library."

Hasagawa looks both proud and slightly surprised. "A fellow book lover?"

I nod. "I'm lost without a good book. Did I see a copy of *The Great Gatsby* on your shelf? 1925, first edition?"

He nods and smiles even broader. "I'm impressed. Most people these days seem more interested in their optics than reading a good book."

I turn and look back towards the bookshelves. "There were some great authors in twenty-five. Well, twenty-five from the last century. Hemingway, Fitzgerald, Agatha Christie."

Hasagawa offers me a patient smile. "Do tell."

"Did you know Paul Bunyan was written in 1925?" I ask.

Hasagawa laughs out loud at this. "A piece of literary trivia that I will no doubt use at dinner parties for the rest of my life."

The assistant lightly touches her boss's arm. "Mr. Hasagawa?"

Hasagawa acknowledges the assistant with a nod. "Yes, of course, I shouldn't ignore my guests." He looks back to Audrey and me and gives us a short bow. "Ladies, if you'll excuse me." And then he gives me a quick smile. "Break a leg," he says before he turns and leaves.

As he passes into the study, I spot him through the door taking notice of the monitor playing *Death Warrant*. It doesn't take a mentalist to notice the negative change in his body language. He gives a terse command

and the monitor blinks off. With a short shake of his head he regroups and leaves my field of vision.

I look to Ms. Nichols. "He's not what I was expecting," I say.

The assistant nods and smiles. "A common refrain."

"Seriously!" I say. "He's like, I dunno, a regular guy. Someone you'd want to have a beer with."

"I know, right?" pipes in Audrey. "You'd never know he was crazy rich, except of course for the thousand-dollar shoes."

I throw Audrey a withering glare. The assistant leans in conspiratorially and whispers, "Three thousand, actually."

Both Audrey and I do a double take on this, but I regroup and get back to business. "I don't suppose my performance will be recorded, will it?"

"Not recorded, but the performance will be on camera. They're located throughout the house."

"And the video feed will be sent to monitors elsewhere in the house?"

Ms. Nichols gives me a puzzled smile. "Yes. The signal will be sent to monitors throughout the house so that the kitchen staff and other service employees may be able to watch as well. Why?"

Now it's my turn to give the coy smile. "You'll see."

She seems to find my answer acceptable and gestures for us to follow her. She leads us through a series of halls until we enter what I must presume is the ballroom. And calling it merely a ballroom does not do it justice. It should be called the exquisite room. First off, it's enormous, the size of a royal wedding reception hall, with floor to ceiling windows lining the far wall with a spectacular view of the city below the west hills. The floor is arranged with about a dozen round event-style tables, each covered in burgundy linen with extravagant blown-glass center pieces, each different from one another. The crowd is scattered throughout the room, some sitting, some standing, all dressed to the nines. Mr. Hasagawa, the birthday boy, is comparatively underdressed. But that's understandable. Nobody wants to come to a Grayson Hasagawa shindig and be the one wearing blue when everyone else wears black. And when the party's for you, at your house, and you're footing the bar tab, you can wear whatever you like, thank you very much. Audrey's dress fits in reasonably well. My outfit? Not so much.

But I don't mind, I know my place.

I'm the help.

Ms. Nichols tells me, "You will be performing in," she checks her watch, "ten minutes. Will that give you time to prepare?"

I nod. "Yes, that will be fine. Thank you."

"Excellent." She gestures to the room. "Please make yourselves at home. I will announce you when it's time to begin." She then turns to Audrey. "And now for your gin and tonic? Come this way."

She leads Audrey away who peeks over her shoulder at me with one last wide-eyed look. I'm glad she's enjoying herself.

I wander the room aimlessly, trading polite grins here and there. That game I play at the Zombean? Guessing customer's stories? I could have a field day in here. Everyone here is either a mover or a shaker. Some probably both. The formal attire makes it more challenging—everyone's dressed similarly—but I've found that the well-heeled tend to put on airs and try a smidge too hard to be charming. They're like the girl who wears too much makeup, too high of heels, and too short a skirt trying to look pretty only to end up looking cheap, tawdry, and desperate. It's a Hamptons version of the same thing. The diamonds are a tad bigger than they have to be. Watch a few conversations, see who's avoiding eye-contact with whom, who's pointing and whispering, and who's being a little too touchy-feely and it doesn't take long to dial in who's in Dutch with the Mrs., who's sleeping with someone else's wife, or who wants to. Of course, sometimes you even get to see it all play out in real time, complete with the gasp, the drink thrown in the face, and the dramatic exit from the room. It's good theater. But frankly, I'd rather not have the competition.

Speaking of competition, I notice a few guests giving furtive glances to their optics, clearly trying to get in sneak peaks of the *Death Warrant* episode playing at that very moment. Nobody wants to be caught watching television during a Grayson Hasagawa party, but even the rich and famous have morbid curiosity. The looky-loos are few and discrete. I am glad, for nothing is worse than trying to hold a crowd's attention when half are looking at their optics.

I scan the room to see if there are any ideal candidates to bring up on stage. I spot a few possibles. A quick check of my watch tells me it's almost show time, so I start moving my way back to the front of the room near a microphone stand. I set my purse over at the foot of a gloss black baby grand piano sporting some propped open sheet music. Rachmaninoff's Piano Concerto

No. 3, supposedly one of the most technically challenging piano concertos ever. Don't ask me how I know that. Another useless piece of trivia that made a nest in my head. I wonder if Hasagawa can play the Rach or if it's only for show. Before I can give this deeper consideration, Ms. Nichols steps up to the microphone.

"Ladies and gentlemen, if you would please take your seats, our entertainment is about to begin."

The crowd begins herding to the tables and the air is filled with the sound of chair feet scraping out and back in. Grayson Hasagawa is sitting front and center next to an astonishingly beautiful woman who undoubtedly is his wife. She's probably in her mid-forties but could pass for a decade less. Her hair is slate gray but still thick and lustrous. She has laugh lines that could have easily been erased with Botox, but she evidently has the confidence to wear them with pride. She's wearing a deep red dress that looks like it was poured out of a bottle of pinot noir. The perfect complement to her hair. And peeking out from the hair that's gathered on her slim shoulders are diamond stud earrings that are large enough to capture your attention but not so big as to feel like they're shouting. A tasteful platinum necklace drapes elegantly below her neck, drawing your eyes to what's below. But here's the kicker: She doesn't have big boobs. It almost seems like a prerequisite for the arm candy of super rich alpha males to have significant others who can also double as a floatation device. Hasagawa's squeeze? B-cup, maybe. But perfect. At least from my eye, and I've seen my share of boobs over the years. She casually rests a hand on his knee.

It says, "mine."

The crowd has quieted, and everyone's attention is front and center. This is the moment that I relish, where the room is filled with equal parts curiosity and skepticism.

"Thank you," says Ms. Nichols. "And now, may I please introduce your host, and the man who refuses to reveal his true age—" She holds for polite laughs. "Grayson Hasagawa."

The crowd gives the appropriate amount of cheers and applause as the guest of honor gives a peck on the cheek of his wife, walks to the front, and takes the mic from his assistant.

"Thank you, Devon," he says to her as she steps back respectfully, stage left. Hasagawa then turns to the crowd. "And thank you for joining me for yet another of one too many birthdays." The audience responds with slightly excessive laughs. "I have a special entertainment for you tonight. As many of you know I am fascinated with magic. Illusionists, mentalists, magicians, I love being . . ." He pauses here, searching for the right word. ". . . surprised. No, better yet, astonished." He turns his eyes toward me and says, "And I can't wait to be astonished tonight." He turns back to the crowd. "May I introduce to you Ms. Frankie Percival."

The crowd gives me a warm welcome and I stride across to the mic, give Hasagawa's hand a quick shake, and turn to face the curiosity-seekers. When performing on stage at a theater, the spotlights make it nearly impossible to see the faces of your audience outside of the front few rows, but here in this room I can see everyone. The closest table is only 15 feet away and the furthest maybe 50. And all eyes are on me.

I stand for a moment and slowly run my eyes across the crowd, making eye contact with as many people as possible, finding that connection, putting them at ease. When you're sitting in the audience before the performance begins, you always wonder if the person on stage is going to stink, and you have this little zing of unease. I channel all my energy into one quality: charm. Get them to like you right out of the gate and the battle is halfway won.

"What a fine-looking collection of men and women. It's like a convention of the beautiful people. My goodness!" I always like to slip in a "My Goodness" or a "Heavens to Betsy" when I can. Charm. "Tonight is going to be all about time. And as a wise man said many, many years ago, aside from Velcro, time is the most mysterious substance in the universe." This, as always, gets a chuckle. I then slip into my slightly more serious face. My imparter of sage wisdom face. "Time is free, but it's priceless, and we all are obliged to spend it. But spend it wisely because contrary to popular belief, time is not money. You can always earn more money, but you don't get more time. Time is finite. But . . ." At this point I hold up my right index finger and pause for effect. ". . . it is predictable. It is consistent." I then turn my eyes to Mr. Hasagawa. "And it is weighing heavily on the mind of one particular person in this room, right Mr. Birthday Boy?"

Hasagawa chuckles and nods. The crowd laughs along.

I walk toward him, my eyes never leaving his, while I continue my patter. "Birthdays are the one day that, as we become older, we simultaneously celebrate and curse." I stop right in front of him. "So, let us take this evening and bring time to its knees. To show it who's boss." I hold out my hand to Hasagawa. "Come with me." He glances at his wife, who nods permission, and then he takes my hand and allows me to lead him back out in front of the crowd. We turn and face the room. Most mentalists like a high-speed patter. I guess they feel it keeps the energy up and attention spans filled. That's not my style. I move at a more deliberate pace. I want the audience to feel a sense of wonderment that you can't create if you're talking a mile-a-minute. "How do you feel?" I say to Hasagawa.

"Great!" he replies.

"You feeling good? Feel fine? You look fine."

"I feel like a million bucks," he says.

I can't resist this softball. "Probably more like a few billion," I say with an eye to the crowd. They all roar at the cheap gag.

Hey, you can't ignore fruit hanging that low.

"Do you have a watch?" I ask.

He holds up his wrist. "I do," he says.

It's big and chunky. Probably worth more than what I pull down in two months' time. "Excellent. If you would be so kind, please take it off for a moment," I say. "What time is it right now?"

He looks at it. "7:05."

"Very good," I say. "First, look at me. I want you to connect your mind with mine. Just mine. No one else's. Mine and mine alone. Can you do that?"

Hasagawa stares directly into my eyes. "Yes."

We hold like this for a moment before I break away. "Fine. I think we've made the necessary connection. Now, I want you to reset the watch to a random time. Give the dial plenty of spins. Don't pick an easy time like three o'clock or midnight, pick a time that's a little out of whack."

He pulls the dial and begins to turn it.

"That's it," I say. "Plenty of spins, plenty. You're doing fine."

I then step away from him and face the crowd. He's behind me and to my right. I then say, "Now set the watch to the random time you chose." I pause. "Done?"

"Done," he says.

I still don't face him but keep my attention forward to the audience. "Good. Now take your watch down to your wife and show her the time. Then show it to the person next to her. And then the person next to that person."

Hasagawa walks past me, and I purposefully turn my head away when I spot him in my peripheral vision. I make a show of it to ensure everyone sees I'm not trying to catch a glimpse of the watch face. Once he's well past, I see him show the watch to his wife and the others around her. I say, "Nobody say what time the watch is set for, okay? Now I want the people who have seen what time the watch now shows to tell the person next to them. It's going to be like a great big game of telephone."

I watch as the members of the audience quietly whisper to the person next to them. Only a few moments pass before the information has spread to the far corners of the room. I then invite Hasagawa back up front with me. I physically maneuver him to my side. I've found that most people like having hands laid on them. They enjoy being touched by another person. Some are uncomfortable with it, but by and large most seem to like the human connection. I glance back over my shoulder at my handbag and say, "Spencer. Music." At which point the optic in my bag begins playing a low, hypnotic tune. I turn to the crowd. "Spencer is my optic," I say with a wink and a smile. They all nod and smile in return. I think most people name their optic. I then say to Hasagawa, "May I sync Spencer with your home's sound system?" Hasagawa nods and I say, "Spencer, sync with home system." Suddenly the quiet, tinny sounding music fills the room, lush and full, but not too loud. Just enough for ambience. I spent months searching for the right cuts of music for my shows. Did research, studied, spoke with audio engineers. I wanted to make sure it had the proper effect on the audience. Based on what I am seeing in the eyes of the crowd, it is doing the job. The musical notes, ethereal without being eerie, wash over the room like an incoming tide. The engineers I spoke with referred to this as deep theta wave music. No drums, no rhythm to speak of, simply electronically produced tones that blend and weave like an aural tapestry. Evidently certain frequencies affect the human brain extremely specifically. There's a happiness frequency, a sadness frequency. Pretty much every emotion you can think of there's a frequency for it. Right now, I am doing the audio equivalent of slipping the audience a mickey. Subtly drugging them with music, releasing their serotonin. I am enchanting them.

I turn to face Hasagawa and place my hands on his shoulders. I look deeply into his eyes. I'm giving him the full treatment. I stare slightly longer than what is comfortable. Making eye contact for an appropriate length of time is a delicate balancing act. Too short and we look shifty, too long and we seem overly intimate. I learned that the preferred gaze duration is a tad over three seconds. Give or take. At about four seconds I shake my head like I don't like the signal I'm getting.

"What time would you have chosen?" I ask rhetorically. "What time would be important to you? How would you choose a time?"

I turn my gaze back to him and say, "I want you to think of the time you set on the watch. Can you see it? Can you see the time?" My speech pattern is gathering steam, becoming ever so slightly more insistent. Hasagawa simply nods his agreement. He is fully engaged. "Look into my eyes. See the time in your head. Now, project that time directly into me. Project it into my head. My soul. My very being." Right on cue the music swells a bit. My timing is freaking awesome. Hasagawa stares lasers into my eyes and I return the gaze, never blinking. I tighten my grip on his shoulders. The audience can see it. They can see that my concentration is physically taxing me. At that moment I let go and stagger back, shaking my head. I bend at the waist and place my hands on my knees, like the exertion was too much. I take three deep breaths, straighten up, take one last deep cleansing breath, take another step back, and roll up my shirtsleeves. Shit's getting real.

I turn back to face Hasagawa, pause, and tip my head slightly. I hold up my right index finger and wave it at him, like I'm scolding him. "You're blocking," I say. "You're blocking the image." Hasagawa raises his hands in a helpless gesture and shakes his head.

I turn to the audience, give them a look that might say, "Bullshit" without saying bullshit, and give my head a shake again. I run my hands through my hair, recheck my rolled-up shirtsleeves, and then realize I need to get serious here. I crack my knuckles and begin unbuttoning my vest. I slip my arms through and proceed to walk toward the piano where my bag sits. The moment my back is turned to the audience I hear gasps. Approximately, a hundred, all in unison. I stop and turn to face them, looking utterly confused. I hear a few voices from the crowd involuntarily speak.

"The time!" they say. At which point the murmuring begins, followed by the laughter, followed by the applause and cheers.

I stand there looking even more perplexed, then peek over my shoulder to my own back and there it is, a piece of paper pinned to my shirt with the time 9:25 printed in large, bold, handwritten characters.

"Huh," I say. "Forgot about that."

The room erupts. Nailed it. The old guess-the-time bit always floors them. Of course, it never occurs to them that I scrawled that note an hour ago. Or that I had a conversation with Hasagawa in the library and mentioned the numbers nine, two, five, or twenty-five twelve times within one minute. Or that I slipped in the words "fine," "time," "mind," and "mine," which all sound remarkably like the word "nine" over twenty times in the lead up to the bit. It's amazing what you can persuade people to say. I swear, sometimes I feel like an Australian Shepherd herding sheep.

I continue with the clueless act and step back over to Hasagawa, who is smiling and shaking his head in wonder. I place my hand on his shoulder and turn to face the crowd. "Let us now continue with our theme of time." I then turn back to Hasagawa. "Let's see that watch of yours again." He dutifully holds up his wrist. "What time is it now?" I ask.

"Uh, 9:25?" he says and gets a laugh.

"Shoot. That's right, I forgot about that." I turn to the audience. "Anyone, the time?"

One shouts back, "7:07".

"Eight," corrects another.

"Okay," I say. "7:08." I then look back at Hasagawa, "Please reset your watch for 7:08." He does so, and I check it. "Good." I then give him a drawn-out look along with a deep exhale, clueing in the audience that something big is about to take place. "You ready for the big stuff now?" I ask him. He nods. I then take my hand off his shoulder, take a step back, and gesture toward the crowd with a dramatic sweep of my left arm. "In the next few moments, I am going to drastically alter time and space within the confines of this room. How?" I ask. "By making every person in this room except our birthday boy here vanish. Again, how? By jumping forward to the time when everyone's gone home for the evening." I fix Hasagawa with a pointed stare, "But to you it will happen in an instant. To you they will be here, and then they will be gone, quite literally in the blink of an eye." I then glance coyly back at the crowd. "But I couldn't live with myself if I ruined such a good party, so I'll bring everyone back again just as fast." I turn once more back to Hasagawa. "Interested?"

"This I have to see," he says.

"But that's just it," I reply. "You won't." I step away from him and fetch an empty chair from a forward table and set it down by my subject. "Please, have a seat," I say. "You're going to be out for a few hours, so I want you to be comfortable." I pause like I'm giving what I just said some thought and say, "Well, I'm compressing those few hours into a single second, but it'll be a few hours in the purest scientific sense. Ready?"

He shrugs like he doesn't have a choice and takes a seat. At which point the real fun begins.

I squat down next to Hasagawa and say to him, "Have you ever been hypnotized?"

"Never," he says.

"I believe you have. Have you ever been on a long drive on some lonely road that keeps going and going? And suddenly you realize you missed your exit fifteen minutes ago? You have experienced Highway Hypnosis. It's a real thing. Your conscious mind begins to drift, and your subconscious mind takes the wheel. Or how about when you're so deeply focused on a book or TV show that your wife will smack you on the shoulder and say she's been yelling at you going on a minute and you never heard a word she said. Okay, that's just being a husband, but again, it is a form of hypnosis." I spin in my crouch to face the crowd. "Time for a quick history lesson. Hypnosis is ancient, been around for over four thousand years, invented by the Egyptians. Hypno means sleep and nosis means knowledge. Feel free to drop that bit of info at your next trivia night." I glance back over my shoulder at Hasagawa. "You're a pretty sharp man, yes? Well-educated? Of course you are. That's good." Back to the audience. "Smarter people make better hypnosis subjects. People who are dumber than a cubic foot of gravel don't hypnotize worth a damn. In a moment I'm going to be telling my subject here to relax, focus, and listen to the sound of my voice and only my voice and block out other sounds around him. It takes at least a marginal level of intelligence to do that." I look back at Hasagawa hopefully. "You do qualify, yes?" He nods and smiles. "Good, then let's get started."

I'm back up on my feet again and ask Ms. Nichols, who has been standing dutifully in the wings, to please dim the lights. Within seconds the room darkens to the equivalent of dusk. I step forward a couple of feet and squint into the crowd and say, "Is Mr. Hasagawa's lawyer in the audience? Yes? Okay, don't worry, I won't make him do anything he isn't willing to do. Nothing that's going to create a scandal on social media by tomorrow morning." This prompts a slightly nervous laugh from the crowd. "Everyone has a built-in toggle-switch in their head, a safety-valve that won't allow you to do something under hypnosis you wouldn't normally do when you're not hypnotized." Back to Hasagawa. "Do I have your consent to be hypnotized?"

"You do," he says.

I pause a moment, look him dead in the eye, giving him an extra beat to reconsider, but he stares right back with a smile. I believe he's looking forward to this. "Okay then, let's get this show on the road."

I slowly pace around my subject. "Did you know that when you are hypnotized your brain is flatlining even though your senses are increased by about four-hundred percent? It's true. I am about to kick your subconscious mind into overdrive."

I stand behind Hasagawa and say, "Please put your feet firmly on the floor and your hands on you lap."

The process of hypnosis—putting people under—can happen in as little as a few minutes if the subject is willing. Ideally, I will take upwards of seven to ten minutes to put someone into a trance. Sounds quick, right? On stage it's an eternity, but you find ways to keep the audience engaged while you go through the process. It's lots of repetition—listen to my voice and my voice only—that sort of thing. Hypnosis really is just getting the subject to relax and then cranking the power of suggestion up to eleven. Anyone can learn the basics in a few hours. I, on the other hand, immersed myself in the discipline deeply for a full year when I got into my profession, and I'm constantly honing my craft and studying to keep me sharp.

I could put Hasagawa out in a couple of minutes if I really stepped on the gas, but this is a big fish, and I don't want to mess it up. I take my time.

Grayson Hasagawa lives in a state-of-the-art house which means the heating and cooling systems are beyond those of mortal men. But even top-of-the-line AC takes a few minutes to adapt to a room of a hundred people. That many people in close quarters means the temperature goes up. A slightly warm room helps with hypnosis. My music slowly tapered off a couple of minutes ago, so the room is deathly quiet. Another necessity. The crowd is doing their part by not so much as coughing. I've got the ideal environment and it pays off. Hasagawa is out in short order, and I tell the audience as much.

"Ladies and gentlemen, Mr. Hasagawa is currently in a deep state of hypnosis and is open to suggestion." I pause. "Any employees want a raise?" Scattered laughter ripples through the room. "No? Okay, thought I'd check, because he's ripe for the picking." I then shift back into a more serious demeanor and step around behind Hasagawa, speaking to him. "When I count to three you are going to wake up and feel as though nothing has happened. You will have no recollection of being hypnotized, however you will still listen and go along with everything I say, okay? I will also ask you what time it is. When you check your watch, you will not notice that five minutes have passed since you last checked. To you it will be as if you sat down here on stage a moment or so ago. Lastly, when I say the word *Perfect* you will fall back asleep. The word *Perfect*. Ready, one, two, three." And I snap my fingers. Instantly Hasagawa's eyes blink open, and he smiles. I turn back to him. "How are you feeling?"

"I feel great."

"Ready to be hypnotized?" I ask.

"I've been ready," he says. The crowd chuckles. Hasagawa has no idea that he's already been under.

"Excellent," I say. "Now, to begin the time/space compression I will need you to check your watch. What does it say?"

He looks. "7:15."

I say, "Perfect." He goes out like a light. I then turn to the audience and say, "Ladies and gentlemen, now things will get interesting for Mr. Hasagawa."

GRAYSON HASAGAWA WAKES up and looks around the empty ballroom. Empty except for myself, sitting by the piano. When I see him looking my way, I stretch my arms above my head and yawn. "Back again? Good." I rise from my chair and walk over to the clearly puzzled birthday boy.

"Where is everyone?" he asks.

"Gone," I say.

He looks at his watch. "One in the morning?" He looks at a clock on the wall for confirmation. He then rubs his eyes like that will magically help. "I don't understand."

"What don't you understand?" I ask evenly.

"They're all gone," he says, pointing to the empty chairs and tables.

"Can you blame them? It's late."

"But, but they were just here." His voice is remarkably calm. For most people, having a room full of close personal friends and relatives vanish in the blink of an eye would be a tad unsettling, but Grayson Hasagawa handles it like a boss.

"Yes, they were here . . . four hours ago. When you fell asleep it seemed a shame to end the party so early, so we carried on. And you looked so peaceful sitting here that no one could bring themselves to wake you up. I hope you don't mind."

I'm seeing clear confusion in his eyes and that's usually a precursor to panic, so I place my hand on his shoulder and say, "I'm supposed to tell you that everyone had a wonderful time. It was perfect."

He goes out like a light.

Grayson Hasagawa's confusion is understandable. That confusion is also why I have a job. A person accepts the world that they are presented. People are very believing, especially if they choose to believe. To Hasagawa, a ballroom full of people vanished in the blink of an eye. Why would he think that he'd been out for only several minutes? Why would he presume that all his guests were herded out of the room and watching on monitors in adjoining rooms?

Or that timepieces were reset?

Because I told him otherwise.

Grayson Hasagawa wakes up and looks around at the full ballroom. He blinks and shakes his head like you see people do in the movies when they can't quite grasp what they're seeing. I'm standing to his left looking down at him, completely neutral.

"I said, what time is it?" I say.

Hasagawa looks at his watch, looks up at the clock on the wall, and then looks up at me with the most blank stare you can possibly imagine. "7:15," he says flatly.

"Good!" I say brightly. "Then, are you ready for me to do the whole time/space thing?"

"But . . . but you just did," he says.

"Excuse me?" I say. "I haven't done anything." I turn to the crowd. "And don't you think we owe it to your guests to show them what I already promised? You don't want to make me out to be a *liar liar pants on fire*, do you?"

"No, no, no!" says Hasagawa. "A moment ago, I was sitting here, I closed my eyes for an instant and suddenly everyone was gone. The room was empty."

I look perplexed. "Empty," I say with no question mark. A statement. "This room. Empty. No one here."

"Yes!" he says. "They were all gone. I checked my watch, and it was one o'clock in the morning. The room was empty. There was no one here but you."

"Hmmm. That is strange," I say. "Maybe the whole time/space thing really did happen and all of us aren't even aware of it." I motion to the crowd. "Did any of you notice anything happen?" They all shrug and murmur amongst themselves. I turn back to Hasagawa. "See? No one else noticed anything weird going on. You sure you didn't imagine it?"

Hasagawa shakes his head firmly. "I didn't imagine it. It happened. You were standing right there and suddenly you were over by the piano, and everyone was gone. You said I was asleep the whole time."

"I did? Okay, now you're freaking me out. How is it that I don't remember any of that? Wait, is it possible I hypnotized myself? Wow!" I turn to the audience. "You were here. You saw everything. Is that what happened?" Lots of shrugs and shaking of heads. "Ladies and gentlemen, if that is true then you have just witnessed something that until now was said to be impossible—a hypnotist hypnotizing themselves! And wouldn't you know it, I slept through the whole thing. That's perfect." Out goes Hasagawa.

GRAYSON HASAGAWA WAKES up and looks around at the full great room with the entire audience on their feet clapping and cheering. I stand in front, bowing. I turn to see Hasagawa smiling and looking remarkably refreshed.

"How are you feeling?" I ask.

"I feel great!" he says.

The audience dies down and I say to Hasagawa, "Would you like to know what just happened?"

"Yes, please," he says.

"You said please, so I will tell you." I shrug. "Nothing much, really. I tried the whole time/space bit, but it didn't take. I didn't want to disappoint the audience, so I went with Plan B. I got you to squawk like a chicken, then I made you think you were a martial arts expert. You had some damn fine Kung Fu moves if I do say so myself. After that, some run-of-the-mill hijinks. You know, made you think your feet were frozen to the floor. That was particularly funny. You kept pulling at your legs, trying to move, and they wouldn't budge. You eventually took your shoes off, so you could move. We gave them back, of course. Everyone seemed to have a lovely time, isn't that right everyone?" I turn to the audience and the place erupts. The cheers are deafening. Frankie 1, non-believers 0.

AUDREY AND I enjoy the drive home in companionable silence. No words necessary. When I drop her off, she leans back in on the rolled down window.

"Dead fookin' brilliant."

I don't recall ever hearing anything that's made me happier.

CHAPTER 8

"Crushed by a falling safe?" offers a woman between bites of a jelly donut.

"What are we making, a cartoon?" replies the man across the table. He crunches up his coffee cup and tosses it onto the table with the half dozen other crumpled cups. "We already did the falling piano bit. Why not drop an anvil on her or a large crate stenciled 'Acme?'"

"It'd be funny!" the woman offers. "Go viral instantly!"

Sheila Graveman lets her creative team banter back and forth. They've been at it for a good thirty minutes and even though she's already decided how Frankie Percival is going to shrug off her mortal coil, she likes to allow her team to stretch their creative muscles.

"Bow and arrow. Totally medieval!" shouts jelly donut.

"Decapitation from a flying pane of glass," replies the coffee crumpler.

"Parachute mishap!"

"Shark attack!"

Sheila has to give them credit; they think outside the box, just like she taught them. Letting them kick around ideas like a soccer ball is good mental exercise, but it was time to rein things in. "Splendid ideas, all of them," says Sheila, "but the good Ms. Percival has already provided the method for us."

"What do you mean?" asks jelly donut.

Sheila taps the table and fresh data appears on the surface. "These are the notes from her meeting with Myrna. Pay attention to the areas I highlighted."

The two team members read the notes to themselves. Within a minute they are grinning from ear to ear.

Coffee crumpler looks up. "You're bringing in the secret weapon?"

Sheila simply nods.

"I can totally see it," says crumpler. "It's appropriate."

"It's poetic," says donut.

Sheila Graveman crosses her arms across her chest and allows herself a self-satisfied smile. "It's perfect."

CHAPTER 9

MARCH

Today I visit my brother which means I will be *had*. That's the emotion I have named: *had*. Happy combined with sad. I suppose I could have gone with another hybrid, sappy, but that's already a word and doesn't apply here.

I pull off the main road into the now familiar entrance and start looking for that most elusive of creatures, the mythical close-by parking place. The main building slowly passes on my right, large, white, very hospitally, which makes sense because that's what it is. Although I do have to give the architect credit for making an effort; the building is not at all intimidating, which is probably a good idea, being that it's a children's hospital.

Don't get the wrong idea, my kid brother is not a child, he's, as he likes to say, well-seasoned. And he's not a patient, he volunteers.

Yet again, I do not find the mythical parking beast, in ten years never have, and instead find a narrow spot between two hulking SUVs whose drivers clearly didn't understand that the purpose of the stripes on the pavement is to park between them. I'm a good three blocks away from the closest entrance and begin hoofing it. Five minutes later I'm panting through the sliding glass doors into the lobby. I've always liked the lobby here; the designers knew what they were doing. The walls depict a kid-friendly forest, and stylish artificial trees sprout from the colorful industrial carpet. Nature and animals are the recurring themes throughout the hospital. You can't turn a corner without running smack-dab into a sculpture or sign in the shape of a friendly furry creature. I sign in at the front desk and say hi to the receptionist, Lou today. He's an elderly man, gotta be pushing eighty, who also volunteers. Lou greets me with his standard,

"For no more beautiful face shall grace these halls than that of the fair Frankie."

Lou's a peach.

"How's it hanging, Lou?"

"Low and to the left," he says. "Say hi to the boy for me. He was already here before I started my shift."

The boy. That's how Lou always refers to my brother. Not Galen, his name, just "the boy." Maybe because Lou is old as dirt and any male under sixty is considered a boy in his book. I take the elevator to the third floor and head over to the Hippo wing of the hospital. All the wings are named after cute animals—there's the Hippo wing, Panda, Dolphin and Koala. I wonder if the hospital staff know that hippos are incredibly dangerous and kill around three thousand people a year. Probably not.

Although the hospital does everything in its power to make the Hippo wing as bright, cheerful, and non-threatening as possible, it's impossible to hide the fact that it's the grimmest wing in the building. The cancer wing. This is where small children are treated for adult, unfair diseases. I find Galen in the "hang-out" room. It's a big rec room with bean bag chairs, a ping pong table, and card tables. Currently the card tables are covered in arts and crafts supplies: scissors, glue sticks, glitter pens, colored paper. It always makes my heart glad to see that kids can still enjoy making things with their hands in this digital world. Sitting at that table is Galen and a young girl. At least, I think it's a girl. With a bandana covering the no-hair head it's a little tough to tell. Especially when the kids haven't reached puberty yet so there are no physical clues to suggest male or female.

Once I'm within ten feet, I can see it's a girl. Great cheekbones and no Adams apple. She's carefully cutting out some shape from a piece of orange construction paper, utterly focused on making her cuts precise, as evident by the slow, methodical cuts and her tongue peeking out the side of her mouth.

Galen looks up when he hears me shuffle forward.

"Ah, a guest!" he chirps.

He's wearing sunglasses, so I can't see his blue eyes. His hair is its typically unkempt shaggy, dishwater blonde, about shoulder length. His cane leans unneeded for the moment against the table. I can see the ivory handle peeking up to the left of his leg.

"Hey, Galen," I say, trying to sound more upbeat than I feel. "Who's the kid?" I always try to be casual and a little flippant around them, they're hit with so many serious people there.

Galen provides introductions as the girl looks up from her project. Her hazel eyes flicker with polite curiosity. "Chloe, meet . . . uh . . ."

"Frankie," I say, filling the void.

"Yes, Frankie," says Galen as the girl gives a smile and wave and goes back to her precision cutting work.

"Whatcha making, Chloe?" I ask.

"Poster," she says without looking up.

"Poster for what?"

"Inspiration," she says.

Galen jumps in. "What's it g . . . gonna say, Chloe?"

"Never!" says the girl and she raises her fist in the air with a triumphant smile.

"That's right," says Galen. "Never. As in never quit. N . . . Never give up." He then turns his sun-glassed gaze to Chloe. "Because, what are you doing?"

"Kicking Luke's ass!" says Chloe.

Galen leans in and stage-whispers to Chloe. "I don't think you should say ass in front of guests."

"Sorry," whispers Chloe back with an insider's grin. She then looks up to me. "Luke is leukemia."

"Ah," I say as if being let in on a deep, dark secret.

Chloe grabs a glue stick, pops the top and gives the base a couple of twists. "Nuts. Out of glue." She hops up from her chair. "I'm gonna restock," she says. "Back in a few," and she scampers out of the room.

Galen watches her leave like a proud father, then turns to me and pulls out a chair. "Take a load off," he says.

I sit and look around the room. It's empty now. "Kinda slow today," I say.

"Yeah, it gets busy here around lunchtime, after morning chemo sessions." He stops for a second, regrouping his thoughts. "D . . . Did you know that what time you receive chemo can be a m . . . major factor in the effectiveness of the treatment and side effects?"

"No idea," I say.

"It's true," he says earnestly. "It has some . . . something to do with our, our . . . what's-it-called clock?"

"Circadian?" I offer.

"Y . . . yes, circadian clock. How our daily rhythms line up. Evidently bodies respond better in the morning. I don't know the details," he says with a wave of his hand.

"I'll take your word for it," I say. My eyes drift down to his right hand resting on the table. It's shaking slightly.

"Galen, buddy?" I ask, nodding toward his hand, trying to sound casual. "You taking your meds?"

He slips his hand back into his lap and gives a noncommittal shrug before changing the subject. "So, what's new in the world of uh . . ."

"Mentalism?" I've become used to filling in the gaps for him. It's now second nature. "Had an amazing show the other night. Performed for Grayson Hasagawa himself."

"No kidding? And Grayson Hasagawa is . . . ?"

"Richest guy in town? Richest guy on the west coast. Top five richest guys in America?"

"Got it. Rich guy," he says.

Every time he blanks on stuff it's like someone stabs me with a little needle. Used to be daggers but over time has become needles. Doesn't hurt so much, but still smarts.

"I'm also moving ahead with Bosco," I say.

"Oh yeah, your big trick."

Why he remembers some things and not others is a complete mystery to me. But the fact he remembers at all is a small victory. I take what I get. "Exactly," I say. "The big trick."

"Still not sure how you're going to p . . . pull that off without burning off your eyebrows, or, you know, l . . . losing a limb or something."

"Don't you worry about me; I'm going to have everything buttoned down. Failure to prepare is preparing to fail."

"Your motto," he says.

"That little girl, Chloe? For a kid with leukemia, she's remarkably happy."

Galen smiles at this. "Amazing, isn't it. I'm always astonished at how r . . . r . . . resilient kids can be. If I were in their shoes, I'd be a blubbering wreck around the clock. They're tough."

"So are you," I blurt out quietly, involuntarily.

"What's that?" he says.

I fix him with a smile. "Nothing." I give him an appraising look. He's thinner than last time. His clothes are hanging on him, but I don't comment. I rise out of the chair and walk over to the windows and look out. It's a fine view of the city. I'm surprised no developers have tried to buy the building out from under the hospital owners, so they can replace it with condos. "You must really like it here," I say to Galen while facing the window. I hear Galen's chair scrape and his slightly off-kilter footsteps. I turn and watch him walking my way. He leans supportively on his cane with his left hand. His right foot drags enough to be noticeable. His cane is gloss black hardwood inlaid with silver filigree and mother of pearl. It looks more like something from a museum. It should, it cost me a fortune. Custom made. I figured if my brother was going to have to walk with a cane it was going to be most badass looking cane in the world. And it's practical in more ways than one; hidden in the shaft is a twenty-inch pigsticker, a sword. When I bought it for him and pointed out the feature, he obligingly unscrewed the handle, withdrew the sword, and made a few thrust and parry moves to make me happy.

"You're walking better," I tell him.

"Am I? Feels the same."

"Pretty soon you're not going to even need that cane anymore."

"Nah. It's part of me now. Even if I could walk . . . uh . . ."

"Normal?" I say.

"Yes, normal, dammit. I was going to finish it eventually."

"Sorry, don't have all day. People to see, things to do."

"You are a world-class bitch," he says with a smile.

"Yes, but I'm your bitch. Wait, that didn't come out right. You know what I mean."

We both smile. I love these moments.

And it's nice to see he's having one of his "good" days. We stand there enjoying the comfortable silence for a moment, and then . . .

"So, how's mom?" he asks.

Shit. "Mom's dead, Galen," I say, point blank for the umpteenth time in the last ten years.

He looks at me for a sec then nods, a subtle flicker of remembrance appears behind his eyes. "That's right," he says in a tone like he just remembered that he had a dental appointment later that afternoon.

Chloe shuffles back into the room, freshly stocked up with glue sticks. I take that as my cue and jump at the opportunity to change the subject. "Well, I better split. You've got posters to make and Luke ass to kick."

Galen looks back at Chloe. "That we do."

He gives me a hug and I tell him that I'll see him later. I stop off at the table on the way out. "Keep on rockin' it with your bad self, Chloe," and offer her a knuckle bump. She smiles, and we tap fists.

CHAPTER 10

THE CHAT WITH MYRNA

"Tell me about your family," says Myrna.

"Really?" I say with arched eyebrows. "I thought you guys had a thorough file of me the moment I walked through the front door."

Myrna gives a tiny shrug. "True, but we don't know everything. Besides, we can glean a lot from one-on-one conversation. How you talk about your family speaks more than any data we might collect."

"Fair enough. Where do you want me to start?"

"How about your parents?"

"Okay. My dad died when I was two, liver cancer, so I never knew him. My mom, though, mom was something special. She was cool."

"Was," says Myrna. "She died."

"Yes, the year after I graduated from high school. Breast cancer. Cancer sucks."

"It does indeed. You lost both your parents to cancer, so you of all people understand how devastating the loss of a family member can be."

"I do."

Myrna glances at the glass tablet. "You have a brother."

"Yes."

"And yet you are prepared to put him through that experience again. He's already lost both parents and now you want him to lose his sister?"

Ouch. "I, uh, look, it's for the best." It sounds much lamer than I would hope.

"How?" asks Myrna flatly.

"This money will completely turn his life around," I say.

"How?" asks Myrna again.

I take a deep breath. "Your records probably already show that he was in a car accident, years back."

Myrna looks at the tablet, she makes a couple of swipes, reads for a moment. "Yes. Ten years ago."

"How much detail is there?" I ask.

"Not much. We can't access medical files."

I'm not sure I buy that, but I play along. "Okay. Well, it messed him up pretty bad. Shattered leg, punctured lung, but the biggie were the head injuries. He was in a coma for a week before he woke up, but he's never been the same."

"How so?"

I consider the question. "To answer that you need some backstory on my brother. See, Galen was the even one, I was the odd one. He was smart, talented, he was the character in the movie who everyone roots for. He got a 4.0 in high school without any effort. He was the kid who would show up for class and say, 'A test? Today?' and still ace it. Class valedictorian, it all came so easy for him. He was blessed with my father's academic genes and my mother's social skills. He wasn't just smart, he was likeable. He had a way of connecting with everyone he met. He liked to help out. You're supposed to serve something like forty hours of community service by the time you graduate from high school, right?"

Myrna shrugs.

"Well, he had about two hundred. It was ridiculous. You try living in that shadow."

"Must have been difficult," says Myrna.

"But that's just it, it wasn't," I say. "I loved that he was so good. I loved that he was so smart. I was so freakin' proud of him. Simply being his sister made me look good. And he and I were tight! Brothers and sisters are supposed to fight a lot, but we didn't. He got me. He got my weirdness and encouraged it. Just like my mom."

"So, what happened?" asks Myrna.

"He graduated from high school and went off and joined the Peace Corps, of all things. But then, get this, he got chomped by a mosquito and got malaria. Bad. By the time he was on his feet again he figured he could help more people by being stinking rich, so he bailed on the Corps and applied to a bunch of high-end colleges. Ended up going to Brown University. You know, the forgotten Ivy League school? Costs something like $125 thousand a year before room and board. Within four years he was in debt close to $700 grand. No worries, he thought. He's earning an economics degree, top of his class, he'll be able to pick and choose where he works, pull down six-figures right out of the gate and be debt free in no time flat."

"And then?" asks Myrna, knowing full well what happened then.

"And then everything went to hell," I say. "The car accident. Tire blew out crossing a bridge, car flipped and went head-first into a support structure. They had to pry him out."

"It was an accident," says Myrna compassionately. "A tragic one, but an accident, nonetheless."

I don't comment on that, which is not lost on Myrna.

"That must have been devastating."

I give her a "no shit" look.

"But also left you angry," she follows up.

Again, I don't comment.

"How long did you stay that way?" she asks.

"Years. But over time that anger dissipated and was replaced with acceptance. But it was hard. The damage to Galen was significant. His memory is crap, he can't concentrate for any length of time. He's like an early-onset Alzheimer's patient. In other words, his career as a money-making machine in the world of high finance was over before it even began."

"And he's saddled with nearly three-quarters of a million dollars in debt," says Myrna sadly.

"Bingo," I say. "And no way to pay it off. Oh, sure, he's had a few jobs, greeter at Costco, cat wrangler at a pet shelter, bagger at a grocery store, and he volunteers at Children's Hospital, but he doesn't earn enough to put a dent in his debt. Hell, the interest alone is more than he usually makes in a month. I help him out as much as I can but it's like a bottomless pit. No, the only way out for him is if he lands a big fat windfall."

"And that's you," says Myrna.

"And that's me," I reply.

Myrna nods sagely. "I can understand your reasoning. But aren't there programs for Galen's situation? To help him out of his debt? What you're doing is such a drastic measure."

"Bankruptcy's out. Evidently, there's some bullshit legal exemption tied to his circumstances that prevents him from filing. Ever since financial institutions won that Supreme Court case fifty years ago giving them carte blanche to create their own rules, it's damn near impossible to plead no dinero. I've found some other loan forgiveness programs, but even with their help he'd be making payments for the rest of his life, and the lives of his kids, if he ever has any. Instead of being 100% financially screwed, he'd only be 80% screwed. In other words, he's still screwed. So, I like to think I'm helping out at least two full generations by signing up to be whacked." I put a smile on this last one to soften the conversation. Myrna picks up on my efforts and gives a smile in return.

"I understand," she says. "I just want to make sure you've exhausted all other avenues before you go down this road."

"Trust me," I say, "I have been trying to figure out a solution to this mess for ten years now. In my eyes, this is for the best." I pause for a moment. "Let me ask you something, do you have kids?"

This question does not seem to trouble Myrna. "I do. A daughter and two sons."

"And if one of their lives was on the line and the only way to save it was for you to offer yours in their place, would you do it?"

Myrna doesn't miss a beat. "Without hesitation."

I hold out my hands. "I rest my case."

"But Galen's life isn't forfeit," she says. "It will just be more difficult."

"Semantics," I say. Her comment pisses me off, and I let it show. "Think about it. Imagine being so deep in debt that you can never get out. Ever. Financial prison. No escape. No one should live like that." She doesn't reply to this, allowing me to vent. "My death, he can recover from. But day in, day out, living with the stress of wondering if you can afford to keep your lights on, your heat . . ." I take a deep breath, my voice dropping. "He's not taking his meds. He's not eating. And I know why. He won't admit it, but I know the reason. Money. He can't afford it." I shake my head. "No. Just, no."

"Your brother has a generous sister," says Myrna kindly, easing the tension. "I hope he fully appreciates the sacrifice you're making."

"He sure as hell better," I say, "or I'm going to come back and haunt his ass 24/7."

"Tell me more about your mother," she says. "It sounds like you were close."

"Yeah, we were close."

"How so?"

"Mom was a character," I say. "She really encouraged us to be who we were. She was the artistic director for a local community theater, so you can see where I get my hamminess. She loved performing and the discipline that went into it. Community theater is usually where you find people who think they can act but aren't good enough to do it for a living, but mom overcame that by putting on performances that overshadowed the lack of talent. She wasn't staging *My Fair Lady* and *The Iceman Cometh*, she went epic. She was producing *Ben Hur* and *Gone with the Wind*. You should have seen her stage the burning of Atlanta. The fire marshals were pissed. When she needed extras to fill out her 'cast of thousands'—okay, cast of dozens—she'd tap the local high schools and soup kitchens. If a person could stand and raise a fist, or hold a sign, or keep a semblance of tempo, she'd find a use for them. Her productions became a thing. Sold out every time. Became must-see events. Sort of a 'Hey, let's go see how the crazy drama lady pulls off the D-Day invasion from *Saving Private Ryan* with some duct tape and baling wire.'"

"You sound proud of her," says Myrna.

"I was crazy proud of her," I say. "She could have moved up to bigger theaters, more recognized production houses, but she wasn't interested. She always said that the bigger the theater the more rules you have to obey, and she hated the idea of some stakeholder telling her what she could or couldn't do. It's funny, she hated rules but loved discipline. She always told Galen and me, discipline yourself and others won't have to. She absolutely demanded good manners and always drove us to create our own destiny."

"Sounds like quite a woman."

"Yeah, she was," I say. "Quite a woman. In fact, my brother and I have a tradition around my mom."

"Oh? What's that?"

"When we were growing up, mom always made a big deal out of her birthday. She'd circle it on the calendar and write 'most important day of the year' on it. We'd always whip up a big dinner together and my brother and I would buy a present that we knew she would absolutely connect with."

"Like what?"

"Well, let's see, one year we flew in her best friend growing up. They hadn't seen each other in probably twenty years. That one was special. Another time my brother went online and found a playbill from the first show she was in. We framed it. She got pretty teary about that one. So, yeah, her birthday is a big deal to us."

"But now that she's gone?" Myrna asks gently.

"Nothing's changed," I say. "It's still a big deal. My brother usually doesn't remember but once I remind him, he gets excited about it. Since mom died, we get together, cook a big dinner, usually become sloppy drunk, raise a toast to mom, and watch her favorite old movie."

"Which is?"

"*Auntie Mame*. 1958. Rosalind Russell. Closest character I've ever found to mom. You seen it?"

"I have not."

"Mame is a free spirit. An absolute force of nature. Her mantras were 'Life is a banquet and most poor suckers are starving to death,' and 'Live! Live! Live!' That was mom, through and through."

"When is her birthday?"

"July 7th."

Myrna gives me a smile that's tinged with sadness. I already know what she's going to say.

"I hope you get a chance to celebrate it. At least one more time."

CHAPTER 11

After leaving my brother, I stop by the Zombean Apocalypse for my medium chai and find a table by the window. There's a copy of some magazine called *Mad*. On the cover is an illustration of a freckled red-haired guy with a big gap between his front teeth. I flip through a couple of pages and realize it's a humor magazine aimed at teens and young adults. I stop on a bit called Spy vs Spy made up of two cartoon characters with long triangular faces and wide brimmed hats. They look identical other than the fact that one spy is dressed in white, the other black. Evidently the whole bit is about each of them trying to kill each other. In this cartoon, one tries dynamite while the other uses a tank. Tank wins. While paging over to the next gag I glance up and freeze. The guy from before is here. You know, *the guy*. The one with the impossibly blue eyes. The one who wears flannel and jeans and is left-handed. Not that I was paying attention.

He is looking out the window, so he doesn't see me gawking at him. Am I gawking? I don't think so; it was just a momentary look of surprise. Either way, the look has been tamped down to practiced indifference. He's three tables down from me, also along the window, so I consider trying the old angle-of-incidence-angle-of-reflection trick. You know, where it appears as though you're looking out the window but are really looking at the other person's reflection. The light is coming through strongly, so it should pose a good reflection. But then it occurs to me, what if he's already trying the old angle-of-incidence-angle-of-reflection trick on me? If I try it when he's already doing it then I'll be totally busted. I keep my eyes fixed on my magazine and feel for my cup, find it, and take a sip, as casually as can be. Nothing to see here, just enjoying a little quality me time, reading a kid's magazine and debating boy/girl nonsense that hasn't crossed my mind in forever.

What are the rules these days? I haven't played the game in a long time. Do I look at him until he looks at me? Do I smile? Grin? How big? Teeth? No teeth? This is brutal. How did it become so warm in here? Who puts a stupid fireplace in a café? It occurs to me that I have been staring at the same page of Mad magazine for an insanely long time and haven't read a single word. I decide to tear off the band-aid and try for the reflection bit. I look out the window at the necessary angle and shift my focus from the traffic passing to the reflection on the glass. My eyes adjust, and the guy's features defuzzify, only to find his reflection looking right back at me. Bastard! Before I can put physical motion to my momentary panic, he smiles. A simple grin, no teeth. Good grief, he has dimples. Are you kidding me? I look away, completely out of my depth, and try to formulate a plan. I come up with absolutely nothing. Not a damn thing. So, I do the next best thing, I grab my cup and take a swig of my chai. It tastes like ashes in my mouth. I involuntarily look back in his direction, not by way of reflection but directly at him. He's looking right back at me with that idiotic grin on his face. My face feels hot enough to ignite a moist towelette. My stupid body has taken on a life of its own and has decided to do things of its own accord. Right now, it's decided to grin back and then chuckle.

My body is a complete idiot.

I turn my gaze back down to my magazine and die several hundred thousand deaths. Out of my peripheral vision I see movement from his direction and lift my head to see him walking my way. He seems to be moving in slow motion. He's wearing a gray graphic tee shirt with two words in large block text: Save Ferris. I did not just see that.

There is no way this guy is wearing a tee shirt with a quote from one of my all-time favorite movies. No chance. He's still moving my way, still in slow motion. When he reaches my table he stops and sets a magazine on it, right on top of the one I'm reading.

"I think you might like this one," he says. He pauses for the slightest of beats and then continues on his way, pushing open the door and walking out. Exactly like last time.

My brain screams at me to do something, but I freeze. It's like my body has gone into torpor, like a frog in a fridge. I look out the window at him as he jogs across the street. Before he leaves my field of vision he glances back over his shoulder in my direction. He smiles.

He glanced, and he smiled. He did. I know he did. I saw it with my own eyes. Why do I feel like I just ran a marathon? My heart is zipping along at a decidedly un-Frankie pace. I slump back into my chair like a puppet whose strings have been cut. It's like, suddenly, my muscles all relaxed at the same precise moment. I didn't even realize I was wound so tightly. I take another hit of my chai. It's warm, smooth, and sweet.

But then it hits me, he left.

He didn't pull up a chair, didn't introduce himself, didn't do diddly-jack-squat. He was supposed to stop, say hi, ask me my name, sit down, provide a clever comment, I would laugh, the ice would be broken, and we would spend the next two hours making small talk and it would feel like it had been two minutes. That's what was supposed to happen. That's how it plays out in the movies. But all he did was drop off a magazine. The magazine! I look down at what it is. It's a weathered old copy of . . . let's see . . . Rolling Stone. Another mag that's been purely digital for decades. The band on the cover, Vermicious Knids, were all the rage when my mom was in her prime. She played them for us when I was a kid. I wasn't even that big a fan of their music, but I liked that they named themselves after a reference from Willy Wonka and the Chocolate Factory.

And that's when I see it. Written with surprising neatness next to the lead singer's head, a phone number printed in blue felt pen. I reach for my chai without looking. And knock the contents all over the magazine.

CHAPTER 12

Would it have killed him to use a ballpoint pen? Jesus. A felt pen. Who the hell uses a felt pen? My chai did a number on his phone number. I can make out three numbers clearly, two numbers kinda sorta, but the other five numbers are simply a blurry blue mess. If I can determine the two sorta numbers, then my odds of cracking the other five will be down to 90,000 to 1. To steal a line from *Dumb and Dumber*, "So, you're telling me there's a chance."

But I don't like mine. I am pissed, and whenever I'm pissed my best therapy is work. And wine. Wine works too. But the wine will have to wait. I need some serious Bosco time, so I pull on my big girl pants, race home, gather up my schematics and head over to the studio.

My studio space is in the warehouse district of town, down by the waterfront on the eastside. It's one of those neo-industrial buildings—a combination of brick and etched glass. One of the few that hasn't been torn down and replaced. Forever ago it was probably an ice factory or coal warehouse or some other forgotten industry from a darker age. But these days brick is hip and with a few well-placed bits of stainless steel, a rundown box of a building receives a new lease on life. This particular place bills itself as "the space you need with the budget you have". According to their website they offer tenants "the ability to collaborate with and contribute to the creativity of the local entrepreneurial landscape" or some such crap. You can rent a desk space, an office, or like I, a bigger, more industrial space for larger projects. I've often wondered how many of the rooms have cots in them and serve as places of illicit rendezvous for hobbyists, writers, and engineers who "can't possibly work at home, honey, I need a quiet place to work." Uh-huh.

My space is a perfect 20 feet by 20 feet box with a roll up garage-style door on the ground floor. I've poked my head in on a few of the other spaces, just being nosy. I've seen a pretty wide variety of uses: fashion designers, boat builders, model train enthusiasts, sculptors. But I've also discovered a few unusual businesses as well. I peeked into one space with a sign on the door that said "Threesome" which of course piqued my curiosity. Inside was an earnest young man doing battle with a stack of cardboard boxes armed with a tape applicator, the two-inch-wide kind you see in mailing rooms and post offices. He was closing and sealing the boxes, all of which already had pre-paid postage stickers on the sides. Turns out his business was socks. Sold not in pairs but in threes for when you lose one. Brilliant.

But the one business that really takes the cake I stumbled upon recently. I was walking into the building on my way to my space when I saw this portly woman, maybe 60, struggling with a loaded hand truck, trying to roll it over a curb. She was dressed in polyester slacks and a floral print romper that you only usually see worn by characters on TV shows to indicate to the viewer that said character is woefully behind the times and utterly uncool. The frumpy aunt or the quirky spinster neighbor with nine cats. She was carefully trying to ease the wheels up and over while not sending the hand truck cattywampus and tipping her load. I rushed over and offered to help, which she gladly accepted. With an extra set of hands to hold the boxes in check, we got over the curb easy-peasy.

She thanked me, and I asked her where her space was. She told me second floor, south end. I asked what she did there, and she said she ran a small business out of there on account her garage wasn't big enough anymore.

Being the curious cat that I am I continued to pry.

"You were running your company out of your garage?" I asked.

"Indeedy-do," she said without any consideration to the fact that nobody says indeedy-do except for the TV characters I alluded to earlier. This observation from somebody who just thought "cattywampus" and "easy-peasy." "Me and the mister," she said, "that would be Ned, God rest his soul, we were looking for a way to pass the time after Ned collected his gold watch and pension—they still did that at the power company. Forty-years my Ned toiled there, and finally figured it was time to stop and smell the roses instead of the solar grids. But Ned discovered golf wasn't his game and we weren't much into travelling; seems like no place is safe anywhere in the world these days, am I right?"

I nodded, unprepared for her dissertation.

"Always something horrible happening somewhere," she goes on. "Busses blowing up, tourists kidnapped, robo-mech servants turning on their owners."

She stared off into the middle distance, lost in the unholy mess that has clearly become of our world in her eyes. She snapped out of it and turned back to me. "Well, we weren't about to leave our safe little nest and go traipsing off to some foreign land only to end up a side note on the evening news when some terrorist with a bug up his behind about America decides to make a political statement at our expense. No siree Bob."

I again nodded along like a bobblehead, wondering how one simple question prompted more information than I would expect on a first date.

"Anyhoo," she went on, "one night we were settling in to watch some TV, Jeopardy's our show, never miss it; always makes me feel so smart when I get the answers right. Pardon me, questions right," she said with a wink, apparently mistaking me for a Jeopardy aficionado. "Their 20,000th episode was about to air, a big darn deal, don't you know, and me and the hubby were all settled in. The national news was just ending, and they were doing a story on how terribly smoggy it is over in China, the big cities. There we were, sitting in our Barcaloungers watching this video of people walking down the streets with those masks on like people wore during the pandemic decades ago. But in this case, it wasn't because of any old virus. Ned turns to me and says 'Look at those poor souls. No one should have to live like that. Here we are breathing the freshest air with which God felt fit to fill our lungs and there are people who can't even take a breath without worrying about getting black lung or some such. That is just not right.' And I says half-jokingly, 'It's too bad we can't give 'em some of our air. It's not like we're using it all ourselves.' And suddenly Ned gets this wild gleam in his eye. I'd been married to that man for forty-two years and trust me when I say I know that gleam when I see it. And just like that he's on his feet and off to the family room and I can hear him typing away on our computer. Yes, you heard me right; he still used a keyboard. Call him old-fashioned, he won't mind," she adds with a cackle. "He was a two-finger hunt and pecker; never did learn how to use the other eight. I figured he'd eventually get around to telling me what he's up to, so I watch my Jeopardy and wait him out."

Which is exactly what I was trying to do by this point, wait her out, but she showed no sign of wrapping things up, so I reinforced my interested face—the one with the slight tilt of the head and furrowed brow that reads "I am fascinated," and sucked it up.

Miss Indeedy-do (Mrs?) carried on. "So, at about the same time the defending champion is betting the farm on biblical figures in Double Jeopardy . . ."

"What was the question?" I blurted out. "I mean the answer."

"He was commanded by God to sacrifice his son, Isaac," she said with zero hesitation, clearly glad to find someone presumably equally enthralled with the game show.

"Who is Abraham?" I said instinctively.

Miss Indeedy-do practically beamed. "Look at you! Someone knows her Old Testament. Sadly, the defending champion did not. He bet it all on Elijah."

"Dummy," I said.

"I know, right? Cost him the game. So, where was I?" she asked me earnestly.

"Ned. Typing."

"Yes! Thank you. So, Ned waltzes in during Double Jeopardy, and after I shushed him to wait for the question, which he did, he tells me he's got an idea. 'What idea?' I ask him. He says, 'A crazy idea!' I say, 'Tell me more.' And so, he does. He proceeds to tell me that he wants us to take a big fat chunk of our retirement and start a business. 'What kind of business?' I ask. 'The selling kind,' he says, as if there's another kind. 'Selling what?' I ask, playing along. 'Selling air,' he says. Now, you could have knocked me over with a feather. 'Air?' I say. 'Ned, my dear, you have officially crossed over into la-la land. At least I won't have to worry about dementia creeping up on you, it jumped on with both feet!'"

At this she let out a little whoop and a laugh and slapped her polyester-encased thigh. I chuckled along.

"Well," she said, dabbing at the corner of her eye, "the joke was on me. Within the year we had gross sales of seven-hundred and fifty thousand dollars."

"I'm sorry, what?" I blurted, giving my head a quick shake, like that would change what I heard.

"Yes, indeedy, and according to my accountant, we—I'm sorry, I still refer to the business as *our* business, probably because it was Ned's idea—we expect to break two-million in sales by end of Q4, the fiscal year."

She stood there, plump and beaming, her hands clasped in front of her like an elementary school teacher whose star pupil had just aced the spelling bee by nailing Antidisestablishmentarianism.

"Two million. In one year." I said, slack jawed. "Selling air."

She giggled and held a hand to her mouth. "I know, pinch me, right? Our biggest seller is the 8-liter aerosol with mask that provides upwards of 160 shots." Then she started reciting value-props that sounded like they were ripped straight from the marketing one-sheet. "No CFCs, no propellants. Our famous 2-in-1 built in mask crafted for precision delivery, allowing for maximum enjoyment of our products. A breath of fresh air for those living in areas of high air pollution."

"Air," I said, still slack of jaw.

"Air," she replied simply. "And that isn't even the half of it. Once we offered discounts for returning the empty bottles and masks—appealing to the green-nicks you see," she said with a proud-of-herself wink, "we make even more since the discount is so much less than the cost of making new ones. We went from 'saving the environment,'" she says using air quotes, "to saving for a boat! Isn't America wonderful?"

This seemed to have put a pin in the topic, and I jumped at the chance to beat a retreat. I helped her straighten her hand-truck load, gave her the thumbs-up sign to indicate she was clear for take-off, and spun on my heels. But then I whirled back around. I had to ask, even though there was a chance I might have to listen to another long-winded explanation.

"You're selling two-million dollars-worth of air canisters out of that little storage unit on the second floor?"

Miss Indeedy-do gave a "don't be silly" wave and said "Heaven's no. We have warehouses in Seattle, Dallas, and Lisbon. I only keep this little unit for sentimental purposes. Ta-ta!"

And with that she rolled out of sight. The only thought in my head . . .

"Lisbon?"

CHAPTER 13

Back in my workspace, I kick off my shoes, roll up my sleeves—even though I have never seen anyone in real life roll up their sleeves before tackling a job—and command Spencer to set the mood. A beat later the room fills with the melancholy rhythm guitar strums of "Pigs on the Wing (part 1)" from Pink Floyd's *Animals* album.

I unpack my updated schematic drawings onto the counter and set my keys on one corner, and three rocks that I keep in here for exactly this purpose on the other three corners to keep the paper from rolling back up. Don't ask me why I don't have four rocks, I frankly don't remember, but the keys work fine as the clean-up hitter. I look down at my pencil sketches—not bad for someone with no practical training in architectural drawing—and then back up at the early stages of Bosco in the center of the floor. At this moment, Bosco is nothing more than a thin framework of carbon fiber tubing in the shape of a large rectangle with Saturn rings. Bosco stands a good 8 feet tall and 4 feet wide. Bosco is my ticket to the bigger time. Notice I didn't say big time. I believe in hedging one's bets and making dreams reachable. I am the sort who makes New Year's resolutions that can be achieved by sunset of January 1st, not December 31st. Then I feel accomplished when I reach my goals.

There's a code among those in the performing arts of legerdemain. It's a brother/sisterhood thing. Like Free Masons or Harley riders. We stick up for one another, support one another, give each other a knowing nod when we cross paths. But at the same time, we're competitors. We want to outdo each other or come up with the next big thing that separates us from the pack. With the close-up magicians it's the card trick that hasn't been seen before. For illusionists it's the big splashy disappearance or transportation that brings the crowd to its feet. For mentalists it's the mind reading trick that leaves audiences shaking their heads in disbelief. But at the same time, magicians are a reasonably bigoted lot, at least toward the other disciplines. Sleight of hand artists look at mentalists as charlatans, mentalists look at sleight of hand artists as hacks who couldn't cut it as mentalists, and everyone pretty much hates the illusionists. Cocky bastards.

No subtlety to their craft.

Everything is jumbo sized. Illusionists are to magic what slapstick is to comedy—big, over the top, in your face. And yet here I am attempting to cross over to the dark side. I am building a stage-piece illusion for my act.

What made me decide to dip my toe in the bedazzled world of large-scale stage illusion is simple. I was jealous. We hate illusionists because we're not illusionists, at least not in the technical sense. Illusionists receive the highest billing, draw the biggest crowds, earn the most money. They're the major leagues while the rest of us are the AA and AAA players toiling in the minors. Illusionists travel first class; we fly with no leg room. Illusionists get room service; we eat at Mickey Dees. Illusionists are known by single names—Houdini, Copperfield, Ravenwood; we are known by our close circle of friends and family.

At least that's what it feels like. I take my jabs at illusionists, but I sure wouldn't mind their W-2s. I started feeling the itch when I was in Vegas a few years back. I was there strictly for fun. It wasn't a girl's weekend to get away from husbands or boyfriends for a spell because that would necessitate more than one girl and I am decidedly a solo act. This was before I hired Audrey to pretend to like me. I was staying at an off-the-strip hotel with the incredibly clever name of "Vegas, baby!" Complete with exclamation point. I can't help but think that people book rooms there for the sole purpose of having sex and getting knocked up so that they can say they had a baby in Vegas at the Vegas, baby! I've stayed at my share of the downtown Vegas hotels and casinos—Bally's, the Flamingo, Paris, New York, New York, even once at the Mandalay Bay, which is normally out of my price range, but it was my 29th birthday—my twenties swan song—so I treated myself. I always have a good time in Vegas, and it never ceases to amaze me how many people gladly hand over their hard-earned dollars to the billionaire casino owners. Vegas is not a place for winners, it is built for losers. It's almost impossible for the owners to lose money because of the law of large numbers. This is a theorem that describes the result of performing the same experiment many times. It's all about probability. A casino might lose a large chunk of change on a single spin of a roulette wheel, but in the long run, they win incrementally. And keep winning. The games are always built in their favor. In roulette the house has a 5.26% edge. The longer you play, the better chance they will win. That's why casinos are designed to keep you hanging around as long as possible, why there are no clocks visible anywhere, why there are no windows, so you won't know if it's daytime or night. And they love it when you drink. God, do they love it. Anything to help knock a few points off your common-sense score works in their favor. There's an old saying, the safest way to double your money in Vegas is to fold it over once and put it back in your wallet. Roulette, backgammon, slots, any games of chance are tilted toward the house. They're for suckers. Poker, however . . .

Poker is about math and interpretation of non-verbal cues, two things I have in, pardon the pun, spades. I've always been good with numbers, and as for the non-verbal cues, it's what I do for a living. In my profession, it's all about reading people. That's a handy skill at the green felt table. Don't get me wrong; I could never make a living playing cards, but let's say I usually win more than I lose.

I try to zip off to Vegas once a year and when the spirit moves me, I'll check out a mentalist if one's performing. This time there wasn't any but there was a new illusionist who'd set up camp at a freshly erected hotel and casino called the Empire. It had an ancient Mesopotamian theme with lots of big pillars painted to look like weathered marble, carved alabaster mural reliefs and muted-toned frescos of men, gods, and beasts painted on all surfaces. The magician's name was, as expected, singular—Marco. Not the Great Marco, or Marco the Magnificent, just Marco. The show was in the Empire's spectacular main auditorium, which seated no less than two thousand people—half the size of Caesar's Palace's stadium—but impressive, nonetheless. And it was a full house. Word had already started to spread about this up-and-comer, and it wouldn't be long before he had his own TV special. What made Marco stand out among other big stage illusionists was his lack of flamboyance. He carried himself with a remarkable stillness on stage, which is anathema to most illusionists. They too often rely on sweeping arm gestures, grandiose posturing, and dramatic music stings. But not Marco. He went about his business as if what he was doing were commonplace. The stage was minimalistic, as was the music. But it worked. God help me, it worked. His grand finale was a staggering, emotional piece, complete with a fully developed story arc that had men and women alike in tears, only to bring them charging to their feet moments later with a raucous roar and what seemed like a ten-minute ovation. The grand illusion acted out the story of an elderly father and his young son who were set upon by the devil in an ancient forest. The devil demanded a young soul, the boy's. The father, old but quick-witted, made a deal with the devil whereas if he could best the devil in a challenge, they would be free to pass. If the devil won, he could take the boy. The devil agreed on the condition that if he won, he would receive both their souls. The father, with no leverage, accepted the terms. The devil said he would choose the challenge. The father, reasonably requested that he should get to choose, being that he had more to lose in the challenge. Again, the devil accepted. The father, knowing the devil to be a creature of guile and craft, knew he had to be careful with his choice. The devil, knowing the ways of men, expected a test of strength or wills. Instead, the man took a simple sheet of parchment out of his satchel along with a stick of charcoal. He held them up with his shaking, palsied hands and said the challenge was to draw a perfect circle. The young boy broke down in tears, knowing of his father's shaking affliction, and begged the devil to reconsider. The devil, feeding on the boy's grief and puzzled by the father's seemingly simple challenge, accepted. Seeing the old man's unsteady hands, the devil demanded to go first. The father agreed, to the dismay of the boy, and the devil, confident, bordering on cocky, put charcoal to paper and with a flourish drew his circle. It came out more oval than perfectly circular and overlapped at the end, giving it a little tail. The father nodded appreciatively and said, "Not bad, but I like to think of myself as a sporting fellow, I'll give you a second chance." The devil, never one to pass on an easy mark, took him up on his offer. He took a second pass and this time the circle was rounder, tighter, and with only the smallest inkling of a tail. He was clearly pleased with his effort and held the paper up proudly. The father, shaking his head with awe, was clearly impressed by the devil's efforts, and took out another sheet of parchment from his bag. The devil, arms crossed, looking pleased with himself, watched as the man with trembling hands laid the paper down, placed the knuckle of his pinky finger in the center, and lightly touched the charcoal to the paper. He then slowly turned the piece of paper. Behold, a perfect circle. The devil was furious at being deceived and vanished in a fiery cloud of brimstone.

This simple tale was woven seamlessly through the magician's illusion, writ large on stage using rear screen projection and shadow puppetry resulting in Marco himself as the devil vanquished in a fiery finale only to reappear as the elderly father. The parchment and charcoal imagery, cleverly and artistically realized, were a good ten feet tall themselves. It was captivating, it was storytelling, it was grand, it was breathtaking. In other words, it was magical. And I became a believer in the art of large-scale stage illusion. Much to my dismay.

In my 20 feet by 20 feet workspace I stand before the skeletal beginnings of Bosco, my own illusion of grandeur, and smile. I know Bosco won't be anything close to what I saw on stage that night in Vegas but, hey, baby steps. Regardless, it's going to throw people for a loop. "Wait'll they get a load of you," I say to the room. Pink Floyd's David Gilmore backs me up singing the opening lines of "Dogs." "You gotta be crazy, you gotta have a real need," apropos of something.

CHAPTER 14

Grayson Hasagawa's office is located atop a steel and glass edifice that's the pride of the city. Tall, stately, with an elegant curve, it rises above the skyline like a vertical scythe blade. I arrive ten minutes before the requested time—if you're early you're on time; if you're on time you're late, my mom always said—and take the elevators to the 75th floor. Well, technically to the 70th floor, at which point I hop off the elevator and ride a separate, private car for the last five floors where

Hasagawa's senior leadership team congregates. I punch in the code provided me and the elevator smoothly carries me upward. With a cheerful ping the doors open into a spacious lobby that quietly whispers understated elegance. The thick, deep pile carpets feel like I am walking across a landscape of slate gray moss. A small burlwood reception desk sits discreetly across the way in front of a pair of tall, deeply lacquered doors. As I approach, I notice there isn't a receptionist but instead a large monitor that rises out of an inset in the tabletop. There must be some motion detection device at work. By the time I reach the desk, the monitor is fully upright and an attractive brunette of indeterminate nationality, her hair in a professional bun, greets me with a pleasant smile.

"Good morning, Ms. Percival, Mr. Hasagawa is expecting you. Can I provide you anything? Cucumber water? Iced tea? A coffee, perhaps?"

"Uh, no thanks, I'm good," I say. I always find it a bit unnerving talking to holos and faces on monitors. Not sure why. It feels . . . impersonal.

"Very well. Please enter the doors directly behind me. And thank you for taking the time to visit us today."

I walk around the desk and to the large, lacquered doors, wondering again why Hasagawa wants to see me. When my agent called me with the request I was stunned. It's not often a lowly subject gets a personal audience with the king. My first inclination was that Hasagawa wanted to know how I did the time travel bit at his birthday party, and he hoped I'd spill the beans. Not gonna happen. I reach up to knock but before I can, the doors open inward. I step through into what I can honestly say is the coolest office I have ever seen. First off, it's big. Huge. You could play pickleball in here. Fifteen-foot floor to ceiling windows take up the back and left side wall, offering a spectacular view of the city and surrounding hills and river. The furnishings are sparse but absolutely kick-ass. A full suit of samurai armor stands in the corner. Made of cloth, leather, and wrought iron colored red, brown, black, and gold, it's clearly the visual cornerstone of the room. Your eyes go right to it. There's a button-tufted deep orange velvet settee flanked by two gold hued wingback chairs surrounding a high gloss black lacquered coffee table with a glass top. There's something funky about the top but I can't put my finger on it. The room's furnishings are an odd combination of ancient Japanese simplicity crossed with the panache of a 1920s speakeasy.

And for some crazy reason, it works.

And then there's the desk on the far side of the room by the windows. The desk with the crowd of people around it. The crowd looking at me. I take that as my cue to quit gawking but I'm not sure if I'm supposed to wave, bow or what. I end up doing an awkward hybrid and wait for some instruction.

Grayson Hasagawa, standing on the far side of the desk, smiles broadly at me. "Ms. Percival, thank you for joining us. Please, come in."

The woman from Hasagawa's party, his assistant—what was her name? Devon something. Dimes? Pennies? Nickles? Nichols! Devon Nichols, that's it!—She breaks from the group and crosses the room toward me, a professional but warm look on her face. When she reaches me, she shakes my hand and offers to take my coat. I thank her but tell her if it's all the same to her I'd like to keep it on. I get cold easy. She accepts with a nod and escorts me back toward the desk. As I walk past the coffee table, I can see what was funky about the top of it. From back by the door, I could see that the top seemed to shift and change ever so slightly, but upon closer inspection I can see that under the glass top is water. And in the water are several white and orange koi slowly cruising around. The man's coffee table is a fishpond. I really need to make more money.

Other than Hasagawa, there are three other people at the desk, a woman and two men. The man on the far side of the desk is in his mid-thirties, athletic, trim in a well-tailored dark gray suit.

To his right, the other man is a touch older, maybe 40, with the beginning of salt-and-pepper in his hair. He too is sporting an immaculate suit, this one black with a crisp white shirt and a surprisingly high-wattage orange tie. The woman to Hasagawa's immediate left and closest to me is tall and statuesque in a fashionable dusty rose blouse and form fitting navy skirt, the kind I couldn't pull off in a million years. You must have super model legs to make it work. Perhaps that's what she was in a former life. She's got the looks, fading though they may be. She's probably around fifty but could get away with saying forty.

Whatever moisturizer she's using, I want it.

Hasagawa begins introductions.

"Everyone, this is Ms. Frankie Percival, as you already know, a remarkably talented mentalist." Gesturing from me to the others around me, "Allow me to introduce you to several members of my team." He nods to gray suit. "This is Mark Peters, my marketing director." To orange tie, "Stephan Triviano, my communications manager." To supermodel, "And this is Marjorie Temple, my director of corporate events. I think you remember my assistant Devon Nichols."

I shake everyone's hands and slip in a nice to meet you. The desk is one of those interactive models where the surface also acts as a computer screen. About half of the tabletop is clear but the other half is covered in papers.

Clearly Grayson Hasagawa doesn't realize we've supposedly become a paperless society. I guess he didn't get the memo, as the gag goes. The open part of the table/computer screen shows what looks like a schematic or map of an event space, perhaps a large auditorium. There's what looks like a large stage at the front and hundreds, perhaps thousands of seats taking up the rest of the room.

Hasagawa sees me looking at the table and gives me a smile.

"You're probably wondering what this is all about. Why I asked you here."

"Pretty much," I say with a smile, keeping it light.

Hasagawa gestures again to his team and says, "We're in the process of ironing out the final details for our annual corporate event. It's where all—well not—but most of our employees get together to hear me blather on about the state of the company, and become inspired about the upcoming year. We have guest speakers, symposiums, lots of networking."

Marjorie Temple, the events director says, "It's called Zenith . . ."

"Like the old TVs," I say without even thinking.

Everyone stares at me like I've grown a second head. "I'm sorry?" says Marjorie.

I can feel my face bursting into flames. "Uh, Zenith. They made TVs back in the day. My grandma had one."

Marjorie smiles at this, "Okay then. I have learned something new. My day is now complete." There is no bitchiness to this comment. She truly sounds like she is happy to have learned a new piece of trivia that she can pull out at cocktail parties. She glances down at the layout of the auditorium. "This year's event will take place in Los Angeles and will last three days. We expect to have somewhere in the neighborhood of twenty-five thousand in attendance. Mr. Hasagawa's keynote address will be in the Dolby Theater."

"Where they used to hold the Oscars, when they were a thing," I blurt out again. I really need to work on my impulse control.

"Precisely," says Marjorie without missing a beat. "Approximately 3,400 people will be there for Mr. Hasagawa's presentation."

"It will also be simulcast to all the employees who are not able to attend, perhaps another two-hundred thousand," fills in Salt-and-Pepper—Stephan the communications manager.

I let out a low whistle upon hearing this. "Crimeny, that's a lot of people." I look up at Hasagawa. "What's it like being in front of an audience that big?"

He smiles and says, "I'm hoping you'll find out firsthand. That's why I've invited you here."

I glance from Hasagawa to the others trying to wrap my mind around what he just said. "Pardon?"

"What Mr. Hasagawa is saying," says Orange Tie—Mark Peters—"is that he would like you to perform at Zenith."

You ever heard that term about being so quiet you can hear a pin drop?

Everyone looks to me, smiling happily, and I stand there with my mouth hanging open with what most likely passes for the most vacuous expression ever witnessed by mankind.

"Me," I say. A statement.

"You," says Marjorie.

"We all were at Mr. Hasagawa's party where you performed," says Mark. "You were remarkable."

"It was all anyone could talk about afterwards," says Stephan.

"When I pressed Mr. Hasagawa on who we should have perform at the event, he immediately suggested you," says Marjorie. "I have to admit, I was a bit surprised by his suggestion. I mean, normally we have only national names and arena-filling musicians on the docket."

"Three years ago, Dark Star Supernova played," says Mark.

"Two years ago, we had Pricilla Esperanza," says Stephan.

"And last year, Pencil-Necked Geeks," says Marjorie.

"I love the Geeks," I say absentmindedly, still trying to fathom what was taking place here.

"Everyone loves the Geeks," says Hasagawa with a laugh. "Oh, sure, we'll have a big-name act opening for me; I'm not at liberty to say who at this moment."

I glance at Mark who does the twist-the-lock on his lips and throw-away-the-key gesture.

"But this year leading up to my keynote," continues Hasagawa, "I want a curve ball. Something no one is expecting. And frankly and selfishly speaking, something that I know that I'll enjoy. And that something is you. Are you interested?"

All eyes lock on me. I am having a hard time processing the information—my mind is acting like a crappy airport rental car on a steep hill—chugging along, taking its sweet time, but eventually getting me there. I feel like I am experiencing one of those flash-forward scenes in movies where the heroine sees her future unfold before her eyes in a quick montage of deliriously happy scenes over the course of about ten seconds. And in those ten seconds, I see opportunity. Hell, who am I kidding? I see fame. I see dollar signs. I see my ship coming in. I see myself on talk shows and the national morning news programs during the entertainment segment. I see paparazzi. I see myself on the cover of the few magazines that still exist, gloriously misquoted and not caring.

See, here's the funny thing. Ever heard the term starving artist? There's a reason for it. I've done pretty well in my profession; never had to wait tables as a side gig. But I've also never reached the point where I felt comfortable with my savings account. I've always felt I was one gall stone or burst appendix away from being on the skids.

I rally all my self-control, which still fails miserably, and my face explodes into the biggest, most sincere grin imaginable.

"Yes, very much so." I say, beaming, walking the razor's edge of tears.

Everyone exhales together and trades smiles.

They must be feeling what it's like to grant a wish to a kid with terminal cancer. Right now, I'm the kid and this gig is my trip to Disneyland. And Disney World. And Universal Studios. And every other theme park the world over.

"Excellent!" says a beaming Hasagawa. We'll draw up the contract and begin promoting you immediately."

"We're actually pretty late in the game," says Marjorie. "Normally we have all of our talent locked in nearly a year in advance, but there's still time."

"When is the event?" I ask.

"Oh, we're still a good four months away," says Stephan. "It's not until July."

My heart does a little skip. "When in July?"

"The event runs the 4th through the 7th," says Mark.

My heart starts to fibrillate. "And Mr. Hasagawa's big presentation is on . . ."

"The seventh," says Marjorie. "The grand finale."

My heart completely folds in upon itself and collapses inside my chest. Evidently it shows on my face because everyone looking at me takes on a confused and slightly concerned expression.

"Are you all right?" asks Stephan.

My eyes are downturned, my lips pursed. It's my default expression for when I'm faced with decisions. I'm thinking about what's being handed to me and the consequences of the next words that are about to spill from my mouth. After the initial shock it occurs to me that I'm perfectly okay with my answer and knowing that I'm okay with it bolsters my confidence. I feel my head rising and my back becoming a little straighter. I look to each of them, one after the other, before I turn my focus to Hasagawa and say with a sad smile, "I'm busy that day."

Remember that pin dropping? It's happening again. Marjorie, Stephan, and Mark all wear identical blank masks. Their faces don't show surprise or shock, it's still too early in the process. As if they heard what I said but their brains are wondering if they heard it correctly. They're simultaneously sporting an expression of incredulity. But the incredulity is swiftly changing over to chagrin, like someone told a deep and clever joke and they're just now getting the punch line. They exchange glances with one another and then begin to smile and chuckle nervously.

"Very good, very, very good," says Mark wagging his head. "You got me on that one."

The others give little snorts of acknowledgment and start to laugh, but their laughs die in their throats when they look back at me and I'm not laughing along with them. It's right about then that they can tell I'm not joking.

"What do you mean you're busy that day?" asks Marjorie. Her expression is shapeshifting before my eyes. Warm, playful, pleasant Marjorie is becoming puzzled, dubious Marjorie.

I hold my hands out in the universal gesture of "Hey, whattayagonnado?" without saying anything.

"We are giving you this opportunity. An opportunity of a lifetime." Marjorie's tone showcases her disbelief.

"I don't think you fully understand what we're offering here." Disbelief is now supplanted by marginal hostility.

The only person who doesn't look like they want to hang me from a rusty meat hook is Hasagawa. He's taking everything in thoughtfully. "What's the conflict?"

"It's my mom's birthday," I say.

Marjorie lets out a derisive snort. "Are you fucking kidding me? Your mom's birthday?" Pissed-off Marjorie has sent warm, playful Marjorie home for the night. "We're handing you the chance of a lifetime and you're turning it down because it's your mom's fucking birthday?" Marginally hostile Marjorie has fully transformed into angry, pissed-off, take-a-blowtorch-to-me Marjorie within a span of about three heartbeats.

"Marjorie . . ." Hasagawa says softly, trying to defuse the situation, but Marjorie is having none of it.

"I've got the biggest event of the year in four short months and this crazy bitch just shat all over it!" Marjorie turns from Hasagawa to me. "Your mom's birthday? Are you out of your fucking mind? Do what everyone else does, buy her a card, send her some fucking flowers, call her on the goddamn phone!" The temperature of the room is rising noticeably, presumably from the blast furnace that has become Marjorie Temple. Her face has taken on the hue of a bowl of tomato soup. "But. Do. Not. Fuck. With MY Event!"

Hasagawa places a calming hand on her shoulder, which she doesn't seem to feel, and with an air of remarkable calm guides her away from the desk and over toward the office doors.

At the door she spins and points at me with an impeccably manicured nail.

"I will burn you down, bitch! Do you hear me? You are dead! Dead!"

And just like that, she is gone. Hasagawa strolls back toward us with an embarrassed smile. "She's a tad excitable but the best event coordinator in the business. I wouldn't worry about her."

"Worry about her?" I ask. "She was talking murder in the first!"

Hasagawa waves it off with a shrug. "Figure of speech."

Mark and Stephan are busy collecting the papers from the desk, seemingly unfazed by Marjorie's outburst. "That's not one of her better flip outs," says Stephan.

"Not even top five," says Mark. "You should have seen her when the Geeks demanded Evian bottled water at precisely 36 degrees for their dressing rooms."

"Thought she was gonna have a thrombosis," says Stephan. "Scared the hell out them though. They said tap water would be just fine."

They finish tidying up, head for the door, and a moment later it's only me, Hasagawa and his assistant, who's been virtually invisible the entire time.

I am expecting the third degree or at least a request for a deeper explanation, but instead he says, "She must be a special woman, your mother."

"She is," I say.

Hasagawa nods and says, "Please contact me if you reconsider."

CHAPTER 15

Hello, my name is Frankie and I'm a career suicidalist. Suicidalist? Is that even a word? If it's not, then I just created the perfect scenario for it to exist.

> ***Career suicidalist** [kuh-reer soo-uh-side-uh-list] noun*
> A person who destroys one's own interests or prospects.
> *"Turning down that once-in-a-lifetime offer was the work of a career suicidalist."*

What was I thinking? Honestly, I know exactly what I was thinking, and I'm still okay with my decision. But still, what was I thinking! These thoughts swirl around in my head as I enter the Odeon theater. The Odeon is my home base for performing. It's an old-timey place, full of what I like to charitably refer to as *character*. The owner, an affable but chintzy guy by the name of Dak Presley who's as much of a theater romantic as me, runs the place with a childlike wonder and a shoestring budget.

In all my years of performing at the Odeon, never once has Dak called me by my name. As a matter of fact, I don't think I've ever heard him call anyone by their name. When he's addressing me, it's always Toots, Hon, Doll, Kiddo, Sis, or the always crowd-pleasing Peaches. The guys are always Sport, Slick, Boyo, Pal, Bud, Tiger, Kid, or Dude. At first, I wondered if Dak even knew my name, but he must because every week my name's on the marquee and because every month I receive a deposit in my bank and the name on the account isn't Peaches. I suspect a lot of women would be offended being called Angel or Sugar but, frankly, it doesn't bother me in the least. Probably because Dak's such a lovable character. I honestly don't think it even occurs to him that it's not PC. My guess is that he says it because the nicknames are easier to remember, and he probably thinks they sound better than "Hey, you!"

The Odeon is a weird hybrid of nightclub and theater. Dak books bands Wednesday, Friday, and Saturday, and has open mic night on Sunday. The Odeon is closed on Mondays, as Dak likes to say, to observe the dagnabest day of the week unencumbered by the weight of employment expectations. Dagnabest, the verb version of Dagnabbit, is as close to swearing as Dak gets. When he's upset, we hear Rats, Dang it, Frack, or Jiminy Crickets. When he's good and truly pissed it's Son of a Trucker, Balderdash, or my personal favorite, Cheese and Crackers!

Tuesdays and Thursdays at the Odeon are all mine. Well, not all mine. Believe it or not, I've got an opening act, a college kid who's a bit of a vaudevillian. Sometimes he's spinning plates on sticks, other times he's doing broad, physical humor. I've seen him do a ventriloquist bit, magic, a little song, a little dance, a little seltzer down your pants. I'll give him this much, he's always fresh.

For whatever reason, the kid and I make a good pairing and have somehow struck a chord with the younger crowd. I think they see us as a throwback act. We're retro, which evidently qualifies us as cool and hip. At least that's the way it's been for a good stretch, but crowds are notoriously fickle, and I've already begun noticing a growing number of empty seats of late.

As I walk through the lobby, I give a nod to Big Wave Dave, the custodian. He's only been working there a couple of months, but it didn't take long to realize that you don't talk to Dave, you simply acknowledge him. I tried chatting him up one time and got nowhere. It was like trying to talk to a fifteen-year-old. I got a couple of grunts and one-syllable responses but that was about it.

He's called Big Wave Dave because he's a hard-core windsurfer. I don't think I've ever seen his van without a board strapped to the roof. And it's not even spring! Word is that when he's not mopping up the previous night's spillage in the village, he's strapped into his board pounding through whitecaps and 20-knot ice cold winds. And he looks it. The dude is ripped. If the place had an official bouncer, Dave would be it, but it's not necessary because just having him walk around keeps the idiots in check.

The evening crowd has already begun trickling in. The Odeon has a sweet happy hour which helps fill seats and prime the audience. Someone once said the best audience is intelligent, well-educated and a little drunk.

True that. I try to gauge how many people are there and it feels meager. There's too much vacant space between bodies for my taste. I spot the kid opening for me; he's at the bar nursing a Coke and watching a ball game on the TV mounted in the corner.

"Hey, Baltic," I say as I walk up to the bar. Seriously, that's his name, Baltic. He's of that generation where parents were going overboard trying to come up with unique names for their kids. You have no idea how desperately I wanted his last name to be Avenue. You know, from Monopoly. I was bitterly disappointed to learn it was Jones.

"Hey, Frankie," he says with a tip of his glass in my direction. "Ready to baffle the masses?"

I look around the bar. "Let me know when the masses arrive."

"Yeah, it's been kind of thin lately, hasn't it?"

"Bordering on emaciated," I say.

"Yeah, well, things will turn around. It's a cyclical business," he says, like he's been thirty-years in the business and not a fresh-faced kid who's probably still living with his mother.

The bartender—an elderly chap named Scotty who I can refer to as a chap because, A: His name is Scotty, and B: He's much older than me—slides a healthily poured high ball glass in my direction without request. Scotty fully understands the concept of being a bartender. I take a sip. Gin and tonic. The tonic is merely incidental.

"What have you got in store tonight, Baltic?" I ask, sincerely curious.

Baltic sets his glass down and rotates in my direction, his face a mask of even-handed composure. "Oh, I got a great bit tonight. Been working on it for a while. It's an oldie, been around for a million years, but it's pretty cool." The kid clearly needs work on his hyperbole.

"So, tell me," I say.

Baltic spins back away from me. "Nuh huh. Not telling. You'll have to wait and see." He steals a smug glance in my direction and looks immensely proud of himself.

"Fine." I shrug. "Be a punk. See if I care. I'm sure the ten people in the crowd will be blown away."

Turns out the crowd isn't as sparse as I had feared, but still far from what I would call robust. At showtime the stage lights dim, the spotlight snaps on and follows Dak as he walks on from the wings, and stops behind the mic stand. He taps the mic a couple of times; it lets out a short squeal of feedback and he gives an embarrassed chuckle.

"Ladies and gentlemen, thank you for joining us at the historic Odeon theater. We've got a great show for you tonight. In a few minutes you will be astounded, bewildered, boggled and confounded through mentalist powers beyond your imagination by way of the mystical and mysterious Frankie!"

Okay, this is the one time he uses my name, and it always makes me cringe. "Frankie" is not mystical, nor mysterious. Ezmeralda? Lucinda? Minerva? Absolutely. But Frankie? Not so much. Marketing never was my forte. Dak soldiers on with his intro.

"But first, prepare to be astonished and mesmerized, stupefied and entranced by the man of a thousand acts, who brings tears and laughter in equal measure, who enthralls and delights every man, woman, and child who has had the privilege of witnessing his act fit for kings and royalty the world over, our very own Baltic Jones!"

I gotta hand it to Dak; he's a cheap bastard, but he knows his stage introductions. The crowd gives a polite round of applause, and the curtain raises to reveal an empty stage, save for a hat rack set in the middle. It's one of those old school racks with the bent wood pieces sticking up on top for hanging hats, and right below where they're screwed to the main mast, they curly cue out for where you can hang a coat. At this moment both ends of one of the bent woods are serving their purpose. A fedora sits on top, while a long black coat on a hanger hangs from the curl. At a glance, it could pass as a person standing there wearing a hat. Ethereal music pipes from the speakers. With mandolin and accordion it has a distinctly Roma sound to it.

Like you'd hear sitting around a campfire in the Balkan steppes. While on acid.

Baltic enters stage left. He's dressed like a janitor, pushing a broom. Baltic did a little makeup job on himself. He looks decidedly older. His posture and body language seal the deal. He looks like a man who's accepted his lot in life, not the life he imagined. With music and stage presence, Baltic has beautifully managed to sketch a rough outline of this man's past in mere seconds. I see a person beaten down by life, a solitary figure, probably living alone in a run-down but tidy three-story walk up. I'd wager he owns a dog, a small one, perhaps named Mitzy or something equally generational, maybe named after a lost love. He had ambitions as a young man, but through poor choices or circumstance, his ambitions never materialized. He took the janitorial job because it was all he could find but chose to do it to the best of his abilities. Dirt in his hallways? No siree Bob! Not on his watch.

Baltic pushes the broom across the stage, oblivious to the hat rack. The Odeon's an old theater and has a trap door set in the stage floor back from its vaudeville days. I'm always afraid someone's going to step on it and fall straight through, but Baltic walks right over it without a thought. When he reaches the front of the hat rack he stops, leans on the broom, and wipes his brow, a man on a well-deserved break. He finally notices the rack out of the corner of his eye and turns to fully consider it. He glances around to make sure no one is watching; after all, the help isn't supposed to intermingle with the building's property. Satisfied that the coast is clear he walks to the hat rack and looks it over from stem to stern. Something on the coat catches his eye and he leans in for a closer inspection. He shakes his head, a "this won't do" gesture, and produces a clothing brush from his pocket. He gives the front lapels a few swift swipes and then picks off an imaginary speck of lint. He moves in closer, to the point where he's right up against the coat. He opens it up and gives the insides a few brushes, then tries to clean the right sleeve. He reaches in with his right arm to give the sleeve some substance to brush against, and then slips it all the way through until his hand is coming out the other end. At this point he basically has the coat halfway on. It looks like he's in front of a person wearing a long black coat and hat. The illusion is beautiful. He has the brush in his left hand but when he brushes the sleeve down to the end, the right hand sticking out of the sleeve takes the brush from him. Baltic stops, slightly alarmed, and takes his left hand away, unsure what to do. The right hand coming out of the sleeve moves incrementally toward him with the brush, trying not to scare him. The hand with the brush reaches up and swipes at Baltic. Baltic jumps back slightly and the hand with the brush stops. Baltic looks at the hand, which tips ever so slightly back and forth, looking for all the world like it's saying, *"May I?"* Baltic nods and the crowd laughs. He's only two minutes in and he's already got them in the palm of his hand. The black-sleeved hand gently reaches up and brushes at Baltic's coveralls. After which the hand places the brush in Baltic's coat and slowly reaches up towards his face. Baltic's eyes go a little wide at this and he pulls back. The hand freezes, then opens its palm as if to say, *"It's all right."* The hand inches in closer and Baltic allows it. The hand reaches up and places it gently on Baltic's cheek and strokes it. Baltic leans into the intimacy, his eyes closed. The hand eases down Baltic's cheek to his neck, travels over his shoulder, and slips under his arm, reaching across his body, holding him in an embrace. Baltic's left hand has reached across, holding the empty but living coat in the same manner. The music wafts over the scenario, dusting it with longing and melancholy. I feel myself tearing up. The sleeved hand eases back, pats Baltic on the chest, a sort of, *"I must be going now"* gesture, and drops back to its side. Baltic slips his arm out of the coat quickly and steps back from the rack. The coat and hat hang there, lifeless, as if the previous moments had never happened. Baltic picks up his broom and shuffles back across the stage. When he reaches the far side, he turns and looks at the coat longingly. He gives a shy wave, and as God as my witness, the sleeve of the empty coat raises and waves back. The crowd gasps and cheers as Baltic exits the stage and the curtain closes.

CHAPTER 16

My show goes well but I can't help but feel it ran a distant second to Baltic's performance. Backstage I find Baltic sitting peacefully by himself, looking shyly radiant if that's even possible.

"Nice show," he says to me.

"Thanks." I stop and consider him for a long moment, trying to sum up the proper words to describe how his performance affected me, because that's exactly what it did. It affected me, deeply. I decide to gush. "Baltic, your show rocked. I'm serious, it was spectacular." Baltic blushes a deep red and takes to staring at the floor. "I've seen variations on the bit before," I say, "but you nailed it. It was moving, sad, beautiful. It did all the things we as performers hope to achieve but seldom do."

Baltic is clearly thrilled by my praise but holds it in check.

"Thanks," he says, "that means a lot to me coming from you."

At that moment Dak ambles up, an odd expression on his face. Dak has always been one of our staunchest supporters and is never short of high praise when he sees an act that he likes. After Baltic's he must be beyond thrilled, but for some reason he's not looking as happy as I would normally expect.

Dak stops beside Baltic and gives him a reassuring pat on the shoulder. "Great bit, kid, you killed." He then looks over at me and says, "You too, sis, as always." He looks between us and says, "Both of you, terrific. I couldn't be prouder, which makes what I have to say even more difficult."

Shit. This can't be good. I look at Baltic and he looks right back at me, a "*beats me*" look on his face. I turn back to Dak, and he's got his hands dug deep into his pockets.

He's rocking back and forth on his wingtips, clearly not enjoying the moment.

"It's just that, well, as you've probably noticed lately, we haven't exactly been packing them in."

I notice that he said *we* not *you two*. Dak Presley stands by his performers.

"We've been losing at the gate for some time, and I have to take measures. The bands are still breaking even but unfortunately Tuesdays and Thursdays have been working at a loss. I've tried to hold out as long as possible, waiting for things to turn around . . ."

"It's a cyclical business," Baltic adds helpfully.

"It is indeed," says Dak. "But unfortunately, the wheel hasn't turned yet." He can see our faces slowly crumbling and quickly holds his hands up. "Hold on now, I'm not ditching you guys, but I am going to have to cut you back to one night a week until things pick back up." He can see that this last bit of news isn't stemming the tide and his hands drop to his sides. He turns to each of us. "I'm sorry. I really am, but I have to do what I have to do to keep the theater running."

I allow a few seconds for the disappointment to register and settle into place and I try my best to pull up my big girl pants and handle the news with as much grace as

I can muster, if for no other reason than to show Baltic that this isn't the end of the world.

I fail miserably.

"But Dak, didn't you see how the crowd reacted to Baltic's performance? He had them eating out of the palm of his hand! When word gets out, you're going to be throwing up the Sold-Out sign on a regular basis." I look at Baltic and he's calmly nodding along, not nearly as excited as I would hope he would be. "And on top of that, I've got a new bit coming too! Wait till you see it, it's going to blow people away. I'm adding a whole new level of flash to my show." I can feel the uncomfortable tone of desperation creep into my voice, but I don't care. It's Go time and I'm not about to lose for lack of bullets fired in defense. "You've always said you felt I should snazz up my show, right?" I turn to Baltic for support, and he wholeheartedly agrees.

"Absolutely!" he says, looking from me to Dak. "Just what you said. Snazz it up!"

I pile on. "And this is world class snazz we're talking here. Next level snazz. This is Vegas snazz. Atlantic City snazz. I've poured my heart and soul into this new bit, and I promise you it will knock you for a loop!"

There. Bullets spent.

I find myself slightly out of breath. I haven't made a pitch like that in years and it shows. I feel like I just ran up three flights of stairs. I look to Dak to see who came down with my desperation pass, the receiver or defender.

Dak slowly shakes his head. Shit. The defender.

"I'm sure it's going to be great, Frankie," he says. "On Thursdays."

Holy crap, he used my name. Now I know it's over.

BACK IN MY apartment, I do a reasonable impression of Hurricane Frankie, storming about, using just about every swear word I can think of, most directed (unfairly) at Dak and (fairly) at the cruelty of life in general. I do all of this between sips. Eventually I toss the empty bottle of white into the waste basket. It lands on the other empty bottle that I finished an hour earlier. I lie on the couch and stare at the popcorn ceiling listening to Roger Waters lament about how he doesn't need no arms around him, and he doesn't need no drugs to calm him.

I, on the other hand, will have to disagree with Roger on this last one. I take another sip of the grape and take on the physical characteristics of Roger's song.

I am most definitely feeling comfortably numb.

I have a hunch that tomorrow, however, I will not be so lucky.

CHAPTER 17
THE CHAT WITH MYRNA

"You like old movies," says Myrna.

"And music," I say.

"What's the attraction? Why do you think you connect with them?"

I've found I like talking with Myrna. She virtually never loses eye-contact and always seems sincerely interested in what I have to say. I wonder if she's like this off the clock. I can't imagine. That would be exhausting. At least for me. I have a hard-enough time carrying on a conversation with anyone for more than ten minutes before I start becoming antsy. You'd think it'd be easy connecting with people given how well I can read them, but somehow that makes it seem like work, doing it off stage.

"My mom turned me on to them growing up."

"For example?" prompts Myrna.

"We always had music playing in the house. Always. Her collection was ridiculous. In the basement we had a room decked out to play every musical platform you can think of: record player, reel to reel, 8-track, cassette deck, CD player, Mp3, Laser, aural projection. We practically needed a room just for her vinyl. She was even more old school than me. She would constantly be teaching me about musicians and songs, giving me backstories and insights. She was a walking encyclopedia. My brother and I would try to stump her, by naming a musician, band, or song, thinking we could find one she hadn't heard of. Failure. Every time."

"That's impressive," says Myrna.

"Did you know Elvis Presley recorded more than 600 songs but didn't write a single one? Well, maybe a couple. I can't confirm."

"I did not."

"You familiar with the Beatles?" I ask.

"I am," says Myrna. "My grandmother saw them live."

"Cool. Know the song 'Yesterday?'"

"I think so."

"Did you know that after Paul McCartney came up with the melody, he didn't have any words yet, so he put in placeholder lyrics."

"Okay . . ."

"Scrambled eggs," I say.

"Excuse me?"

"Those were the opening lyrics to Yesterday until Paul took the time to write the real lyrics."

"Scrambled eggs," says Myrna,

"The opening working lines were Scrambled eggs, oh my baby how I love your legs, not as much as I love scrambled eggs."

"Seriously?"

"That's the kind of stuff my mom taught us. Made music so much more fun."

"Who's your favorite musician?" asks Myrna.

"Musician or band?"

"Let's say band."

"Which era?"

"Uh, favorite band, current century," she says, enjoying this interplay. It's starting to feel like a game.

"Let's see. That would be a toss-up between Bangla Dash and False Liberty, depending on my mood."

"Last century?"

"Easy. Pink Floyd. Nothing else close." I say with conviction and finality.

"Why?"

"Floyd's music is rich, theatrical, complex, even psychedelic. Back in their day it was called psychedelic prog-rock, progressive rock, ahead of its time. And according to the history books, everyone in that generation was drugged out of their mind, so the music was perfect for the times."

"And here we are, one hundred years later, and it still speaks to you."

"I think it's because they tell stories with their songs. The music takes me places. It makes me feel."

"And you think you need music to help you feel things?"

"I didn't say that." I sound defensive to my own ears. "It's just, dredging up feelings and emotions on my own isn't easy. Floyd does the work for me."

Myrna is silent. She looks like she's weighing the value of pulling on this thread, but eventually decides this is not a sweater she's ready to unravel. She changes tack.

"Let's talk movies," she says with a note of cheer in her voice. She already knows this is the sweet spot for me. Bring it on.

"Let's," I say brightly.

"I won't insult you by asking you your favorite movie."

"Points for you," I say with a nod of respect. "When people find out you're a movie buff that's always the first question they ask."

Myrna rolls her eyes, as if she totally gets it. "Like you can pick one."

"I know, right? It's like asking a parent to pick their favorite kid."

"I don't know," says Myrna with a smirk, "I think I could pick a favorite out of my crew, easy." We both get a chuckle out of that. Damn she's good. Self-deprecating, says things most people would never admit to, she lets you right in and you gladly check your defenses at the door.

"But a favorite actor," I say, "that I have."

"And?"

"Actor, Tom Hardy, actress, Emma Stone," I say.

"Hardy," wonders Myrna aloud. "He sounds familiar. Has he done anything lately?"

"No, he's passed on. Emma still works though. She makes an appearance now and then, usually as the saucy, wise-cracking grandma. She's still got it though. Did you ever see any of her stuff when she was young? Man, she was something."

"Nobody currently? No contemporary actors that impress you?" asks Myrna.

"Oh, there are lots of actors working today that I think are terrific, but I dunno, there's something about actors from yesteryear that, that . . ."

"Connect with you?" helps Myrna.

"Yeah."

Myrna considers me a moment with a mischievous grin. "You, Frankie Percival, are an old soul."

I smile back. "I like that. An old soul." I slouch down into my chair and let that label roll around in my head for a moment. I like the way it fits. Frankie, the old soul. Catchy. Christ, where was this woman ten years ago? I could have been so much more well-adjusted if I saw her once a week. When she talks, I listen. When she asks questions, I answer. I've revealed more of myself in the last hour than I have in the last decade. Somehow, someway, Myrna coaxed it out of me. It's like she's one of those master burglars who quietly unfolds her velvet kit of lock picking tools, makes a selection, jiggers my locking mechanism and click! Lock springs, door opens, and out pours my soul. The question now though is whether my soul is good TV.

CHAPTER 18

Between my job, social life, and brother issues I allow myself to be a little fed up. Fed up with all this rain on my parade, so I turn to my all-purpose mood-turning umbrella: a flick.

I'm at the Mission theater in ten. Audrey's already there. She's sporting her requisite black boots and, of course, they go perfectly with her stylishly ripped black jeans, bright orange tee shirt and bomber jacket. It actually looks like a real bomber jacket. It's weathered and has the kind of fleece collars you saw buzz boys sporting in World War II movies, except it couldn't be from that era. Thing would be moth eaten and rotted through by now, so it must be a replica. She's got a hint of cat-eye eyeliner going on, which sets off her deep red lipstick perfectly.

What I wouldn't give to be able to pull that off.

She gives me an air kiss and we stroll in. It's a particularly sparse crowd so I'm not surprised to see my fave love seat available. I throw my coat on it and we fetch our drinks. Tasteless fizzy water for Aud, IPA for me. The timing works out so that we come in about ten minutes after the end of the previous showing so there's a good fifteen more minutes to kill before they start playing the coming attractions. The clean-up crew, all one of him, is sweeping up wayward popcorn into a dustpan. I watch the guy mill about and feel myself zoning out. I'm watching but not seeing. My mind is drifting off to everything that's been going on lately but before I can start peeling away onion layers, I feel a sock in my shoulder.

"Earth to Frankie, earth to Frankie. Permission to come aboard," says Audrey robotically.

I turn to Audrey, who is looking at me with a mix of concern and bemusement. It's the kind of look that says,

"Are you okay?" but starts with "Hey, dipshit." It's the kind of look only friends can pull off. Even paid ones.

"What? Oh yeah, I'm okay. I guess."

"Uh huh," says Audrey, taking a pull on her not-quite soda. She delicately sets her drink down, on a coaster, of course—I love this woman's manners—with overly exaggerated precision. She adjusts the glass to be perfectly centered once, twice, until it meets her critical eye. She then slowly turns to me, places her hands neatly in her lap, bats her outstanding cat eye lashes and says, "So, tell auntie Audrey who peed in your cereal."

"That obvious?" I ask.

Audrey raises a single perfectly plucked brow.

Suddenly everything starts flooding out of me like someone took their finger out of the hole in the dike. I tell her that Dak cut back my days at the Odeon and that Grayson Hasagawa wrote me my meal ticket and I tossed it back in his face.

Audrey ruminates on this for a moment. She has the look of a woman in a grocery produce section weighing the virtues of two cantaloupes. Eventually she says, "That sucks donkeys." Audrey the poet.

I simply nod. Audrey takes a drag on her fizzy water and says, "The Odeon thing, that's bollocks, yeah? But it couldn't have come as too much of a surprise to you. You'd said yourself the crowds have been down."

"Yeah," I say, deflated. "Just that the timing couldn't be worse."

"And as for the Hasagawa dealio, well, I wouldn't sweat that too much. Personally, I think you done right proper by your ma. Course, she woulda said you were daft to do it, but, you know . . ."

She takes another draw.

Audrey's British slang tends to increase when she's waxing philosophical. It makes her sound strangely more reassuring.

"And you know what I think?" she asks. "I think he'll come back."

"Why would he do that? I turned him down flat."

"Because he's a man, and men like what they can't have. Plus, you said that he said to let him know if you change your mind."

"But I'm not going to change my mind," I say spontaneously. The fact that it came out so quickly and easily tells me I made the right choice. Sometimes your heart makes choices your brain can't comprehend, and logic takes a back seat.

Evidently this is one of those times.

"Well, either way, I think it's way cool that you basically got asked out by the richest man on earth and you told him to take a piss."

"He did not ask me out and I did not tell him to take a piss, but I like your analogy anyway." I hold up my IPA and say, "Here's to stupid decisions that will haunt me for the rest of my life."

Audrey hoists her fizzy water, and we tap plastic cups. Without the clink of glass, it totally cheapens the moment, but what the hell. "Cheers," she says with a nod of agreement.

After we take our toast sips, I start to say something but then change my mind. Audrey notices and fixes me with a stare.

"What?"

"What what?" I say, trying to look innocent. A look I am decidedly ill equipped to pull off.

"You were gonna say something."

I debate whether to bring it up and eventually figure, what the hell. "I saw a guy," I say.

"You saw a guy," Audrey says back at me.

"Yes."

Audrey looks around, points across the way, and says, "See that guy over there?"

The guy she's referring to is an older gentleman sipping a glass of red wine and nibbling on pretzel bites. An odd combination, even for me. "Uh, yeah," I say.

"Good. Now you've seen two guys. Congratulations."

"No, that's not what I mean. I met a guy," I say, a little flustered.

"You met a guy?" Audrey asks, showing the first signs of interest.

"Well, I haven't exactly met him, but I've seen him, and he's seen me."

"This has got to be going somewhere," says Audrey. "You've seen a guy and he's seen you, but you haven't met him, and this is a big deal because . . ."

"Because I noticed him, and he noticed me!" I say with no small amount of frustration.

"Oh," says Audrey matter-of-factly. "Okay, remind me why that is a big deal?"

"Guys don't notice me," I say.

"Guys do too notice you," says Audrey giving me her best supportive friend eye roll.

I shake my head. "No, guys do not notice me. Guys have never noticed me. Know what they called me in high school? Texas highway."

"Texas highway?"

"Way too straight, way too flat."

"That's pretty funny." Audrey laughs, which earns her a straight right to the shoulder. "Ow!" she says. "Blimey, that hurts!"

"Good!" I say. "You're supposed to be sympathetic, dummy!"

"I was getting there," she says rubbing her shoulder. We're silent for a moment, which we fill with awkward sips of our drinks. Eventually Audrey puts a pin in the silence. "Yeah, well, you're no longer flat and you're no longer straight."

"Wait," I say, trying to piggyback on her efforts to lighten the mood again, "are we back to lesbian talk again?"

"Are you hitting on me?" says Audrey with a hand to breast, in her best mock-shock.

I cock my fist. "One wasn't enough?"

She holds her hands up. "One was plenty."

We both smile. All's well again.

"So, what's the story?" she says.

I give her the rundown.

"Damn. Bring back the donkey. You spilled tea on his phone number? That sucks even more," says Audrey. "But don't worry."

"Don't worry? It's been ages since I went on a date, but I still think the universal rule is that if you call, you're interested, if you don't call, you're not. And I can't, because I'm a klutz and a spazz and he's going to think that because I'm not calling that I'm not interested which isn't the case and I'm going to go another twenty years before a man gives me his phone number and by that time, I'll be too senile to remember to call." I'm babbling but it feels good to get all this out.

It's been more than one presidential term since I've had girl talk like this.

"What did I tell you about men? They want what they can't have. If you don't call you think he's going to throw in the towel? Not a chance. He'll be back for another swing, trust auntie Audrey." She sits back with a decidedly smug look on her face. "Besides, he knows your watering hole. He'll be back. Mark my words."

The lights dim but my mood lightens.

THE MOVIE IS a noirish thriller called *L.A. Confidential.* One of my faves. After it ends and the credits roll, Audrey and I exit the theater. "What did you think?"

"Me like," says Audrey. "Particularly Officer Bud White. He's a dish, in a baser instinct beat-the-shit-out-of-you-if-you-screw-with-a woman way. The blonde chick wasn't bad either."

"Kim Basinger," I say. "She won an Oscar for the part."

"I wasn't talking about her acting," says Audrey with a look.

"Men or women, for Christ's sake. Have a preference."

"What fun is that? And cut my chances for a date in half, yeah?"

I couldn't argue with her there. Audrey is one of those women who appeals equally to either sex. She is hot, no question there, I can see why guys would want to her. And she has the slightest masculine edge to her, maybe it's the boots, I'm not sure, but whatever it is, it has a similarly magnetic effect on women. I've seen the stolen glances on more than one occasion. I think if I wanted to cross that line, Audrey would go along to the accepted degree, but that's not part of the package I signed up for. Like I said, you're not allowed to use the service for intimate relations, but human nature being what it is, it didn't take long for the blurry line to get crossed when the companion services first went public. There were numerous news stories about police busting

BFFH organizations because it was becoming too brazen and out of hand. In fact, at one point it became so flagrant that the Feds decided to move it to the top of their hit list. I guess that happens when countless senators are caught with their pants down. It's bad PR. A republican president had just been elected and the woman made it her personal project to bring holy hell down upon BFFH agencies the moment she finished picking out the White House china. The easy fix would have been to simply make the service illegal, but the online dating lobby is so powerful they make the NRA look like the proverbial ninety-eight-pound weakling. The Feds and Mrs. President folded like cheap lawn chairs. Well, not folded completely. Evidently smoky backroom deals were brokered because BFFH services were still allowed to operate but the Fibbies made a big hoo-ha of making it public knowledge that they were infiltrating the services and that the vetting process was so rigorous that anything that even sniffed of ill repute could go badly for the person who raised the red flag. Automatic ten years in the slammer for trying to screw your BFFH, consenting or otherwise, cleaned up the business right quick. You can sign up for a romantic BFFH, but the interaction stops at second base.

I dunno, maybe the BFFHs have got an embedded electronic chip that alerts the powers that be if too much hanky-panky goes on. All I know is that stories of people getting busted for crossing the line have become few and far between.

But that isn't an issue here. Audrey and I are besties and that is more than enough for me. At least that's my perception.

"Parting words of wisdom?" she asks.

"Discipline yourself and others won't have to," I reply.

Aud shakes her head. "Not gonna happen."

We share a hug and go our separate ways, but before I can take three steps Audrey calls out to me.

"Frankie, forgot to mention, the agency wants to know if you want to keep paying on an as-you-go plan or go with auto-pay."

"Uh, auto-pay? If that's cool with you," I say uncertainly.

Audrey doesn't seem to notice my tonal change, she's still all smiles. "Auto-pay it is! Ta!" She spins and bounces down the walk, seemingly without a care in the world. I am infinitely jealous.

CHAPTER 19

I'm not sure why, but the last ten seconds of my interplay with Audrey kills my post-movie buzz. Who am I kidding, I know exactly why I feel crappy. The billing comment was a reminder that I am a client, nothing more. I wonder if she has other paying BFFs. I never bothered to ask when I signed up. It's not like I have to pay for a best friend. I mean, I've had close friends before and even have a handful of colleagues and acquaintances in the here and now that I could call friends. Okay, maybe not friends. They smile when they see me and say hi. We chit chat for a few minutes. That's not bad, right? Before I signed up and got paired with Audrey, I freely admit it had been a while since I had palled around with anyone other than my brother. Okay, more than a while. But when Galen had his accident, my world stopped spinning. He became my center of gravity. That's a bad analogy. If my world stopped spinning there would be no gravity, but you get my point. All my time and energy were for him, and I had no problem with that. Whatever meager social life I had—and make no mistake, it was meager—got kicked to the curb. I'm the first to say I signed up for a BFFH because it was easy and convenient. I didn't have to invest any time or effort into building the relationship. I call, she shows up. I look at it the same way I look at food. Why go to the trouble of making lunch when I can go to a drive through and have it handed to me?

However, Galen's predicament gave me purpose—purpose beyond myself. Before Galen's car blew out a Firestone and went pinwheeling, my greatest talent was looking out for number one. I guess that's natural when you're young and single. You don't have a spouse or kids to dote on so it's easy to focus all your attention on your three best buds: Me, Myself, and I. That's where Galen and I were different. He was single, but he was always focused on others. I remember one instance that completely encapsulates our differences. It was during spring break when he was at Brown. He called me up and said, "What do you have going on this weekend?" I said I didn't have a thing in the world going on. He said, "Let's do the big apple!" And so, we jetted off to New York City to do the tourist thing. We did what you're supposed to do in NYC—Empire State Building (and spit off it)—Lady Liberty (couldn't spit off that)—caught a Broadway show (Sophie's Choice: The Musical; I'm kidding. It was a 50th anniversary revival of Hamilton)—bought a real (fake) Rolex from a nice man named Paco—lost $20 in a game of three-card monte (we knew it was rigged but now we can say we played three-card monte in New York)—and successfully made it through Central Park after dark without getting mugged, so I guess it wasn't a completely authentic New York experience.

We went to the United Nations headquarters for a tour, because that too is a thing you do when you're in New York City. We're walking around the main floor, waiting for the tour to begin when my brother steps on something. He reached down and picked up a roll of bills like you see gangsters pull out of their suit pockets. The thing was enormous. He looked it over with an expression that couldn't have shown less interest. He held it up to show me.

I'm like, Holy Crap! But before I could go any further with my assessment, he was already hoofing to the security booth. I chased after, reaching him just as he was tossing it on the counter in front of the female security guard.

"Someone dropped this," my brother said, like it's a quarter and not what might likely be ten thousand dollars in unmarked bills.

The security guard looked at the roll of bills the size of her fist, then looked back up at Galen, then back down at the bills, then back up at Galen. She then looked around, leaned in toward my brother, and said, just loud enough for the two of us to hear, "Keep it."

Galen smiled and held up a hand as if she was offering him seconds on ice cream. "No, I couldn't."

The guard did the whole look down, look up, look down, look up thing again, finishing with a long appraising stare at Galen that slowly turned into a smile. "This is remarkably kind of you," she said. She cocked her head and said, "Are you sure this is what you want to do?"

Galen nodded. "Uh-huh." We then watched as the guard cupped her hand in front of the bills and swept it back off the counter into her other hand.

Whether it went into her pocket or a drawer I'll never know.

As we were walking away, I grabbed Galen by the shoulder and spun him to face me.

"Explain."

He shrugged.

"All I could think of was what if it belonged to some old couple from Kansas who'd saved up their money to visit New York for the first time and it was everything they had."

"Or some rich dude with more money than sense," I said.

"Nah. I like my story better," said Galen and wandered away. I chased after him.

"You realize that that wad of bills is probably now in that security guard's pocket, right?"

He looked at me as if the thought never even crossed his mind. "You think?" He appeared to give it some consideration and then evidently felt it didn't have merit and tossed it aside. "Nah, she wouldn't do that. She seemed cool."

I immediately realized I was looking into the eyes of pure innocence. Or at least unadulterated kindness. Someone else might have seen naiveté or even idiocy, but not me. I recognized purity when I saw it and my brother dripped with it. That was one more incident in a lifetime of incidents that solidified my deep conviction that I would unwaveringly step into traffic for that man.

CHAPTER 20

THE CHAT WITH MYRNA

"If you are chosen, how would you like to go out?" asks Myrna.

"In my sleep when I'm ninety-five in my oceanside mansion with my twenty-five-year-old lover by my side."

"Funny, same here," says Myrna without missing a beat. The woman's good.

"I thought we didn't get to choose."

"You don't. But it gives us another peek into your head. Helps us see what makes you tick. And believe it or not, we do take some of your thoughts into consideration."

"It's not like I'm going to remember anyway, right?"

"Correct," says Myrna. "You'd be surprised how much of the groundwork is laid just from this meeting."

"Some algorithm looking for key words and phrases to help determine the optimum method of termination?"

"Something like that. It's necessary to help speed up the process. We have a creative team that makes the final call, but the data from this meeting weighs heavily in the decision."

I'm tempted to screw with them, offer some ridiculous suggestion like being sucked out of a commuter flight and falling thirty thousand feet to my death. That would be cool. Instead, I give them the truth. They can take it as they may.

"In that case, something big and theatrical. If I'm going to go out, the least I can do is give your viewers a show. Couldn't hurt your ratings either."

"Which would translate to higher advertising revenue for your dependent."

"The thought occurred to me," I say. "But doesn't everyone want that? A splashy job that will draw more eyeballs?"

"Not as much as you might think," she says. "Most want to get it over with. Quick and painless."

"In our look-at-me social media-driven society? That surprises me."

"Me too," says Myrna. "I guess when push comes to shove, more people opt for a touch of dignity."

"Unlike me," I say with a grin.

Myrna matches the grin. "Unlike you. But you're a professional performer. I guess I shouldn't be surprised."

I sit forward again. "I want you to tell your crack team of killers to fire up their imagination. I want them up late, burning the candle at both ends coming up with something that will knock viewers for a loop." I look up at the ceiling. "Hear that, boys?" I shout. "Are your ears burning? Round up your best and brightest and start stoking their creative fires."

Myrna takes in my outburst with a chuckle. "You are a rare gem, Frankie."

"You know something," I say. "When I was eighteen, I had a dream that I would die in some grand and glorious fashion. Who does that? When you're eighteen you don't think of dying. You think you're bulletproof, indestructible." I cock my head and shrug. "Well, when you're eighteen you're kind of stupid."

"I've had teenagers. I can't disagree," says Myrna the wise.

"Hey, question," I say. "Do you ever use people the target knows to kill them?"

"Interesting and insightful question," Myrna says with arched eyebrows. "We have been known to introduce people into the target's life."

"Like a sleeper cell," I say.

"Very much so."

"They gain the target's trust only for that target to die at their hands hours, days or months later? Harsh."

"Reality TV is harsh," acknowledges Myrna.

I have no reply to that, so I change the subject. "I was doing a little research leading up to this," I say. "I read about this shadowy organization back in the late 1800s called the Ring of Fire. Ever heard of them?"

"No. To me 'Ring of Fire' is a Johnny Cash song."

"Myrna! Look at you, pulling out a century-old music reference. She shoots, she scores!" I think Myrna blushes. "At any rate, these guys, they did what you guys do, whack people for a living."

"We don't prefer to see it that way," says Myrna, a touch of indignation in her voice. The closest thing to pique that I've heard from her so far.

She takes pride in her work.

"You're right, I apologize. Totally different. These characters were more like the mafia. They saw the world as one of two things: liabilities and assets. They removed liabilities, for a price. It was purely business."

"No doubt a healthy business," says Myrna.

"No doubt."

"But the Ring of Fire?" asks Myrna. "A less than subtle name."

"Hey, it was the 1800s. I don't think subtlety was all the rage back then. Those were the days when the circus was just becoming a thing. The big top. People wanted a show, to be dazzled, thrilled, entertained. Something to take their minds off their drab late 1800s no-indoor-plumbing lives. I think the Ring of Fire was simply a reflection of the times."

"So, you want a modern-day version of the Ring of Fire?"

"Just a thought," I say, hands raised.

"No promises," says Myrna with a smirk.

The conversation goes on like this for a while before it peels off into new and different directions. Myrna asks me questions about things as seemingly inconsequential as my favorite color, cocktail, clothing fabric. Beats me what it's all supposed to add up to. They must have an interview algorithm that takes all this information, feeds it into a computer, and out pops a psychological and personality profile. I answer all her questions and then some. I'm feeling quite chatty and, frankly, I enjoy Myrna's company. I'm enjoying the exchange. I throw in a constant stream of compliments to her unseen support staff for good measure. Just because they're going to plot out a sophisticated method of killing me doesn't mean they're not people too.

CHAPTER 21

APRIL

I figure the only way I am going to earn back some much-needed money-making hours is to finish my grand and glorious illusion; that which will launch me into the stratosphere of high recognition, high praise, and high earning performers. I head over to the slick brick box warehouse and make a bee line for my studio. I don't see Miss Indeedy-do and count my blessings. Seeing the frumpy millionaire will do nothing for my self-esteem. Seriously, Lisbon? I go into my studio and take in the current state of Bosco. He's further along than I recall, which improves my mood a tick. The carbon fiber tubing, the structure, stands dull and mute. I walk up and give it shake. Solid. Good integrity. Bosco is costing me a small fortune, but I consider it money well spent. I'm investing in my future. I spent months researching, trying to develop a trick, an illusion that hadn't been seen yet, which is no small task. It seems like everything's been done before. So, I did the next best thing, I took a well-known illusion—a popular one—and put a new spin on it. Or will, as soon as I get this blasted thing finished. I step over to my schematics and go down my checklist. I'm pleasantly surprised to see most of the hardware is finished and that it's time to start securing the skin—the outer layer.

There are basically two major considerations for a big illusion, the inside and the outside. The inside is where things happen. It's the mechanics. They must work perfectly, or bad things can happen. Bad things that I don't even want to think about. The outside, however, has to look kick ass and make people pay attention. Think of two girls at a bar, one plain, the other smoking hot. Guess which one is receiving all the attention. Uh-huh. Same goes for stage craft. That's why I'm putting in extra time, effort, and money to ensure Bosco doesn't just work perfectly, but looks amazing.

I put in a solid four hours at the studio and feel feverishly alive with accomplishment. I debate swinging by the Zombean for a late-night celebratory chai, but think, *What if the guy's there? Or worse, what if he isn't?* I flip and flop in the car and somehow it decides to take me there anyway. I try to casually look through the windows to see if he's there. I can only see about half the tables through the window, and he is at none of them. I open the door which gives a little ring of its bell—company's arrived!—and sweep the room. Two couples and three singles, and not a one has insanely blue eyes. I head right back out the door. I didn't really want a chai anyway. Stupid chai.

CHAPTER 22

It's Visit Galen day. I arrive at the hospital, give my regards to Lou, who immediately makes me feel better with his standard greeting, and I weave my way through the wildlife-painted halls to the Hippo wing. I enter the "hang-out" room figuring that's where I found him last time and see that it's busier than before. There are a half-dozen kids of assorted ages scattered about. A couple are crashed on the bean bags studiously inspecting their optics and trading comments. Two are watching an anime cartoon on the large monitor and a couple of younger kids, probably around eight or nine years old, are at the crafts table cutting and pasting God knows what. The girl Galen was with last time . . . what was her name? I tried to lock it in last time by rhyming it. What did I rhyme it with? An old musician. The thin white duke. Bowie. David Bowie . . . Chloe! That's it. She's standing over them offering encouragement and instruction. I look around the room but see no sign of Galen. I walk over to Chloe, and she looks up, spotting me. I can tell by the look on her face she recognizes me but can't quite place the face. Before I reach the table, she figures it out.

"You're Galen's sister," she says with a smile that seems incongruous with her bald head and dark circles under her eyes. She didn't even bother with a bandana today. She's going craniumly commando. "Frankie, right?"

"Good memory!" I say brightly, trying to match her tone. "And you're Chloe."

She looks duly impressed that I remembered as well. "If you're looking for Galen he's not here. Well, not in the hang-out room. He was earlier but left."

"Where'd he go?"

"I think he went to his quiet place," she says.

Shit. Not a good sign. Galen only goes to his quiet place when he's not having a good day. I nod noncommittally and start backing up. "Okay then," I say. "Guess I'll catch you on the flip side." I give Chloe a wave, spin, and speed walk out the door.

Galen's quiet place is exactly as advertised. The sign on the door even says, "A quiet place." It's a room designed for the sole purpose of providing the most clinically calming environment possible. I give a soft knock, even though it's not necessary—it's open to anyone, you can't reserve it—but knocking seems polite. There's no reply so I crack the door and peek in. In the sliver of view that the opening provides I can see Galen standing by the window looking out, leaning on his cane. I open the door the rest of the way and slip in. The room's a small rectangle, about 15 feet by 10 feet, with floor to ceiling windows on the far right. A couch, armchair, and small end table make up the furnishings. Lying on the end table is a pair of headphones. The irony of the room is that it's called "a quiet place" but one of the main uses of the room is to listen to music. I've spent more than my own share of hours in this room waiting for Galen, and I can say without a scintilla of doubt that the couch and armchair are probably the most comfortable pieces of furniture ever made. You sit in them and effectively melt. The room has wall-to-wall carpet that's so soft you leave footprints that would rival those left by last year's astronauts on Venus. I've slept in beds less comfortable than this floor.

I take a couple of test steps into the room and wait to see if Galen acknowledges the fact that someone entered.

So far, nothing.

"Galen?" I ask softly.

He turns and looks at me with a quiet smile. "Oh, I'm sorry, do you need the room? I can leave if you like." There's no inkling of recognition in his face.

"Galen, it's me, Frankie."

Still no sign that he knows it's me. Not even a glimmer. He has the shy but kind look of someone slightly embarrassed in front of a stranger. He glances at the floor and shifts his weight from one foot to the other. He suddenly looks twelve. He looks back up at me and his head does a little tilt to one side, like a dog's. Suddenly, a light in his eyes appears, like a switch got flipped. No slow realization, but sudden, instantaneous recognition. It's almost creepy. What must that have been like for him? Was he looking at a complete stranger and then suddenly the stranger magically transmogrified into his sister in the blink of an eye? My chest takes on twenty pounds of lead weight.

"Oh, Frankie, sorry, my mind must have been elsewhere," he says, blinking and shaking his head briefly as if clearing his head.

I paste on my best big sister smile even though it feels as artificial as clown makeup. My feet take matters into their own hands and drag the rest of me over to him in three quick strides where I engulf him in a hug usually only witnessed between plane crash survivors and their mothers.

"Hey! What gives?" he says with genuine surprise.

I hold on tight, a drowning woman with a life ring. I can feel tear drops springing from my clenched eyes but bury my head in his shoulder and use his shirt to sop up the tears before they can show. "What?" I murmur, my face still pressed deep into his collar. "Can't a sister give her brother a hug without getting the Spanish Inquisition?"

I break away and step back with a short laugh to hide what I'm really feeling. I can't tell if my eyes are red, so I make a point to start rubbing them and offer a lame excuse about how bad the pollen is right now. He seems to buy it. That's the problem with Galen these days, he's utterly transparent. What you see is what you get. But is that really a problem? I ask myself. Normally that would be a virtue, but I have to admit that there are times I want a little white lying to spare my feelings. If I ever did online dating that's what I'd put on my profile—*Wanted: Man who will lie to me when appropriate.*

I shuffle over to the armchair and flop into it like a spoonful of dough dropped onto a cookie sheet. Splat. God, I love this chair. It's like falling into a velveteen hug. I'm convinced this chair alone could cure half the world's illnesses. I lounge there for a moment enjoying the sensation of full blissful engulfment. I finally snap my head around and find Galen looking out the window again.

"Galen?"

He glances back over his shoulder at me. "Yeah?"

I swivel the chair around in his direction. One leg hung over the arm, making myself completely at home. "What's going on? What brings you to the room?"

He sticks his free hand in his jeans pocket and hunches his shoulders up in a shrug, an embarrassed smile on his face. "D . . . dunno. Just needed it."

I consider his answer. It's legit. Everybody needs some quiet time now and then. The difference is that this room is for industrial strength, military grade quiet time. This is the place when you need to completely obliterate the world outside your hula hoop of personal space.

I swing my leg off the arm and give him my complete attention, hands clasped together in my lap. I lean forward. "Talk to me," I say.

He smiles. "Is doctor Frankie now on duty?"

Busted. "Sure. Lie on the couch and tell me your deepest, darkest secrets."

I can tell he's enjoying the repartee, brief though it may be. For that moment it's like the way it used to be, back before life went sideways. He takes a breath and looks up at the ceiling. I can see the machinery at work.

"I miss myself," he says.

I haven't heard this one before. "What do you mean?"

He looks back down at me with arched brows, almost mischievous. "The old m . . . me. The one who used to be pretty g . . . goddamn cool."

"Galen, you will always be pretty goddamn cool," I say instantly.

"Yeah, see . . ." he says with a chilled smile. "it's really not possible to be cool and br . . . brain-damaged at the same time. It's a one or the other."

Self-evaluation was something I'd never heard from him in all the years since the accident. I'd always presumed he'd buried whatever thoughts he had on his accident so deeply away that they were nowhere to be found. That he'd locked up the box and tossed the key into the ocean. But this was a naïve thought. Of course he'd thought about it. Dwelled on it to no end, I'm sure. But he'd hidden it well. He never spoke about the accident. Hell, he almost never even talked about his condition. The counselors had told me on more than one occasion that the human mind has a remarkable ability to pretend shit never happened, or at the very least, tuck thoughts away so effectively as to be practically nonexistent. Not that this is always the healthiest thing to do. The shrinks assured me that once Galen physically recovered, the sooner he accepted his new reality, the better he would be in the long run. Not that it would be easy. They told me to expect a fair amount of denial on his part, but Galen went right ahead and proved them wrong. Once his body had mended, he acted as though his new limited mental abilities were no biggie. His acceptance of Galen 2.0 was immediate and remarkable. His memory and brain capabilities were the exact opposite of new and improved. I guess I thought that maybe that was part and parcel with the brain damage, that he had forgotten what he used to be like. As if there was a cable that ran from what he was to what he is, and the accident had taken a bright, shiny, well-sharpened axe and cut the line with one clean chop. Images and memories no longer able to run from here to there. But evidently that wasn't the case. Images and memories had indeed made the leap, through some synaptic form of wi-fi that could still send and receive.

"I know I'm not who I u . . . used to be. I don't know exactly what I was or how smart, but I know that I'm . . . less . . . than I was."

His words are molten lead poured into my heart. Galen was not a man who recognized sadness. At least not to the degree of everyone else. It had always felt like the emotion simply could not find purchase on him and when it did show its face, it appeared atrophied from lack of use. Galen's version of sadness was a wan, pale form compared to others. Except when mom died. When she passed, Galen's grief was real and vivid, like scar tissue. Right out there for all to see. Since it was such a foreign expression for him, it seemed even more heartbreaking.

Whatever damage the accident did to Galen, his remarkable buoyancy has not changed. He may not remember that he used to always look at the bright side of life, but he still has that gift. And suddenly here I am.

Seeing sadness on my brother's face is so foreign it is even more devastating. Like you see one of your parents cry for the first time as a child. You think, that's not possible, parents don't cry, I cry, and they make me feel better! I want to rush to Galen, wrap my arms around him and tell him everything is going to be all right, but something in his look keeps me rooted in place.

"You're not less, you're just Galen."

Galen looks up and gives a little puff through his nose. "C'mon, Frankie, I'm not s . . . stupid. Well, okay, I am stupid. Stupider."

Good. A joke.

"No, you're not."

"Frankie, my mem . . . memory is for shit, I have a hard time putting thoughts together. Does that sound like genius material to you?"

I take an experimental step toward him. "Why are you saying these things? Where did this come from?"

"What? You think I don't think about my . . . my, uh, shit, what's the word . . . my current situation?"

"I . . ." I start.

"Station in life!" He blurts out. "That's the word. Words. Whatever. S . . . see? Half the time I can't say what I want to say. What I'm really feeling."

"I know, and I'm so sorry. I can't imagine what that must be like for you."

"It sucks ass, if you want to know."

Another joke. Good. I smile at him to let him know it had the desired effect. He smiles back a tiny bit, but then it slowly melts off his face.

"Sometimes I feel sorry for myself. Today is one of those days."

"Galen, honey, anybody else who goes through what you have and they're popping pills by the handful and spending their days seeing only the negative. You are and have always been the most positive person I have ever met." I then add, "And that's why everyone loves you."

Sometimes Galen will ask a question and I'll answer it, and a moment later he'll ask the same question again. Like an Alzheimer's patient. And I'll wonder, if he couldn't remember asking the question and me giving him the answer, how did he remember that he still wanted the answer in the first place? It's like the question and answer are on a timeline and after getting the answer his brain moved backward on the timeline but jumped right over the answer to the question again. It's this type of stuff that makes my brain hurt. After the accident I wore out the Internet researching brain injuries and memory and cognitive issues, but after a while I simply gave in. I'd finally accepted that *it is what it is*, as they say, and there wasn't a damn thing I could do about it.

And for the millionth time my mind goes back to one thought—how a miserable little scrap of metal did so much damage. A piece of metal that shouldn't have been there and wouldn't have been there if it wasn't for . . . but I stop myself. Dredging that up does nothing to help the situation. It only ratchets up my anger and helplessness. Two feelings I've become all too familiar with, the current moment a prime example. Here is my brother, feeling like five miles of bad road, and I can't fix the problem. But what I can do is be here for him at this moment and do what he has done for me a million times over—listen.

And I do, for the better part of an hour. Galen says more in that hour than I've heard him say in a year of Sundays. I am learning that every person has a point where they say Uncle, and for whatever reason, today is Galen's day. He tells me, haltingly, and often repetitively, that he has always been vaguely aware of the quality of his life before the accident. He says it's been like a hologram that flickers in and out. He sees random images that he suspects are from his previous life and over the years has connected enough of the dots to know he's not what he was. The more dots he connects the sadder he's become, hide it as he may. And here I've been stupidly presuming he wasn't that aware. My ignorance is overwhelming, and I only now begin to fully understand how terrible it must have been for him, knowing, or at least suspecting, the spiral his life took. The pain I'm feeling at this moment is the knowledge that I've blithely gone about my life convincing myself that he didn't know. It was selfish. A way to make myself feel better.

I'm an idiot.

While I'm listening, my mind latches onto something I hadn't noticed before, his clothes. Beyond the bagginess of them, Galen's wearing the same outfit I saw him in last time. A hoodie and jeans. Everything wrinkled and threadbare. Clothes Goodwill wouldn't even take. And he hasn't shaved. I look to his hands and again see the subtle shaking. In that instant, it occurs to me what he looks like: homeless.

When Galen finishes, I'm lost for words. I say the only thing I can think to say. "I'm sorry." It sounds so horrifically inadequate and my face flushes with shame. "I wish it were me. I can't tell you how many times I wish we could have switched places."

But then Galen does what Galen always does.

He fixes me with his trademark grin and says, "No you don't."

"Yes, I do," I say a little defensively.

"No, you d . . . don't," he says with a shake of his head, dismissively.

My eyes sharpen, my fists find themselves planting on my hips. "Yes, I do!" I say louder.

His grin breaks into an official smile. The bastard was baiting me, and I took it.

I glare at him. "Mother Fu . . ."

He cuts me off. "I don't remember the accident but I'm guessing it really hurt. Like, a lot. Smashing into a bridge support. No, I don . . . don't think you'd want to do that."

All my anger evaporates. He still has the gift. I toe the carpet, smirking in spite of myself. Then, quietly, pouty. "Yes, I do."

"Then you're a dumbshit."

"And you're a son of a bitch."

"I don . . . don't think mom would . . . would appre . . . appre . . . like that."

I'm defenseless around him. I laugh. Good and hard. "No. No, I do not think she would."

"Speaking of mom, her birthday's in a few months, right?"

The brain is an utterly baffling piece of machinery. Last time I visited he forgot that mom was dead but today he remembers she's got a birthday coming up. There is no pattern to his memory lapses. It's like his brain flips a coin as to whether it's going to remember something at any given moment.

"Yes, she does." I take this turn back toward the positive and try to water it. "And that means we'll have some planning to do. But we've got time."

He acknowledges my effort and pays in kind. "Whose tur . . . turn to cook this year?"

"I cook, you bring the stomach pump. An equal division of labor."

"I love you, Frankie."

CHAPTER 23

MAY

My visit with Galen felt like a wake-up call. Now knowing that my brother is somewhat aware of his past and how miserably his present compares means I need to help him out in whatever way I can. Whatever doctors he's seen before, I need to find better ones. Whatever financial hardships he's facing I need to help mitigate. In other words, I need money. More than I have. Much more. My decision to turn down Hasagawa's offer was foolish and short-sighted, purely based on a romantic tradition that is sweet and important to us, but . . . impractical. That meeting with Galen was a bucket of cold water thrown in my face. I need to quit living in the past and start looking down the road, and what I can see down that road is expensive. Clearly, I have to go back to Hasagawa and tell him I've had a change of heart. But how will he take that? As desperate? He seemed impressed that I turned him down to honor the memory of my mother. Will he think less of me if I come crawling back? When I turned him down, I was a woman of virtue and integrity; I was above petty things like the almighty dollar. But now, I'm like everybody else. Frankie will do anything for a buck. If I return with my hat in hand, I need to do it in a way that still looks like I have some shred of integrity.

I stand in my living room as a tidal wave of insecurities washes over me. I feel weak, insignificant, and impossibly small. Inconsequential—that's it in a nutshell. I feel incapable, as they say in the business world, of moving the needle. There's a film about a young man, played by the late Tom Cruise, who steps out of his comfort zone and uncovers a side of him he didn't know existed. The movie was appropriately titled *Risky Business*. There was one line in the movie that stood out and resonated with me. "Sometimes you just have to say, 'What the fuck.'"

CHAPTER 24

At 4:25 pm, I stand alone in the rapidly rising elevator going over the pitch I'd spent the night rehearsing after my colossal pity party. I must admit, I was surprised when Hasagawa's assistant took my call, and twice as surprised that the great man had a cancellation in his schedule, offering me one small, coveted window of time to right my ship. With a soft ping the elevator reaches its destination and I take a deep, resolute breath.

"What the fuck." Showtime.

At 4:30 on the button, Ms. Nichols escorts me into Hasagawa's office. He is standing beside his desk looking appropriately CEOish in a perfectly tailored midnight black suit.

He beckons me in with a friendly wave.

"Ms. Percival. I'm so pleased. Come, take a seat." He gestures to the wingback chairs by the coffee table. The koi under the glass swim slow circles, oblivious to our presence. I take the closest chair and, for the umpteenth time, go over what I'm going to say. Ms. Nichols, as per usual, stands quietly behind us. Out of sight, out of mind. She gives the impression of a quite lovely and well-trained watchdog.

Hasagawa eases into the chair next to mine, pivots it slightly to have a more direct view, and rests his forearms on his knees, leaning forward, making it abundantly clear that I have his full attention.

"You changed your mind," he says. It's a statement, not a question.

"Kind of," I say, my head tipping side to side.

His eyes show this is not the answer he was expecting. He leans back into the chair and crosses a leg over the other. If I didn't have his full attention, then I do now. "Do tell," he says.

I take a deep breath and dive in. "First of all, I want to thank you for your generous offer. You have no idea how career changing the opportunity to perform at your convention would be."

"And yet you turned it down," he says with what I could swear is a trace of a smirk.

I feel my face flush. "Uh, yes."

"And yet here you are. Why?"

"I would like to provide a counteroffer," I say.

Surprise and amusement brighten his eyes.

He glances from me, over my shoulder, obviously at his assistant, and back to me. "A counteroffer," he says wryly.

I can feel my self-control beginning to crumble, so I put my foot on the gas before I chicken out. "I can't perform at your convention, but I want to perform for you and your friends at another time at another venue, the Odeon Theater." The words tumble out so fast it sounds like I just sucked in a balloon full of helium.

Hasagawa brings a hand to his mouth and thoughtfully taps a finger against his lower lip. "The Odeon. The old theater where you currently perform." Without looking her way, he says, "Ms. Nichols, how many people does the Odeon theater hold?"

In a matter of seconds, I hear the assistant reply. "Five hundred."

"Five hundred," says Hasagawa. "At my convention you would be performing in front of thousands, and hundreds of thousands online. At one of the most important and influential corporate events in the country. But you would prefer to perform at a struggling shoebox theater."

"Exactly," I say.

"Why would you want to do this?"

"Because I won't perform on my mother's birthday. But turning down your offer was . . ." I search for the right words. "Well, really, really stupid. So, I thought, maybe we can reach a compromise."

"And how is performing at a small, rundown theater a compromise?"

This is the moment. It's time to explain my master plan and then wait to see if he laughs me out of the room.

"Because you would be helping save a local institution, and the press loves philanthropy."

Hasagawa stands up from his chair and slowly walks over to the floor-to-ceiling windows. He stares out, speaking to the glass. "A fundraiser, as it were."

"Yes," I say.

"I seem to recall reading something about how the theater had been falling on hard times of late," he says airily.

I don't know if there's ever been an article to that effect, but I run with it.

"Absolutely. Hard times. It would be a shame to see a place that's been home to some of America's greatest performers close up shop." The place has never been the home of even America's second-tier performers, maybe even third, but why spoil the mood.

"I could invite my closest friends and associates," he says. "Charge, oh, I don't know . . . Ms. Nichols, what do you think would be an appropriate cover charge for an event like this, knowing my friends?"

From over my shoulder: "Perhaps a couple of thousand dollars a head?"

"Nonsense, I was thinking closer to five," Hasagawa says with a wave of his hand.

I gulp. Five grand per person? 2.5 million dollars for one performance? Holy crap! Hasagawa turns back to face me. "And for that kind of money we'd want there to be plenty of press. Not just local but national as well. I'm sure we can find an angle." He glances at his assistant. "Ms. Nichols, do you think that's doable?"

She doesn't blink. "Absolutely."

Hasagawa turns back to me. "What do you think, Ms. Percival?"

"I, uh, think that's a swell idea." My heart feels like it's going to leap out of my chest and splat right on top of the koi.

"Would you be performing your standard act, Ms. Percival? I mean, one would think an event such as this demands a little something special, wouldn't you agree?"

Is it my imagination or is there something in his look that suggests he already knows the answer to that? But that's impossible. Nobody knows about Bosco except me, Galen, and Audrey.

"Well," I say, shaking it off, "as it turns out I'm working on a brand-new bit for my act. Very flashy, very theatrical."

Did he know? How could he know?

"That sounds like precisely what this special night would need. Something very flashy, very theatrical," he says. "Now, the big question: when?"

"I was thinking August 18th," I say.

"And why is that?"

"Gives you plenty of time to promote it, gives me time to perfect my new bit, and, well, eighteen is my lucky number."

Hasagawa looks at me with a coy smile. "It just may be."

CHAPTER 25

When I walk out of Hasagawa's office building and hit the sidewalk, whatever holding tanks of adrenaline I have break apart and flood my nervous system. I'm hyperventilating. Where's a paper bag to breathe into when you need one? I take a moment to gain my composure and start walking. I'm not even sure where I'm going, just walking, but within a couple of blocks I realize I'm heading straight toward the Zombean Apocalypse. Clearly my body knows what ails it and how to fix it. In this case, a calming but celebratory chai tea, old magazines, and reading strangers. Mother's milk.

By the time I arrive at the Zombean, my euphoric high has tempered to a nice, pleasant case of the good feelies. I keep replaying the meeting with Hasagawa and decide it couldn't have gone better. He appeared to still hold some respect for me for not caving on my refusal to work on my mom's birthday. And I got the impression that he enjoyed the fact that I proposed a counteroffer. But best of all I was able to create a new opportunity for me: I will perform in front of a packed house of serious movers and shakers with full press coverage, earn me and the owner of the Odeon some serious cash, get me back up to a couple of nights a week, and maybe even create a launch pad to bigger and better venues, and before you know it, I'll book ten shows a week at the Mandalay Bay in Vegas. Sure. With a new act that I've never tried before that could fail miserably, I remind myself.

But I refuse to accept that possibility. Yet. For the time being, anything is possible, and I am not going to ruin it with grim thoughts of epic humiliation.

The world is my oyster.

I stride through the Zombean's front door like I own the joint. Which maybe I will after I strike it rich. I see

Mitzi working the counter. Same inverted bob but with a cool streak of purple. It works.

She sees me coming and her face registers a look of genuine surprise. Which for her is a shade or two above indifference.

"Frankie. What the hell gives?"

"What?" I say, honestly surprised.

"I dunno," she says, eyeing me suspiciously. "You look different. Like you just won the lotto." After a pause, she leans in. "Didja jus win the lotto?"

Yes, I'm thinking. "No, but I did receive some much-needed good news. Guess it's put a pep in my step."

"It has at that. Chai, medium?"

"If it's not too much trouble," I say.

"I live to serve," says Mitzi, already turning to the steamer.

The crowd is about average for the hour, maybe half the tables are occupied. While Mitzi steams the milk for my tea I lean across the counter and give a stage whisper.

"Psst. Mitz. Can ya help a girl out?"

Mitzi's eyes flash around, like a spy receiving a drop from an operative. "Speak," she says, her eyes back to the task at hand.

"There's a guy . . ." I say.

Mitzi's nods her head approvingly. "Ah, so that 'splains the pep in your step."

"No, no!" I say. "That's not it. I'm hoping you can give me some intel. A guy who comes in here occasionally."

Mitzi cracks a smile and blasts more steam into the milk. "Like I said, I live to serve. Gimme his specs."

"A little older than me, six feet, blonde hair, a little shaggy, no product, jeans, flannel, left-handed," I babble.

"Blue eyes?" she asks. "Like, bluey blue?"

"Yes!" I blurt.

"Hmmm," muses Mitzi with a dramatic chin rub. "That sounds familiar. Why? You wanna meet him?"

"Uh, yeah," I say.

Mitzi nods thoughtfully and sets the chai on the counter in front of me. "I can make that happen."

"Really?"

"Sure," she says, utterly offhand. Then her eyes drift off me and over my shoulder. "Mike, Frankie. Frankie, Mike."

Pure glacial ice water fills every molecule of my body, which seems scientifically impossible because my cheeks have spontaneously burst into flames. I stare daggers at Mitzi who smiles back undaunted. I slowly turn around to find he who shall henceforth be called Mike standing at a respectful distance, wearing a crisp white shirt and a bashful smile. He holds out a sizeable hand. His right one, even though he's left-handed. At least, I've been under the impression he's left-handed. Perhaps he's not. But then perhaps he is and knows that most people aren't left-handed and shake with their right and he's being polite. I take his hand and give it a single shake. Grip not too hard, not too soft. His hands are large, muscular. I'd even go so far as to say brawny. Maybe not an entrepreneur. Is he a former baseball player? Does he work on a farm bucking fifty-pound bales of hay? The hand isn't overly calloused. Maybe he likes to work out.

"Pleased to meet you. Again," he says with an impossibly impish grin.

From behind me, Mitzi. "You met before?"

Mike glances over at her. "Kinda sorta," before turning those death-defying blues on me again. "I'd ask you to join me but I'm afraid I have to order and run."

I open my mouth to say something, what, I have no idea. But it doesn't matter. He intercepts me.

"But . . . hold that thought." He looks back over to Mitzi. "The usual. To go."

I hear over my shoulder. "Roger that."

He stands in front of me and seems to take me in without taking his eyes off mine. Finally, "You didn't call," he says, still smiling.

My cheeks could roast marshmallows. "I, uh, had an accident. With the phone number."

"I see," he says. No skepticism. "Would you have? Called, I mean."

"Yes," I say quietly. I feel shrunken, small. I've gone from grape to raisin. Whatever confidence I had moments earlier has escaped like steam from a kettle. I feel like I'm a freshman being asked out by the captain of the football team. Unbelieving, unsure, undeserving. I'm sure there are a few more *uns* in there somewhere but those three seem to cover all the bases.

"I'm glad," he says.

At that moment, from behind, Mitzi, clearly enjoying the scenario playing out before her, "Medium latte with whip." And I hear a cup meet the counter.

Mike gives her a nod and says to me, "Excuse me," and steps past me to settle his bill. He smells terrific, like warm chocolate chip cookies, and crème brûlée. Okay, that's a lie, but try convincing my mind otherwise. A moment later, he's back.

"Shall we try again?" he asks.

"Sure," I say, a little stronger than before. I can feel myself gaining my footing.

He clears his throat and looks around the shop to see if others are paying any attention to the drama unfolding. No one is. They're either deep in conversations or their optics. He looks back at me and asks quietly so that only I can hear him. "Frankie, would you like to go out with me? On a proper date?"

"A proper date?" I ask, emphasis on proper. I'm rising to the game. "Well, as long as it's a proper date then I will say yes."

He nods, and his smile widens. He's clearly enjoying the game as well. "I'd suggest the safe approach, meet for coffee, but it feels like we've already done that."

"I guess we kind of have," I say.

"Dinner?" he asks.

"Chinese?" I ask.

"Perfect," he says. "Fung's on Fourth? 8:30 pm?"

I do the math in my head. It's five-thirty. Three hours. Fifteen minutes to run home, two hours to get ready, fifteen minutes to get there. Thirty minutes of wiggle room. Doable. "I'll meet you there."

He gives a slight bow, like greeting royalty or a Japanese businessman, and says, "As you wish." Oh my God.

He's stealing lines from another of my favorite ancient movies, *The Princess Bride*. He's the Wesley to my Buttercup.

He turns and exits the shop. No glance back. None needed this time.

CHAPTER 26

"Change of plans," says Sheila, briskly walking into Klaus Manfred's office. No sooner have the words left her mouth that she instantly regrets her rash behavior. One simply does not barge into the executive producer's office without a scheduled meeting. The glacial stare he imparts on her only reinforces her misgivings, but she knows better than to let it show.

"What do you mean, change of plans?" asks Klaus, darkly, his German accent evident but sanded down over the years in America. It becomes stronger on two occasions: when he is drinking and when he is angry. At this moment, his accent is slightly more pronounced than usual, and the man does not drink on the job.

"We have to move the event back by a couple of months," says Sheila definitively. She stands in front of Klaus's massive desk, feet planted wide, arms crossed, the portrait of a woman to whom taking shit is a completely foreign concept. She's battled with Klaus more than a few times in her tenure and knows that although imposing, he can be reasonable. He will listen to and consider a well-made argument, but you better not show weakness.

You can earn his respect if you stand your ground and back up your claims. But make no mistake, the man is still scary as hell. He can destroy careers with a snap of his fingers.

And has.

"Why?" he asks, his massive hands resting on his gleaming mahogany desk. Sheila takes notice of the sheer precision of each and every item laid out on the surface. She doubts they've moved a millimeter since the last time she was in there a month before. The desk is a perfect reflection of the man: methodical, structured, and impeccably organized. Traits that have helped catapult the show to stratospheric ratings. "Why do we have to postpone an event?" Klaus continues, dreadfully quiet. "An event that has already incurred substantial costs. And by postponing, incur even greater costs."

"Things have changed," Sheila says evenly. She knows the man doesn't like beating around the bush, but she also knows that the information she has is a game changer, and the opportunity to poke the bear is too seductive. She pauses a delicious moment, seeing his temperature rise, and for a moment fears she may have gone a bridge too far. Sheila plays her ace.

"Her event profile is about to skyrocket."

"The mentalist?" Klaus keeps his eyes locked on Sheila, making it abundantly clear he is not amused. Eventually, he looks down at his desk and taps the surface. Blocks of text, images and graphics appear. He studies them for a moment then looks back up at Sheila. Whatever he saw displayed got his attention. "When did this happen?"

"Just today," says Sheila. She can tell Klaus is intrigued. "We knew she'd performed for Grayson Hasagawa at his birthday party. Evidently, she made quite the impression. Looks like she's becoming his pet project. It's not public yet, but soon will be."

"He's going to be there himself?"

"With five hundred of his closest, richest, most high-profile friends," says Sheila, allowing herself a small smile.

Klaus Manfred is not a man one would consider jovial. In fact, if you asked Sheila at that moment if she's ever seen Klaus laugh, she would be hard pressed to remember even a single incident. That changed. Klaus throws back his head and laughs like a man who has been hoarding them his entire life and has found the proper moment to let them spill out all at once. He roars and pounds the desk with his hand.

After several seconds of this his laughter dials down to a few chuckles and he dabs at the corner of his eyes with one hand and points down at the information displayed on his desk surface with the other.

"This! This is a gift from God. Pennies from heaven," says Klaus. "Hell, millions of dollars from heaven!" He stabs a meaty finger into his desktop. "This will be the single most incredible event we have ever produced." He practically springs from his chair and begins pacing, his fist tapping a staccato rhythm on his chin. He stops and turns to Sheila. "How far are you down the line on the project?"

"Pretty far," she says brightly, caught up in his unprecedented good humor. "We have the method of passing mapped out, the day, the time, the place. The beauty of it is that we can still keep the same plan."

"Just a little later."

Sheila nods. "It was always going to take place at the theater. The foundation is set, we just have to make some tweaks."

"I want it bigger," says Klaus. "This is going to be our Inauguration, Olympics, and Super World Bowl rolled into one. This is our moment to shine."

"Certainly."

Klaus sits back down into his chair and thinks for a moment. "As it was originally scheduled to go down, what was the forecasted advertising take?"

Sheila, without so much as a pause, "Thirty-eight mill. The woman's got a great backstory, engaging personality, interesting profession. Even her reason for the money is uniquely suited to show our service in a good light. She checks all the boxes. Throw in the event location and the people on site and you have a better than average number."

"With this new information what do you think the numbers will be?"

Sheila gives this a moment of consideration. Finally, "This is uncharted territory. Huge international players will be watching it in person. I wouldn't be shocked to see the numbers doubled."

"Neither would I," says Klaus staring off into space. "That would be a new record." He then refocuses and turns back to Sheila; his face softening a tick. "I read your game plan. It's a nice approach. I would even go so far as to call it sublime. You did your homework."

Sheila blushes slightly at this. Klaus Manfred compliments appear with a frequency on the order of Halley's Comet. "Thank you, but honestly, she provided me all the creative content I needed and didn't even realize it."

Klaus cracks the tiniest of smiles. "Very accommodating of her." Then after a beat, "How many assets do you have in place?"

"Several secondary, one primary," says Sheila. "It was going to be a relatively easy play; we didn't need too much infiltration or redirection of behavior. A bit, but mostly for reconnaissance purposes, intel gathering. Everything was going by the book."

"Add some more ground troops. More eyes on her. Discretely."

"We're on it," replies Sheila.

"Good," replies Klaus. "We need to make sure every contingency is covered." Gone was any humor from moments before, replaced now with a face that has gone purely tactical. All business. Klaus gives her a nod. "You've got some work to do."

Sheila smiles, nods back and heads for the door. Exiting, she hears one last question.

"I know you have several assets in place, but who's your primary?"

Shelia pauses at the doorway. "Aubuchon," she says.

"Of course," says Klaus. "The secret weapon."

Sheila takes this as her cue to leave. Just as she's pivoting, Klaus's voice returns. "Oh, and Sheila?"

She stops and turns to find the man back standing to his full, imposing height, his face chillingly blank. "Don't ever come into my office without an appointment again."

CHAPTER 27

It takes fifteen minutes to go from the Zombean to my apartment. I make it in twelve. I have two hours and thirty-three minutes to get ready for my proper date. I begin the process by pacing. It seems the appropriate action. What am I feeling? Excitement? Fear? Happiness? I conclude that it is all the above, also known as anxiety. But why am I so freaked out? It's not like I haven't been on a date before. I have, but it's been a while. Who am I kidding, it's been more than a while. I'm pretty sure it's more than six years but less than ten. The lifespan of four hamsters. When I was younger, I knew of girls for which dating was an expectation. Something was preposterously wrong if it was Friday night and they didn't have a date or plans with a group of friends. For a while I was jealous of their absolute confidence that they would have someone else planning their activities for the night. I was the classic invisible girl. The beige human being in a world of dun-colored sand. I wasn't alone. There were many of us and we all knew our place in the cosmos. We drifted through space, reasonably content in our existence, knowing we didn't have the necessary genetic code that made it possible to be invited to the keggers, or asked out on dates. We of the invisible tribe had our own little circles of friends, much smaller than the populars, sometimes only one or two others in the group, but we were generally cool with that. We were residents on the Isle of Misfit Toys, and that, in and of itself, meant we were part of something. We were the ones who were a little too nerdy, a little too unattractive, couldn't dance, weren't up on popular music, wore socks with sandals, didn't know that there were some colors you couldn't wear together or didn't really get into the whole social media thing. That was the ultimate sin. If you weren't connecting through the latest and greatest apps, then you might as well be living in a Siberian gulag. I wouldn't say you were a leper; lepers are shunned. You simply didn't exist. You were a cipher. A black hole.

As I grew older, I grew more comfortable in my skin. I branched out, met more people, found my sub-culture, went on dates, even got laid when I felt like it. I remember reading somewhere, maybe a book on clever quotes, that when a man goes out on a Friday night he wonders if he's going to get lucky, whereas a woman already knows. I am and have always been the below-mediocre girl but even I learned the truth to that comment. If I really felt like I wanted to end the night with a walk of shame, all I had to do was put out the vibe that I was open. I've had my share of one, two and three-night stands. I've even had bona fide boyfriends, where the phrase was used by at least one of us. I think maybe three, but don't hold me to that. However, it's been many moons since I lived in that world. Like I said, more than six years, less than ten. I can honestly say that I do miss sex, but only when I think about it, which really isn't that often anymore. I didn't make a conscious decision to live a nun's lifestyle, it happened organically, naturally. As for missing it? It's like altering your eating habits over time. At first you only drink whole milk, and then you work your way down to 2%, then 1%, then skim. After a while you don't really remember how much you liked whole milk. Skim is perfectly fine, thank you very much. Or so you tell yourself. I've heard that when someone goes vegetarian, they end up losing their taste for meat and eventually find it gross. Hope I haven't gotten to that point yet.

I know exactly when my social life became an after-thought. It happened the day I got the phone call telling me Galen had been in an accident and might not make it. It's not like my social life stopped cold turkey on that day, but it was the beginning of the end. My priorities changed: Galen first, my job second, nothing after. That was ten years and three months ago. Like I said, more than six years, less than ten.

But that streak is coming to an end tonight. I think. I glance nervously at my optic. What if it rings? What if he cancels? I remember overhearing a girl back in high school talking to her friends about dates and dating protocol, subjects that to me were beyond exotic. One girl instructed the others that if your date calls on the day of your get together, don't answer it, because it can't be good. He's most likely bailing. That stuck in my head. Phone calls on date night equals bad. I stare at my suddenly malevolent optic, wondering if it was simply biding its time before springing on me, observing me with cold intelligence and calculating the time when ringing would cause the optimal emotional damage. I can feel my anxiety level increasing, until it occurs to me that I've never given him my number. We just planned on meeting at Fung's. He can't call to cancel! Ha! I was feeling better already. With that anxiety tamped down I have one more to contend with, but at least I know how to address it. Time to call in the cavalry.

CHAPTER 28

Moments later, but what seems like an ice age, I hear an insistent knock at my door. I fling it open and Audrey bursts through, a small case in her hand. She sets the case on my kitchen counter and turns on me. "How much time have we got?"

"Just over two hours," I say.

Audrey considers this for a moment. "That's not much time but I think we can do this. Show me your options."

I introduce Audrey to what I call my wardrobe. It's a closet. Five feet wide, half full. Audrey stands before it, hands on hips, then looks at me.

"Where's the rest?"

"That's pretty much it," I say sheepishly.

She turns to my dresser, points at it. "What have you got in there?"

"Underwear, socks, a few tee shirts," I offer feebly.

Audrey looks at me, her expression blank, then turns back to the wardrobe.

She plants her feet a bit further apart, her hands go back to her hips like she's bracing for something or preparing for battle.

Her eyes scan my meager collection, and she says thoughtfully, "Well, then, I guess this will have to do, won'it?"

Within moments virtually every shirt, blouse, skirt, trouser, vest, tie and hat are laying or hung on what few pieces of furniture I have in my bedroom. Audrey slowly walks the small space, one arm across her chest, the other propped on it, a knuckle tapping her lips.

"What's the impression you're trying to convey?" she says, her eyes trained on a pale beige, hopelessly masculine button-up oxford dress shirt.

Impression? Jesus, I don't know. "Uh, non-psycho?" I offer.

Audrey nods approvingly. "I can work with that."

"Aud, I know I've been out of the game for a while, but since when do you have to concern yourself with a certain impression? Can't I just be me?" I ask what seems like a perfectly reasonable question. But judging by Audrey's snort and scoff you'd think I'd asked if it was appropriate to mix stripes with plaid.

"Look luv," Audrey says, speaking like she's trying to explain basic arithmetic to a third grader. "Of course, you want to be yourself, but what version of yourself? You want to project Frankie but not look like you're trying to project Frankie."

I have to think about her answer for a minute. "I want to look like myself but not look like I'm trying to look like myself?"

"Exactly."

"That doesn't even make sense," I say.

"Think about it. Are you perfectly content with how you present yourself to the world? Nothing you wouldn't change?" Audrey asks with an arched brow.

"What's wrong with how I present myself to the world?" I ask indignantly. I know perfectly well I'm nowhere near the height of fashion. I dress . . . uniquely. Eclectic-chic. And I don't give a rip if anyone likes it.

Audrey takes my face in her perfectly manicured hands and looks at me sympathetically. "Nothing. Not a thing in the world. You present yourself as the Frankie we know and love and the rest of the world can sod off, yeah?" She drops her hands from my face, turns to the articles of clothing scattered about like casualties on a battlefield. "We just want to make sure it's the bestest, most kick-ass Frankie the world has ever seen." And then back to me. "Without looking like that's what we're trying to do."

My clothing options are not what you would call diverse. Everything would fall under the umbrella of *similar*. It's like when you're at the paint store and you pick up a swatch that has six shades of the same color? You get the idea. My clothes aren't terribly vibrant, not a lot of bold colors. They tend to be a bit autumnal—differing shades of browns, golds, and greens. Funny, I've never even thought about it. Probably because this is the first time in close to a decade that I've seen my entire wardrobe laid out before my eyes. There are a few articles in blues, grays and even a couple of deep reds, but the most glaring omission is what I've come to learn is the hallmark of all fashion-forward American women.

"Where's the black?" she asks, her eyes scanning the room.

"Don't have much," I say blankly, my eyes following her optical path. I've got a few ties, socks, a singular vest and one set of slacks, but that's about it.

"Ya think?" She does some mental gymnastics, figuring out options. I can practically see the machinery at work. It's like watching an autistic savant do a seven-figure math problem in their head over the course of three seconds. She points to a handful of clothes. "That, that, this, that, annnnd that. Go!"

I gather up the articles and scamper off to the bathroom. A moment later I step out for inspection. I stand uncomfortably before her scrutiny.

She's back to the arm-crossed-arm-propped-knuckle-at-lip pose. She twirls a hand. "Spin," she commands. I slowly turn around, arms akimbo. The outfit is an ensemble of pleated ivory linen trousers, cuffed, a soft gold blouse, forest green vest and cream pumps. No tie. No hat. I've owned these pieces of clothing for who knows how long and yet I've never worn them in this combination. I glance over at my reflection in the wardrobe mirror.

Damn, I think to myself, that's not half bad.

Why didn't I ever think of this combo? I steal a look at Audrey, who doesn't seem as taken with the look as I.

"Nope," she says definitively and looks around the room again. "That, this, this, and that. Keep the shoes."

I do as ordered and return a moment later with this latest mix and match. I again am startled by how the clothes magically work together, like some fresh new life has been breathed into them. My clothes are probably silently cheering, thrilled that someone with a modicum of taste has pieced them together the way they always knew they could and should be. Audrey and I continue this dance over the next sixty minutes. Her assembling what to me look like utterly disparate combinations and me perfectly shocked that they fit together like puzzle pieces. The more outfits we try the more I get into the process. I become giddy with excitement. It's like I'm preparing for the prom I never went to. Of course, the fact that we break out the wine fifteen minutes in doesn't hurt.

At precisely 6:45 p.m. I step out of the bathroom and stand before my clothing mentor waiting for her assessment. It takes all of one second.

"Fookin' Brilliant," she says with quiet authority.

I look myself over. Charcoal slacks, flared, crisp white men's dress shirt, untucked, sleeves rolled twice, burgundy vest, loose black tie, gray pork pie hat with the brim popped up. It's me, only better. Audrey takes a few steps left then right, eyes scanning, looking for chinks in the armor. She suddenly takes several bangly bracelets off her wrist, grabs mine, and slips them on. Then she takes a long, loose, medium-weight silver necklace that's double hung around her neck and slips it over her head. It's a good three-to-four-foot loop with a two-inch crescent moon at the end. She breaks the clasp, reaches around my waist, and fastens it like a thin silver belt, the moon hanging down below the vest, left of center. Audrey steps back to inspect her handiwork and gives a satisfied nod.

I look at myself in the mirror. The bracelets, the necklace-cum-belt? Somehow, they work.

"How did you do that?" I ask amazed.

"What?" Audrey asks back, sincerely puzzled.

"That!" I point to myself in the mirror. "This!" I point to myself. "These!" I point to the jewelry. "What form of sorcery is capable of taking those . . ." I sweep my arms across the scattered remnants of mismatched clothing, ". . . and making this?" I sweep my hands from my head to my waist and then out to the sides, indicating the whole package.

"I dunno," Audrey says with a shrug. "I just see it."

I've heard a similar response before. From my mom. She was one of those freaks who could sing harmony. I'd listen to her sing along with a song on the radio, a song she'd most likely never even heard before, and suddenly she'd be singing the harmony. I'd asked her how she did it. How did she know what notes to sing that complimented the melody without the benefit of sheet music? How did she know to go high when the song went low, and have it blend seamlessly? How did she know to hit an A flat instead of a B minor? She shrugged exactly like Audrey and said, "I just hear it."

Aud looks at her optic, checking the time. "We've got one hour. Time for the war paint."

Full disclosure: I'm not a makeup gal. I know, shocking, right? Doesn't mean a girl doesn't want to get dolled up now and again. My makeup experience is almost exclusively limited to stage makeup; the kind that helps me look okay from the 25th row but up-close like a two-dollar hooker. I show up like that and it'll be the shortest date on record. In the bathroom, I turn to Audrey and say, "If you think my clothing collection was weak then you really don't want to see my makeup kit."

Aud replies by holding up the small case she arrived with. It's about a foot long, six inches wide, and six inches deep, like a tiny suitcase. It's light pink with shiny silver clasps and covered in vintage travel stickers, the kind seen on steamer trunks and suitcases of well-heeled globe-trotters in a more gracious era. Stylish declarations of social status, recalling an age when travel promised luxury, adventure, and excitement. Where men in brass buttons and red caps stood at the curbs of swank hotels and loading docks waiting to portage mountains of fine leather cases to suites and staterooms. Rome, Cairo, London, Amsterdam, and Zurich! the labels shout. A couple of stickers touting Cunard-White Star steam ships round out the collection. The pink makeup kit is as sophisticated and elegant as its owner. Even without seeing its contents, I know I am in capable hands. Forty-five minutes later I behold a visual best-case scenario of myself. Eyes brighter, lips fuller, cheek bones sharper, but none of it glaring or obvious. My face is a masterpiece of subtlety. Never in my life have I been so readily prepared for a proper date. For once, I look more like the after picture in the shampoo commercial.

Audrey looks me over from head to toe and bequeaths upon me her ultimate praise.

"Drop dead you are. Fookin' deadly."

CHAPTER 29

Audrey offers to give me a ride to Fung's on Fourth. She has two reasons. The first is so that she can give me dating advice and the second is so that he'll be forced to give me a ride home afterwards which can lead to "snogging," as Aud puts it.

"But what if the date sucks and I don't want him to give me a ride home and snog me?" I ask.

"Then give me a call and I'll pick you up."

She pulls up to a curb a block away from Fung's.

She says she wants to give me a few pearls of wisdom before I enter the lion's den. She looks at her optic. "It's quarter after, that gives you fifteen minutes. Normally I would suggest you arrive a couple of minutes late, five max. That way when you walk in, he'll already be at a table and if he's a gentleman, he'll stand."

"I hate being late. It's rude," I say.

"I know you do. And I know how important manners are to you. That's why by being only a couple of minutes late you're not out of bounds and you can gauge his basic manners right out of the gate with the stand-up thing, yeah?"

"Good point."

"But this is a slightly different scenario, we can't play it that way. You don't know this guy from Adam so we're going to plan defensively."

"How do we do that?" I ask, using the royal we.

Audrey has her eyes locked on mine, all business. She's in her no bullshit mode. "You arrive ten minutes early. If you get there five early there's a chance he'll already be there and that queers our plan before it can even begin. Chances are he's not going to get there ten early. In fact, I'll bet you a pint of Scotch he's sitting in his car right now looking at his optic trying to figure out exactly how early to arrive. He's listening to the car radio and looking at the optic every minute, sweating if he should be there five minutes early or at 8:30 straight up."

"Seriously?"

"Guaranteed," says Aud with 100% conviction. "So, you get there ten early and grab a table right away. It's Fung's and it's past the dinner rush so that won't be a problem. Don't meet him in the waiting area. Get a table where you can see the entrance and sit with your back to the wall."

"I think you're being a teensy bit paranoid," I say with a light laugh.

She doesn't laugh back. "First date. Don't know dick about him. He could be an axe murderer."

"He's too handsome to be an axe murderer," I say, trying to steer the mood back to positive, happy, shiny thoughts.

"Aren't they all," says Aud with a touch of a smile. "It's not bad to be extra safe." Audrey pauses for a moment, and I see something in her eyes I haven't seen outside a blood relative in a long time—sincere tenderness and concern. It warms my heart. "I worry about you, is all," she says.

"Okay, okay," I say, hands raised in acceptance. "Back to the wall."

"What do you want our code word to be?" she asks, shifting effortlessly back into dating coach mode.

"Code word?"

"You know, what word do you want to text me if things are going to shit and you need to escape."

"Crap. I hadn't thought of that."

"I know," says Audrey with a snap of her fingers. "Gelato."

"Gelato?"

"Yes. At precisely 9:30 I'll shoot you a text confirming our plans for tomorrow."

"We don't have any plans for tomorrow," I say.

"Shut up. Something like 'Still on for tomorrow morning?' If you need to escape you reply with something like, 'Absolutely. My turn to buy the gelato.' That looks legit in case he reads the message."

"I get it. If I reply with 'Gelato' that tells you I need to roll. No 'Gelato' means things are going well." I pause. "So then, how do I escape?"

"At 10 p.m. I call you. No text, a call. I sound frantic. Make sure you hold your optic far enough away from your ear so that he can hear my panicked voice. I'll act the hell out of it. I'll say there's been an emergency with your cat, Buster, he's shaking uncontrollably."

"I don't have a cat named Buster."

"He doesn't know that. And if between 8:30 and 10 p.m. he asks if you have any pets, you tell him you have an adorable Siamese Blue named Buster. Love of your life."

I nod with my deep appreciation of her deviousness. "You're good."

She shrugs it off and checks her lipstick in the rear-view mirror. "It's a gift." She turns back to me. "Have you done a background check yet?"

"What? He asked me out three hours ago!"

"Shit. You're right. No worries. We can do one later. Okay then, have you at least figured out a few questions to grill him with?"

"Not really." I feel like a rank amateur in front of a seasoned pro.

"Start with the light stuff. Fluff. Nothing threatening. Job, where he's from, siblings, kids, you know. And don't get too cute too early. You know how you can be around new people."

I know exactly how I can be around new people. I offer some comment, trying to be funny to diffuse the tension and often it makes me look like the weird person no one wants to sit next to on a plane.

"I can do that," I say with complete confidence.

"Then work your way up to past marital status. Find out if he's ever been married and if so, how many times."

"Is that a big deal? He's a borderline middle-aged man. Odds are he's been married."

"True. Then see if you can find out about his parents. If they're still married, divorced, how many times."

"His parents? What the hell does that have to do with anything?"

"I was out with a guy. Seemed cool. He lets slip his mom had been married four times. First date became last date. In my experience the apple doesn't fall far from the tree."

"Harsh," I say.

"Reality," she counters. Audrey takes another peek at her optic. "Game time." She looks up at me and says, "Okay, baby bird, time to leave the nest. Remember who you represent and make good choices." She licks her thumb and flattens out a loose hair that's strayed from its appointed place. Classic mom behavior.

"This time it's my turn to give the words of wisdom," she says.

"Which is?"

"Don't give up the booty."

"Thank you, sensei," I say with a smile and dash in with a hug. I break away, take one last deep breath, check my teeth for lipstick in the mirror, and then exit the car. As I'm walking away, a spectacularly loud whistle stops me in my tracks. I look back and there's Audrey leaning out the driver's side window with a show-stopping grin.

"Fookin' deadly," she says and peels away from the curb.

CHAPTER 30

I firmly believe Fung's on Fourth was made specifically for Americans who want Chinese food that's never graced a plate in China. I have a hard time believing that Chinese families feast on Chow Mein, Chop Suey, General Tso's Chicken, and Beef with Broccoli. Another quirk about Fung's on Fourth is that it's on Fifth Avenue. When Fung's first opened eons ago it was on Fourth but sometime in the last who-knows-when city construction went a little wacko and Fourth got redirected. The owner, Frank Fung, who was about as Chinese as NASCAR, fought city hall, and predictably, he got squashed. Fung's on Fourth was now on Fifth. Legend has it that at first the name/street confusion did a number on his business but then he hired a clever ad agency who had a creative director with a good sense of humor. The CD crafted a commercial campaign that made fun of the fact that Fung's on Fourth was actually on Fifth. It played like an old-time comedy bit. The public ate it up, and before you knew it Fung's on Fourth became *the* place to eat fried won tons.

And now I am standing in front of it. Its enormous over-the-top neon sign bathing me in a flaming red glow, more a warning than a welcoming endorsement. I scamper inside before I'm radiated like a pork chop in a thermal pulse oven.

Inside, the décor is all reds and black. Faux-Chinese artwork depicting cherry blossom trees, dragons, tigers, and white-faced women in kimonos cover the velvet-patterned walls. I peer into the restaurant and see that it's about half full—a couple of small groups, a single or two, and several couples, one with a baby in tow. Who brings a baby to a restaurant? I shake it off and spot the perfect table, opposite the room of the baby couple.

A young Asian woman meets me at the host's check-in stand. Her name tag says Becky.

"Table for how many?" Becky asks cheerfully.

"Two, please." I point to the table I'm hoping for. "Can I have that one?"

Becky looks it over, checks her chart, says no problem, and walks me there. I grab the seat against the wall. I've got a clear view of the entire restaurant. I check my optic. 8:22. Eight minutes early. Still no sign of him. I begin figuring out my pose for when he enters. Left arm draped on the table? Too casual? Both hands in my lap? Too stand-offish? Sipping my water? Always a good option. I opt for left hand in lap, right hand resting on table near the water glass so that I can use it as a prop as need be. I can pick it up, trace the foot of the glass with my finger, tap it . . . it gives me options. At 8:25 on the dot I see my proper date enter the restaurant. I feel my core temperature jump up a degree along with my anxiety. Jesus, what am I, a teenager? Mike, whose last name I still don't know, spots me and breaks into a broad smile. Do I stand? Shake his hand? Wave? Hug him when he gets here? I'm at a total loss. I opt for a smile and wave, seated.

He's dressed in jeans, a plain black tee shirt, and dark blue sports coat. His hair, not unruly but not brushed flat. I think it's what's officially called tousled. He strides over confidently. "You beat me!" he says and pulls up the opposing chair.

"I just arrived a second ago," I say with what I'm hoping is a demure smile. I'm not well practiced at demure.

He takes me in from head to table, his sea-blue eyes practically sparkling. "You look great," he says, and it feels like he really means it.

What I really want to say is, "Thanks, so do you," but for reasons I will never quite understand what instead comes out of my mouth is, "What? No corsage?"

Jesus Christ! What the hell did I just say? Why did I say that? I'm a fucking idiot. My heart rate jumps to triple time and my cheeks take on the shade of a stop sign.

If he's put off by my monumentally stupid comment it doesn't show. In fact, he doesn't skip a beat. His eyes don't lose an ounce of sparkle. Instead, he looks thoughtful, and begins patting his coat pockets. His eyes brighten, and he pulls something out of his right coat pocket.

"Something better," he says and proceeds to set a small plastic bottle on the table in front of me. Inside is a thick, clear green liquid. "Shampoo I stole from the hotel I was staying in last night. Smells like spearmint. My gift to you."

I look at the bottle then back up to my date who evidently doesn't think I'm a complete whack-job for making a crack about him not bringing a corsage. I could like this guy.

This time my mouth doesn't hijack my brain, and something appropriate spills out. "Thanks. I like spearmint."

He sets his large hands on the table. Nails not manicured but neatly trimmed. Did he cut them before he came? "Where do we start?" he asks.

"How about names?" I hold out my hand. "Frankie Percival. Well, technically Frances Percival. Frances Grace Percival." I'm blathering.

He takes mine. "Hello, Frankie. Mike Empire."

I let go. "It is not."

He chuckles. "You're right. Though I always thought that would be a cool name. Then when I reach my goal of world domination, I can call it Empire's Empire."

"Catchy."

"I know, right?"

"And your secret headquarters would be in the Empire State Building."

"Naturally." He nods appreciatively. "And if I can pull off my world domination using vampires . . .

"Empire's vampire empire," I say. "And what would your title be?"

"Emperor, of course," he says.

I laugh. So far so good. Fun, playful, testing the waters, he's checking to see what kind of sense of humor I have. I feel confident that the first thirty seconds have gone well.

Onward.

"Actually, it's Dalen. Michael Dean Dalen," he says.

"Like an off-brand name version of my brother Galen. Or better yet, Dalek," I say, taking a stab at obscure humor. It works. He perks up.

"You watch Doctor Who?"

"When I was a kid. The twenty-fifth version of the Doc. Dalen will be an easy name to remember," I say.

"Okay," he says, "names have been established. What's next on the itinerary?"

"Uh, jobs?" I say, a little unsure.

"Good idea. Safe topic. Who goes first?"

"You," I say quickly. I still need time to warm up and it gives me a chance to listen and learn, two things I've found to be critical before opening my mouth, my corsage comment notwithstanding.

"Teacher," he says. "Sixth grade."

"You're a sixth-grade teacher?" I ask, honestly surprised. "Boy, was I wrong."

He looks bemused by this. "You already took a guess? Tried to peg me? What did you think I did for a living?"

"Entrepreneur," I say.

"Why?" he asks.

I explain my little game at the Zombean and what I tried to divine about him by watching for a few minutes.

"Well, you got the left-handed part right," he says. He then looks around the restaurant. "What about the people in here? Want to take a stab?"

Now we're talking, I think to myself. We're playing in my ballpark.

Did he ask this to put me at ease?

"Pick one," I say.

He looks around and settles on a man sitting by himself over by the fish tank. He's African American, elderly, probably late sixties. He's sitting quietly, no optic in hand, watching the fish in the tank slowly do their fishy thing, waiting for his food to arrive.

"Him," he says. "Fish guy."

"Okay," I say and feel myself slipping into observation mode. It's smooth and effortless. Frankly, relaxing. "He's a regular. Widower. He and his wife used to come here a lot. Now that she's gone, he comes to find some peace, good memories of their times here. He's not looking at his optic. Doesn't even have one on the table, which is truly rare, so that tells me he's not that much into tech. Also, he seems perfectly content to watch the fish in the tank so he's clearly comfortable with silence and a lack of activity, another rarity. He has a job where he goes long periods of time without anything of consequence happening. He has infinite patience. He could be a bridge tender or a zoologist, or . . ." I pause and give it a little more thought and look to Mike. "An educator. Perhaps special ed." Mike smiles at this. I continue. "His clothes are off the rack so he's most likely not anything too white collar-y. His shoes are Mephistos, made for being on your feet all day. Not terribly stylish but comfortable. They're expensive, a luxury for him, but also a necessity. He's a practical man. Knows that you should pay more for things between you and the earth—mattress, tires, and shoes."

"That's good. Mattress, tires, and shoes. I like that. Never heard that one before," says Mike.

"Advice from my mom," I say. I settle back in my chair and feel the warm glow I always get after a deep study. For me it's better than yoga.

Mike then says, "So, let's find out," and before I can say another word, he's off his chair and across the room to the man by the fish tank. He walks up and quietly introduces himself. I see him gesturing to our table. The man looks over at me and gives a nod and looks back to Mike. I can't hear the conversation over the white noise of the restaurant but it's evident the man doesn't think Mike's a loony for approaching him. While I watch, the baby from across the room begins to fuss, but their parents give it no mind, not about to cave to some minor disturbance on most likely a rare night out. A few of the other patrons glance nervously their way, clearly wondering if the ticking time bomb baby will go off. But the child self-soothes and quiets again, and my attention returns to Mike's mission. The man he's speaking with gives a few short answers, Mike asks a couple more questions, and after another short answer from the man, Mike shakes his hand and strolls back, an interesting look on his face.

When he sits down, he fixes me with a look of clear fascination, like I'm a side show carney who just guessed his weight.

Which I guess I am to some degree.

"How did you do that?" he asks.

"How close was I?"

"Close enough to be scary. He's a bachelor, not a widower, but he and his sister used to come here every week until she had a stroke and had to be moved into an assisted living facility. He's not a bridge tender or a zoologist or a special ed teacher but an occupational therapist. Yes, those are Mephistos, and yes he treats himself to a new pair every year."

Mike sits and looks at me with a look that pretty much says, "Damn." He's impressed, and I am glowing.

"I'm guessing that display has something to do with what you do for a living. Either that or it's your go-to party trick," he says.

"It is part of what I do, yes. And it does make a for a good party trick."

"All right, I'll bite. So, tell me Frankie Percival, what is it that you do for a living?"

"I'm a mentalist."

"Shut up! You are not!" He practically shouts and then looks around, slightly embarrassed by his outburst. "Really? A mentalist? Read minds and stuff?"

"Well, read people, really," I say, with no small amount of pride, and take a swig of my water and crunch ice.

Mike sits back. "That is way cool." I know what's coming next, the inevitable question, can I read his mind?

"Where do you perform?"

I am pleasantly surprised. "The Odeon theater. You know it?"

"Sure," he says. "I've seen a few bands play there over the years."

I smile at this, and it occurs to me that I'm thoroughly enjoying his company.

So, this is what a date feels like. I'd forgotten. Whatever tension I'd been feeling earlier has ebbed away. I'm liking this feeling. Evidently, Mike can see something shift in my demeanor.

"What?" he says.

"I was just thinking it's been a while since I've been on a date."

He then looks at me with those sapphire eyes, and with a quick nod of his head, "Well, you're on one now."

There is no pretense to this man. He's casual, funny, compassionate, not bad looking. Why the hell is he single? I'm waiting for the shoe to drop, to find out some horrible thing about him, like he moonlights as a mob hitman or something.

After our food arrives, we spend the next half hour touching on exceedingly trivial small talk. Just enjoying each other's company and Americanized Chinese food.

Then at precisely 9:30 my optic chirps. A message. I'd completely forgotten about Aud's escape plan.

I let it chirp.

Mike says, "You want to check that?"

I shrug it off and say it's probably just my friend confirming our plans for tomorrow.

"Go ahead, ping her back, I don't mind."

"You sure? It's really no big deal."

He waves it off and I grab my optic. Sure enough, there's a message from Aud asking me if we were still on for tomorrow and if we could meet at the gelato place near her apartment.

I show the screen to Mike. "Yep, my friend Audrey. Okay if I reply to her?"

"Be my guest," he says.

"Mind if I voice it?"

"Not at all."

I hit the voice command button and say, "Aud, sure, tomorrow's fine but no gelato for me. Watching my girlish figure. How about I meet you at your place?" I hit the send button.

I give Mike a tight smile and try to steer the train back on track. "Where were you that you got to steal hotel shampoo?"

"Up in Seattle. I was visiting my son. He broke his hand playing baseball, so I drove up to give him a little moral support."

"Hope he's okay," I say.

"He's fine. Kids are resilient."

Just then my optic chirps again. I ignore it. It continues to chirp.

"Uh, you want to get that again?" Mike asks. "Sounds pretty insistent."

I feel my teeth clenching and check the screen. Audrey again. "Are you sure you don't want to meet for gelato?" I hold up a finger to Mike, a just a second gesture, and hit the voice button. "Yes," I say, a little more forcefully this time. "No gelato. Positive." I stab the send button, look up at Mike and smile.

"Your friend must really like gelato," he says.

"Gelatoholic, that's her. Lives for the stuff."

Luckily at that moment our fortune cookies arrive, and we both stare at them, then at each other.

"Who goes first?" he asks.

"You," I say.

He picks the one closest to him and breaks it in two. He takes out the strip of paper and reads it aloud. "Your date is smoking hot."

"Shut up!" I say and try to smack the fortune out of his had but he pulls back, and I miss.

"What?" he says, innocently. "That's what it says."

"It does not."

"Okay, okay. It says, A foolish man listens to his heart. A wise man listens to cookies."

I nod, giving my approval. "Damn. That's a good one."

"Your turn," he says.

I crack mine open and read it. "Master your circumstances or they will master you."

He smiles at this. "I like that. I'll have to remember that for my students."

I read the fortune again, to myself, "Words to live by."

WE ORDER ANOTHER round of drinks and continue gabbing. It's weird, I can be a Chatty Cathy but I'm not too social. I'm quite particular about whom I open up to. But with Mike I am fully engaged. I don't remember the last time I've felt like this. There's so much I want to learn about him, so many questions I want to ask. It's like I'm an anorexic who's been cured and is standing before an all you can eat buffet. And then the baby bomb goes off. In full wail mode. All eyes snap to the instantly regretful parents as they break out all their baby-quieting tricks, but nothing's working. And then a small mercy: our check arrives. I offer to pay my share, speaking in a half-shout over the critically annoyed baby, but Mike will have none of that.

At that moment my optic chirps. Mike and I both look at each other. Mike, I'm sure, is ready to make a crack about Audrey's gelato-olicism, when we notice the chirp came in plural from throughout the room, Mike's optic included. We glance around. The sounds of clinking flatware and glasses diminish to nothing. Even the baby magically quiets, leaving a brief black hole of silence. Only one thing has this effect.

"*Death Warrant* notice," says Mike quietly, looking from table to table. Virtually every person in the room, wait staff included have their eyes burned into their optic screens and the inevitable murmur of excitement begins to grow, like a dial being turned. Electricity fills the space like a physical being.

Mike turns back to me. "Do you tune in, too?" he asks. It's an off-hand question. Nothing leading about it. Like asking if I liked a certain band.

"Sometimes." I shrug, trying to be casual, but the pings and response of the other customers fill me with unease. As it always does.

He gives his head a sideways tip, quizzical. "Ever feel guilty about it?"

I purse my lip and nod. "Every single time. You?"

"Not as often as I should." He takes a hit of his old fashioned. "Would you ever do it?"

For a split second I want to say yes, but instead. "No, never." Why did I even consider it? It feels like one of those subliminal messages that's slipped into a video, where they put in one frame of what they want to embed in your mind. For one frame my brain wanted to say yes.

"Never?" prods Mike.

"Well, I guess I can never say never. Just seems like an extreme measure. What do you know about it?"

"Same as everybody else, nothing. Creepy, huh? With social media and everything it's impossible to keep secrets, yet they do. Makes you wonder what's going on behind the curtain."

I look around the restaurant again. People still excitedly chattering about the upcoming kill, their food forgotten, the baby bomb forgotten. I hear several simultaneous gasps. New information is coming out.

"It's a woman!" someone says.

The only person who doesn't seem to be engaged is the gentleman by the fish tank. He glances around at the activity and our eyes meet. They're empty, nothing there. I'm just a face he has paused on for a moment. Or is there something more? It's rare to see someone that disinterested in *Death Warrant*. The anticipation is notoriously contagious. Yet there he is, the indifferent calm amidst the storm of morbid curiosity. His eyes leave mine while the room vibrates with anticipation. I envy his disinterest.

Mike says, "Would you ever want to know?"

My eyes are still on the man by the fish tank. Mike's question brings me back to the moment. "I'm sorry, what?"

"Would you ever want to know when your time was up. I mean, not like cancer where you have to live with the dread of knowing you're going to die within six months or something. I mean, would you want to know that your life will end abruptly and when it will happen?"

I'm awash with the strangest feeling of déjà vu. Like I've had this conversation before. I consider Mike's question. It's a strange question. Frankly, the first one of the evening that feels out of place.

"No, I wouldn't want to know." The mood has dipped back into somber mode. I try to lighten it up. "I want my obituary to read, 'She never knew what hit her.'"

This coaxes a smile from Mike. "You want to be here when it happens?" he asks. "Not your death I mean. The poor gal who's about to get killed on TV."

"Not really," I say. But before either of us moves to leave, I hold up a finger. Mike takes my cue and waits to see what I have to say. Frankly, I'm not completely sure myself. I take a breath to collect my thoughts. Do I really want to go down this road? What the hell. "Let me ask you something. Do you believe in coincidence?"

Mike instantly recognizes that my question has stepped beyond typical date chit chat and has some weight behind it. He gives his answer a thought. "Yeah, I guess I do."

"I don't," I say. "Ten years ago, my brother Galen was in a terrible car accident. Blown out tire on a bridge. Crash. Coma. Brain damage. The works."

"I'm sorry to hear that," says Mike. "How is he now?"

"A shell of himself, if I'm being honest." I pause, again wondering if I'm about to reveal too much information for a first date. But it only takes a second for me to reach my conclusion. "The bridge where Galen crashed?

There'd been a half dozen accidents on it in the previous fifty years. Suddenly there's three in six months. Galen's being one of those three."

"And you don't think that was a coincidence?" Mike asks gently.

"I don't."

"What do you think happened?"

"I think something was wrong with the bridge or the surface. Something that caused Galen's accident. People involved in the previous accidents filed lawsuits, but nothing came of it. No negligence was found on the part of the bridge contractors or the state."

"And you felt . . . ?"

"Pissed. I was sure there had to be some reason other than pure happenstance that, for all intents and purposes, my brother's life was destroyed."

Mike lets my response settle for a moment before continuing. "And you think something other than wear-and-tear made the bridge unsafe?"

I nod.

"And what do you think it was?"

This is the moment where I should shut up if I want Mike to keep thinking that I am a rational human being. But I don't.

"*Death Warrant*." There, I said it.

Mike's eyebrows jump. "*Death Warrant*?" I can tell he's beginning to wonder what he's gotten himself into by asking out the crazy lady.

"In a *Death Warrant* episode that took place several months before my brother's accident, some poor guy met his end when his brakes gave out and he rear-ended a tanker truck at full speed. I guess I don't have to tell you where the accident took place."

"On the same bridge?"

I nod again. "Left a fair amount of structural damage. But *Death Warrant* being *Death Warrant*, they tidied it all up as nice as you please."

"And you think that accident led to your brother's?"

"That's what's nice about not having a nine-to-five job," I say. "Leaves you with a lot of time to investigate and poke around."

"And what did you find?"

I look into his eyes, wondering if I've completely blown it with this man. I shrug. "Nothing I could prove in court."

He lets my answer sit, considering it. "So, needless to say, you're not a fan of the show."

I shake my head.

"And yet, you have the app and receive push notifications."

I let out a sigh. I know precisely how nuts I must sound. "Guilty."

He nods, eyeing me, like he's weighing how to reply. Finally, "I don't think they'll mind if they have two less viewers for tonight's show, do you?"

I return a sad, appreciative smile. "I don't."

When we get up, I excuse myself to go to the ladies' room before I'll meet him at the door. I don't really have to use the bathroom, well, at least not for, you know, that. I just want to recompose and do a mirror check-up. Plus, I want to take a break from the grimness that invaded our date. I walk in, the bathroom's empty. I go to the sink and look in the mirror. Audrey's handiwork is still in effect. I reach into my bag and take out my lipstick and do a once over lightly. At that moment the door opens, and another woman walks in. She's probably barely legal drinking age. I don't remember seeing her in the restaurant. Maybe she's just arriving. She steps up to the sink to my left and gives herself a once over as well. She's striking. But of course, she is, she's at that age when you will never look better in your life. Her face is smooth, not even a rumor of a wrinkle. Her pores are non-existent. Her figure is nothing short of dynamite and her dress accentuates the positives. There are a lot of positives. Standing before the mirror, our reflections side by side, my heart drops. Just when you think you're looking pretty good, reality steps up and shows you what good really looks like. The comparison between us is, frankly, no comparison. I wonder if this girl fully appreciates what she has at this moment in her life.

I doubt it.

To her, what she sees is simply business as usual. She looks at that face and figure every day of her life. It's standard operating procedure. Gravity and life have yet to have their way with her. She is ignorant. Even on my best day in my youth I never looked like her. Not by a sight. She catches me glancing at her reflection and gives a polite smile. I smile back but there's nothing in my smile. It's perfunctory. The girl seems satisfied with what she sees, repacks her lipstick, and clacks back out the door on a pair of Christian Louboutin shoes that cost more than my entire ensemble combined.

It had been a great evening until I let *Death Warrant* invade our conversation and began comparing myself to a woman at least a decade younger than me. In fifteen minutes, I went from feeling like the prom queen to feeling like the kid picked last for dodgeball. I chastise myself for feeling like that, but I can't shake the buzzkill. Why'd I have to open my mouth about my crazy conspiracy theories? And why'd I have to go the damn bathroom? Why? The answer to the first one is more complicated. But the second one? Vanity. I look my reflection straight in the eye. All I see are wrinkles, crow's feet, age spots, thinning hair, and a dull complexion. Whether any of them exist or not. How did I age twenty years in two minutes? When I leave the ladies' room, I see Mike waiting patiently at the front door. He smiles when he sees me, and I paste on my own in response. My face hurts from the effort.

When we walk out into the night, I wonder how he's going to respond to the evening's events. His first question smothers all my fears.

"You want to go somewhere else for a drink?" he asks hopefully.

I think on that for the briefest of moments, but then answer. "No, thank you. I've had a great night. Frankly, a better night than I've had in a long time, and I want to keep it the way it is."

"I'm glad you enjoyed yourself. So did I." We stand in slightly awkward silence for a moment. He begins staring at his shoes, hands in pockets, looking like a little kid. "Does that mean then that you wouldn't mind if I called you sometime?"

"I would like that very much," I say. Simply being around him again makes me feel better, my mood warms back up a degree or two. We trade numbers on our optics. Like strangers who met in a bar.

"Can I give you a ride home?" he asks.

"I'm good, but thanks," I say.

With that he steps closer and takes my hands in his. It strikes me how gentle he is, although his hands are so large and look so powerful. My mind races back to the first time I saw him in the Zombean. Hay bailing hands, I thought back then, not teacher hands. Hands that could crush mine like an egg. But they are tender hands right this minute, and they pull me in for a kiss. It lasts only a moment, but I can instantly feel endorphins kicking in, the rush of being wanted.

He turns with a smile and walks away. But after a few steps I call after him.

"Mike!"

He turns back to me, quizzical.

I stand there, trying to figure out how to ask this, but then give it to him straight. "Why'd you ask me out?"

This seems to puzzle him.

"Why?" he asks. He takes a couple of steps back toward me until he's five feet away. "Because you caught my attention," he says.

"Yes, but how? I'm not exactly a swimsuit model. I'm a fashion-challenged woman you saw in a coffee shop. What was the attraction?"

He thinks on this for a moment, again, hands in pockets. "I dunno. Something about you caught my eye."

My insecurities flood to the surface. "But what? I'm not pretty."

He steps closer, only a couple of feet away. Those ridiculous eyes resting on me. How can eyes that piercing be that comforting?

"To me you are. And besides, you're more than pretty. You're interesting."

CHAPTER 31

Sheila Graveman loves auditions. It's a part of her job she finds exceptionally satisfying.

She's gathered her creative team together to view and judge the latest prospective talent that will soon be set loose into Frankie Percival's universe to act as the eyes and ears of *Death Warrant*.

It's a decidedly low-tech approach, but highly effective. Good old fashioned shoe leather reporting.

"You'd think they'd be suspicious," observes Brent Haesham, Sheila's associate creative director. "The actors responding to the cattle call aren't even told what they're auditioning for."

"You ever acted before?" asks Xi Park, a seasoned writer and producer on Sheila's team. Haesham shakes his head. "Trust me," says Park. "Half don't care what the role is. All they want is the job."

"Kind of ironic, then," says Haesham with a smile, "that they won't ever be able to put it on their resume."

"Won't even know they auditioned for it," notes Park, "once we hit them with the mind sweeper."

"Mind sweeper," nods Haesham. "That's a good one. Who came up with that?"

"Beats me," says Park, her eyes back on her tablet, reviewing the laundry list of acting hopefuls. "But it's appropriate. Their mind will be swept clean of everything related to this audition." Park looks up thoughtfully. "I wonder if they know they auditioned for something but it's made blurry so they can't quite remember what it was they auditioned for?"

"Heck if I know," says Haesham. "I gave up trying to understand the whole memory wiping thing long ago. It's black magic."

"Hey, boss," Park says in Sheila's direction. "What are the roles we're filling today?"

"Most are nothing overly demanding. Low level stuff. Invisible characters. The kind you see every day of your life and never notice."

"In other words," says Haesham, "the best moles."

"But we have a couple of roles that will require a little more finesse," says Shieila. "We'll need some talent with particular skill sets."

"Don't we already have enough assets in place?" asks Addy Selma, the newest producer on the team, adjusting the camera that will be used to record the auditions.

Sheila gives her a pointed look, but then shakes her head with a smile. "Team?" she asks the rest of the room. "What's the number one rule around here?"

"You can never have too much data," the other members respond in unison.

"Precisely," says Sheila, and then with a smile to her new producer, "And because my boss demanded it." Sheila looks around the room. "We good? Ready to go?" Everyone nods. "Okay, then. Who's our first future star?"

Haesham looks at his tablet. "Missy Collinsworth. Aspiring actress of stage and screen."

"Show her in," says Sheila.

A moment later a woman, maybe late twenties, steps in, confident and bright-eyed.

"Hello, Ms. Collinsworth. Did you bring your resume and headshot?" asks Sheila.

"Yes," says the woman. She holds up her optic and gives it a waggle. "I transferred it to your assistant's tablet when I came in," she says, indicating to Xi Park.

"Excellent," says Sheila. "So, this role shouldn't be too much of a stretch for you, being that you've spent a fair amount of time in theaters."

The actress nods and smiles at this. "More than my fair share."

"Exactly." Sheila looks at her tablet. "It says here you are good with accents and dialects."

She nods. "French, German, British, to name a few. My specialty."

"And from what I see here you have some stagecraft technical experience as well."

"I've been a stagehand, and a lighting tech."

Sheila smiles. "How convenient."

CHAPTER 32

JUNE

I wish I could have been there when Dak got the call from Hasagawa's assistant to book the Odeon and demand that I be the headlining act. Word has it that when she dropped fifty thousand dollars as a down payment, he almost fainted. All I know is that it got me my Tuesday nights back. He's been prodding me about who Devon Nichols is and why her client has requested me specifically, but I play dumb for now. The glorious details will come out soon enough.

Speaking of glorious, that would sum up my current mood quite nicely. Business has been, shall we say, good. I've picked up a disproportionately large number of private bookings on top of my twice a week at the Odeon. Suspiciously so. It crosses my mind that perhaps Hasagawa is putting a quiet word out to his colleagues looking for party entertainment, but I have no proof of this. None of the gigs have been for overly lavish events. In fact, one was for working the crowd at a local car dealership's grand opening—not Lexus or Prestidio, but Toyota, so I have my doubts Hasagawa had anything to do with that. However, the fact that I've landed more work lately hasn't gone unnoticed by me. The extra work is another reason why I haven't had as much time for Mike, which has become, as Audrey might say, a bit of a sticky wicket.

When he dropped by today, unannounced, it irritated me, but I know he was just being spontaneous. Trouble is, right now I don't have time for spontaneous.

"What a surprise!" I say, trying not to look at the time. Time that seems to be moving at an alarmingly quick rate lately.

"I thought maybe we could do lunch," he says hopefully.

"I'd love to but . . ." That's as far as I get before he begins nodding, already knowing where his grand gesture will end up.

"I know, I know," he says. "Your other boyfriend awaits."

"That's not fair. You know how important this is to me."

He steps over to my couch and mindlessly adjusts a pillow. A casual gesture that shows how far we've come in so short a time. "You're right, you're right. It's just that as a teacher I've got a whole summer with nothing to do and there's no one other than you I'd rather do nothing with."

I want to melt in the warmth of his blue eyes, but I want to tackle my career by the horns more. I have too many good things lined up and I wish he could understand why that's so important to me. I wish I could tell him—without hurting his feelings—that after being single and independent for so long I've gotten used to my time being MY time. Making time for another person is more delicate than I remember. I start the balancing act. Again.

"Mike, you know I want to see you more, and I will, soon . . ."

"After the show. I get it," he says, with no shortage of frustration in his voice. "But surely you can take a break for lunch, right? I mean, you do eat occasionally?" He says this last line with a smile, hoping to lessen the tension.

"Yes, I eat," I say, but before I can continue, he intercepts me.

"At the studio. I know. Between measuring, cutting, and grinding away at your ticket to stardom." He isn't trying to be mean, but it smarts, nonetheless.

"And rehearsing," I say.

"Of course. How can I forget," he says, not even trying to hide his frustration.

I've developed a new thirst for updating my act. I'm researching new bits, studying, throwing myself into my work whole hog. Failure to prepare is preparing to fail. I have made it my own personal mission to blow Hasagawa's cronies right out of their goddamn seats on August 18th.

Mike stares me down, waiting for me to crack, but then a light appears in his eyes, and he plants his fists on his hips and says, "Show me."

"Show you?" I ask, puzzled.

"Yes. Show your boyfriend the big, damn, life-changing act that's taking up all your time. I don't think that's an unreasonable ask."

Crap. If there's anything more irritating than your significant other being right, I don't know what it is. In my mind I try to conjure up a defense for why I haven't shared the details of my act with him but, frankly, I don't have one. If I had to guess, fear, mostly. Fear of what he might say.

"Okay," I say. "You asked for it."

Thirty minutes later, Mike and I are outside the warehouse. As we enter, we walk past the studio with the Threesome sign.

Mike jokingly points at it.

I tell him it's not what he thinks and his face falls in mock disappointment. Before we reach my space, I hear an unmistakable voice.

"Yoo hoo!"

I turn and there's Miss Indeedy-do, waddling her way down the hall. She's all polyester double-knit and a toothy smile, waving to us.

"I am so glad to see you again!" Her enthusiasm is breathtaking. "I was just saying to my friend Mildred at our water aerobics class, Mildred, I said, this nice young woman helped me out of a pickle a while back and I have yet to see her since." She turns to Mike like they're old friends. "I was beginning to wonder if I'd imagined the whole thing!" She then turns back to me, beaming, "And then here you are!"

"Here I am," I say trying my best to match her glow. I begin introductions and immediately realize I don't know the woman's name. "Mike, this is . . . uh . . ."

Miss Indeedy-do holds out a meaty hand toward Mike. "Cloris. Cloris Bellweather."

Of course it is.

"And now that you mention it, I don't think I've had the pleasure of knowing yours either," says Cloris, of the warehouse district Bellweathers.

"It's Frances Percival. But you can call me Frankie."

"Ooh, Frankie! How fun!" gasps Cloris with a bend in her knees, hands clasping to her cheeks.

"How are things in the air business?" I ask.

"Peachy! Absolutely peachy! We just got in a big order from Taipei."

"Taipei," I say.

"It's in Taiwan," offers Cloris helpfully. "Northern tip of the island. There was a volcanic eruption on Datun mountain in Yangminshan National Park. They thought it was dormant but evidently the mountain had other thoughts!" Cloris repeats the knee-bend and hands to cheeks thing and lets out a high, girly laugh. Mike and I stare. Cloris begins fanning her face. "I'm sorry, I shouldn't find pleasure in other's misfortune, but golly, the first shipment was for a hundred gross." She sees our blank expressions and says to Mike with a reassuring hand on his elbow. "A gross is a dozen dozen, one hundred forty-four. Times one hundred . . ."

"Fourteen thousand four-hundred," I finish.

"Yes, indeedy!" says Cloris. "With more orders on the way. The Taiwanese government has been most appreciative." She turns back to Mike again. "Have you ever been? Taiwan, I mean." But before Mike can answer Cloris plows on. "I hear it's lovely," and then with a knowing glance my way, "not that I would ever go there myself. I'd probably only last a day or two before I'd be snatched up by some terrorist organization preying on wayward Americans." Turning back to Mike. "Am I right?" Mike nods dumbly. Cloris takes on a faraway look. "Godless creatures."

"Actually," I hear myself saying, "they're mostly Buddhists and Taoists, so technically their version of God is nirvana."

Cloris looks at me like I'm speaking in tongues. At this moment, Mike finally takes the initiative and steps into the breach.

"Couldn't agree with you more, Cloris. No one's safe outside America's borders."

Cloris smiles like she's just met a long-lost brother. "I know, right?"

"Indeedy-do," says Mike and I throw him a warning glance.

"And what brings you here today?" asks Cloris.

"Oh, you know, making sure my girl isn't using her studio to tomcat around on me," says Mike with a wink. He knows his audience.

Cloris does the knee-bend thing again and waves a hand in Mike's direction. "Aren't you a stitch!" She looks to me. "Isn't your friend a stitch? Heavens."

"Oh, he's a stitch all right. Well, Cloris, it's been great seeing you again, but I've got to get to work." I start taking slow steps away.

"Well, don't work too hard," says Cloris. "You know what they say, all work and no play . . ." She gives Mike a friendly nudge with her elbow.

Mike, stealing my bit, forms guns with his fingers and fires off a few shots at Cloris. "Back to the salt mines for us, Cloris. See ya round."

"Not if I see you first," says Cloris and bursts out laughing.

When we arrive at my studio, I turn to Mike. "That was Cloris."

"You don't say?"

We step inside and I flip on the overhead lights. Bosco takes up the center of the room, a hulking shape covered with a tarp.

"Ready?" I say.

"Bring it on," says Mike. "I've been waiting a long time for this."

I grab the tarp and draw it off to puddle on the floor. I kick the tarp aside as Mike stares with unvarnished wonder. "What do you think?" I ask.

"Holy crap!" says Mike. "You made this?"

I nod.

Mike does a slow circle around Bosco. He reaches out to touch it, pauses and checks with me to see if it's okay. I give him a nod. He runs his hands along the surfaces and then steps back to take in the full effect. "What's the bit?" he asks. "Do I finally get to know?"

I ignore the dig. "It's a take on the old disappearing woman trick," I say. "But with a twist."

Bosco is about eight feet tall and five feet wide. The main structure is a simple tall rectangle box with two large rings encircling it, like a pair of crossed Saturn rings. The rings are polished metal tubing. Well, painted carbon fiber, but they'll fool the average Joe. The rectangle walls are painted to look like a night sky, all blacks, blues, and purples.

"Watch this," I say and walk over, turn off the overhead lights, then come back and hit a button on the side of the contraption. Instantly, a constellation of lights winks on over every surface of Bosco. The effect is purely magical, dreamy. The lights, tiny, some dim, subtle, others brighter, shift and change before our eyes. "I've got them programmed to move with whatever music I choose. Oh, and there's one more feature," I say and punch another button. Instantly two quick jets of flame burst upward from carefully hidden nozzles in the top-front corners of the box. The flames lick out a good five feet, like fiery horns, and just as quickly vanish.

Mike's eyes are filled with complete wonder and then he steps back and lets out a whoop. "Killer!" He steps in closer and reaches for the door placed within the circle.

"Uh-uh," I say, blocking him. "No peeking."

"So, what does it do? Other than look pretty and possibly roast marshmallows."

I turn off the starlights and turn the overhead lights back on. "Like I said, it's a spin on the disappearing woman bit. I step inside the glass chamber, the closet, as it were, and eventually I will disappear in an interesting manner.

The difference is that you see me the whole time. I'm always there right before your eyes in full view. I will then be incinerated, again, right there before your eyes."

"Burned up in the box?"

"That's the plan," I say.

"In plain sight, behind the glass door?"

"For all the world to see," I say with a smile "Turned to charcoal briquettes in seconds."

"Sounds dangerous."

"If you don't know what you're doing," I say nonchalantly.

Mike fixes me with a look. "And do you?"

"It's always a little dicey when you're working with propane," I shrug with a nod toward Bosco, "but I've been studying. So far so good."

"Wait, you're not working with trained professionals on this? Fire experts?" Mike asks dubiously. "You're winging it on your own?"

"I don't know about 'winging it,'" I say, doing air quotes. "I'm being careful."

"Christ, Frankie, there are people who do this for a living. People that put in hours and hours of training to ensure they don't blow up. And you're doing this on your own?"

"Everything I need is on the Internet," I say. "It's really not as complicated as you might think. Mostly it's basic engineering and then crossing your t's and dotting your i's. If you do what you're supposed to do it works fine."

"So, you've already tested it?"

"Define tested." He can be so easy to needle.

Mike buries his face in his hands. "Am I going to have to clean up your remains using a whisk broom and a pan?"

I dust off my hands. "Sure hope not. That would suck."

CHAPTER 33

For the next week I tolerate Mike's incessant worrying and go about my rehearsals. He's being mother hen-ish about the whole thing, which, I must admit, I kind of like. It feels good to know someone's that concerned about me. I was just giving him crap about not testing Bosco. I'd tested it numerous times already. I like getting a rise out of him.

Revealing my act to him has done wonders for our relationship. He's more understanding of my time commitments, and I'm more understanding of the subtle workings of a relationship. To celebrate our new-found dynamic, he's coming over tonight, so I start closing up the studio.

As I'm giving the room a quick once over to make sure I don't forget anything, something catches my eye. It's nothing really, a T-square that I keep on the work bench. I only notice it because it's sticking out a few inches from the countertop. I'm nothing if not a slightly anal creature of habit.

Every day when I'm in the studio part of my routine is setting things just so.

And that T-square is out of place. On my first day here, it was sticking out and I caught my hip on it, knocking it to the floor. From that point on I always kept it flush with the edge.

But here it is sticking out a few inches. Did I forget to line it up last night? Granted, I've been putting in a lot of hours here and have been a little fuzzy at times. Did I forget? I arrange the T-square properly, edge flush with the counter's edge. Nice and precise. I then roll up my schematics and tuck them under my arm and head for door.

I feel better already.

BACK AT MY apartment, I'm tidying up for my dinner with Mike when Spencer chimes in. "You have a call coming in."

"Who is it?" I ask, not expecting one.

"Audrey."

Audrey? "Put her through."

Audrey's face appears on my wall monitor. Her eyes are red and puffy. I can see she's outside my apartment.

"Hey, Frankie," she says with an apologetic tone. "Got a minute?"

"Of course, come on up." I buzz her in.

A moment later there's a timid knock on the door and I open it to see a completely unfamiliar version of Audrey on my landing. She looks smaller, fragile. A far cry from the brash woman I thought I knew.

"Come in!" I practically shout, wrapping an arm around her and leading her into the living room. "What's going on?"

She settles into the corner of the couch and pulls a pillow to her chest, holding her arms around it like a teddy bear.

She looks all of ten-years old in my eyes.

She takes a deep breath and looks to the ceiling, like she's trying to compose herself. "Me gramps died."

"Oh, honey, I'm so sorry. Were you close?"

"He was me fave," she says, her English accent more pronounced than ever. "Always called me on me birthdays. Took me to the fair every summer."

"Was it unexpected? His death, I mean."

She nods and I settle in next to her, pulling her head to my shoulder. "I'm so sorry," I repeat, not sure what else to say. I remember when I was young how when the husband of one of my mom's friends died, she went over "to sit." I couldn't understand that. Why she would go over simply to sit with her friend.

I now understand.

Sometimes it's not necessary to say much of anything, you need to be there for the person. You need "to sit." And so, I did, slowly rocking her.

"I didn't know who else to call," she says quietly. "I've never lost anyone close before. I guess I felt if anyone could relate it was you."

I'm touched by this. It's never occurred to me that the death of my mother or what happened to Galen could ever put me in a position to be viewed as an expert on suffering.

"I know how much it hurts," I say, and I mean it. "It's like a piece of you is taken away." My eyes begin to fill with tears.

Audrey lifts her head and looks at me with those red, but still perfectly made-up eyes. "That's exactly what it's like. I knew you would understand." She then glances across to my kitchen space and spots the place settings and wine glasses. "Shite, you're expecting company," and pulls away a little.

"Just Mike. Coming over for dinner," I say.

She jumps to her feet and runs her hands through her hair. "No, no, no. I need to leave. You've got a date."

"It's no big deal, really. He's not coming over for at least fifteen minutes. Probably closer to thirty, if I know Mike," I add in with a weak attempt to brighten her spirits, even if only a little. It works. She breaks into a small, girlish grin and then begins to wave her hands in front of her face, like she's trying to cool herself off.

"Look at me, yeah? I'm a sight." She holds her hands to her face, pinching her temples and gives a squint. "And crying all day has given me a rager. I don't suppose you got something for a headache, do ya?"

"Of course, absolutely. Give me a minute," and I hotfoot into the adjoining bathroom, making a beeline for my line of pill bottles. I grab the first, ibuprofen. Empty. I move to the second, acetaminophen. Empty. I grab the third, aspirin. Empty. "How the hell did I not replace any of them when I took the last ones?" I grumble to myself. "Spence, do we have any aspirin?"

"Did you recently purchase any?" he asks.

"No."

"Then no."

"Thanks for nothing," I mumble again. "Nightstand," I say with a snap of my fingers and exit the bathroom for the bedroom. "Hang on, Aud," I half-shout, passing between the two rooms. A moment later I find a half-empty bottle of Naproxen. Bingo. I make a quick stop in the bathroom to fill up a glass of water and return to the living room to find Audrey leaning over my worktable, peering at my schematics. She appears startled by my sudden appearance, but I chalk it up to her emotional state.

"Are these for your new act?" she asks.

"Uh, yeah," I say, handing over the pills and water and slide some papers over the plans as casually as I can.

She downs the pills and water and fixes me with a disarming smile before wrapping her arms around me. "Thank you, Frankie," she whispers into my ear. "You're a true friend."

After Audrey leaves, I step back over to my table and slide the papers away from my schematic. There's Bosco in all his glory, virtually every detail mapped out. I walk back over to the kitchen and check the time. I still have a few minutes before Mike arrives. I crack open the fridge and take out the chilled bottle of white. I pour my glass and catch a glimpse of myself in the reflection of the glass covering one of the movie prints on my wall. I reach a finger up and wipe away some of the mascara that's run down my cheek, courtesy of my tears.

"Audrey's been crying all day," I say to myself. "And yet, *her* makeup is still perfect." How does she do it? I'll never know.

CHAPTER 34

JULY

The bouquet of roses, complete with a touching thank you card from Audrey, are a pleasant surprise. As I read her thoughtful words, it takes me back to what she'd whispered in my ears: You're a true friend.

The week after her grandfather's death I couldn't shake a niggling feeling that Audrey's visit had felt . . . peculiar. But that feeling evaporates at the delivery of the roses, as they have the desired effect. My heart swells. And the timing couldn't be more perfect. For today is

July 7th, that most important day on my and Galen's calendar.

If mom had been alive today, she would have cracked the same joke she made every year, except each year the punchline was slightly different. On her fiftieth birthday she told us, "If Jesus was alive at my age, he'd a been dead for seventeen years." The next year it was eighteen, then nineteen, etc. etc. Today it would have been thirty-two. Mom would have been sixty-five.

I had to remind Galen of mom's birthday again, but once he remembered he was excited. I am on dinner patrol and the special of the day is chicken alfredo with Rice-a-Roni as our side dish (herb & butter flavor, mmm) and a loaf of garlic bread, heavy on the butter. It's pretty much carb central. The wine is a mid-shelf chardonnay. Galen's in good form today. His memory isn't too bad, and his spirits are high. He even shaved.

"How's your b . . . boyfriend?" he asks.

My ears are still recovering from the Tricentennial celebrations three days prior. Seemed like every firework in America was going off at once. Every city tried to outdo one another, and as a result it was explosion central from coast to coast. I cynically half-expected some poor sap to be blown to smithereens by a wayward skyrocket on a patriotically themed *Death Warrant* episode but was pleasantly surprised that they took a pass. Despite my diminished hearing, I could still hear what Galen said.

"My boyfriend Mike is doing great," I say. "Thanks for asking." *I like that title,* I think. Boyfriend.

"So, he is your boyfriend? Officially?" asks Galen with a sly smile.

I take a hit of my wine. "Yeah, sure, why not. I've got a boyfriend. Happy now?"

"Wanna hear something w . . . weird?"

"I always want to hear something weird," I say.

"I'm seeing someone too," he says, looking both proud and embarrassed.

I nearly drop my wine. "No way!"

"Way."

"Who is she? What's her name? What are her specs? Give!" I blurt out.

"Her name is Tonya. She works at the hospital in pediatrics. She's a n . . . nurse."

"When do I get to meet her?"

"Anytime you want," he says. "Next time you come by t . . . to visit."

"Done." I hold up my glass of wine. "To the fair Tonya."

"Hear, hear!" says Galen and we clink glasses.

We enjoy the moment, swill our wine, and clean our plates. While we tidy up, Galen asks me about the big show. That's what I call it, The Big Show. Right after everything was confirmed with Hasagawa, I raced over to tell Galen and he was thrilled for me. At the time I didn't have many particulars but now I do. I go over everything with him and he listens attentively and even asks surprisingly astute questions about the financial aspects of it. Evidently not all his capitalistic education was erased with the accident.

"You and Tonya will have front row seats. The best in the house," I declare over a sink full of suds and dirty dishes.

"Wouldn't miss it for the world."

After clean-up we repair to the living room, all of fifteen feet away. Galen flops into the corner of the couch closest the window while I take up the other half. I'm into my fourth glass of wine and am feeling just north of fine. I look at Galen. His face is bright red, as per usual after only a couple of drinks, and his smile is deep and satisfied.

We are both in our happy place.

He holds up his empty glass. "Oh, waiter?"

I reach across with the bottle and give him a healthy refill. He settles back into the couch, closes his eyes, and murmurs with the slightest of slurs, "What would I do without you."

For some reason it freezes me.

I sit there staring at my brother, the bottle poised above the table. His eyes are still closed so he's oblivious to my reaction. Why did that comment jolt me so? It was like a tiny zap of electricity that short circuited my wiring. What would he do without me? It's a question I've asked myself countless times over the past decade, but for some reason hearing it come from his own lips . . . I don't know. I splash another finger's worth into my own glass and try to shake the thought from my head. Tonight is a celebration. No time for downer thoughts. In that moment a completely different thought leaps forth. It occurs to me that a thousand miles to the south, Grayson Hasagawa is probably preparing to walk on stage in front of thousands of his devoted employees. And I was going to be the opening act.

I picture in my head Hasagawa stepping out from the wings and walking into the spotlight only to hear the gathered masses chanting my name for an encore. Frankie! Frankie! Hey, if you're going to daydream, dream big.

I take a stiff swig and smack Galen on the leg.

"Hey, wake up! We got stuff to do."

His eyes creep open and his lips curl into a mischievous grin. "We certainly do."

You would think that as part of celebrating our mom's birthday a major proponent of it would be rehashing old memories of her. We try, but with Galen's issues it's usually just me spouting stories and Galen occasionally chipping in. He'll surprise me sometimes by bringing up an occurrence with mom from way back when, but those moments are few and far between. Even so, he enjoys the custom we've created which in turn makes me happy.

"Spencer," I bark. "Movie time. Wouldest thou play Auntie Mame, prithy?"

"I wouldest," replies Spencer dryly. "And how are you this evening, master Galen?"

"I am w . . . w . . . I'm good," says Galen and we both burst out laughing. We spend the next two hours and twenty-three minutes in perfect wine-infused contentment with our favorite cinema aunt who better than anyone other than our mom knew how to Live! Live! Live!

CHAPTER 35

The talent gathered in the *Death Warrant* production studio would put any other network to shame. This was the cream of the crop, and Klaus Manfred wouldn't have it any other way. It was less than a month before what he openly considered the most important event in the program's history, and he made sure every signature position was held down by an all-star. There was too much riding on this.

"Status update," he says, turning to Sheila Graveman.

She'd been putting in fifteen-hour days for the past few months and felt she and her team had considered every contingency imaginable. They weren't going to have to rely on an act of God if something went wrong this time around. Because nothing would go wrong.

Herr Manfred had made that abundantly clear.

"We're right on schedule. Surveillance has been exceptional, and all of our intelligence indicates that Ms. Percival is still unaware of her participation in the upcoming episode." She says this last line with a small smile. It's a well-worn joke in the *Death Warrant* inner circles. The participant never knows. And never will know if any *Death Warrant* employee knows what's good for them. Klaus Manfred casts a long, terrifying shadow.

Sheila turns to an utterly unremarkable woman sitting to her left. Unremarkable other than her air of supreme self-confidence. Whatever she lacks in defining physical characteristics she more than makes up for it with an aura of invincibility.

"You all know Ms. Aubuchon, our point person and primary asset for Ms. Percival's passing."

The others nod appreciatively in her direction, even Klaus, which speaks volumes to the regard in which he holds the woman.

Her given name is Marguerite Aubuchon, but she is known by another name around *Death Warrant* water coolers: the secret weapon. The woman has several rare gifts that lend themselves quite nicely to *Death Warrant*'s needs. Coming out of high school she was all prepared to go to college on a dramatic arts scholarship. Her natural ability to pick up dialects being a huge plus. She also had a chameleon-like ability to shift and change as the role demanded.

Marguerite was ready to hone her dramatic craft at the local state university when the strangest thing happened. She got a visit from two suit-clad gentlemen from the Central Intelligence Agency. They informed her that they had seen her test scores and profile breakdown and felt she could do much better than preparing for a world of cattle call auditions. They told her she would be trained by the finest dramatic instructors around but for a much more noble purpose—they wanted her to trade her aspirations of the Great White Way for defending the great American way.

Marguerite bought in. Fully. She enjoyed the discipline and the challenge, knowing that if she didn't sell her character completely there could be dire circumstances. On the stage or screen the worst you could expect was a scathing review. In her new line of work, lives were at stake. For years she quietly went about her business assuming identities all over the world and added a few other skillsets along the way as well. The CIA likes specialists but they're not above a little cross-training when they feel it can benefit them. Surprisingly, Marguerite showed a remarkable aptitude for one particular skill set that changed the course of her life. It was a particularly useful skill in eliminating liabilities with minimal collateral damage. Marguerite could blow stuff up like nobody's business.

She was having a successful career with the CIA when the second strangest thing happened to her. She got a visit from an imposing suit-clad man who claimed to be a television executive producer who told her that her combination of skills would translate seamlessly into a new project he was working on. He presented a convincing argument. For the last five years she has freelanced for this man. Every six-to-nine months, she receives a call requesting her services and she does her thing. It's the perfect part-time job. And the pay is exceptional.

Sheila Graveman says, "Are you still comfortable with the time frame, Ms. Aubuchon?"

Marguerite merely nods. "All is in order."

Klaus rubs his chin thoughtfully. "A shame the episode couldn't have taken place on Independence Day. The fireworks would have made nice cover."

Marguerite softly shrugs. "We can't have everything."

The television program's director, Paola Sabatini, gives his hand a subtle raise. "Concerning the method of termination, the close proximity of civilians won't be a concern?" he asks. "This will easily have the highest risk factor you've been asked to account for."

Coming from anyone else it might have been insulting to Marguerite, but she knows and respects the director. Like everyone else at the table he understands no detail is insignificant.

Paola Sabatini's background is in sports broadcasting, particularly soccer, or football as it's called everywhere else in the world. He was recruited by *Death Warrant* after Paolo's last stint during the World Cup tournament. Coming in he expected the productions to be similar to other live events he'd directed, but soon learned these productions took a much lighter touch, due to the sensitive nature of the content. Blood was kept to a minimum, which was a frequent challenge. That is why he has concerns now. He knows of his colleague's skill, but it is still his job to be prepared for any eventualities. He doesn't want to be cutting to a reaction shot of a bystander only to see bodies mangled in a stampede.

Marguerite Aubuchon nods respectfully to the director. "The exceptional risk factors will not be a concern. They will in fact be a highlight." When she says this, she looks around the table, a gleam in her eye that no one can ever recall seeing before. It gives Sheila a quiet thrill.

"Excellent," says Klaus. "I would expect nothing less." He turns to Sheila. "I want status reports from our other surveillance assets on an even more frequent basis moving forward, is that understood? I want to know everything Ms. Percival is doing, and when she's doing it, up until the moment of truth."

Sheila doesn't blink. "They haven't let us down yet."

CHAPTER 36

Three weeks before the show, the promised press coverage begins, and my stress levels rise. When Grayson Hasagawa calls for an audience, he gets one. Every local reporter, blogist, vlogist, and columnist is there. And some not so local. There must be twenty microphones picking up his every word. I'm astonished by this response. He's holding a fundraiser for a second-rate local theater and the headliner's fame barely even registers on the Northwest scene. Hasagawa plays the role of the philanthropic patron of the arts, doing his small part to keep the local theater culture alive and well. He even offers vague hints that he may do this in other cities as well. Whoever wrote his script knows his stuff. If you didn't know better, you'd think the Odeon was a historic monument from the golden age of theater. At one point he actually used the words, "In her heyday, our beloved Odeon was the region's most magnificent temple of theatrical grandeur." You would have thought the greatest acts in the land were beating down its doors to play there instead of has-beens, bar bands and novelty acts. But the press eats it up. Every TV and radio station gives the story extended coverage. Hasagawa makes himself remarkably available for numerous one-on-one interviews. And needless to say, I'm a primary beneficiary of this full court media press. I can honestly say I am doing more interviews in one week than I have done in my entire life. So, this is what celebrity feels like.

I read some of the stories. Most treat me as a curiosity. Why is Hasagawa holding this big event, inviting some of his closest friends, and entertaining them with a Bar Mitzvah mentalist? He can book the most popular musicians on the planet, but instead he insists on a fortune teller, a mind reader, someone you hire for parties.

I stand off to one side, doing my best to look confident and professional, while Mike provides my emotional support, hovering behind the scrum of reporters flashing me an occasional thumbs up or goofy face, hoping I'll crack up.

I give him no such satisfaction.

Hasagawa handles the throng like the seasoned media vet that he is, all smiles with just the right touch of gravitas.

"I had the pleasure of having Ms. Percival perform at a party of mine some months back, and it was astonishing," he says with a nod in my direction. "At one point she stopped time. Or at least gave me the impression that she had."

Many of the gathered press members roll their eyes, but Hasagawa presses on. "You have to witness her stage presence yourself."

I'll say this for Hasagawa, he knows event promotion. His praise sounds utterly sincere. I glance down toward Mike for his reaction, expecting to see him joke-gagging, but he's not where he was the moment before. I scan the area to the sides and back of the gathered media looking for him but come up empty. Huh. That was ninja-like. I continue my visual sweep, trying to be as subtle as possible—I don't want to seem rude to my benefactor—while Hasagawa continues heaping praise.

"And . . ." he says, holding up a finger. "She is taking her performance art to a completely new level." His voice builds with emotion. "The lucky attendees will be witness to the world premiere of a new addition to her act. And from all reports, it will leave the audience questioning their own senses."

All reports? What reports? He's never seen my new act, and neither has anyone else. No one has even seen my schematics of Bosco . . . except . . . Audrey . . . At my apartment after her grandfather died, she did lean over the drawings . . . No way . . . she wouldn't. I quickly shake that off as just another instance of my overactive imagination and obsessive observation. I turn my attention back to Hasagawa. I feel like I'm watching an old-time carnival barker whipping up the masses. The man has a gift. And the byproduct of that gift is the greatest marketing and advertising coup imaginable . . . for me. People often wonder what's the secret to hitting it big. How does a video go viral? How does a book become a best seller? All it takes is a person of influence singing your praises. It really is who you know. And Hasagawa's support is a gift from the gods. I foolishly almost let this chance slip away once. It won't happen again. I allowed emotion to color my judgement and get in the way before, but now I know better. This is business. All I have to do is *not* totally screw the pooch and my meal ticket is punched. That's the good part. The not so good part? Some of the Internet trolls are really teeing off on me. I can't believe some of the horrific things that are being written. I fall somewhere between Satan and that nanny that killed the six kids she was taking care of. I'm being called a hack, a loser, a tramp, a side-show act, a joke, and a slut. Evidently, I've slept my way to this opportunity, or I have incriminating photos of Hasagawa and a goat. The comments are so poisonous and personal that I quit reading anything I see posted. I have sworn off all media and am wrapping myself in a cocoon of ignorance. So, this is what celebrity feels like.

When the dog and pony show wraps up, Hasagawa draws me in for the requisite photos of us shaking hands, waving, and performing other artificial poses usually reserved for politicians. And that's when I spot Mike. He's tucked behind one of the free-standing room dividers near the back. I can see him speaking into his optic. And by the looks of it, it's a serious conversation. I can see his furrowed brow from across the hall. I step down from the dais and weave my way through a few straggler reporters and the clean-up crew. I'm more than halfway there when he spots me. He says something into his optic, pockets it, and waves.

"Where'd you go?" I ask. "One minute you were there, the next, poof!"

"Yeah, sorry 'bout that. I got a call from my son. About his broken hand. He wanted to tell me about how he's learning to eat left-handed. I couldn't exactly blow him off, and you were doing perfectly fine up there," Mike says with that maddeningly disarming grin of his.

"No," I say with an apologetic wave of my hand. "Of course, you should have taken the call. It's just that it was so sudden. I got a little concerned, that's all." I pause for a moment. "Hasn't he already got the cast off? I mean, it's been a couple of months. Broken hands don't take that long to heal, do they?"

"Oh, yeah, normally," Mike says dismissively. "But he had some complications. Didn't I mention that? Huh. Well, nothing to worry about." His grin then amps up to his best thousand-watt smile and he wraps an arm around my shoulders, turning me to the exit. "But I'm honored and touched that my disappearance caused you emotional turmoil. That's the sign of a healthy relationship."

I chuckle at his efforts to sweep it aside as we leave the building and head over to his car.

AT THE THEATER, Dak is beside himself with glee. When he found out the theater was going to be on the receiving end of a healthy chunk of the 2.5-million-dollar gate, he cried like a little girl. And who can blame him? This theater is his pride and joy. The man sweats blood to keep it afloat and as much as we like to gripe about his penny-pinching ways, we respect the effort he puts in to keep the doors open. Even with the upcoming windfall, I admit I am a little surprised that Dak hired some new bodies to fill out the theater. Technicians, stagehands—it's starting to feel like a legitimate theater.

As we inch closer to the big gig, Dak and my agent Mel are doing something remarkably smart. They're making me scarce. Dak's pulled my weekly shows until the big event. He says he doesn't want to water down the impact by having others see it beforehand. Mel says he's getting inundated with requests for my act, sight unseen, and he too is begging off until after the 18th. By doing this they've both now made my act a hot commodity.

It's the classic case of you want what you can't have. I can't live on hopes and dreams, so I insist that I still be paid for the turned down or cancelled gigs. Much to my surprise they agree. They tell me they're looking at that money as an investment for the inevitable demand after the big gig. Suddenly I'm a wise and practical monetary solution.

Who knew?

Both Dak and Mel have been in this business a long time so I'm taking them at their word that the demand will materialize. Dak's filling the Tuesdays and Thursdays with local bands and other acts that are suddenly begging him to consider. Hasagawa has agreed to let Baltic open for me and the kid is surprisingly non-plussed by the news. When I tell him he smiles, gives me a short nod, and says, "Then I guess I better not screw up."

I'm thinking the same thing. Don't screw this up.

CHAPTER 37
THE CHAT WITH MYRNA

"Are you truly prepared to die?" Myrna has taken off her tangerine specs and is cleaning them on her blouse.

"Yes," I say with virtually no hesitation.

Myrna inspects her lenses, and, appearing satisfied, places them lightly back on the bridge of her nose. "I want you to think of this as suicide. You're seeking a permanent solution to a temporary problem."

"I guess I don't see years of Galen's future struggles as temporary. This money will improve his life more than having me around."

"I doubt your brother will agree with that."

I can feel my frustration beginning to boil to the surface.

"This isn't something I decided on over the weekend. It's been brewing in my head for a long time. I've looked for other viable solutions, and guess what? There aren't any!" I grind my teeth. "I know what it's like to lose someone close. It takes a while, but eventually the pain subsides. It'll be the same thing for Galen when I'm gone. But that money will soften the blow. He'll be able to get the kind of help he isn't getting now. Mark my words, his quality of life will improve."

Myrna listens patiently and taps out a few more subtle notes on her table. Finally . . . "But look at what you'll be missing? Relationships . . ."

I flip a hand, dismissively. "Don't have any. Not any that really count, other than Galen's."

"But that could change. You never know what life will bring." Myrna is trying her best to get me to look at the positives, but so far, it's not making a dent. "What about your friend Audrey?"

"Bought and paid for," I say a bit unkindly. "A week after I'm gone, she'll have a new client and will be cashing someone else's checks."

"You don't strike me as a cynic," says Myrna, inspecting me with those perilously deep brown eyes. From anyone else it would sound as a reprimand, but Myrna being Myrna it comes off as merely conversational.

"Look," I say, "I don't doubt Audrey would miss me. But at the same time, it's not like we go way back. We're not sorority sisters or grade school pals."

"I don't know," says Myrna thoughtfully. "Even if you are merely a client, as you put it, I can't imagine she hasn't grown fond of you. I would wager you're closer than you want to admit."

The words carry weight.

It's like Myrna expertly slipped her stiletto smoothly between my ribs to reach a vital organ. An experienced hand. I don't have a response and default to shrugging it off, hoping that might put an end to this line of questioning.

"When was the last time you looked around at the world, Frankie? I mean truly looked around. There's an awful lot of joy and beauty still to be found. I still think you're capable of seeing it. What do you think?"

"I think you're good at your job, Myrna."

She smiles at this but is content to wait me out. I oblige her. "I've lived a good life," I say. "No regrets."

"None?" she says.

I dip my head slightly, looking up at Myra. My voice goes soft, thoughtful. "I've seen things you people wouldn't believe. Attack ships on fire off the shoulder of Orion. I watched C-beams glitter in the dark near the Tannhäuser Gate. All those moments will be lost in time, like tears in rain." I pause. "Time to die."

Myrna nods her head, her brow furrowed. "That was . . . extraordinary."

"Thank you," I say. My demeanor is all seriousness.

Myrna crosses her arms across her chest. "What the hell does it mean?"

My face gives up a smirk. "Sorry. It's the Roy Batty death soliloquy from one of my favorite old movies. A sci-fi flick called Blade Runner."

"I like it," says Myrna simply. "But what about you? Real life?"

"Real life is over-rated," I say. "Roy Batty's speech is from a movie, but it doesn't mean I can't relate to it. I've had a good run, experienced love, loss, the whole shebang."

"In real life or on movie screens?"

"What difference does it make?" I say, trying to sound indifferent. "I still had the experiences."

"There's a difference between living them and watching them."

"That is a matter of opinion. I've been to funerals that left me unmoved, yet I've seen movies that leave me in tears. Which one had the greater impact?"

"It is not the funeral that leaves the impact," says Myrna soberly, "it is the person the funeral is for."

I have no response other than a feeble shrug.

Myrna lets the silence hang for in the air longer than is necessary. She's making a point, and I am trying to ignore it. Eventually, she taps out a note on her glass tablet.

After a moment she looks up at me and says, "It is in my professional opinion you would make a strong candidate for the show, Frankie, and that saddens me."

"So, what are you saying?" I ask, blinking, a bit startled. "Does that mean I'm in?"

"I can't tell you at this moment," says Myrna. She really does look sad. "All I can say is that I will recommend that you would most likely draw an excellent audience. Your backstory, your personality, your profession, it all adds up to a likely ratings winner." Myrna pauses a moment to remove and polish her glasses. She looks back to me. "In the world of reality television, it's all about the personalities. Compelling personas drive the numbers. I've been doing this for some time now. I've learned that I'm quite good at knowing what the viewing public likes, and you, my dear, they will like very much." Myrna hands me the glass tablet. "Please place your hand on the surface for a thermal imprint. This gives us permission to move forward with the deliberation process."

I can feel my heart racing as I take the tablet and bring my palm to the glass but pause before I touch it. "Huh," I say.

"What?" asks Myrna.

"I'm literally signing my death warrant." I press my palm to the glass and hand it back to Myrna.

Myrna offers a wry but sad grin. "If I had a nickel for every time I'd heard that." She sets the glass tablet on the table between us and stands up. I follow her lead.

"Any more interviews? Tests?" I ask, somewhat surprised that our interview is coming to an end. I was enjoying it. Well, most of it, beyond the Galen guilt trip.

Myrna seems to have aged over the last few hours.

Her shoulders are more slumped, her demeanor somber. "No more tests, Frankie."

"You get enough information from talking with me in just these past hours to determine whether I'm of sound mind and body and whether I'm not lying my ass off about everything I've said? Are you really that trusting?"

"There is more technology within a fifty-foot radius of where we're sitting than you can possibly comprehend. And it's all been focused directly on you."

"And I didn't feel a thing," I say, trying to cheer her up. It works, a little.

"I can't begin to tell you the number of hours that have been spent developing the questions I have been asking you. They have been tested and retested to reveal even the subtlest responses. For all intents and purposes, you have been laid bare."

"Really," I say, my tone laced with doubt.

"Really," says Myrna with a sad nod of her head.

We stand in silence. "Well then," I say. "Is this the time when you guys wipe my memory?"

"The process has already begun," she says.

"No shit," I say quietly. I look around the room. "Airborne?"

Myrna nods. "Tailored to your biology. Doesn't affect me."

"Huh. Am I going to start becoming more and more confused over the next few minutes or will I not even notice it?"

"You won't notice it."

"How long before . . ."

"In a few moments you will have forgotten who I am and where you are. I will escort you out. You'll be a bit puzzled but not alarmed. By the time you reach your car, the better part of this entire day will simply not have existed. And the thought of even coming here will never cross your mind. You will think, 'Oh, what was it I needed at the grocery store?' and off you will go, oblivious, ignorant, at complete peace."

"And my . . . death? It will happen when?'

"If you are chosen . . ."

"Which sounds like a foregone conclusion," I say. "Ratings, remember?"

"For legal reasons I am not at liberty to say at this point in time," says Myrna.

I reach out to shake Myrna's hand, but instead she moves in and hugs me, deeply. In my ear she softly says, "Goodbye Frankie."

CHAPTER 38

AUGUST

The night before the show I can hardly sleep. I try everything, I play virtually every hypnotic, trance-forming Pink Floyd tune I can think of to help me drift off, but I don't think I find a wink until well after 3 a.m. Then, when I do nod off, it's fitful. I'm awash in a toxic cocktail of stress, dread, and excitement. I fade in and out until I finally give up around 9 a.m.

"Big day today," intones a male voice, unusually cheerfully. It's not Orson's or Spencer's.

"Got that right," I reply with a grin to Mike, who's standing at the bedroom door, nursing a steaming cup of coffee in those massive hands of his. Hands, it occurs to me, that I feel immeasurably safe in.

"Can I interest you in a shower?" He asks haughtily. "102 or 104 today? A tad warmer to help loosen you up for tonight?" Mike asks, mimicking Orson surprisingly well.

"What are you, my mother?" I ask. "102 will be fine. But thanks for thinking of me."

"As you wish," he replies with a Wesley to Buttercup bow and turns for the bathroom. Over his shoulder he says, "I'll have a fresh brewed cup waiting for you when you get out."

I smile, lying in my bed, sprawled out, staring at the ceiling, wondering for the millionth time how I got here. My career is about to go full turbo, and I've got a guy in my life who makes me coffee and worries about the temperature of my shower. Despite my worry and sorrow over Galen, my life is as stable as it's ever been. It's beyond stable. "Life is good," I say to the ceiling. What a difference a year makes. Hell, nine months!

After breakfast I send Mike on his merry way so I can spend the rest of the day practicing my patter, going over my cues, and rehearsing down at the theater.

"Remember, Mr. Hasagawa said he was going to send a car for you, Galen, and Audrey at 5:30. Don't make me look bad by being late," I chide him with a smile.

"You kidding?" he says, practically glowing. "Biggest night of your life, you think I'm going to be late? And late to get a ride in a limo? Not a chance."

BEING ABLE TO rehearse with Bosco at the theater instead of my studio has made a huge difference. Everything feels different in the theater. There's a richness to the experience you can't get in the studio. Plus, the space is decidedly larger. I have room on stage to work, to pace, to find just the right angles. I worked it out with Dak that no one was allowed in the theater proper while I was rehearsing other than the lighting crew. I built Bosco on small caster wheels, so moving it around is a breeze—silent and smooth. Once it was into the building and backstage, I could literally move it out on stage myself. I even started coming in late at night after the theater was empty, so I could practice on my own. Well, almost all on my own. I still saw Big Wave Dave on a couple of occasions. I had no idea he worked that late or what he could possibly be doing at that late hour. Eight hours before showtime and I'm finally feeling good about everything. After the third walk-through, the lighting crew has their cues down tight.

After the final run-through I go home hoping for at least a couple of hours of R & R. No dice. I'm a nervous wreck. Mike leaves me an appropriately over-the-top pep talk message on my optic. How tonight is going to be the show of my life.

I love it.

He says he'll meet me in my dressing room.

At 3 p.m. Audrey arrives and does her fashion voodoo. I've still got my eclectic-chic going on, but the loving Audrey touch magically takes it up a notch or two. Of course, it helped that she brought a few articles from her own collection to breathe some fresh air into my ensemble. She breaks out her sorcerous pink box of war paint and takes ten years off my face. I roll up to the theater at 5 p.m. and touch base with Tim and his team one more time. Everything is a go.

I stroll out front to the theater lobby and enjoy the pre-show silence. Well, semi-silence. The theater staff are giddy with excitement and Dak is pacing a trench in the rugs. I see Baltic at the bar with Scotty and pull up a seat.

Scotty whips me up a Gin Fizz. No other acknowledgement.

Baltic meets my gaze evenly.

"How you feeling?" I ask him.

"Feeling good," he says.

I look him square in the eye and see no sign of nerves. What is it with this kid? We sit quietly, sipping our drinks, enjoying the calm before the storm. Dak steps lively back into the lobby, eyes fixed on his watch.

"Five minutes, people! Five minutes till we open the doors."

On any other night I'd sit tight and happily chat up audience members at the bar until maybe thirty minutes before the show started, but tonight I make an early exit. I give a nod to Scotty, clap Baltic on the shoulder, and peel off toward the theater. When I walk into the main hall, I stand beside the steps that lead up to the stage and take in the space. The ushers are doing last minute checks, same goes for the stage and light crews. Everyone is laser focused.

"Frankie."

I look to my left and see Tim, the lighting chief walking down the aisle toward me.

"What's up, Tim?"

He stops before me, hands on hips. "Me and the fellas have a little something extra for you during your show tonight." He sees the shift in my eyes and that I'm about to say something and he quickly places a reassuring hand on my shoulder. "Don't worry. Nothing out of our normal cues. Think of it as simply an extra layer of light, a little spice for the meal, courtesy of the house." I obviously still have a look of incredulity on my face because he steps back, hands up in supplication. "Trust me."

"You know I don't like surprises, Tim. I like to know exactly what's going to happen when it's supposed to happen. You don't spring something like this on me right before showtime."

Tim still hasn't lost his smile. He slow steps backwards up the aisle. "Trust me."

There's nothing more for it. I suppose I could demand that he not do whatever he is going to do but I've known Tim a long time and the guy's aces. A lighting whiz. I do trust him. Of course, he knows that if his lighting shenanigans blow up in my face, I'm going to hunt him down and gut him like a fish.

I mount the steps, walk to the center of the stage, and look out upon the empty seats. It occurs to me one last time that in a couple of hours my life will be different. I wonder how much it will change. If the show goes the way I hope, my prospects will undergo a tectonic shift. If I fall on my face? Well, I try to avoid letting my mind wander down that path. I turn and head to my dressing room. Time to get my game face on.

My dressing room is more akin to a generously appointed closet. It's so small, as the joke goes, I have to step outside to change my mind. When I approach the room, I see a Dak flourish that's never been there before: a star on the door, just like you see in the movies, with my name above it. I whip out my optic and take a photo because evidently, I'm more of an emotional sap than I'm willing to admit.

My dressing room is made up of a table with the requisite mirror framed with makeup lights, a rack to hang clothes, and an extra chair. Thus endeth the nickel tour. I suspect church confessionals are roomier.

I set my optic on the counter and ask Spencer to play me my new pre-show playlist. I've been working on it for a while, precisely curating the tone and mood I feel I'm going to need tonight. There's a movie from I think the early 2000s called *High Fidelity* where a record store owner played by John Cusack takes tremendous pride in creating mix tapes, back when music was played on tapes. There's a scene in the movie where he goes over the subtle art, the rules, of creating said tapes. The rules don't necessarily apply to my current situation, but I can appreciate the sentiment. My mix runs the gamut, but I finish it with "The Great Gig in the Sky" off *Dark Side of the Moon* for no other reason than it's my favorite Pink Floyd song and totally kicks ass. The song has no lyrics, for the most part it's singer Clare Torry wailing along with the instrumental. Allegedly, it's about death and dying, but I've always felt it sounded more like an extended orgasm. All I know is I love, love, love it. I turn the lights off, kick back, prop my feet up on the other chair, close my eyes, and let the music have its way with me.

When I finish listening, my emotions have been thoroughly wrung from me. As the last chords of the piano and Clare's voice dissipate, I slowly open my eyes. After a moment, the silence is broken by the artificial intelligent voice of my optic, Spencer, who sounds completely in awe.

"Damn."

A SOFT KNOCK at my dressing room door brings me back to the moment.

"Come in," I say.

The door cracks and the space is filled with red roses. The roses speak.

"Delivery for you, Ms. Percival." Missy, the quiet, unassuming new stage tech steps through, carrying what looks to be her weight in flowers. She sets the enormous bouquet on the counter along with several notes and several other smaller bouquets of flowers.

"Thanks, Missy," I say, but what I'm thinking is, Shit! No flowers before a performance! It's an old theatrical superstition. Flowers after, great. Flowers before, bad luck. But I keep this to myself. As Missy shyly edges back toward the door she says, eyes cast down. "This is so exciting, Miss Percival."

"Thanks again, Missy. I appreciate it. More than you know. Now, go give Baltic his pep talk."

She slips out the door, leaving me in a tiny room that has suddenly become even tinier, taken over by a substantial floral convention. I try to shake off the pre-flower juju and pick up the notes. The first one, the one that came with the huge bouquet of roses, is from Grayson Hasagawa, wishing me luck. The second, attached to a smaller, but equally pretty, collection of white and yellow roses is from Mike. It says break a leg, or knock 'em dead, or whatever it is that fancy-schmancy show biz people say before a show. Below the message and above his name he drew a little heart with an arrow through it. Touching. But I wonder why he didn't wait to give me the roses in person. I look at the time, it's still early. He hasn't even been picked up yet. I debate giving him a call, but do I really want to be the needy girlfriend? I can wait.

The last bouquet is made up of bright, happy looking daisies. They're from Audrey wishing me well and reminding me that I'm fookin' brilliant. I read a handful of other notes from assorted other well-wishers. One, however grabs my attention. It's big, bright, and gaudy, with two words across the front in large red block letters that read Hey, You! I open it up and inside are three other words, small, centered, printed in Galen's unmistakably careful hand: Don't screw up.

CHAPTER 39

The *Death Warrant* operations room is filled with technicians, engineers, and the full complement of television crew members. It is a study in controlled chaos, people milling about, orders shouted into headsets, deep conversations held in tight groups, all with a singular purpose: to put on a smooth event and air a clean show.

Sheila Graveman takes her usual seat near the back of the operations room where she has a clear view of all the monitors that fill the wall. There must be at least fifty screens, all currently active. It takes a small army of camera operators and well-hidden autonomous cameras to capture the event in its final moments. She checks the time: 5:35 p.m. They would send out the notification in thirty minutes. She likes to arrive early to help answer any questions the director might have leading up to the execution. She found it ironic that this really was the only word they could use to describe what they were attempting to pull off. They were executing a task, a job, while at the same time they were executing a person. Or rather, they were participating in the "passing" of a "soul." This event has been a particularly challenging and enjoyable project to work on. It has been seven months in the works and gone through a bit of a redirect halfway through. By her estimation her creative team has outdone themselves on the method of the termination, with Frankie's help, she has to admit. It has tremendous artistic flair. She knows the ratings are going to be off the charts.

She watches impassively as a heated argument grows between the director, executive producer, and a small, mousy woman she doesn't recognize. Best to keep above the politics was her attitude. From what she can hear, the argument is around the black-out space. The director, Paola Sabatini, clearly feels that his points can be made stronger by making his arm and hand gestures more expansive, in true Italian fashion. The executive producer, Klaus Manfred, stands with arms crossed, patiently tolerating the director's gesticulations. Perhaps he is waiting for him to tire himself out. The small mousey woman interjects every now and then when the director takes a pause to catch his breath.

"This is a decision that should have been made weeks ago, not two hours before airtime. We have crews posted all over the city!" says Sabatini.

The director hates unknowns. The only person who dislikes them even more is the large man standing across from him, Klaus. The big German has listened to Paolo's concerns quietly, yet intently, and is about to make an executive decision.

"Three-hundred-mile blackout," says Klaus.

"Three-hundred miles? Are you crazy?" barks the small woman, her mousiness all gone. She only comes up to Klaus Manfred's chest but at this moment she seems to fill a larger space. "Do you have any idea how many people will not be able to watch because of your excessive blackout? We're not only losing the Portland market, but Seattle as well! Those are top-twenty-five markets!"

Sheila now knows exactly who the woman is: the sales director. If there is anything Sheila has learned in her dealings with the business world it is that you do not fuck with the bottom line.

Klaus Manfred is not impressed.

He hates salespeople. He understands the importance of the financial aspects of the business, but he also understands the assorted other moving parts that make it possible to charge the exorbitant rates the woman before her charges.

"It's a necessary precaution," he explains in a tone he feels is conciliatory. "Very famous, very important people are attending this event. The moment we go on the air and show the location, people will try to communicate with anyone they know in attendance. These people have a higher-than-average web of contacts. Even if nothing beyond 911 calls can go in or out of the blackout ring, people have been known to try to make contact. You're lucky I'm only making it a 300-mile blackout. With this audience, even that may not do the trick. If I had the means, it would be even bigger. I'm trying to hedge our bets and still get the biggest audience possible."

"But 300 miles? That's absurd! We've never imposed anything this large before. Not even close. The FCC is going to have a fit! The police will have a fit!"

"We'll fix that bridge afterwards," says Klaus. "We have the opportunity of a lifetime here and all it will take is one over-zealous fan to screw it all up. Trust me, the moment this goes public, people will jump in their cars or Lear jets and race to the theater to get up close and personal. With a three-hundred-mile blackout radius someone would have to leave within minutes of getting pinged, know exactly where they were going, and not run into any traffic. So, technically I should be imposing a 400-mile blackout radius to be perfectly safe."

"That is unacceptable," says the sales director defiantly.

Klaus Manfred neither has the time nor the inclination for this. He most decidedly does not like having to explain his actions, and this little twig of a woman is starting to get on his nerves. When he next speaks, his accent is much more pronounced, as are the tendons on his bull neck. He uncrosses his arms and leans down to be eye to eye with the diminutive sales director, and then speaks in a low but powerful voice that anyone within the room can hear, "I'm giving you two choices: You either shut the fuck up right now and leave, or I can promise you beyond any promises you have heard in your pathetic money-grubbing little life that staying in this control room and bugging me with any more black-out radius bullshit will be the worst decision you have ever made or will ever make. You will look back on this day while you're standing in the unemployment line wondering how you fell so far so fast. I will make it my personal mission to lay a strip of napalm across your career and then salt the earth where it once stood. I will go Old Testament on you."

The sales director doesn't blink an eye. The woman has sand. All she says is, "Okay, then, make it a good show." She turns and walks out of the control room with absolutely no sense of urgency.

Remind me never to screw with either of those two people, thinks Sheila Graveman.

The in-house drama concluded; Sheila notices another woman across the room. It's the secret weapon, Marguerite Aubuchon.

She is the one freelancer with which Sheila has had frequent personal contact. Since the creative all hinges on the execution, it is necessary to communicate directly with the person pulling the metaphorical trigger. You don't want to lose anything in third-party translation. Sheila joins Paolo and the two of them walk up to Marguerite.

"Ms. Aubuchon," says Sheila respectfully. "Glad you could join us."

"My pleasure," says Marguerite.

"Paolo tells me everything is in place on your end, as per usual. I can't thank you enough for your attention to detail. It's always a joy to work with professionals such as yourself."

"Thank you, and I would also like to say I've been impressed with your creativity on this project. It really is a stroke of genius. Blowing up the client in a fiery explosion at the precise moment she and her audience are expecting to see her engulfed in flames? I can't help wonder how many in the audience are going to wonder if it's all part of the act."

"I was wondering the same thing," admits Paolo. "The viewers will know she's been blown up for real but the people in the theater will have no idea. Priceless."

"How are you able to manage an explosion that tightly controlled? Grayson Hasagawa and other notables will be sitting barely ten yards away. Is there any concern of them being injured by flying debris?"

"Well, I can't say there's no risk, but I feel I've mitigated it pretty thoroughly. The explosive charge is set to blow up and back. The heavy velvet stage curtain behind her should protect the backstage crew and little of the box that she's in should blow forward. We still want good visuals, so I've woven, for lack of a better term, "confetti" into her stage prop, so that there will be a fair amount of detritus falling in the air afterwards. It's going to look like right after the Super World Bowl. The concussion will radiate almost exclusively upward with a blast radius of only about thirty feet. It's some of my best work, I must say. I'm immensely proud of what I've created here."

"And it will be appreciated by what I'm guessing to be a record audience," says Sheila. "Your work will be part of an historic event. Tonight, we're creating high art."

CHAPTER 40

At precisely 6 p.m. Pacific Standard Time, 8 p.m. local time, Michael T. Gaines is standing in the parking lot of The Old Grind Restaurant in downtown Lindsborg, Kansas (aka Little Sweden, pop. 3473) on a break. He is all alone and dwelling on how dead the little town is and how boring mid-western life can be, especially for a seventeen-year-old. Michael glances down at the ground and counts the Nic-Sticks. Seven of them. All his, all from this week. When cigarettes and vaping went by the wayside, there was no lacking in companies ready to fill the profitable addiction vacuum. Thus, Nic-Sticks. Michael can't be sure, but he believes he may be one of only a handful of "Nics" left in the Lindsborg city limits. Seems like everyone has caved to the incessant anti-nicotine campaigns that litter the airwaves and Internet. Even his old man, a hard-core Nicker in his prime and the man who'd led Michael down the addictive road, had thrown in the towel. Of course, the cardiac event that had landed him in the ER might have had something to do with it. At 6:05 Michael T. Gaines' optic chirps. And keeps chirping. Michael looks at it and immediately drops his stick. It's a *Death Warrant* notification. Someone is about to take the dirt nap. It's the first show in months. Michael rushes inside, and sure enough, more than half the staff and customers have their eyes riveted to their optics. Saturday night isn't going to be so boring after all. All over the world, millions of people watch TVs, video monitors, optics, and whatever other device they can to see how some poor soul is going to meet their maker.

As people watch they see that the star of tonight's show is a woman by the name of Frances Grace "Frankie" Percival, a professional mentalist of all things. They learn that she committed to the show to help provide for her younger brother. The viewers learn of the brother's early promising life and career and how it was brought down amid a pile of twisted metal in the blink of an eye. The piece, interwoven with old photos and footage of Galen, along with hidden camera clips of him at the children's hospital, paint him as nothing short of a saint. People all over the world weep openly. Frankie receives equally glowing coverage. A story of a determined, but altruistic woman who pulled herself up by her bootstraps, making a career for herself on the unforgiving stages of the theater world. But her days of scraping by had finally come to an end. She had been handed the keys to the castle, the goose that laid the golden egg, she had been offered the opportunity of a lifetime—a command performance by none other than one of the richest and most influential men in the world, Grayson Hasagawa. There was no question that her career was about to shoot through the stratosphere. If only she wasn't going to die that same night. The irony is breathtaking.

CHAPTER 41

Klaus Manfred stands in back of the *Death Warrant* control room taking in the show. With a wave of his hand, he calls over one of his junior producers.

"Cue the accidents," whispers the big man. "Do you understand?"

The junior producer nods and whispers back, "Not a single car will get in or out of Portland through any of the major highways for the next two hours." He turns on his heel and is out the door. No one notices him leaving the room. All eyes are fixed to the screens. Within fifteen minutes, three massive accidents paralyze traffic outside the city proper. One, a tanker spill, another a four-car pile-up, and the third, a distraught man threatening to leap off an overpass.

Within thirty minutes, the backups are two miles long. In forty-five, six miles.

PAOLO IS IN his element. The prepackaged pieces are beautifully produced and set the proper tone for the evening. His eyes dart from screen to screen without conscious thought. He is in the zone. He knows which cameras to cut to purely on instinct. Everything feels like it is moving in slow motion. It is all coming together effortlessly.

Sheila Graveman stands in back halfway between Klaus and Marguerite Aubuchon. Everything she's painstakingly crafted for the show is falling into place. The beauty of it all is that the viewer has no idea how the grand finale is going to play out. They don't know if Frankie is going to take a bullet or be attacked on stage by a knife-wielding maniac, or what. It is the suspense that makes the show such a winner. She can't wait to see the reaction shots of the general public that always find themselves posted online right after a particularly surprising ending. Tonight, the Internet is going to be overflowing with them.

Sheila peeks down at Marguerite. The woman is as actively engaged in the show as anyone. Sheila edges down to where Marguerite is sitting and sidles up next to her.

"Enjoying the show?"

Marguerite, her eyes never leaving the monitors says, "Outstanding." She turns to Sheila, true, raw emotion in her eyes. "Truly outstanding. You should be proud."

Sheila basks in the woman's compliment before turning her own eyes to the wall of screens. In a moment the Odeon's opening act will be taking stage. Forty-five minutes until all of Sheila's long hours of work come together.

"May I ask a professional question?" asks Sheila.

Marguerite turns to face her, giving Sheila her full attention. She loves explaining her craft. "Of course."

"How long did it take you to install the explosive device into Ms. Percival's set piece? What did she call it?"

"Bosco," says Marguerite. "The installation only took a few nights. It was the reconnaissance and pre-production that took well over three months."

"I have to say, the character you played, well, let's just say I was an instant fan. And your performance? Brilliant. Oscar-worthy," says Sheila.

"Thank you, I liked her as well."

"You vanished into her so completely. It's hard for me to reconcile the woman you are sitting here with the woman you were playing. What was her name?"

"Cloris. Cloris Bellweather," says Marguerite Aubuchon with a smile.

CHAPTER 42

I've never been part of an event like this so I'm not sure if I want to stick with my normal pre-show routine. On any other night I would have hung out in the lobby with the crowd to take their temperature, see how they look, how they feel, maybe get a sense of who might be a good volunteer to bring up on stage. But not tonight. My adrenaline is redlining as it is and I'm afraid if I look out front and see a packed house full of swells, knowing full well that my career is about to rest in their manicured hands, I might get a bad case of the oh-my-gods and freak. I could sit tight until my five-minute warning and then take the stage sight unseen but then I wouldn't see Baltic's set and I would never forgive myself if I missed that. Tonight's my night but Baltic's got skin in the game too. If he does well, it could also raise his profile. Even if I didn't mix and mingle with the crowd, I was at least hoping to see Mike before the show. Have him settle me down. But he still hasn't called back. I determine that I can't dwell on that right now. Gotta keep my eye on the ball. Maybe his optic's battery died. He's notoriously lax about charging it. I take one last look at myself in the mirror, give myself a short salute, and head out the door.

We're ten minutes before Baltic is scheduled to perform and I find him standing in the wings talking with the stage manager; he's in full makeup and costume. His new performance is clown based, but not the circus ha-ha type you might be thinking of. His is more in line with the cirque clowns, those that are drier, more thoughtful.

He was telling me his routine is based on an old Russian clown's performance from decades ago. Baltic is dressed in massively oversized clothing, all pale blues, and whites. He's swimming in his clothing. His makeup is simple with little adornment. A whitewash with colored cheekbone highlights, his hair a white fright wig sticking out in every conceivable direction. He looks like the bastard child of Albert Einstein and, frankly, I'm not sure who. Some woman with equally crazy-ass hair. He sees me approach and flashes me a preternaturally calm looking smile.

"Ready, kid?" I ask.

"Guess I better be," says Baltic.

We both drift over to the edge of the stage and look out to the portion of the theater that we can see from our angle. Nearly every seat is filled, and the crowd is passing the time making small talk. I watch a few lucky photographers snapping off photos of the who's who in attendance, their cameras quickly panning left and right. I'm guessing no matter which direction they aim their lenses will fall on someone whose photo will fetch a price.

I can see Hasagawa in the front row next to his stunning wife. He's leaning into her, whispering something that evidently, she finds funny. The seat on the other side of him which was reserved for his assistant sits empty. Further down the row I see the seats for Mike, Galen and his freshly minted significant other, Tonya, also empty. Odd.

They should have been here by now. Been here more than half an hour ago. Traffic can't be that bad. Flat tire? I can't help but feel a slight sense of worry drifting toward full on concern. I check my optic again. Nothing. I'm about to go down to ask Hasagawa, but an excited voice stops me.

"Heck of a night! Heck of a night!" I hear from over my shoulder, and I turn just in time to see Dak striding up, practically aglow. "By golly, this one's going to be for the record books, as sure as I'm standing here." It's like his excitement has cranked up the levels of his G-rated exclamations. He looks over at Baltic. "Ready to knock 'em for a loop, Sport?"

"Yep," is all Baltic says.

Dak turns to me. "And how about you, Miss How-do-you-do? Ready for the first day of the rest of your life?"

I do my best to regroup. "Ready as I'll ever be, Dak."

"Fire and Ice! Great theme for the show. Can't wait to see how they react," says Dak excitedly.

"That makes two of us," I say. The fire and ice thing he's talking about is how we promoted the event. I'm the fire, Baltic's the ice. My routine has a flame element and Baltic's evidently has a chilly angle to it.

I haven't been able to see his rehearsals; he was as secretive as me, but I know it's cold-related to keep to the theme.

Dak slaps his hands together and rubs them like he's trying to keep warm. "So, we're all good? Excellent. Good." He's not really sure what to do or say after that so he turns on his heel and rushes off to expend a few more ounces of nervous energy.

I glance over at Baltic. He's looking at the crowd on the backstage monitor, a peaceful look on his face. There's a wide-angle lens on the camera that's set centered above the curtain, so the edges of the crowd curl up a bit on the screen.

"Aren't you the least bit nervous?" I ask.

Baltic glances my way, a small grin bends his lips. "Naw. Not really," he says.

"How?" I ask. "How is that possible? I feel like I'm going to need a paper bag to breathe into any minute, but you look like you've popped a Valium. What gives?"

"Don't get me wrong," he says. "I'm excited, just not nervous. Want to know why? Because I've left nothing on the table. Virtually every waking hour since you invited me to join in on tonight, I've been practicing. Like you. I can do my bit in my sleep. I can do it backwards. I can do it blindfolded. I haven't been on a date, I haven't seen my friends, this is all I've done, prepare for this."

"Failure to prepare is preparing to fail," I say.

"That's good," Baltic says with a smile. "That should be in a fortune cookie."

I involuntarily laugh. "Then the show is in good hands," I say. I think about what Baltic just said. He's spent virtually every waking hour preparing for this. Have I? Before I met Mike, absolutely. Since then? The show's still been my priority, but it occurs to me that it hasn't been my entire life. I happily admit to myself that regardless of tonight's outcome, he's still going to be there for me. Hopefully to celebrate with instead of picking up the pieces. So where is he? And Galen? With a subtle shake of my head, I bring my mind back to the present. "Are all your props ready?"

"Yep," he says. "And I've gone over all the blocking and timing with the stage and lighting crews until they're sick of me."

"Well, then, guess we better get to the starting blocks."

"Guess we better," he says with a smile. Before I turn away, he says, "Hey, Frankie?" I stop.

"Yeah?"

"Give 'em hell, tonight."

"Hey," I say with a smirk, "I'm fire. That's what I do."

FIVE MINUTES BEFORE showtime the backstage warning lights blink off and on a couple of times, our cue to hoof it to our places. I walk around back to where Bosco is standing idly, waiting for his big moment. Missy, the new stagehand, was kind enough to offer to keep an eye on it, and prying eyes off it while I was in my dressing room. I thank Missy and send her on her way before I give Bosco a once-over for the thousandth time. Everything looks copacetic. I weave through the busy stagehands back to the wings, so I can watch Baltic's performance. I can't wait to see how it plays. The stage lights dim and the crowd ebbs into silence. I steal one more look toward Mike and Galen's seats, but it's too dark to see anything. A disc of light appears stage right at a microphone stand and Dak Pressley steps into the light from off stage.

"Ladies and gentlemen, I am Dak Pressley, owner of the Odeon Theater, and I cannot tell you how happy we are to have you here tonight for this remarkable evening." He turns his focus to Hasagawa in the front row. A smaller spotlight lands on him. "And we have Grayson

Hasagawa to thank for that." The crowd applauds and Hasagawa waves appreciatively. Dak continues. "With his help, and your kind participation, we have raised enough money to keep the Odeon and the local arts alive for the foreseeable future." More applause. Dak raises his hands to quiet the crowd. "And now, without further ado, may I introduce to you a performer you may not know, but whose name soon will be on the lips of every man, woman and child who still have a passion for the lost art of the laugh. Who find wonder in a smile, and who understand what the late great Charlie Chaplin meant when he said a day without laughter is a day wasted." Like I said, Dak knows his introductions. "Ladies and gentlemen, may I introduce to you, the icy half of our Fire and Ice performance tonight—Baltic Jones."

The crowd cheers heartily as the velvet curtain rises to an empty stage. The music begins. It's a jaunty piece, playful and old. The primary instrument, a calliope, has a vintage circus vibe to it. Baltic appears stage left dragging an immense suitcase. It's nearly half his size. He pulls it a few feet, wipes his brow, and turns to look up, like a man evaluating the sky for rain. He holds his hand out, palm up and immediately takes on a look of consternation. Clearly the existing weather simply will not do. He lays the suitcase down, pops the latches and opens it up. He reaches inside and takes out a large piece of paper which he then proceeds to tear into tiny bits. He throws the bits of paper high into the air, and they begin to flutter down around him like snow. But the snow continues to fall. It's like the bits of paper multiplied and have created their own little weather system around him. A soft sprinkling of flakes drifts down from the rafters and lightly swirls around him. He looks around seemingly satisfied and reaches back inside his suitcase. He then proceeds to extract from it a wooden folding chair and a ridiculously elaborate multi-layered white frosted cake. He balances the cake precariously in one hand while he tries to unfold the chair with the other. The chair is being uncooperative. He uses one of his feet to pin part of it down while trying to open the chair and only succeeds in becoming more entangled with the chair. It's the classic scenario: the clown doesn't see the simple solution to extricating himself from the chair and unfolding it. The tension exists from what the audience can see but the clown can't. Add to that the constant fear that he's going to drop the gorgeous cake at any moment, and you can practically see the audience members' sphincters puckering up. The room is fully engaged in the on-stage battle between man and chair. If you've ever heard the term Chaplin-esque, this is it in spades. The routine goes on for a few minutes and the penultimate moment comes when Baltic must set the cake on the chair seat so that he has both hands free. You can practically hear the audience groan with delight when they realize he's unaware that he's going to sit on the cake. He stops short, of course, with a wag of his finger to the audience—breaking the fourth wall—as if to say, "Ah, ah, ah, nope." At which point he picks up the cake, eases himself into the chair, produces a fork out of one of his many pockets, gently takes a bite . . . and then spits out the cake like it's made of rat poison. All that work and the cake is lousy. The crowd roars. He looks at the traitorous cake and promptly throws it across the stage where it lands perfectly inside the suitcase which then magically closes on impact. The crowd erupts in cheers.

Baltic's portion of Fire and Ice is a thirty-minute set. He runs through three more thoughtful, beautiful, and frequently hilarious bits, each more compelling than the last, and all are performed throughout his gentle snow shower. But it's his finale that's for the books. He's finishing up his final routine which centers around his interaction with a dancing and multiplying ball of fairy light that seems to have a personality all its own—it's a spin on the iconic Disney Sorcerer's Apprentice with the fairy light taking the place of the animated brooms—all the while accompanied by the quieter and more passive yet menacing portions of the unmistakable "O Fortuna" from Carl Orff's *Carmina Burana*. It's a cut of classical music every person on the planet has heard at one time or another, most likely during a movie trailer for an epic blockbuster. Right when the song hits the big operatic portion with the now dozens of fairy lights bewildering the hapless Baltic, he finds himself entangled in huge waves of white gossamer, like a cocoon, while the back curtain opens, and an absolute blizzard of snow-like confetti powered by enormous hurricane force fans and blinding light blast out past the struggling Baltic, engulfing the audience in a massive snowstorm. It is epic! The audience are thrilled and flabbergasted by the spectacle and showmanship. No one saw it coming and they are loving it. Me included.

After a moment the storm subsides, and the crowd is on their feet cheering while Baltic stands, smiling bashfully on stage amid a slowly dying stream of fluttering white.

And this I must follow.

When Baltic walks off stage, I'm the first to meet him with a nonchalant tipping back and forth of my hand, the international signal for Not Bad. But I can't keep up the charade. I break into a huge smile and engulf him in a hug.

"I have witnessed greatness!" I yell into his ear just as several other backstage hands and managers descend on him.

I peer back out onto the stage to see Dak step out from the wings into the spotlight, letting the audience know that there will be a short intermission as we clean up the snowstorm and prepare for the Fire portion of the evening. The crowd applauds as one while the auditorium lights come on and the patrons excitedly talk amongst themselves at what they just saw.

As stagehands position Bosco behind the second curtain, I take a few minutes to go over my patter and focus. It is at this instant that I have a moment of astonishing clarity. I know that it will be Baltic who is the star of tonight, not me. He's the one who's going to earn the headlines, the one who's going to be catapulted into stardom. When it's all said and done everyone will be wondering why I wasn't opening for him. There's a scene near the end of the classic movie *The Hustler*, where

Paul Newman's Fast Eddie is playing pool against Jackie Gleason's Minnesota Fats and after hours of play Fats says, "I can't beat you, Eddie. You're too good." That's precisely what I'm thinking. Baltic is the headliner and I'm the warmup band. Or will be after tonight. And here's the weirdest part of this epiphany: I don't care. For months all I've ever wanted was for this night to launch me into the topic of conversation. Instead, it's going to be someone else. Someone more talented, more disciplined, and more deserving. And I couldn't be more pleased. I have Mike. I have Galen. I'll still have a cool job. I think back to my moment in bed that morning staring at the ceiling. "Life is good," I say to myself with a growing smile.

I look over Bosco one last time, running a hand over his surface and say, "Well, Chief, let's go down swinging. Let's try to at least make it a coin flip by the time it's all said and done."

CHAPTER 43

Dak's introduction for me is no less colorful than the one for Baltic and no less full of hokum and humbuggery, which I appreciate. I look out across the audience feeling strangely calm, a far cry from where I was a mere hour ago. Perhaps seeing Baltic absolutely crush it took the edge off. All I know is that I'm completely and totally at ease. I am in my element. I look down at Hasagawa and give him a wink. I then look over to Mike and Galen's seats and find that they're still empty. In a split second, all sorts of bad-ending scenarios flash through my head. But the scenarios are short lived. They both had flowers sent to my dressing room, after all. They must be here somewhere. They could be in the bathroom for all I know. I regroup and soldier on.

There's still electricity in the air, residue from Baltic's performance. The crowd is thinking if the opening act is that good the headliner must be a killer.

I dive right in to try to prove their hopes are not unfounded.

The first bit focuses on me bringing a couple of people up on stage and me asking one of them to write down a vacation that was a particularly big deal to them, while I have the other write out a series of numbers that pop into their head.

I won't bore you with the details, but it involves multiple people on stage, felt pens, manila envelopes, puzzlement, confusion, and finally gasps and applause when the revealed numbers—8,3,7,1,2,3—when inverted have the approximate shape of letters that spell out the vacation destination—B,E,L,I,Z,E.

One bit down, four to go.

THE NEXT SEGMENT of my act is some good old-fashioned hypnosis. Always a crowd pleaser. See, mentalism is not bright and shiny yet it captures people's imagination. It's all about wonderment, something we lose as we get older, yet desperately miss. I live for seeing astonishment and joy on people's faces. And, tonight, I get to dish it out in healthy portions.

I take an elderly and dignified looking gentleman who is most likely some Forbes magazine captain of industry and proceed to hypnotize him into thinking he's a belly dancer. I convince a matronly woman that she's a pro wrestler heel called the Shadow of Death. I then take a local television news anchor and within minutes he's bobbing his head, flapping his wings, and clucking like a chicken. It's all harmless good fun and makes the audience absurdly happy. Silliness will never go out of style. But it's time to ratchet up the holy-crap factor before we reach the finale.

Remember what I said about John Cusack in the movie High Fidelity talking about the rules of making mix tapes? It's the same for laying out a performance. You want to start fast, grab attention, then dial it back a little, lull the audience into a false sense of security before ramping it up at the end to culminate in the closing explosion.

It was time for the ramp up.

THIS ONE'S NOT an overly big bit, again, not flashy, but never fails to make an impression. I begin by lugging out a book. But not just any book, it's got to be a big book. Big, intimidating and a book everyone recognizes. That book, of course is *War and Peace*. Tolstoy's epic 1,225-page tome broadly focusing on Napoleon's invasion of Russia in 1812. The book everyone knows but few have read. For the act I found the largest copy I could find, thus the lugging. It's a good foot and a half tall, six inches thick and weighs about the same as a newborn baby. A fat one. I make a big show of dragging it up onto a small table, center stage. It lands with a satisfying boom that most likely is heard in the lobby.

"This is *War and Peace*," I say. "How many of you have read it?" I ask the audience. A couple dozen raise their hands. "Liars," I say dismissively, which garners a good laugh. "I need someone to volunteer another volunteer. In other words, volunteer your friend, husband, wife, whatever." I do this to help alleviate any suspicions that I'm picking a plant. I mean, I still could do it that way, but allowing an audience member to make the selection seems more credible. I point to a woman about halfway back, right-center audience. "Who would you like to embarrass?" She indicates to another woman next to her who looks appropriately red-cheeked. I point to the woman and tell her to stand up. "Your name?"

"Rebecca," she says.

"Do we know each other? Have we met?"

"No."

"Very well, Rebecca. I'd like you to pick a number between one and three."

"Three."

"Now a number between one and fifty."

"Eighteen," says Rebecca.

"Now a number between one and twenty-five," I say.

"Eleven."

"Excellent," I say. "Rebecca, you may take your seat. Thank you. You passed the test." I pace a little to the right side of the stage. "Three, eighteen, eleven. Those were Rebecca's numbers, yes?" The crowd indicates to the affirmative. I then take the right-hand stage steps down to the audience. The auditorium seats are broken up into three sections, left, center, right, with aisles running down between them. I point to the left section.

"One," I say. I point to the center section. "Two." And then to the right-hand section. "Three." I then walk up the right-center aisle counting the rows as I go. When I reach row eighteen, I stop. I then start counting seats beginning with the first seat on the aisle. "One, two, three . . ." When I reach seat eleven, I tell the person sitting there to stand up. A handsome middle-aged man with receding slate-gray hair and a sharp sports coat rises to his feet. "Your name, sir?"

"Ramon," he says with a hint of a Spanish accent.

"Ramon, if you would be so kind as to join me."

Once on stage I turn an appraising look on Ramon, complete with my go-to thoughtful pose: one crossed arm and my other elbow propped upon it, my knuckle at my lip.

I consider Ramon for a few seconds. Long enough for him to become uncomfortable.

"Ramon, are you a book guy?"

"I read," he says with a shrug.

"Then that officially makes you a book guy. Wonderful. The reason I ask is that for this to work I need someone who's really in tune with books. Someone who gets books and gives off a strong book vibe. Is that person you, Ramon?"

Ramon smiles and looks decidedly embarrassed. "Sure, I guess."

"Ramon, here's how this is going to work. I want you to join me here with this book." Ramon does as instructed. "I am going to start fanning through the pages of this enormous book, and you tell me to stop whenever you want." I open the book and, using two hands because the book is so thick, I begin riffling the pages. Within a couple of seconds Ramon tells me to stop. I'd made it through about an inch of pages. I lay the book open to that page. "Which side do you want me to use, left or right?

"Right," says Ramon.

"Now, I'm going to run my business card down the page, and you tell me when to stop." I'm about a third of the way down before he stops me. "Okay, Ramon, tell me the biggest word on that line."

Ramon steps over and peers at the page. "Humiliated," he says.

"Very well. Now, Ramon, I would like you to go down the steps and walk over to the center section of the audience." Ramon walks down, turns, and faces me, awaiting further instructions. "You see that woman there?" I'm pointing to a striking platinum blonde three seats to the right of Hasagawa. Ramon nods. "Please stand up, ma'am." She does. "Ramon, look at her seat." He pauses, the crowd laughs. "Her chair, Ramon. Her chair. Geez." Ramon looks under the woman's chair and removes a large piece of paper that was taped there. He holds it up. "Please bring it here." Ramon climbs the stairs and returns to me, center stage. "Ramon, please show the audience what's written on that paper." Ramon looks at the paper and flashes me a look. Sort of a, "You sure you want me to?" look. I nod to him, and he holds up the paper. I instantly turn to the crowd with a flourish, arms raised in a Ta-da! manner. But the crowd is silent. It's worse than silent. The only sounds are a few quiet groans and the odd squeak of springs as people shift uncomfortably in their chairs. I glance nervously in the direction of Ramon holding up the paper. On it in large hand-printed type it reads EMBARRASSED. If you've ever looked up the definition of irony you will most likely see a picture of me at this very moment. My face falls, my mouth stands agape. My hands drop to my sides, and I stride purposely over to Ramon and snatch the paper from his hands. I stare at it, then look back up to Ramon. "This wasn't the word?"

"No," says Ramon, looking thoroughly uncomfortable.

"You sure you didn't read it wrong?" I ask, sounding a little panicky. "I mean, embarrassed, humiliated, they mean virtually the same thing. You sure you didn't transpose them in your head? That can happen you know." Ramon shakes his head. I quick-step it back to the book and stare at it. I lean in for a closer look. I then try to wrestle the book off the table. The thing weighs a ton and I barely lift it off the table when I drop it to the stage floor. It lands with a resounding boom. I step around, placing myself between the book and the audience and squat down to pick the book back up. In that instance the audience erupts as if the Pencil-Necked Geeks had unexpectedly walked on stage. But I'm oblivious. I'm still squatted down, hunched over struggling with the book, trying my best to slip my fingers under it, but failing.

Ramon sees and hears the crowd erupt and with a curious expression walks over right in front of where I'm crouched down. He looks down at me and the puzzle pieces all come together. With me in this undignified position my blouse has hiked up and my pants have hiked down, revealing a large expanse of lower back and plumber's crack. And printed in large hand-printed type, right over the top third of my ass, it reads HUMILIATED. The applause hasn't died.

I finally give up on the book, still hunched over I turn and look back at the audience with an expression that basically says, "What the hell?" I stand up, dust myself off and with hands deeply in pockets, and looking decidedly abashed I thank Ramon for his help and apologize to the audience for my obvious failure as a mentalist.

When the crowd finally settles down, I take a deep breath and say, "Then I guess the only way I can redeem myself is with the grand finale. Trust me, it's going to be worth it. Totally make up for that epic failure."

And with that, the lights dim and two stagehands wheel Bosco out onto the stage. Baltic's performance was dynamic, theatrical, and finished on a decidedly high note. Now it's my turn.

CHAPTER 44

I instruct the audience that I am a mentalist, not a magician, but have decided to step into the world of illusion. Basically, adding an extra course to the evening's meal. I take Bosco by a corner and slowly spin it around, so everyone can see all sides of it.

Once back in its forward-facing position I begin my spiel.

"The world is made up of the elements: earth, air, fire and water. Tonight, let me introduce you to fire." On cue two short bursts of flame erupt up from Bosco's top, which elicits the prescribed response of oohs and ahs.

"We live in a world where perception and reality are frequently at odds. What you see is not always what is truly happening. Allow me to give you a demonstration." I open the front glass panel door of Bosco to reveal the compartment within. "What is one of the most destructive forces in nature?" I ask. Again, on cue, a burst of fire leaps out of the top of Bosco. "Correct," I say. "Fire." I pause for effect. "And tonight, I shall demonstrate just how destructive it can be, particularly to the human form." On that cue several jets of flame shoot into the open compartment from the encircling walls. No doubt the people in the front row can feel the heat. They lean back, startled.

The flames halt and I close the transparent front door. I then rap on the glass. "Ceramic glass. It can withstand temperatures of up to 1400 degrees. The walls within this box are also insulated ceramic. The heat can go in, but it can't get out. It's basically a blast furnace. An oven. And tonight, I will step inside this oven, and you will witness my cremation. Or at least, that's what you will perceive. As for the reality?"

I let the answer hang in the air.

I step back to the side of Bosco, raise my hands above my head, spread them wide and then bring them together with a loud clap. On the clap, the character of the entire theater changes. The stage goes dark all except a dim pool of light around Bosco. The constellation of lights adorning every square inch of Bosco bloom into life, glowing, pulsing, faintly chasing. Bosco becomes a living, breathing entity of light. At the same time the auditorium is awash in a cavalcade of mixing shades of purple, blue, orange, and white. It's like the light filling the space has been filtered through a multi-colored lava lamp and witnessed through a nervous system shot through with two tabs of acid. I wasn't quite expecting this; this extra layer of wow must have been orchestrated by Tim and his lighting magicians. I approve. The music accompanying all of this I've been curating and crafting for weeks. It's a milky tapestry of different aural tones. Nothing you can quite wrap your brain around as there is nothing to hold on to. It swirls, dances, moves like the equivalent of musical mercury. And it's building. The music then begins to take form, you can feel the elements of an orchestra bubbling to the surface. Before long, it has left its nebulous world and has become more recognizable. There's actual rhythm and cadence. And bass, lots of bass. You can feel it in your back teeth. It's a foundation of doom, of dread. When this happens, I open the glass door and step inside Bosco's closet-like chamber.

ON MOST OF the monitors in the *Death Warrant* control room, Frankie steps into the large starlit box on the Odeon theater stage. The tension and excitement in both the theater and control room is palpable. Paola is shouting instructions to half a dozen people. It is almost go-time, and every crew member must be completely dialed in. Paola checks with several of the camera operators who are hidden throughout the theater to ensure they have their shots ready and what to do after detonation. The cameras are next generation tech—so small and obscure they're virtually impossible to detect. Marguerite sits forward on her seat. This is her moment to shine as well. She's been doing this for quite a while, but still always has moment of doubt right before things go boom. She's never once had a misfire, but with anything mechanical, it's always possible. Paola glances over his shoulder at Marguerite, a smile on his face and she responds with a thumbs up. All systems are go. Marguerite had gone to great pains to rig the detonation trigger in a manner that posed the smallest threat of misfire. For most jobs she ties it to a simple switch or button. Push the button or pull the switch and boom. She has that as a back-up, but this time the primary triggering mechanism is heat activated. No buttons necessary. When the propane jets of flame blast into the main chamber and once a certain temperature is reached, the explosives are activated. The test blasts that Frankie did before she climbed inside primed the pump, as it were. Once the flames are fired for a second time and run for a couple of seconds, the temperature will reach its necessary threshold, and then, as play-by-play announcers say at the end of sporting events, it'll be all over but the shouting.

On the screens, Frankie stands inside the box with lights strobing and swirling about the theater. The music rumbles and builds. The atmosphere is truly enchanting. Startled audience members avert their eyes against the strobing lights, but the flashing ends only moments after it began. Within the glass fronted coffin, Frankie is clearly visible, standing perfectly still. She closes her eyes, and then the chamber is filled with jets of flame, engulfing Frankie to the point where you can barely see her through the fire. It truly is an astonishing effect. She throws her head back and screams as if sheer volume could douse the flames. Her hair ignites, her skin blackens and peels. Audience members gasp, scream and throw up their hands in alarm. Marguerite was as curious as everyone else in the control room how the mentalist was able to withstand the flames. Not that it would matter. She counts in her head. One, two, three . . .

And then it all blows to hell.

As far as explosions go, it is beautiful. Exactly the right amount of flame, a gorgeous blue/orange mix that just falls short of the theater ceiling. The concussive blast is equally impressive—loud, but not damaging. The box that seconds earlier had been holding Frankie is simply no longer there, replaced by a pile of flaming debris. The shrapnel field extends out thirty feet in every direction, falling short of the first row of seats. The air is filled with smoke and small bits of paper that twist and drift throughout the theater, reminiscent of Baltic's snowstorm effect. What else fills the air is screaming. Lots and lots of screaming. But these are screams of panic, not injury. Not a single paying audience member receives as much as a scratch. Marguerite could not look prouder if she had just given birth.

CHAPTER 45

"What the f. . . ?" That's all I get out of my mouth after a large, heavy body lands on top of me, knocking the wind from my lungs while my ears are ringing from a massive explosion right above my head. Until that moment, everything had worked perfectly. I'd climbed inside Bosco and waited for the strobes to kick in. With the sudden and rapid changes in light, the audience did not see the moment I dropped through the trapdoor. All they saw was the projected image of me in the exact location, in the exact same pose. They may have seen a short blur of movement, but with the chaotic lighting effects, it would be negligible. To their eyes, I was standing right inside the glass door, ready to be blasted with fire. I dropped through onto the three-foot-thick foam pad below and was preparing to finish the effect by racing out the below-stage-room side door only to appear in one of the theater aisles, perfectly unscathed, when I was buried by this enormous body.

That's also when the massive explosion happened right above me. Pieces of scorched wood hammer all around me, like they have been shot out of a cannon. Whoever this person on top of me is, their back just got blasted with shrapnel. As quick as the explosion happens and dissipates the body is off me and a powerful hand takes mine and pulls me to my feet. It takes me a moment to regain my bearings. Everything sounds dull in my ears, like my hearing is running at about 25 percent. The person lets go of my hand and proceeds to slap away pieces of smoking debris that are lodged in his clothing.

It's then that I realize that he's wearing something large and bulky, like an olive-green padded space suit. A second look confirms to me what it really is, a bomb-disposal outfit. When he takes off his helmet, I can see his face and I become even more confused. The face looking back at me is that of the theater's custodian, Big Wave Dave.

"Are you hurt?" he asks, while at the same time turning me around, inspecting me for damage. I can barely make out his words, but dumbly shake my head no. "They sealed the trapdoor, but we anticipated that, and I got it operational again. Nick of time too."

"What . . . ?" is all I can say.

"I'll answer all of your questions soon, but first we need to get you out of here. Do you understand me?"

What may be confusing me more than anything else is how much dialogue I'm hearing from Dave. I don't think I've ever heard more than two words out of his mouth at any given time, so this is one more layer of weirdness to this already surreal moment. I nod yes to his question and allow him to physically move me to wherever he wants. I'm not about to question the man who just kept me from being turned into a scattered jigsaw puzzle. Dave moves me along as fast as he can in his cumbersome outfit, out the door and down a hall that leads to the backstage entrance. Even with my limited hearing, I can hear the mayhem inside the theater auditorium.

Outside the door wait two nondescript sedans. Dave directs me to the first, opens the rear door, and pushes me in.

"Ms. Nichols will take you from here," says Dave in a remarkably calm but urgent voice. "I'm glad you're safe. Good luck." And with that he closes the door, and the car pulls away from the curb. I look out the back window to see Dave climb into the back seat of the following car, which then peels off in a different direction.

I look at the driver, and sure enough, there is Devon Nichols at the wheel.

"Where are you taking me?" I yell, not realizing I am yelling.

Without taking her eyes off the road, "Somewhere safe. Everything will be explained to you there." I open my mouth to protest, but she calmly reiterates her message. Her demeanor is so placid, and my brain is such a jumbled mess that I shut up and take her at her word.

For the next ten minutes, I sit quietly in the back seat, trying to make sense of the complete and utter senselessness I just experienced. The car drives into an underground parking garage, and a minute later Ms. Nichols is escorting me to an elevator. I catch a glimpse of the building we entered; it is one of a hundred other downtown apartment complexes. When we exit the elevator on the fourteenth floor, we walk halfway down the hall and stop at an apartment door. Ms. Nichols clicks on a key fob, and the door's lock releases with a snick. Inside is a nice, if unimpressively furnished apartment. It has the comfortable blandness of a two-star hotel. I sit down on the edge of the bed and Ms. Nichols walks over to the closet and opens it. Inside are several outfits hanging up.

"You will probably want to shower and change. I'm sure this has been quite traumatic for you. Nothing like soap and water and a fresh outfit to reestablish some balance," she says with a comforting smile. I nod and sleepwalk to the bathroom.

When I step out of the shower, one of the outfits is draped on a hanger on the door. I change into it and come out to find Ms. Nichols sitting patiently in one of the chairs by the window.

"Ready for some clarity?" she asks.

I am more than ready. Even my hearing has returned to some degree.

"I'll do my best then," says a different voice within the room. Hasagawa's. He is standing right inside the door dressed in the same outfit I saw him wearing at the theater, but it is slightly worse for wear. The fabric is smudged and wrinkled, and I can smell the smoke coming off it from across the room.

"You were there during the explosion!" I gasp. "Are you okay? Was anyone hurt?" Upon seeing him, my mind starts racing and the reality of the previous hour bubbles up like a geyser.

"Other than ringing ears, I'm fine," he says. "And from what I understand so is everyone else. I can't say the same for the theater stage though."

"What happened?"

Hasagawa replies with a quiet smile and turns to look at his assistant, Ms. Nichols. She returns a softer version of that same smile. The woman is nothing if not professional. Never one-up your boss. Hasagawa turns back to me, looks around for a chair, takes one near the desk and brings it over. He sits down with a look that seems to say Where do I start?

"First of all, congratulations."

"Congratulations?" That was not what I was expecting. "For what?"

"Frances Percival, you are the first person to ever survive *Death Warrant*."

I stare at him for a beat or two, trying to comprehend what he just said. Finally, "What are you talking about?"

"*Death Warrant*, the TV show? You survived it."

"What do you mean I survived it? I wasn't on it."

Hasagawa reaches over and takes my hands in his. "Yes, you were."

There's something called aphasia; it's an impairment where you have difficulty understanding speech. That's what I experience at this moment. I could hear what he was saying but it was not making any sense. I was on *Death Warrant*? Bullshit. I wasn't on *Death Warrant* or ever had any inclination to be on the show. Evidently my confusion is showing because Hasagawa quickly steps back in.

"I know this is going to be hard for you to understand or even comprehend but tonight, during your grand finale, you were to be killed. Blown up. All on worldwide television." He can see I am about to protest, but he holds up a hand. "But you beat them. You won. You didn't die. You're perfectly fine and everything moving forward is going to be wonderful."

"But, how? How is it that I have no memory of anything?"

"That's a longer story, one that I'll get to, but right now the most important thing for you to know is that everything is all right."

"But if I was on the show, I should be dead. No one ever lives."

And that's when Hasagawa smiles the type of smile I suspect only his closest circle of friends ever see. "Not anymore. You beat those bastards! Well, we beat them. I have to admit I played a part."

"You?"

"Yes. I suppose the easiest way to explain this would be to start at the beginning . . . which would be two years ago. As you know, I'm a fan of magic, illusion and mentalism. Two years ago, I saw you being interviewed on a local TV talk show."

"Sure, *Wake Up Call*. That was the name of it. Still on, I think. That was pretty much the only press I'd ever gotten in my career. And it helped. I landed a few good gigs after that," I say.

"Your interview caught my attention. You were talking about hypnosis and the power of suggestion and how you can persuade people to follow your lead because of your suggestions. You said that you weren't so much a mind reader as a mind influencer."

"Yeah, so?"

"You were confident. You sounded like you completely believed it."

"I do believe it. People are open to suggestion."

"And that is why I contacted you."

"For your birthday party, I know. That I remember."

"No, I first contacted you almost two years ago."

"You did? Then why do I not remember that?"

"I'll get to that soon enough. I contacted you with a proposition. I wanted you to help me bring down *Death Warrant*."

"Wait. What?" I say utterly perplexed. "You contacted me to help you beat a TV show?"

"Not just a TV show, an abomination. A show that's an embarrassment to humanity. Except we've become so numb to it, so accepting that we don't even realize how far we've fallen. I wanted to change that."

I let that sink in. "Wait, don't you own a TV network?"

Hasagawa glances at his assistant looking for help. He doesn't receive any. He turns back to me looking slightly shame faced. "I do. I admit, *Death Warrant* is on a competing network."

"So, it wouldn't hurt you financially to see the show that kicks the hell out of every other show fail."

Hasagawa shrugs. "It wouldn't hurt."

I think on that for a moment.

"Okay, I can't blame you. But if you hated the show so much why not start a movement or bring together some of your incredibly rich and powerful friends to shut it down. I can't help but think you've got the financial and political pull."

Hasagawa reveals a bit of a grin. Shark-like.

"Why merely beat an opponent when you can completely eliminate them in humiliating fashion?"

I can see how he got to where he is in the business world.

"So, you've been plotting this for two years?"

"Oh, much longer than that. I'd been researching the show extensively for quite a while. I've found it is best to learn the rules so that you know how to break them properly. However, two years ago I saw an interview that changed my thought process on how to bring the show down. When I heard what you had to say and how sure you sounded, I thought, okay, I need to reconsider things. The first thing I had to do was convince you to participate, which was surprisingly easy."

"It was?" I say.

"You hated *Death Warrant* as much as me."

He had me there, but it wasn't exactly common knowledge.

"Go on," I say.

"You blame the show for your brother's accident. You feel the damage on the bridge where your brother's tire blew out was a direct result of a *Death Warrant* episode from months earlier at the same location."

"But how would you know that?"

"I didn't. But once you knew what I wanted, you told me your suspicions."

"Yeah, I don't believe in coincidences. But no one could prove anything. The bridge contractors were found to be non-negligent," I say with disgust in my voice.

"And who do you think supplied the legal teams for the bridge contractors?" asked Hasagawa.

"*Death Warrant*?"

"Silent partners, as it were. They have a way of getting what they want. Making things disappear. They are the proverbial 500-pound gorilla," says Hasagawa. "When I told you my plan to bring down the show, you were more than willing to throw your hat in the ring."

"But how? What was your plan?"

"I only had a hunch, not a plan. You provided the plan with your spectacular confidence," says Hasagawa with a laugh. "You were convinced that if you committed to be on the show, you could use your powers of suggestion to manipulate their team to try to kill you in a particular way, on a certain occasion."

"Evidently I knew my shit," I say with no shortage of chutzpah.

Hasagawa smiles. "You did indeed. I found it remarkable that you were willing to risk your life on that confidence."

I shrug at this. "Besides wanting desperately to bring *Death Warrant* down, I'm guessing money was also a factor. I die, someone in my family gets a fortune. Galen, I presume, being that he's my only living relative."

"Correct."

"So, if I die Galen is set up for the rest of his life and then some."

Hasagawa merely nods.

"But if I live, which evidently, I did . . ."

"He still gets the payout. It's in the contract."

"Holy shit," I say more to myself. Then suddenly, "Galen was at the show! Is he all right? And Mike! And . . ."

"They're fine, all fine. Mike, Galen, your friend Audrey. I sent Ms. Nichols to pick them up and then she took them to a remote location, out of harm's way. They never saw the show. You'll see them soon."

I look at his assistant.

"How did you explain it to them? They were all set to see the biggest moment of my life, and some woman they've never met before drives them off to a mystery location and tells them the most insane story imaginable. They must have freaked. And how come none of them called me to tell me they were being kidnapped?"

"Two reasons," says Hasagawa. "Because Ms. Nichols is immeasurably convincing, and because of the *Death Warrant* communication blackout. No calls can be made within a set distance and a set time leading up to the killing. They don't want their target being warned."

I feel like I have officially fallen down the rabbit hole where nothing makes sense. Down is up, left is right, and salt tastes like pepper.

Hasagawa places a steadying hand on mine.

"Perhaps this will help you believe what I'm telling you."

He motions to his assistant who nods and turns to the video monitor on the wall. "Play video," she says. The monitor blinks to life and there I am in all my glory, staring back at myself. I can tell that this clip is from a while ago as my hair is a tad longer and in a style I was experimenting with for my thirtieth birthday. After looking at my image I remember why I did not stick with the style.

I begin speaking on the screen.

"Hello, Frankie, it's me, Frankie. If you're watching this that means we beat those sons of bitches." I see myself on the monitor look off screen and give a knuckle-bump to a fist that reaches in.

"You were knuckle-bumping me," offers Hasagawa.

"This video is to help you understand the fact that you did indeed work with Grayson Hasagawa for over two years to take down *Death Warrant*. It was a risky plan and took a lot of work, but I never doubted for a second that we could pull it off. You're a terrific mentalist if I do say so myself."

I glance at Hasagawa. "She's humble, but I like the cut of her jib."

Me on the screen continues. "Grayson's going to explain in more detail how we pulled it off, but rest assured, I'm proud of you . . . me . . . us, whatever, for what we did. I don't know about you, but I can't wait to be a world-renowned mentalist. Ciao!"

The screen goes gray, and I'm left feeling overwhelmed but with a strange sense of accomplishment. Hasagawa pulls out his own optic and makes a few taps and swipes.

"We practiced for months before you applied at *Death Warrant*. We mapped out a thorough plan and you developed an incredibly precise script of what you wanted to say during your interviews to suggest to them how to kill you, where to kill you, and when to kill you. And let me tell you, if I had any doubts before, I don't anymore." He pauses for a moment, lost in thought. "This is precisely what you did with me at my birthday party, right? The bit where I was supposed to come up with a time on my watch."

"9:25," I say.

"That's right. You still remember that. You made suggestions to me beforehand in the library, suggestions that instilled that time in my head, yes?"

"Do you really want me to give up my secrets?" I ask. He stares at me. I guess he does. "Okay, fine. Do you remember us talking about some of your books? One in particular? The Great Gatsby. What year did I tell you it was published? 1925. I said the date several times. Really ingrained the number 25 in your head. Then I kept slipping in words that rhymed with nine—fine, sign, time—before the show and during the show. By the time I asked you for a watch setting, nine and twenty-five were the numbers that were top of mind for you. Your mind gravitated to the quickest numbers it could think of. Bingo. You've been suggested."

"I still can't figure out how you made my entire birthday party audience disappear though. That one still has me stumped."

"Good. And no, I'm not telling." I steal a glance at Hasagawa's assistant. She gives me a subtle shake of her head. My secret is safe with her.

"So, what did I say in my interview with *Death Warrant* that got them to do my bidding?" I couldn't wait to hear what my master plan had been. It's so weird for me to be asking questions of myself in the past tense.

Hasagawa looks at his optic. "Here are portions of your script that we rehearsed ad infinitum."

"Failure to prepare is preparing to fail," I interject.

Hasagawa simply smiles and nods. "Indeed." He holds out the optic for me to see. "You'll note the key words and phrases. This is when you were being interviewed and monitored by their team of creatives and analysts." He draws the optic back and clears this throat. "Ahem," he begins, "'I want you to tell your crack team of killers to fire up their imagination. I want them up late, burning the candle at both ends coming up with something that will knock viewers for a loop. Hear that, boys? Are your ears burning? Round up your best and brightest and start stoking their creative fires.'"

"Ah, instilling the theme of fire and circles."

"Very good," says Hasagawa. "You wanted them to blow you up and you put the circle imagery in there for when they saw your stage device."

"Bosco."

"Yes, Bosco. You built it with huge rings around it."

"I did. And it shoots fire."

"Here's more," he said and looked back at his optic. "You said, 'When I was eighteen, I had a dream that I would die in some grand and glorious fashion.'" He looks back at me. "Here you're reinforcing the image of killing you in a theatrical fashion."

"Yep," I say.

Hasagawa lowers the optic saying, "You then went on to talk more about the 1800s, the circus, three rings, dazzling audiences . . ."

I nod. "Continuing to reinforce the number eighteen, the ring/circle theme, and the theatrical angle again," I say. "Yep, that's exactly how I would have done it."

Hasagawa slips his optic back inside his coat pocket. "There's more but I think you get the idea. Your interview was a non-stop barrage of suggestion. For hours you planted words and images in their heads, over and over. Then all it took was for you and me to ensure all their decisions were easy by offering up exactly what their minds had been trained to look for—a big theatrical event with fire and rings on a date of the 18th. They then did exactly what you basically told them to do." Hasagawa opened his hands out in a "And that's that" gesture. "You, of course, have no memory of the interview because they use a powerful combination of hypnosis and drugs—incredibly top-secret stuff—to make sure you didn't know what's coming. To know you were going to be killed."

"It evidently works. I don't remember any of it and had no idea I was targeted." I drift off, my mind wandering.

"But *our* plan worked too," Hasagawa says. "Beautifully."

I snap back out of it. It's all too clean-cut. My brain is still looking to poke holes in how this all came together. "All right. Then what I don't understand is why I have no memory of our prior meetings and plans. How were you able to wipe my memory? You said their process was top-secret, proprietary, and no one else has the capabilities or knowledge of how they do it."

Hasagawa tips his head slightly and smiles. "Do you really want me to give up my secrets?"

Touché.

"So now what?" I ask.

Hasagawa turns a look to his assistant and stands up. "And now the spectacular organizational and planning skills of Ms. Nichols are brought to fruition. She has been mapping out the aftermath plan for over a year. And I must say, it's brilliant. You will stay here for . . ." he looks at his assistant. ". . . how many days?"

"Two," says Devon Nichols.

"Yes, two days," says Hasagawa. "That will allow enough time for the police and coroner's office to investigate and fully realize that there is no trace of Frances Grace Percival in the wreckage that once was her stage performance equipment. Also, during this time, the good people at *Death Warrant* will be sweating bullets when they receive these same results. After two days, you will magically appear and reveal how this was all part of your master illusion. The greatest illusion of all time. You will then tell the world how you beat *Death Warrant*—in vague terms, of course—more details will be forthcoming—stay tuned! But we won't wait too long. We need to start having you prepare for your Vegas shows." Hasagawa begins walking toward the apartment door.

"Vegas shows?" I ask, completely dumbfounded. "I don't have a Vegas show."

Hasagawa stops at the door and looks back at me. "Did I mention that among my many business interests, I also own a casino?"

CHAPTER 46

The mystery location to which Mike, Galen, and Audrey were squirreled away is an apartment building as non-descript as the one Devon Nichols had taken me to for my briefing with Hasagawa. Evidently, the super-rich have their own version of safe houses at their disposal. The only giveaway, to my eye, are the operatives that pepper the garage, lobby, and halls. Plain-clothes security personnel. They're good, too. The only reason I spot them is because I was looking for them.

Standing before the apartment room door, my heart pounds. The whole way over I experienced a veritable kaleidoscope of emotions, mostly painful ones. Would they forgive me for what I put them through? When the door opens, I am greeted by the hulking presence of Big Wave Dave wearing something I have never seen before on him, an ear-to-ear smile.

"Hello, Frankie," he says warmly. "I think there are some people here who would like to see you." At which point he steps aside.

Audrey is the one who hits me first. Literally, hits me. Full force with a running hug. Practically knocks me to the floor.

"Bloody hell," she yells as her arms wrap around me. "When we saw the explosion on the telly we were so scared." She then steps back and slugs me in the arm. Hard. Then calls me a "fookin' bitch," followed by a laundry list of British insults, ranging from "wanker," to "tosser," to "daft cow." It is wonderful. When she finishes, my heart sings to see her mascara running.

And then I look over her shoulder. Mike and Galen stand side-by-side, both smiling, both wiping tears from their eyes. Audrey steps aside and I rush toward them.

"I'm so sorry," I whisper aloud as I collapse into both.

When I pull back, Galen is the first to speak.

"M . . . money? You almost got yourself killed for money?" And he is pissed. Pissed like I have never seen in my life. "What the hell?" he yells.

"I know," I plead. "It was stupid. Crazy. I don't know what I was thinking."

"No shit, Sh . . . Sherlock!" he says, before dropping down, sitting hard on the edge of the bed, the explosion of emotion draining him. He holds his head in his hands. "What would I have done without you?" he asks quietly.

I kneel next to him. "Just like mom and Auntie Mame taught us to do: Live! Live! Live!"

This brings a nod, and a reluctant smile to his lips.

I then look up to Mike still standing to one side, patiently waiting his turn. He holds out one of his massive hands, a gesture, which at this moment strikes me as the most tender, and loving thing I have ever witnessed in my lifetime. I take it and he gently pulls me to my feet.

I look into those cloudless blue eyes, afraid of what I might see.

"Will you ever forgive me?" I ask.

He reaches up and holds my face in his hands. "As you wish."

CHAPTER 47

All performers have the look-at-me gene. We're wired to crave attention. Ever since I was young, I wanted to be famous, to be a household name. Now, I finally get my wish. It is no stretch to say that I am the most famous person on the planet. Hasagawa created a nice protective cocoon for me; kept me hidden away for the promised two days before letting the cat out of the bag.

He also assigned a nice young woman by the name of Hazel to be my personal assistant until all the fuss died down, which understandably took a while. She's handled all the interview requests, scheduling, you name it.

I have to say it's been pretty damn cool.

By the time the smoke had cleared, and it was determined that the reports of my death were greatly exaggerated, *Death Warrant* went into crisis mode and lawyered up right quick. Of course, they kicked and screamed about having to cough up the money to Galen, but they did. Their lawyers weren't that good.

I don't know if Hasagawa and I will get our wish and the show vanishes from the airwaves, but it's most definitely going on hiatus until the court of public opinion weighs in. The show was now flawed. Trust was broken.

Perhaps people will look at it with fresh eyes. I honestly don't know which way the scales will tip, but I'm glad I got people at least talking about whether public assassination should be part of our entertainment culture. Perhaps we the people have lost our taste for bread and circuses.

IT'S NOW FOUR months past and the Zombean is busy, sporting a full complement of stories for me to decipher.

I'm at my special table taking in each customer, seeing what they can tell me without actually talking to me. Mike sits across the table quietly sipping a latte and reading an ancient issue of *Sports Illustrated* with the World Series winning Seattle Mariners on the cover.

I quietly analyze a half dozen patrons before breaking to take a hit off my chai tea and flip through a weathered copy of *Entertainment Weekly* that has a white-coifed Lady Gaga on the cover. This from back when she was young and spry and still singing, before the whole vocal nodes thing ended her music career, and she went to live out the rest of her days on an island off the coast of Maine. I'm about two pages in when I notice someone has approached and stopped at my table. I've grown accustomed to autograph seekers and the run-of-the-mill curious.

Mike and I look up to face the most compassionate deep brown eyes you can possibly imagine. Offset by the loveliest looking tangerine framed glasses.

"Hi," I say. I've been working on my chit chat with strangers who approach me. It's taken me a while, but I've come to understand the dynamic better. I don't know them from Adam, but they've seen me so often in the media that they feel like they know me. I try to give every person who stops me at least a couple of minutes of my time. "What's up?"

The woman with the tangerine frames regards me with a look of what I can only describe as bemusement. "I just wanted to let you know how proud I am of you," she says. "What you did and what you accomplished was nothing short of incredible."

I blush at this, and Mike smiles and places a hand on mine. I've heard similar comments from people over the past few months but for some reason this woman's words touch me more deeply. Her sincerity is breathtaking.

"Thank you," I say. "What's your name?"

"Myrna."

I perk up. "Like the old movie star? Myrna Loy?"

"You know of her?" she asks, genuinely surprised.

"Star of the silver screen! *The Thin Man* with William Powell? *The Best Years of our Lives*? Another *Thin Man*?"

"*Shadow of the Thin Man*?" offers Mike. I'm slowly indoctrinating him to old movies.

"Evidently my grandmother was a fan."

"What is it you do for a living, Myrna?"

She smiles at this and says, "I'm between jobs."

"Oh, I'm sorry to hear that."

"Don't be," she says.

I look at the cup in her hand. "What are you drinking?"

She looks down at it and then back to me. "A medium Frankie," she says with a wink.

"A woman of exceptional taste!" I say and raise my own mug in a toast. We clink ceramic and paper and take a sip.

Myrna says, "I don't want to take up any more of your time, but you sound like you're a bit of a movie fan."

"I am indeed," I say.

"There's a film playing over at the Bagdad. That little repertory theater in southeast, on Hawthorne. Are you familiar with it?"

"Sure. What's the movie?"

"It's an old one, but I have a hunch you of all people might appreciate it." She reaches down to me to shake my hand. "Frances Grace Percival, it has been a distinct pleasure to meet you," she says with the warmth of a weighted blanket.

We shake and without another word she turns and heads out of the shop, never looking back.

I AM NOT one to turn down a movie challenge. After Mike and I leave the Zombean, we head straight for the Bagdad. It's a sister theater to the Mission, so I know I'll most likely enjoy whatever they're showing. We find a parking place a couple of blocks away and start walking up Hawthorne. It's only a couple of weeks before Christmas so the shops are in full holiday mode. Virtually every window is festooned with twinkle lights that cast a watery technicolor smear across the wet pavement. Walking up the street I'm wondering what film Myrna thinks I would appreciate. My first instinct is one of the old Final Destination horror movies; they're about a group of people who cheat death. At least for a little while. That wouldn't be a bad choice, but Myrna doesn't strike me as the type of person who would recommend a horror movie. She seems more like someone who recommends hot chocolate and snickerdoodles. And down comforters and fireplaces. And puppies.

We reach the Bagdad and I look up at its old school marquee, the kind where the movie title is often missing a letter, or a 5 replaces the letter S. But tonight, all the letters are there, big and red and perfectly aligned. I read the title and can't help but wonder, how did she know? I couldn't have picked a better movie if I tried. We walk up to the ancient ticket booth. There's a college-age girl sitting in the small space, sipping a coke, and scrolling through her optic. She looks up when we approach and much to my chagrin gives me her full attention. If she recognizes me, she's not showing it. Good for her. "Two please," I say. "Seven o'clock show." When the girl hands me our tickets, I make sure to say thank you. Mike and I walk into the lobby past a large poster touting the night's film. There's Jimmy Stewart picking up a smiling Donna Reed, her legs kicking girlishly behind her. Below the happy couple in large red type: *It's a Wonderful Life.*

ABOUT THE AUTHOR

Bryan Johnston worked 25 years in local network television as a writer/producer before jumping ship to explore the world of corporate video. He is now the Creative Director for a Seattle-based creative agency. He has authored several books and written for numerous magazines and websites.

Bryan lives in the Seattle, Washington area with his wife, two kids, and one large Goldendoodle. His one great hope is for the Seattle Mariners to make it to the

World Series before he dies. He predicts they hit paydirt in 2024.

He is a devout movie lover, sports fan, and avid reader. In his day, Bryan used to have surprisingly good pop from the right side of the plate on the softball diamond, a passable post-up game on the basketball court, but couldn't shoot to save his life. He is currently a mediocre golfer, but at least has a hole-in-one to his credit. So he's got that going for him. Which is nice.

If you enjoyed

Bryan Johnston's *Death Warrant*,

you'll enjoy

Madison Lawson's *The Registration.*

DAY ONE

Lynell feels the sun cutting into her skin, a harsh reminder of her own mortality. She coughs, bites her lip, rolls forward onto her toes, and holds her hand up against the sun. The motion puts an old scar on her forearm in her direct line of sight. Her stomach clenches and she drops her hand, moving into the shade.

Dallas is busier today than on a usual Thursday. The first Thursday of the quarter, April 4th, brings promises of vengeance, clarity, anger, and in the odd case, love.

It's Registration Day.

Lynell pushes herself against the wall of the building and leans her head back. She flattens her palms against the stones, which are hot to the touch. Hundreds of feet pound the pavement and the streets are congested with honking cars and a dozen people on the phone.

An old man walks out of the large glass door across the street Lynell has been staring at for two hours now. He's crying as he folds a piece of paper and slides it into his back pocket. She considers whom he just Registered. A business partner who screwed him over? A drunk driver who accidentally killed his grandchild? A wife who can no longer breathe on her own?

She's brutally pulled out of her fantasies when a gunshot rings. A young girl screams and a few college kids jump or duck. Lynell, like most of the adults walking the streets, doesn't even flinch.

She looks up to see a middle-aged man lying in a pool of his own blood and a woman, the same age, standing over him holding a small, smoking gun. Almost instantly a pair of Elysian regulators rush to her side. Lynell can't hear what they're saying, but after the woman holds up a piece of paper and the officers dig in the man's coat, they nod. A lengthy phone call later, the regulators leave.

If the Registration had been completed anywhere else, officers probably would have arrived first. But since she's right outside a Registration office, there are plenty of regulators around.

The woman kneels next to the man's side. Lynell can't tell if she's crying, but probably not. On a normal day, the Sanitary Crew would likely have dispatched a team within a few minutes.

Today, however, the busiest day of the quarter, Lynell knows it will probably take them a few hours to reach the destination.

In the meantime, pedestrians simply avoid stepping in the blood.

No one talks to the woman who just completed her Registration.

Lynell turns away from the sight and stares at the tall glass doors again.

She takes a deep breath.

Not for the first time, she considers going home and taking advantage of her day off work. She has most of her life to Register. After all, she's always been told "Never Register before you turn thirty. Chances are, you'll need that Registration when you're fifty more than you think you need it when you're twenty."

But Lynell is twenty-four and she's been wanting to Register the same person for nearly two decades. She doesn't think she will ever have anyone better to Register. And now, with the news that he's getting married at the end of the year to a woman with three daughters, Lynell knows she needs to do it soon. If not for her own sanity, then for the safety of those girls.

She could still wait until the July Registration Day, though.

Lynell looks at the old scar on her arm. One of the oldest decorations to the canvas that is her body.

She pushes off the wall and walks across the street toward the glass doors. She's thankful for the recent measures Eric Elysian requested and the government placed that made picketing and protesting against the Registration illegal. She's not sure she would have been able to walk past a crowd of ignorant people calling her a murderer.

Lynell knows that without the Registration, their world would have disappeared into chaos and violence. Without it, they probably would have nowhere to live. The already overcrowded streets would be too full to move around. Without the registration, they would never know true love or have anything to test it with. It's the only thing that saved them after the war. The entire country owes a life-long debt to the Elysian's for saving them.

The Registration is a gift she's held onto her entire life. Not everyone has this gift. Most do, but those unfortunate few have parents that either didn't or couldn't pay the fee to give them a Registration.

She remembers when her mom had explained it to her when she turned five.

"You see, Lynell, life is not always as easy as it was meant to be. It does not always give, but sometimes it takes. In order to find order in such chaos, the Registration is necessary. One day you'll learn exactly how important it is. You'll recognize the blessing that is your own Registration."

Elizabeth didn't have that blessing. Lynell believes if her mom did, their life would have been better. Her childhood would have been different.

Almost seventy years ago when Gideon Elysian proposed and created the Registration, everyone—regardless of age, origin, color, title, or class—had the option to pay the fee to get one Registration. Once signed, you have two weeks to kill that person or immunity is forfeited, as is your chance for another Registration. If the Registration is completed during the cooling off period, after the two weeks and before the next Registration, then it is considered murder and charged as so.

After those initial few years of madness, the government put a law in place, much to the Elysian's chagrin. The parents of newborns have to pay the fee, or that child will never be allowed to legally Register another human being.

That's why you need to know. That's why you have to be sure that this is the person you want to Register. You can't waste such a gift.

Lynell looks at the scar again, thinks of those three young girls, takes a deep breath, and pulls open the large, glass door.

"You can't do it! Please, you can't Register her! Give her another chance!" A young girl, maybe twelve, yells at a boy, around eighteen, in the corner of the room. Lynell rolls her eyes and closes the door behind her. Looking around, she notices they are the youngest people there.

The Registration room is littered with people. Most of them are older, though there is a woman who looks to be about Lynell's age holding two babies in her arms. A man halfway through the line leans on a cane, his legs shaking and his glasses balancing precariously on the edge of his nose.

It's a large room, made completely out of white marble. Probably twenty to twenty-five yards wide. There are eleven windows, each with their own long line. Above each window are two letters. The first window, on the far-left side, says A-B. The next says C-D. And so on. Some, such as X-Z, have much shorter lines. Lynell knows what to do: You need to stand in the line coordinating with the last name of the person being Registered. She's walked inside the building and stood in line twice before, always chickening out last minute.

There are hundreds of people dispersed throughout the room. Lynell turns to see the boy drag whom she assumes to be his little sister to the U-W line. They stand behind a short, black woman who pulls her shawl tight, glancing around nervously. Lynell almost wants to follow them, grab the young boy's shoulders, and scream, "Why, why are you using your Registration so young?" but then she remembers she's hardly older than him and has no place to talk.

She filters out the sound of the young girl crying and pulling on the boy's sleeve and steps forward to the M-N line. There are probably thirty people ahead of her. Thirty people Registering. Thirty people being Registered. Thirty deaths in the next fourteen days. Thirty cleansings. Thirty moments where lives end and lives get the restart they desperately crave.

Lynell holds up her left arm and looks at the watch securely fashioned on her wrist. It's almost 3:30, which means everyone in the city only has an hour and a half to Register before they are forced to wait for July.

Lynell lowers her arm and sees a small scar peeking out from under her watch. Her stomach churning, neck sweating, and heart palpating as if her own name were about to be Registered, she pulls down her sleeves. The unrelenting summer heat is no longer barreling down on her and the air-conditioned building starts cooling the sweat clinging to her skin.

She zips up her hoodie, tucks her fingers under the sleeves, and pulls up the hood as if to put up a shield between herself and the world.

She has no reason to hide. The Registration is good, pure, and right. People would not look down on her for Registering Alan.

She knows this, but she doesn't lower her hood.

Sounds from the large building assault her ears as she rocks on her feet with her hands hiding in the pockets of her hoodie. Pens scratching on pages. Names spoken with a chilling finality. Crying. Whooping. Rustles of bags as people search for IDs. A cough from a small, frail, old woman clutching to her husband two lines over.

Lynell watches the couple make it to their window. She listens as the man speaks, through tears, that he wants to Register his wife. She stands next to him, clutching his arm in support, smiling up to him with so much *gratefulness* that Lynell wants to sob. That is what selfless love looks like, she thinks. Ending your best friend, your partner, your teammate's life because it is too unbearable to keep living. Because you love them enough to let them go.

The line Lynell stands in moves forward. She looks at her watch again. 3:28.

The line moves again. 3:33.

A small part of her hopes she won't reach the window before the clock strikes 5 and each window clangs shut. But when the line is over halfway finished and her watch says 4:08, she knows she won't have that escape.

She starts shivering. The air-conditioning is blasting and she's standing directly under a vent. She glances up and a strand of deep brown hair breaks free from her bun. Huffing, she tucks it behind her ear and hunches her shoulders.

They move forward again. 4:11.